I never knew love until I met you.

I never knew happiness until I kissed you.

All I want is you…

Other Avon Romances by
Eloisa James

DUCHESS IN LOVE

ELOISA JAMES

FOOL FOR LOVE

AVON BOOKS
An Imprint of HarperCollinsPublishers

This is a work of fiction. Names, characters, places, and incidents are products of the author's imagination or are used fictitiously and are not to be construed as real. Any resemblance to actual events, locales, organizations, or persons, living or dead, is entirely coincidental.

AVON BOOKS
An Imprint of HarperCollins*Publishers*
10 East 53rd Street
New York, New York 10022-5299

Copyright © 2003 by Eloisa James
Excerpts from *Adventures of a Scottish Heiress* copyright © 2003 by Cathy Maxwell; *Flowers from the Storm* copyright © 1992 by Amanda Moor Jay; *And Then He Kissed Me* copyright © 2003 by Patti Berg; *Fool for Love* copyright © 2003 by Eloisa James
ISBN: 0-06-050811-6
www.avonromance.com

First Avon Books paperback printing: August 2003

Avon Trademark Reg. U.S. Pat. Off. and in Other Countries, Marca Registrada, Hecho en U.S.A.
HarperCollins® is a registered trademark of HarperCollins Publishers Inc.

Printed in the U.S.A.

10 9 8 7 6 5 4 3

Acknowledgments

I am most grateful for the help I received while writing *Fool for Love*. Frances Drouin and Melissa Lynn Jones answered my desperate queries for historical information with aplomb. Pete Dennett and the Hanneford Family Circus, and Tony Usher and the Knutsford Ornithological Society were particularly helpful in response to specific queries.

In Which Simon Darby Receives Undesirable News

28 Park Lane
London

Some men turn into walruses when they're angry: all bushy and blowing air. Others resemble pigs, with pillowy cheeks and small eyes. Simon Darby turned into a Cossack. His eyes took on a slanted look. High cheekbones that spoke of generations of Darbys turned formidable, angular, and altogether foreign. To Gerard Bunge's mind, the man looked positively savage.

The last time the Honorable Gerard Bunge himself could remember being so enraged was when his doctor informed him that he had caught the pox. Even remembering the moment made him queasy. There was that uneasy sense of heavenly retribution, not to mention the unpleasant treatment lying ahead.

But even less would he like to be told that his inheritance had disappeared. After all, diseases come and go, but life is so expensive. Even handkerchiefs are prohibitive.

Darby was probably in shock. So Bunge repeated himself. "There's no question about it. Your aunt is increasing."

When Darby still didn't answer, Bunge strolled over to the litter of china dogs lining the mantelpiece and thought about poverty versus the pox again. Definitely syphilis was preferable.

"I said, Lady Rawlings is *enceinte*. I mean to say, the Countess of Trent paid her a visit in the country, and described the lady as waddling. Did you hear me, Darby?"

"They likely heard you in Norfolk."

Silence.

Bunge couldn't stand silence himself, but it wasn't every day that a man had his inheritance snatched out from under his nose by an unborn babe. Tossing back his deep cuffs, he pushed the china dogs into a neat row. There had to be fourteen or fifteen of the lolling, garishly painted little things.

"I suppose these belong to one of your sisters," he said over his shoulder. The thought of Darby's sisters made Bunge feel a bit uncomfortable. After all, if Esme Rawlings's child was male, they had just lost their dowries.

"Actually, the dogs belonged to my stepmother," Darby remarked.

Quite the mortality rate in Darby's family, Bunge reflected: father, stepmother, uncle, gone in under one year. "I wish your aunt weren't increasing, damned if I don't," he said, displaying a rare flash of generosity.

He swallowed a curse as the sharp edge of his starched linen collar nipped him in the neck. He had to remember not to turn his head so quickly. The new high collars were the devil to wear.

"It could hardly be construed as your fault. I gather my uncle and aunt had an unexpected rapprochement before his death."

"Startled me to the gills when I heard he died in his wife's chamber," Bunge agreed. "Not that Lady Rawlings isn't a beautiful woman. But your uncle hadn't lived with his wife for years. He was snug in Lady Childe's pocket when I saw him last. I thought Rawlings and his wife weren't even on speaking terms."

"As far as I know, they rarely spoke. Presumably they engaged in heir-making without speech."

"Some are saying the child isn't Rawlings's, you know."

"Given that my uncle died in his wife's bedchamber, he and his wife likely engaged in activities that led to this child. You will please me by squashing any such rumors." Darby's eyes now wore their customary expression of detached amusement.

"You're going to have to get married," Bunge pointed out. "Course that won't be too difficult for you, catching a rich one. Heard that there's a wool merchant putting his daughter on the market this season—everyone's saying she's a woolly breeder." He erupted in a cascade of high-pitched laughter.

But Darby's eyes hardened into distaste. "An unappetizing possibility." He gave a little half bow. "Much though I adore your company, Bunge, I have an appointment this afternoon."

Cool bastard, Bunge thought to himself, but he let himself be propelled toward the door. "Are you going to tell your stepsisters?"

"Naturally. Their esteemed aunt is going to have a baby. Josephine will be delighted."

"Does she know that the babe will do her out of a fortune?"

"I fail to see why inheritance issues should disturb a child still in the nursery."

"And you never know. Lady Rawlings might have a girl."

"A pleasing thought, under the circumstances."

"You're a cool one. Don't know what I'd do, if I had two girls to get off on the market, and—"

"You would do admirably." Darby rang the bell, and his butler, Fanning, appeared with Bunge's coat, hat, and cane.

As he walked back into his study, the mask of detached amusement fell from Darby's face. He had choked back his rage in front of the painted popinjay who had so delighted in telling him of his aunt's pregnancy. But anger swelled in his throat.

"God-damned *bitch*." The words burned like poison in his mouth.

Whatever his uncle was doing in his wife's bedchamber, it didn't involve fornication. Rawlings had told him last July, just before he died, that the doctor had ruled out connubial acts—and since he'd been a little in his cups, he'd added that Lady Childe was agreeable. No need to mention his wife, and he hadn't. His mistress, Lady Childe, was the only person remotely interested in Miles's ability to shake the bedsheets.

And yet he died in Esme Rawlings's bedchamber a week or so later. Suffered a heart attack in his wife's bedchamber. And now the woman was increasing—waddling, even? Doubtless the child would be born on the early side. The house party took place last July. If the child were Miles's, his wife was six months along at the most. And why would the elegantly slim Lady Rawlings be *waddling* at only six months, with three long months to go?

Damn her for a lying jade. He didn't believe for a moment that Miles slept in her bed. Likely she sprouted the babe with another man and lured Miles into the room in order to confuse the issue of paternity.

Miles never deserved that hussy of a wife he married. But he stuck by his wife, never flinched as Esme Rawlings created scandal after scandal. Refused even to consider divorce.

There were people in London who thought Darby was an uncaring, dispassionate man. They judged him an Exquisite, given the eccentricity and elegance of his clothing. They noted the ease with which he played the fashionable games of the *ton* and the trail of broken hearts that followed him, judged him by whispered tales of debauchery and degenerate friends. Told each other that the only emotion *he* ever displayed was vanity.

Belying the gossips, Simon Darby stared at the mantelpiece with a look of such savagery that it was a wonder the china dogs didn't shiver into pieces.

The man who pushed open the door to the study didn't seem to notice as he loped into the room and slung himself into a chair facing the fire. He was an olive-skinned, broad, brawny brute of a man whose only signs of his aristocratic birth lay in a crumpled neck cloth and a pair of fine boots.

Darby glanced at him over his shoulder. "I've not the inclination for company."

"Stubble it." Rees Holland, Earl Godwin, accepted a glass of Madeira from the butler with the grimace he used for a smile and tossed off the glass, only to break into a fit of coughing. "Dammit, where did you get this hellacious wine?"

"I'd rather not discuss household exigencies."

There was a note in Darby's voice that made Rees blink. "You've heard," he said.

"That my aunt is increasing? Gerard Bunge just left the house. He suggested I marry a wool heiress otherwise known as the woolly breeder."

"Blasted little gossip hound."

"Bunge describes my aunt as waddling. There can be little doubt the child was conceived during my uncle's life, if not actually by my uncle."

Rees eyed his closest friend. He wasn't much good on the comfort front, and the fact that he'd known Darby since they were boys only made it worse. He knew just how much his friend loathed pity.

Darby stood at the mantelpiece staring down at the fire, a long lean body of coiled muscle clothed in superb fine cloth. He looked a lord, from his tossled brown hair, to his shining boots, which is what he stood to be, *if* he inherited his uncle's title and estate.

Without the estate, Darby was left with whatever he made from importing lace, and that couldn't be much, in Rees's estimation. Darby had two young stepsisters to raise. Even this house was likely entailed to the little whelp growing in Lady Rawlings's belly.

Whereas Rees himself was a shambling mess, sartorially speaking, and yet had three or four houses, and more money than he knew what to do with.

Darby swung around. He had a face that made women swoon, with lean hollows in both cheeks that emphasized his cheekbones, deep-set eyes, and lean chin. It was a look that was exquisitely aristocratic and dangerously male. "The important thing is that Esme Rawlings is not carrying my uncle's child."

"Doubt it's an immaculate conception. And bastardy is the devil to prove."

"Then a baseborn whelp is going to inherit my uncle's estate. God only knows who the father is. Do you know how much Miles—my uncle—wanted an heir?" It burst from him.

Rees jerked his head. "We never discussed offspring."

"That was the one thing he wanted: an heir. Still, he couldn't bring himself to renounce his wife. Miles was the kindest of men. He couldn't hold the line before an impudent beggar, let alone his wife."

"Beautiful woman, Lady Rawlings," Rees said. "She has a warm manner, all right. I never could understand how she could be one of my wife's best friends. Talk about opposites."

"Your wife is a saint compared to her."

"My wife is a saint compared to anyone," Rees pointed out. "Unfortunate that saints are hell to live with. I clearly remember telling Rawlings that he should have booted Esme out as I did Helene, rather than allowing her to keep the house."

"Miles never would consider any sort of action against my aunt," Darby said. "Nothing. Not divorce. Nothing."

"Any idea who fathered her child?"

Darby shook his head. "She was at Lady Troubridge's house party when Miles died. Could have been anyone."

"Troubridge? That woman with a place in East Cliff who fancies herself an art enthusiast and cobbles together a bunch of actors and dilettanti? She's tried to get me out there by dangling opera singers before my nose."

"Her parties are so ripe with scandal it's a wonder anyone is ever found in his wife's chamber," Darby said. "Why do you think Esme Rawlings got pregnant?"

Rees had taken a screw of paper out of his breast pocket and was scrawling on it. He didn't look up. "Last time I heard, the bedtime waltz was still to blame for children."

"Damn you, Rees, listen. Why do you think she got pregnant *now*? The woman's been catting around London for ten years. Why'd she suddenly get pregnant now, when all the world knew that my uncle's heart was going?"

"Think she did it to secure the estate?"

"What if she did?"

"Hard to say. You'd have to prove illegitimacy, and that's virtually impossible. Better pray for a girl."

Rees was scribbling away again, no doubt messing about with a musical score. "You don't think she did away with your uncle, do you?" he said, almost absentmindedly.

"What?"

"Put him to bed with a shovel so as to cover up a pregnancy?"

"I doubt it," Darby said, after a moment. "She's a light-skirt, my aunt. But I can't honestly say I see true vice in her."

Rees's fingers were flying across the page, and Darby could see that he'd entirely stopped paying attention. Once Rees was following the lure of a musical line, there was no getting him back until it was on paper.

Of course Esme Rawlings wouldn't murder her husband. She was a lady, for all she was a trollop. And in an odd way, she and Miles had got along quite well. She never fussed over his mistresses—well, how could she?—and he never blinked an eye at her consorts. In fact, she seemed fond of Miles in an odd way.

But perhaps she didn't like the idea of giving up the estate.

Everyone knew that Miles's heart was about to give out. Perhaps she got the wind up about moving to the dower house, and cooked up the pregnancy.

Perhaps she wasn't pregnant at all.

That would explain a good deal, such as why Esme retreated to the country after his uncle's funeral. The lady rarely left London. So what was she doing in a half-forgotten estate in Wiltshire?

Walking around with a pillow under her gown, that's what. Scouring the neighborhood for a child likely to pass as Miles's heir.

"What if she's not pregnant, Rees?"

His friend didn't answer.

"Rees!"

At the near bellow, Rees's quill scratched and splattered. "Damn it to hell," he muttered, blotting the ink with his cuff.

Darby watched as Rees's white cuff absorbed spreading blotches of black ink. "How does your valet get those stains out?"

"Haven't a valet at the moment. The man quit in a fit of rage a few months ago, and I haven't bothered to hire another. The housekeeper will buy some new shirts." He finished tracing the notes that had been obscured by flying ink and began flapping the paper to dry it. "Now what are you shouting about?"

"What if Esme Rawlings isn't really pregnant? What if she's planning to fake a birth, and return with a baby she finds in Wiltshire? She could buy one without a problem. Bring him back and set him up as Miles's heir."

Rees's thick eyebrows matched his mane of hair. Generally they scowled; now they looked skeptical. "It's a possibility," he grunted. "I suppose."

"Why is she in the country else?" Darby insisted. "My aunt is the epitome of a London grande dame, for all she's a scandal-maker. It's hard to imagine her away from the comforts of Gunther's, not to mention her mantua-maker. Why is she rusticating in the country unless she's running some sort of racket?"

Without waiting for Rees to answer, he strode to the other side of the room. "I never believed that story about Miles being in her room, never."

"You said your uncle wanted an heir," Rees pointed out. "Why shouldn't he have tried to get one on his wife, if she were willing? You don't need to live with a woman to get an heir."

"Miles wouldn't have taken the risk. Dr. Rathbone himself told him to avoid bedroom activity or his heart would give out."

"Well—"

"No," Darby said. He swung around and faced his friend squarely. "Esme Rawlings is running a racket on my uncle's estate. I'll bet you two hundred pounds there's naught more than a pile of feathers around her stomach."

Rees eyed him. Then he said: "Hire a Runner. He'll find out soon enough."

"I'll go to Wiltshire myself." Darby's eyes were glowing with all the pent-up rage he'd felt from the moment Gerard Bunge had minced into the study with his red-painted heels and unappetizing news. "I'll shake the truth out of her. Hell, if the woman *is* increasing, I want to know who its father is. Even if I can't prove it, I want to know the truth."

"How will you explain your sudden appearance?" Rees asked.

"I had a note from her a few weeks ago about London air and its insalubrious effects on children. Josie and Anabel seemed well enough to me, so I ignored it. We shall all join her in the country."

"Children aren't the kind of thing you move around easily," Rees objected. "For one thing, they come with a plaguey amount of servants, not to mention clothing and toys and the like."

Darby shrugged. "I'll buy another carriage and put the girls and their nurse in it. How difficult can that be?"

Rees stood up, tucking his now dry papers back into his breast pocket.

"Perhaps I can find myself a spouse in the wilds of Wiltshire," Darby said moodily. "I can't raise my sisters by myself."

"I don't know what is so difficult about raising children. Hire a nursemaid each. No need to saddle yourself with a wife."

"The girls need a mother. The servants find Josie particularly difficult."

Rees raised an eyebrow. "Can't say my mother did much for me. I wouldn't think that your mother had much to do with your raising either."

"All right, they need a *good* mother," Darby replied impatiently.

"Still not a sufficient reason to take a wife," Rees said, leaving. "Well, best of luck with your aunt. What was that they call her? Infamous Esme, isn't it?"

"She'll be infamous after I'm finished with her," Darby said grimly.

2

Sugar and Spice and Everything Nice

The High Street
Limpley Stoke, Wiltshire

He was the most beautiful thing she'd ever seen. His eyes crinkled in welcome, and he smiled at her . . . her heart flopped in her chest, and then she was caught in a wave of longing so overwhelming it was like to throw her to the ground.

"Lo!" he said. "Lo! Lo!"

"You *are* a beautiful boy," Henrietta cooed. She leaned down. "Do you have a tooth, sweet one? Is it right *there*?" She put her finger on the baby's chin.

He broke into a storm of giggles and took a step toward her, repeating: "Lo!"

"Lo?" Henrietta asked, laughing back.

"Lo-Lo!" shouted the baby.

A little girl grabbed the baby's hand and pulled him backward. "*She* means hello," she said in an aggravated tone. "Anabel is a girl, not a boy. And she's not beautiful. She's quite bald, in case you didn't notice."

A girl of four or five scowled at Henrietta. Her pelisse was unbuttoned, and she had no mittens, not that it mattered much. It was unseasonably warm for January, and Henrietta

had left her own pelisse in her carriage. The child was wearing a grubby dress that likely started out as pale pink that
morning, but had obviously made contact with the street. In
fact, she had a smelly streak of manure down her front, as if
she'd fallen directly onto a dung heap.

The girl started to pull the baby away, down the street.
That pink dress was fine broadcloth, if it did reek of the
stable.

Henrietta stepped squarely in front of her and then smiled
as if she just happened to block her passage. "You caught
me properly, didn't you? And you're absolutely right. I
know almost nothing about children. Of course, I know that
you're a boy."

The girl's scowl got deeper. "I am not!"

"Never say so! You must be mistaken. I am quite certain
that young lads of about—oh, four years old—are wearing
pink with ribbons this year. I'm quite certain of it."

"I am not a boy and I'm five years old. If you would please
move, you are blocking our way."

Her look of deep wariness made Henrietta blink, so she
bent down, and said, "What's your name, sweetheart? And
where's your nurse?"

For a moment, it didn't look as if the girl would answer at
all, as if she would keep running down High Street, towing
her little sister behind.

"I'm Josie," she said finally. Then, *"Miss* Josephine
Darby. This is my baby sister Anabel."

"Lo!" Anabel shouted. "Lo!" She seemed enormously
pleased that Henrietta had come back down to her level.

"Ah," Henrietta said, twinkling at the babe. "Now I am
Lady Henrietta Maclellan. And I'm hugely pleased to make
your acquaintance. Josie, do you think you misplaced your
nurse somewhere?"

"I've left her for another position," Josie said grandly, and
rather quickly.

"You've *what*?"

"I've left her for another position," she repeated. "That's what the cook said just before she moved across the street."

"Ah," Henrietta said. "And where do you suppose you left Nurse, do you think?"

"Back there," Josie said, her lip setting mulishly. "But I'm not going back there. I won't get in the carriage again, I *won't*!" She looked down the row of mullioned windows that lined High Street. "We've run away and we're not going back. We're looking for a shop that sells ices, and then we're going to walk even further."

"Do you think that Nurse may be worrying about you?" Henrietta suggested.

"No. This is time for her morning tea."

"Still, she must be worried about you. Is she at the Golden Hind?"

"She won't notice," Josie said. "She had hysterics again this morning. She doesn't like traveling."

"If your nurse hasn't noticed, your parents will, and they will be terribly worried if they can't find you and your sister."

"My mother is *dead*," Josie announced. She gave Henrietta a look that implied the fact should have been obvious.

"Oh dear," Henrietta said, rather lamely. Then she rallied: "How would it be if I carried your sister, and we strolled back in that direction?"

Josie still didn't reply, but she did drop her hold on Anabel's hand. Henrietta reached out, and the baby toddled straight into her arms. She was plump and rosy and sweetly bald.

Her whole face broke into a gleaming smile. She patted Henrietta's cheek and said, "Mama?"

Henrietta's heart twisted in its customary, lamentable surge of envy. "Goodness," she said. "You are a darling, aren't you?"

"Nurse says she's a terrible flirt," Josie said in a dampening sort of way.

"Well," Henrietta said, managing to stand up with the baby in arms, "I think I would have to agree with your nurse. Anabel seems to be quite friendly for someone making her first acquaintance with me. Not at all the sort of thing that an older young lady would do, is it?" She smiled down at Josie and began walking slowly back toward the Golden Hind, praying that her weak hip would manage the weight. Anabel was a good deal heavier than she looked.

"Anabel does lots of things I wouldn't do," Josie remarked.

"Yes, I can imagine," Henrietta said. She was conscientiously picking her way along the pavement. It would be dreadful if she tripped and dropped the babe.

"I don't ever spit up, for example."

"Of course not." There was an uneven patch of ice coming up. Henrietta tightened her grip on Anabel.

"I did lose my supper once. It was Easter last year, and Nurse Peeves said that I had eaten too many candied plums. Which is a complete tarradiddle, because I only had seven. I don't think seven is too many, do you?"

"Not at all."

"Anabel, on the other hand, she—"

But Anabel's propensity to spit up became all too clear just a second later. Henrietta had managed to negotiate the broken pavement, and was pausing to let a carriage and four go so they could cross the street to the Golden Hind, when Anabel gave a dry little cough.

"Careful," Josie cried, clutching Henrietta's skirts.

Henrietta looked down at her confusedly. "It's quite all right—" she began.

At which point Anabel threw up down Henrietta's back. Warm—nay, hot—liquid rolled down her back and absorbed directly into her gown.

A second later it turned clammily cold.

Instinctively she pulled Anabel away from her and held

her away from her body. That was a huge mistake, because Anabel's stomach wasn't empty, and a wave of slightly curdled milk hit Henrietta in the chest and swept down her front with sodden violence. She shuddered all over but managed to keep hold of the baby.

She was dimly aware that Josie was shouting. Anabel screwed up her face and started howling.

"Oh, sweetheart," Henrietta said, instinctively pulling the baby back against her wet gown and cuddling her against her shoulder. "That's all right. Don't cry. Is your tummy upset? Don't cry, please don't cry."

She rubbed her back until the baby stopped wailing and put her head against Henrietta's shoulder.

Henrietta's heart twisted with pure longing as she looked down at the bald little head, with one pink ear showing. I must do something about this, she thought to herself prosaically. If I have become so drunk with longing for a child that I admire a creature who just spewed on my best walking costume, I am truly going insane.

Josie was dancing up and down before her. "She's sorry!" she shouted, her voice shrilling into a near shriek. "She's sorry, she's sorry!"

"So am I," Henrietta said, grinning at her. "It's a good thing that I'm not made of sugar and I won't melt."

Some of the anxiety that pinched Josie's little face disappeared. "She ruined your pretty dress," she said, stepping closer and touching Henrietta's pale amber walking gown. "Nurse says that Anabel should have stopped doing that by now. Anabel is almost a year old, after all, and she drinks from a cup. But she can't seem to stop. I don't think she knows how."

"I expect you're right," Henrietta said, snuggling the damp little bundle against her shoulder. "Perhaps we had better find your nurse, though, because Anabel needs a change of clothing."

But Josie shook her head. "Oh, no, she can't change her clothing yet. Nurse Peeves says she must always wear the wet ones until they dry, because otherwise she'll never learn to stop throwing up."

Henrietta narrowed her eyes. "What?"

Josie told her again. And she added, "Could we *please* sit down and wait for the dress to dry? Because that way Nurse would never know, and Anabel hates being smacked."

"That's what I thought I heard," Henrietta said. "I shall not allow your nurse to smack Anabel, but I do intend to have her clothes changed immediately. I am going to have a conversation with your nurse. And your father." She reached out her free hand, and Josie didn't even hesitate, but trotted at her side across the street and into the inn.

A plump man hurried out of the Golden Hind as they picked their way toward the entrance. "Lady Henrietta! What a great pleasure to see you!"

"Good day, sir. How are you and Mrs. Gyfford?"

"The better for your asking, Lady Henrietta, and so I'll tell my wife. But what on earth?" He nodded toward the child. "That child is surely too heavy for you. And whose is it?"

"I can carry her without problem, Mr. Gyfford." That was a lie; Henrietta could feel that her leg was starting to drag. If she didn't put Anabel down soon, she'd begin to list to one side like a ship in a storm. She tightened her grip.

"I was hoping you could tell me to whom these children belong. I found them wandering down the High Street. Josie, do you—"

But at that moment Gyfford spied Josie and his face brightened. "That's one of Mr. Darby's little ones. He has a private parlor. Now, how did you get out of the inn, young lady?"

"I should like to speak to Mr. Darby," Henrietta said firmly. "Would that be your blue parlor, Mr. Gyfford? I mean to have a word with the girls' nurse as well."

The innkeeper bustled ahead of them through the carved archway leading into the inn proper. "Well, my lady, as to that, their nurse has just left."

"Left?" Henrietta stopped in the narrow hallway. "I suppose that explains why these children were wandering down High Street by themselves."

Mr. Gyfford nodded as he opened the door leading to the blue parlor. "Left a short time ago, with bag and baggage and not a word of warning. Said she didn't bargain for leaving London and she didn't like traveling. Quite tearful about it, she was, saying the children were too much for her, and she'd been abused and the like."

To Henrietta's mind, the nurse herself was vicious, given Josie's artless tale about vomiting and wet dresses. The fact that little Anabel was drowsily nodding on her shoulder and obviously quite uncaring about her damp condition was beside the point. The child could have caught inflammation of the lungs. Moreover, given that Bartholomew Batt's *Rules and Directions for the Well Ordering and Governing of Children* maintained that a nursemaid could influence a child's life forever, Anabel's father had been wantonly careless in hiring such a contemptible person to care for his children.

"Go right in, Lady Henrietta. I'll just bring you a cup of tea. Can't have been easy, carrying that child down the street."

"Thank you very much, Mr. Gyfford," she said, walking into the room. "Just a glass of water would be lovely."

The room was empty. Blue carpet stretched quietly to the windows overlooking Limpley Stoke's central square. Henrietta turned around to inquire about the whereabouts of the children's father, but Mr. Gyfford was bowing to the man who just walked in the door.

~ 3 ~

The Throes of Grief

Her first thought was that he was like a Greek god—the intelligent kind, not the pouty, dissipated type. But if he was a Greek god, he must be the patron of tailors, because he was by far the most elegant man she had ever seen. Rather than wearing dark brown, as most men did while traveling, he wore a double-breasted coat with fawn-colored labels and pale yellow trousers. His boots had a brilliant shine and curved tops unlike those on any boots she'd ever seen. Moreover, his neck cloth was edged in lace and billowed around his neck in a complicated fashion.

His eyes flickered over her rumpled dress, and she thought she saw his nose twitch. Undoubtedly she smelled like sour milk and vomit. The odor was making her stomach turn.

But he said nothing, merely shifted his attention to Josie, whose scowling little face was uncannily like to her papa's, with the same golden brown hair and the same arched brows. He showed no particular dismay at the fact that the little girl had clearly measured her length on the ground.

Instead he asked, with an air of mild inquiry, "Did you get so filthy playing in the courtyard, Josie?"

Henrietta's smoldering resentment broke into speech. "I find it difficult to believe, sir, that you regularly exhibit as little concern for your own children as you have displayed today. These two children were not playing in the courtyard. Instead, they had made it a fair distance down High Street, having crossed two thoroughfares. And as it is market day in Limpley Stoke, there are moments when I fear for my own life crossing High Street!"

To his credit, he looked somewhat dismayed. "In that case, I am in your debt," he said, bowing. But his next question made him akin to a devil, in her opinion.

"I gather that *is* Anabel you're holding, then?" he asked.

Henrietta raised her eyebrows with a look of disdain. "Is it too much to hope that you would recognize your own child?"

"There is no special exertion required," he pointed out. "The sad odor that adorns her person identifies her as Anabel. Gyfford, I had no idea that you would be able to locate a suitable nursemaid so quickly, even if she does seem"—he gave Henrietta a lazy smile—"somewhat agitated. I am quite certain that you will be able to keep these creatures in good order, miss. If I might just ask about your former employment?"

Gyfford and Henrietta spoke at the same moment.

"I'm not—"

"She is not a nursemaid," Gyfford said in horrified tones. "May I present Lady Henrietta Maclellan, Mr. Darby. Her father was the Earl of Holkham."

Henrietta narrowed her eyes as Mr. Darby bowed with elegant abandon. She had little interest in further conversation with a dandified fop who didn't recognize his own children. This polished version of a man was just as inept as the rest of his sex.

The man himself obviously had no idea of his iniquity. "I gather that Anabel expelled her lunch with her usual grace," he said, his beautifully shaped nose twitching a bit. "I heartily apologize, Lady Henrietta. And"—he almost looked sincere when he said it—"I am grateful that you rescued these two little wanderers. Their nurse was not herself this morning, and I suppose that they escaped while she was in hysterics." He turned to Gyfford with a charming smile and bowed. "Could you spare a barmaid to accompany us to my aunt's house?"

Gyfford failed to shut the door in his hurry to do Mr. Darby's bidding, so Darby did so himself. He seemed to move with a kind of leashed elegance, like a great cat she'd seen in a traveling circus. A prickle of annoyance moved up Henrietta's spine. It must be so *easy* to be born like that, with a perfect body, from his lean legs to his long eyelashes.

Suddenly she was aware of the hair falling down her back and the stains down her dress. She'd likely never looked worse in her life. But the babe she held reminded her of the truly important issue. Here was a callously neglectful parent. It was up to her to show him the error of his ways. Luckily, ever since she opened the village school, she had ordered every book she could find that offered child-rearing advice.

"A barmaid is unsatisfactory," she announced. "You must find a proper person to care for your children."

He turned back to her. "I apologize. Did you say something?"

"You appear ready to hand your children over to any woman who walks into the room. Perhaps this barmaid will be as careless as your previous nurse. Did you know that the woman has been forcing little Anabel to wear wet clothing in a grossly mistaken impression that it would cure her of vomiting? Were you aware of that, sir?"

He blinked at her as if a tree had broken into song. "No, I was not. And I agree with you that it seems unlikely to solve the problem."

"Children should be treated with kindly intent at all times," Henrietta said, repeating her favorite line from *Rules and Directions for the Well Ordering and Governing of Chil-*

dren. "Why the noted child-rearing expert, Mr. Batt, says that—"

But Mr. Darby was clearly not paying attention to her. "Josie, please do not lean against my leg. I shall be extremely annoyed if your grimy condition transfers itself to my trousers."

Unless Henrietta was mistaken, there was a devilishly mischievous look on Josie's face. Sure enough, the little girl began deliberately rubbing her cheek against her father's pale yellow pantaloons.

He reacted predictably, saying sharply, "Josephine Darby, stop that immediately!"

Henrietta inwardly shook her head. Mr. Batt recommended that children be treated with respect. Chiding them too harshly merely made them recalcitrant.

Josie proved a perfect exemplar of Batt's theory. Clearly she had been gruffly admonished in the past, and had begun acting like a shrew, albeit a small one, as a consequence. She backed up and put her hands on her hips, glaring like a general on parade. "You raised your voice!"

"I shall do so again if you are badly behaved."

"You mustn't shout at me. I'm a little motherless girl!"

"Oh, for goodness' sake, don't start that tripe again," he said heartlessly. "I already know about your motherless state. If you don't pipe down, I'll *give* you to the barmaid."

Heartless! He was absolutely heartless, to Henrietta's mind. Josie must have agreed with her, because she dropped to the floor and began kicking energetically and screaming louder and louder.

Mr. Darby looked pained but not surprised. And he showed no inclination to address the situation.

"Do something!" Henrietta hissed.

He raised an eyebrow. "Did you have a particular action in mind?" He said it rather loudly in an effort to be heard over Josie's screams.

"Pick her up!"

"What good would that do? She's having hysterics. Didn't you wonder why her nurse left? This is probably the four-teeth such episode since we left London three days ago."

Henrietta felt a stab of pain in her right leg. Anabel's weight was making her sway from side to side. Her hip simply couldn't take the physical exertion. "Here!" She plumped the baby into her father's arms.

An almost comical look of surprise crossed his face. For a second she wondered whether it was the first time he'd held his own child.

"Now," Henrietta said. Josie's piercing screams were causing her to feel an unwarranted level of irritation. "What do you usually do in this situation?"

"Wait for her to finish," Darby said obligingly. "Since this is my first— *and* last—trip with the children, my experience is limited to the last three days."

Henrietta raised her voice. "Are you saying that Josie only began this behavior during the trip from London?"

"In fact, I gathered from her nurse that this is a regular occurrence. Combined with Anabel's weak stomach, the nurse felt unable to continue in her employment, and I can't say I blame her."

"The child appears to be in the throes of grief," Henrietta said, watching Josie thrash about the floor. She felt a wave of sympathy, mitigated by fraying temper. Something about Josie's shrieks was particularly unnerving.

Obviously the behavior stemmed directly from her father's neglect. "Perhaps you should value your clothing less and your daughter more," she said, slanting a look at Darby's velvet lapels.

He narrowed his eyes. "If I bought my clothes in Limpley Stoke, I would likely feel as you do."

"Anabel is chewing on your neck cloth," Henrietta pointed out, with some pleasure.

A look of deep horror crossed on his face. Apparently he had no idea that the baby had woken up and was luxuriously rubbing his starched neck cloth against her face. He wrenched it out of her hands, but the cloth had lost all starch and hung limply at his neck, marked with a few streaks of dirt.

"What a shame," Henrietta said sweetly.

"I've already consigned this particular costume to the devil," he said, eyeing her up and down. "I can only suggest that you do the same with your own gown."

Henrietta opened her mouth to blister the dandified Londoner for jeering at her apparel, but Josie's screams were so irritating that she couldn't overlook them for another moment.

Ignoring the sharp pain that lanced her hip, Henrietta bent over and grasped Josie's wrist, pulling her firmly upright. The little girl came to her feet screaming like a penny whistle. Henrietta held her upright for a moment, but there was no cessation of noise. "Josie," she ordered. "Stop this noise immediately."

"I won't!" Josie bellowed. "I won't go to the nursery! I won't eat bread and water! I won't go with the barmaid! I'm a poor motherless girl!" Her recitation had a fluency to it that suggested much practice. She twisted around and managed to kick her father in the leg. It looked as if it hurt, although his wince might have had more to do with the scuff left on his boots.

"I've had enough of this nonsense," Henrietta said, raising her voice over the screams.

Josie's voice escalated. Henrietta felt her temper rising in tandem.

She bent over, looked Josie straight in the face, and said, "If you don't be quiet, I shall do something extremely unpleasant."

"You wouldn't dare!" the little girl said at the top of her lungs "I'm a—"

"Be *still*," Henrietta said, in the most menacing tone she could manage.

Josie tried to wrench herself free and succeeded in twisting Henrietta's wrist. That was the straw that broke the camel's back. Without letting go of Josie's wrist, Henrietta grabbed the glass of water that Gyfford had brought her and poured it over the little girl's head.

There was an almost comical moment of silence, broken only by a tiny snore from Anabel, who had settled down nicely again in her father's arms.

Josephine stared up at her, mouth open, water dripping from her hair.

Darby burst out laughing. "Well, that did the trick. Lady Henrietta, I must salute you. I had entirely underestimated your backbone. I do believe I had written you off as a missish type."

Henrietta's stomach had just fallen into her boots. "Mr. Darby, you must forgive me. I can't imagine what came over me! I'm horrified at myself," she gasped. "What I just did goes against every principle of child-raising that I hold dear!" She loosed her grasp on Josie, who backed toward her father, still staring up at Henrietta.

Darby instantly put out his hand. "Josie, if you convey your wet condition to me, you shall suffer from more than water. Now you had better make your apologies to Lady Henrietta."

Water was dripping from Josie's soiled pink dress. Her hair had formed little rattails around her head. In all, she was the very epitome of a motherless child. Henrietta's heart twisted with reproach. How *could* she have lost her temper in such a way?

"That lady threw water on me," Josie observed. Her tone was more wondering than outraged.

"You deserved it," Darby said callously. "I wish I'd thought of it myself."

"Mr. Darby, I simply cannot apologize enough for my behavior," Henrietta broke in. Her voice wavered with the force of her shame. "The fact is"—she gathered herself together—"the fact is that I have a deplorable temper. You must allow me to make reparations."

He raised one arched eyebrow.

"Reparations?" he repeated. His voice was a husky baritone that held just a trace of laughter.

"I shall find you an appropriate nursemaid. It's the least I can do. If you will be staying in the inn for a day or two, I will contact the employment office in Bath and have candidates presented immediately. I assure you that my appalling behavior aside, I am perfectly capable of finding you a nursemaid. I hired the schoolmistress for the village school, and she has proved quite satisfactory."

Josie tugged on Darby's pantaloons rather as someone might pull a bell cord and demanded, "I need to use a pot."

Mr. Darby ignored her. He was still looking at Henrietta, one eyebrow raised, as if the question of "reparations" had given him some sort of idea. A humorous one, to judge by his grin.

"Lady Henrietta, may I say again what a pleasurable surprise you are turning out to be?"

Josie repeated, loudly, "I need to use a pot. Or I might have an accident."

Luckily Mr. Gyfford entered the room at that very moment, looking rather surprised to find Josie dripping water, and even more surprised when he saw Mr. Darby holding Anabel. "I've brought Bessie from the kitchen," he announced. "She's the eldest of six, and knows all about little ones."

A moment later Gyfford and Bessie had hustled both children out of the room. Henrietta could hear Josie's voice retreating down the corridor, recounting the fact that she, a poor, motherless child, was all wet because. . . .

Henrietta shuddered. She had always had a temper, but she had never, *ever* addressed it to a child. Of course, she'd never been around children, despite the fact that she knew Bartholomew Batt's books by heart.

Perhaps it was just as well that she couldn't have children of her own.

~ 4 ~

Home Truths Are Seldom Pleasant

Darby closed the door behind Anabel and Josie with an acute sense of relief. From the moment he'd embarked on the trip from London, his life had been hell. Josie had been forced into his carriage by Anabel's vomiting, a request he could not deny once the odor in the children's carriage grew pestilent. But Josie's company was not an unmixed delight. It was no delight at all. When she wasn't whining, she was stretched on the carriage floor bellowing to the skies.

Lady Henrietta was still looking distraught. Feeling guilty, he thought smugly. When he first saw her holding Anabel, he felt a pulse of alarm: a nursemaid that beautiful was bound to cause trouble amongst the footmen. His second thought was to discard that possibility. The woman had a beautiful face, but she carried herself gracelessly, with no awareness of her femininity. It wouldn't matter what she was wearing. Plus, she was clearly a virago at heart. No wonder she was unmarried.

"Please accept my apologies on Josie's behalf," he said. "Both children have been inexcusably rude."

The virago bit her lip. It was a remarkably soft and pink

lip, for one so sharp-tongued. "I fear that her bad behavior is tied to your inattention," she said bluntly. "Children who are treated with love and affection are sweet and biddable at all times." She didn't need to point out that Josie hardly qualified for that description.

Darby had never engaged in a discussion of child-rearing practices, nor had he the slightest inclination to engage in one. But stung, he answered. "Your conclusion is unlikely since Josie hardly knows me. I shall hire a nursemaid who can provide the necessary affection. Although I pity the woman."

"A nursemaid cannot supplant a parent," she said, sternly.

Perhaps her lack of inches explained her ferocity, Darby thought. Petite or not, she had a glorious bosom, this termagant who had rescued the girls. Thanks to a thorough dampening, her dress clung to her breasts in a way that outlined every curve. Any other woman would be either flaunting or concealing that fact. Lady Henrietta didn't appear to have noticed.

"The fact is that your daughter hardly knows you. And that is not something to boast of, sir!"

"Josie is my stepsister," Darby said bluntly. "I believe I met her three or four times before unexpectedly becoming her guardian, after my father and stepmother died in a carriage accident. My stepmother probably summoned her from the nursery for a Christmas viewing when I was there, but I really have no recollection of the event." Since achieving adulthood, he had spent the requisite Christmas season with his family counting the moments until he could leave the house.

Henrietta blinked. "Josie is your *stepsister*? And Anabel as well?"

"Yes."

"Why on earth didn't you tell me immediately?"

He shrugged. "If Josie is reminded of her parentless state, she invariably starts bellowing."

"Her behavior likely signals grief due to her mother's untimely death."

"Ah, but is she grieving? I believe Josie's tantrums may be a flaw in her character. Her nursemaid certainly seemed to think so, and I'm sure the woman knew her far better than I."

He could see uncertainty in Lady Henrietta's eyes, which just confirmed his sense that Josie was a budding virago. In fact, a petite version of her dear mother.

"Has her mother been dead for a long time?"

"Just over eight months," Darby replied. "Now if you would excuse me, Lady Henrietta, I assure you that I will take more care in choosing my next nursemaid. My aunt, Lady Rawlings, lives in Shantill House, quite close to Limpley Stoke, and she will undoubtedly be able to locate an appropriate nurse for the children."

He walked toward the door of the parlor.

Henrietta followed and held out her hand in farewell. "We shall likely meet again, Mr. Darby. Your aunt is holding an at-home this evening, and my family has accepted her invitation."

The man transformed before her very eyes into a gentleman of the first stare of elegance. He swept her a bow that might have graced the king himself. Then he caught her hand in his and kissed the very tips of her gloves. "That will be extraordinarily pleasant." His voice took on a practiced husky ring that promised delight.

Henrietta blinked and almost laughed, but she caught herself. "You must have lived in London all your life," she said curiously.

There was something about the warmth in his brown eyes that was slightly unsettling.

"I rarely visit the country," he said. "I'm afraid that bucolic pleasures have held little appeal."

Henrietta could well believe it. Even bedraggled by his encounter with Anabel, he was a fish out of water in Limpley Stoke.

"Will you making a long visit?"

"That depends," he said, his eyes intent on hers, "on the pleasures of the countryside. I must say, I have found myself . . . surprised to this point."

Henrietta nearly laughed again but managed to catch the giggle. It would never do to insult such a fashionable buck, especially while he was in the midst of practicing his manners on her. Of course, he had no idea that his manners were wasted.

As she made her way back down the High Street, her right leg dragging on each step, her sister Imogen bounced down the stairs from the mercer's shop.

"Oh, Henrietta," Imogen called. "There you are! I've been looking up and down." She stopped sharp. "What on earth happened to you? What is that appalling *smell*!"

"Nothing extraordinary happened," Henrietta said, climbing into their carriage. "Although I am afraid that my dress is rather odiferous." She pushed hard on her aching hip with a gloved fist. Her hip was throbbing in a way that promised a marked limp for a day or two.

"How are you feeling?" Imogen asked. "Is your hip causing you discomfort?"

"I'm just tired. I met a young child, and I'm afraid that she spit up on my gown."

"Well, that should cure you of your attachment to the little creatures," Imogen said cheerfully. "You really do *smell*, Henrietta."

Henrietta sighed. Imogen had taken her sixteenth birthday as a prompt to engage in candid remarks that she considered adult.

"You must rest yourself," Imogen continued. "Although I

think this excursion has done you some good. You don't look as pallid as you do normally."

Henrietta knew very well that she normally had the hue of a ghost without Imogen telling her. At least *that* had nothing to do with her infirmity. Papa had always insisted that Henrietta inherited her looks from her mama.

When she was small Henrietta had spent hours staring at the little miniature of the woman who died giving birth to her, wondering if her odd-looking assortment of features could ever turn into something as exquisite as her own mama's face.

The problem was that now she looked well enough, but it didn't matter. She was tainted by her lameness and by her inability to marry.

From the moment she was conscious of herself, she had been conscious of her hip. It wasn't because of pain, either. Unless she took long walks or carried heavy weights, it didn't hurt very much.

But her mother had the same hip, and her mother had died giving birth to her. Henrietta had known that fact for years. If she had a child, she too would die, as her mother had died.

She had cried and cried when she first realized the truth. One day, her father had found her and asked what was the matter. When she finally gulped it out, he gathered her in his arms and promised that she would never, ever be affected by her infirmity, because she wouldn't get married. "You will stay home with me. Who needs a husband?" he said with mock fierceness, and she, at the tender age of nine, had agreed.

"I would never want to leave you, Papa," she had said.

"And you never will," he had said tenderly, kissing her on the forehead.

Now she was three-and-twenty. Her papa was dead these two years. But it wasn't as if there were suitors pounding on her door anyway.

The truth stung. Yes, her father had made it clear that he would never allow her to marry. But men never wanted anything to do with her once they found out about her hip. Who would want a wife who was sure to die giving birth, almost certainly taking the child with her? Everyone said that she herself had only survived due to a miracle.

"Perhaps you should forgo the evening if you are overly tired," Imogen said, checking her curls in a little mirror she carried in her reticule.

Normally, Henrietta would have agreed without a second's thought. But this evening they were invited to Lady Rawlings's house, and there was Mr. Darby. Not that he showed any interest in meeting her again.

But it would be amusing to see him play off his airs and graces with their neighbors. It would be worth it to have a front-row seat when they realized that a swan had found its way into their little backwater.

⌒ 5 ⌒

Infamous Esme

Shantill House
Limpley Stoke

Lady Esme Rawlings wasn't feeling very spry. She stared at her ankles. Through her entire life, her ankles had been a point of pride. When she debuted, she was deliciously aware that gentlemen clenched their jaws at a glimpse of their slender elegance. After the first picture of a Frenchwoman with her skirt looped up at the side arrived on British shores, Esme lost no time looping up her skirts as well.

But now . . . Her ankles were fat and bulgy. She reached forward with a little grunt and poked at the place where her ankles used to be. Her finger sank into puffy flesh. It was unbelievable. Not that it mattered. The only body part in which anyone showed interest was her belly, as demonstrated by the fact that it was regularly mentioned. "Aye, missus, belly's getting on a fair treat, in't it?"

No one had ever discussed her belly until she embarked on this task of carrying a child. In the regular course of life, ladies' bellies were unmentionable.

With a sigh she leaned back in the chaise longue and placed her hands on the rug that covered her belly. When she lay on her back her belly rose straight in the air like an island starting from a river. Thin January sunshine shone on her closed eyelids. Beneath her hands there were faint stirrings.

Well, Miles, she thought, here's your babe.

Perhaps.

In the distance she could hear Helene calling. But she didn't feel like answering, so she lay still, tracing with her fingers the house in which her baby lived, trying to sense whether there were two wee babes there.

The old woman who ran the creamery in the road to the village was fond of predicting that she was carrying two. The idea seemed possible because she was so large. And unlike many women, she knew precisely when she had conceived the baby—well, she had it narrowed to two nights, one after the other. That meant she was precisely six months along: no more, no less.

Yet she was growing bigger by the moment. Her belly looked nearly as large as some women's did at birth—and the babe wasn't due to be born for another three months. Twins was an absorbing, terrifying thought. How could it be? How could it not be twins?

One boy and one girl, she thought. Or two girls. Or two boys. They danced behind her closed eyelids, in the golden warmth of sunshine, small girls in pinafores with ribbons in their curls, boys with rumpled hair—

No! She had accidentally given the boys golden hair. You don't have that hair, she told them silently. You have Miles's nice, brown hair. For a while anyway. Your father didn't have more than a few strands left.

She reshuffled the pictures in her mind. Now she had boys with sweet round faces and rumpled brown hair, already looking a little thin on top although they were only a year or so. That's better, she thought sleepily. Brown hair, Miles's boys.

A cool voice cut into her sleep. It was her friend Helene, or Countess Godwin, as she was known to the rest of the world. "You have visitors, Esme."

"Visitors?" she said, struggling against the impulse to sink into a sleepy daydream.

"Your nephew has arrived for an unexpected visit."

There was a sharp note in Helene's voice that caught Esme's attention. She struggled to a sitting position. "Darby is here? Darby? Truly?"

"He drew up in a traveling coach with his sisters. Looks as if he's been on the road for days."

"What on earth is he doing here?"

"He says the children needed air."

Esme stood up, with just a little help from Helene.

"Esme!" Helene said. "Don't you understand why Darby has made this visit?"

"I wrote him a note suggesting that London air was insalubrious for children. He refused to rusticate himself initially, but he must have reconsidered." She began walking up the slope toward the house.

"Why?" Helene demanded. "Why would Darby change his mind about visiting you?"

"Because London air truly is unhealthy?" Esme said, rather confusedly. Pregnancy seemed to have filled her head with cotton wool. She felt like one of her cousins, the one her mother used to call bacon-brained.

"Use your head. He's suspicious of the child you're carrying. Darby was Miles's heir, wasn't he?"

"He still is," Esme said.

"Not if you have a boy."

Esme stopped and faced her friend. Helene was dressed in a rose woolen gown with a matching pelisse and gloves. Perfect for a winter's day in the country. Her hair was drawn up in an elaborate nest of braids that made her head seem to float, swanlike, on her delicate shoulders. She didn't look tough as nails, but she was.

"We've discussed this," Esme said. "Darby is still Miles's heir. I will not accept the estate."

"Balderdash!" Helene said.

That was the strongest oath she allowed herself, so Esme knew that she was truly perturbed.

"If you give birth to a boy, Esme, that boy will be the heir to Miles's estate. This house as well as the one in London in which Darby is living, if I'm not mistaken. You will *not* disinherit your son. In fact, I'm quite certain that you can't, given the laws governing entails."

Esme laced her fingers over her stomach in unconscious support of the disloyal thing she was about to say. "You don't seem to understand that this babe may not *be* Miles's child."

"You don't know that," Helene snapped.

"You think I would pass off another man's child as Miles's child?"

"Would you deny Miles's son his heritage?"

"Of course not!"

"Then how are you going to know?" Helene demanded.

"I'll just know." Esme could feel her eyes starting to prickle. That was the worst of being pregnant. She, who hadn't cried since her father married her off to a stranger, seemed to cry four or five times a day at least.

"Even I, who know next to nothing about children, know that it's impossible to tell a child's true parentage," Helene announced. "Remember all the dust kicked up last year when the Earl of Northumberland insisted that his firstborn son couldn't have been his because the boy got sent down from Oxford for the fourth time?"

"Northumberland is a fool," Esme muttered.

"Likely not. The countess debuted the same year I did, after all, and I'm sure I'm not the only one who remembers her desperate vows of adoration to a mere soldier. Her father married her off quickly to avoid a *mésalliance*, or so he said. But her babe was born barely nine months after the wedding: perhaps she married quickly for another reason."

Esme scowled. "I can't believe you're telling me all this sordid gossip, Helene. It isn't at all like you."

"I'm trying to knock some sense into your head," Helene said tartly. "There's no way to tell whose babe you are carrying. You have black hair; Sebastian Bonnington has yellow hair; your husband had brown hair. Even if the child had brown hair, it could be just a combination of your and Bonnington's colors."

Esme paled.

Helene pressed her advantage. "You would do a great disservice to Miles if you deliberately allowed his own son to be disinherited. And there is no way to ascertain a child's father."

"Perhaps it will be a girl," she said weakly.

"That would be for the best. Especially from Darby's point of view."

Esme started walking toward the house again. "I forgot Darby! And the children. Where shall we put them?"

"The girls went into the nursery. Darby arrived without a nanny, so it's quite lucky that your old nurse is already here to help with your babe when it's born. She seemed pleased to have something to do. We put Darby in the blue room, at the end of the hall."

"Oh no," Esme said. "Doesn't the fireplace smoke?"

"It serves him right," Helene said with a certain relish. "He's trotted all the way up here just to see if you're bearing a bastard, to call a spade a spade."

Esme felt her spirits droop. "I'd better tell him the truth."

Helene stopped short and grabbed her arm. "You will do nothing of the sort," she said. "To even admit for one second that the babe may not be Miles's is both to desecrate your husband's memory *and* destroy your son—who may well be Miles's child. You don't want to do that."

Esme stared into her friend's eyes. Helene always seemed convinced of an appropriate action. To Esme, this whole issue seemed foggy.

"Now pull yourself together," Helene advised. "You seem to have forgotten that you have an evening at home tonight. Half the county is arriving at the house in a few hours, and here you are, drowsing on the lawn."

"Oh Lord," Esme gasped. "I did forget about the evening."

"You would be the only one," Helene observed. "I still cannot fathom why you wish to outrage most of the county by inviting guests to your house during your mourning period."

"It's only a small at-home," Esme said feebly.

Helene was chewing on her lower lip, and Esme knew with the instinct of a longtime friend that she had something else to say. "What is it?" she asked, resigned to bad news.

"Would you mind terribly if I paid a brief visit to my aunt Caroline in Salisbury? I shan't leave until after your at-home, naturally." Helene's aunt lived a short distance away.

"Of course not," Esme said, feeling that she would mind very much indeed. In fact, she might start crying again at the very thought.

"It's just that Darby is Rees's best friend."

"Why does that matter?" Esme said, trying to summon up a weak defense. "It's not as if your husband is here. Darby is just a friend of his, Helene. Nothing more than a friend. You can't avoid all of Rees's friends." But she already knew that Helene would leave for her aunt's house first thing in the morning. Once Helene had decided on a course of action, it was impossible to dissuade her.

"I don't feel comfortable with Darby. He has always been in Rees's confidence. When we were married, Rees would disappear, and when I demanded to know where he was, he would say *with Darby*. Except that I knew he'd been rollicking about with opera singers. The very women he later moved into my house, as a matter of fact."

Esme grimaced at the keen edge in Helene's tone. "That was years ago, Helene. Years. Lord knows, Darby probably didn't even know that Rees was using him as an excuse."

"Perhaps," Helene said. "But I doubt it. They were always in each other's pockets, those two. Even now, while we were exchanging the briefest of greetings, he mentioned something Rees had said to him. And I . . . I just don't want to hear about Rees."

"But you and your husband separated ages ago, Helene," Esme said, knowing full well that she might as well spare her breath.

"I don't care. I don't want to hear or think about my husband, and unfortunately Darby brings that very subject to mind."

"God knows why they're friends. They're quite opposite, aren't they? Darby dominates the *ton* when it comes to men's fashions, but Rees——"

"Rees is as sloppy in his dress as he ever was," Helene filled in. "You're right about their dissimilarities. Darby is invariably discreet, but Rees hangs out his dirty linen in Hyde Park."

"Couldn't you—*please* rethink your decision?" Esme asked, almost desperately. "I wouldn't ask except that I feel quite lonely here——"

"I cannot bear to be around him. I only have to look at Darby, and I want to scream at him for allowing Rees to move that opera singer in our house!" She stopped. "Which is hardly Darby's fault. But I simply cannot bear to think about my husband. You must excuse me."

"It's my fault for even asking you," Esme said, shaken by the pain in Helene's voice. "You are so composed in general that I tend to forget you have strong feelings about your husband. It's inexcusable of me. I'll be fine. Besides, I think that I've made a new friend."

"Lady Henrietta Maclellan? I like her enormously. I thought she showed a lot of sense at tea yesterday." That was Helene's highest praise. "Will she be here this evening?"

"I hope so," Esme said, as they started walking. "Will you

stay for the evening, Helene, please? If I am indeed scandal-
izing the county by holding an at-home while in mourning, I
would be grateful for your company."

Helene nodded in a tight-lipped kind of way that indicated
that she wished to be gone, but would stay for the evening.

"Thank you," Esme said, kissing her friend's cheek.

"I'll only make a brief visit," Helene said. "I will return
long before the baby is due."

"You probably won't recognize me by then," Esme said
morosely. "I already look like a moving elephant."

Helene laughed. "A very small elephant, darling."

~ 6 ~

Extreme Youth and Scorn Are Close Associates

Holkham House
Limpley Stoke

"I simply can't *believe* that Mr. Darby has come to Wilt-shire!" Lady Imogen Maclellan said to her stepsister. "Who would have thought? Emilia Piggleton told me all about him. She actually saw him at Almack's one night, but of course he didn't ask to be acquainted with her. Do you think I should wear my new gown, Henrietta? It was only delivered yester-day. You remember, the sprigged India muslin. Except that Mrs. Pinnock—"

Her mother appeared in the doorway, interrupting the con-versation. "Good evening, darlings," said Millicent Maclel-lan, the Dowager Countess of Holkham. "We probably ought to begin to make our way to dinner."

"Mama, do you know who has picked out the very same dress as I?" Imogen said, in the affected, rather snappish way she had lately adopted. "Our beloved next door neighbor, Selina Davenport! Mrs. Pinnock told me."

"Oh dear," Millicent said. Selina Davenport was the clos-est thing in Wiltshire to a high-flier. She was married to a squire who cared more for his hounds than his wife. Not that that was unusual, but it was rumored that a pile of dogs shared the ancestral bed, and where Selina slept was an object of everyone's curiosity.

"It's disgraceful," Imogen said scornfully. "I don't know why Selina can't simply accept the fact that she's a married lady, and be done with it. She'll have had the bosom lowered on the gown, and she'll sit there with the tiniest bodice on this side of London. Likely she'll insist on sitting beside me all evening."

"Only to share in your popularity, dearest," Millicent said. "And I don't like your peevish tone. Women will be your greatest ally during the season, but not if everyone decides that you are a sharp-tongued snippet." Imogen had just begun attending local parties, and already had a phalanx of local boys clamoring for her attention. It had had an unfortunate effect on her disposition.

"No one will take a second glance at me when Selina's bosom is hanging out for all the world like a piece of washing!"

"That is a most unladylike remark," her mother said. "Why don't you wear your ivory gauze tonight instead of the sprigged violet?"

"I suppose," Imogen muttered. "What are you going to wear, Henrietta?"

"My Italian crape."

Imogen stared. "I thought you were saving that for something quite special."

"I have changed my mind."

"Lady Rawlings is in *mourning*, Henrietta. There won't be dancing."

Henrietta opened her mouth, but Imogen corrected herself. "Not that the mourning signifies, because you don't dance. So why on earth should you wear your Italian crape? I thought you were saving it for the next assembly in Tilbury."

Henrietta shrugged. "Why should I? As you say, I can't dance. So why shouldn't I wear what I want? It doesn't make a bit of difference."

"No one knows what the future has in store for them, darling," Millicent said, winding her arm around Henrietta's shoulders.

Henrietta smiled affectionately at her stepmother. "In my case, it doesn't include dancing. Or suitors."

"You're more beautiful than Selina Davenport any day," Imogen said with some satisfaction.

Henrietta grinned. "What a hum that is!"

"It's true. None of the girls around here can hold a candle to you. If you weren't lame, they wouldn't have a single beau amongst them. I heard Mrs. Burnell saying that you were getting dangerously beautiful, Henrietta. Imagine that— *dangerously beautiful*! No one will ever say that of me. Not with my unfashionable hair."

Imogen came up behind Henrietta and made a face into the glass. Henrietta's hair was a pale amber marked with strands of sweet lemon and honey gold. Imogen's was a less modish mass of black curls.

"Hogwash," Henrietta said bluntly. "No one cares about the color of your hair if you can't have children."

"Mr. Gell heard of a new doctor," Imogen reminded her. "That bone doctor in Swindon. Perhaps he'll know what to do."

"Papa dragged me to every doctor within forty miles, and they all said exactly the same thing. If I carry a child, I'll likely die in the birth and the child as well. It's better to face the truth, not keep dreaming of a new doctor who might say differently."

Imogen pressed her lips together and for a moment she looked as commanding as a Roman goddess. Or her late father. "I won't settle for it," she said. "There'll be a doctor who can cure you. You'll see."

Henrietta laughed. "I don't want a husband."

"You are always clucking at babies," Imogen said, sounding unconvinced.

"No, I am not," Henrietta said, rather nauseated by the old-maid image. Did she really spend her life clucking at other people's babies? A familiar sense of despair clutched her around the heart. It was so unfair.

If only she were like those fashionable women who had no interest in their offspring. Lady Fairburn boasted that she never saw her children but twice a year. Said it was the best way to raise them. And the oh-so-splendid Mr. Darby didn't even recognize his own sweet sister.

That was the crux of it: she, Henrietta Maclellan, was cursed with a passion for children and a hip that prevented her from bearing them. She was doing her absolute best to convince herself that running the village school was an adequate substitute. And she was blessed—as she tried to remind herself often—with sufficient brain to see how tiresome husbands could be.

"If I had a husband, my life would be utterly tedious," she pointed out. "I would have to pretend that I thought his talk of ferrets and hunting dogs was interesting. Men are self-absorbed idiots. Take that Darby, for instance. He was so absorbed by his own consequence that he actually tried to play his London manners off on me—*me*!"

"That's why you are wearing your crape," Imogen crowed. "I should have guessed immediately! Is he terribly handsome? Emilia told me that all the girls in London were longing to dance with him. With a single compliment, he could make you one of the most eligible ladies in London."

"A more conceited man I never saw," Henrietta said dampeningly. "You should have seen how pained he looked when he realized that his neck cloth was crumpled."

"Darby must have seen how lovely you are. Did he compliment you? Is that why you're wearing your best dress?"

Henrietta burst out laughing. "Oh, Imogen, give over! Why on earth would I change my apparel because a frenchified London beau was rusticating in Wiltshire? The man has no interest in me. And—more to the point—I have none in him. I decided yesterday that I would wear my crape. As I told you, I decided that I'm not saving anything for a better occasion."

"I don't believe you," Imogen said mulishly.

"My hip is really a blessing in disguise," Henrietta told her skeptical sister. "Papa would have married me off the very year I debuted—"

"You didn't debut."

"I would have, if I hadn't this infirmity. And I should have been married off to the highest bidder, likely a man who couldn't remember my name and simply wanted Papa's estate, given as most of it is so obligingly unentailed. By now I'd be a lamentably bored woman."

"I was married before I debuted," Millicent put in. "And I'm not bored at all. I've had two of the loveliest daughters in Christendom to care for, and what what's more, Henrietta, I always found your father's conversation very interesting. He didn't just discuss ferrets; he was a veritable mine of information on the subject."

Henrietta grinned at her stepmother. "You would find that fascinating, darling, because you are the sweetest-tempered woman in this country. But I cannot countenance a droning discussion of hunting in the morning, only to be equaled by the tedium of a list of executed animals recited over supper. I'm afraid my temper would get the better of me."

"Only because you haven't fallen in love," Millicent replied.

"Likely if you had made a debut, you would have fallen in love your very first season," Imogen said dreamily. "A handsome duke would have swept you off your feet and married you out of hand." When Imogen forgot to be irritating, she was a passionate romantic.

"There are no handsome dukes," Henrietta said, laughing. "They're all decrepit." She tried to imagine herself, going to London and being feted by ancient gentlemen. And by all the fortune hunters, a sharp little voice in her head pointed out. After all, her father's title had gone to a distant cousin, but the unentailed portions of his estate had made her an heiress.

She would have spent her time receiving flowers and gifts and dancing with gentlemen as exquisite as Darby. She almost laughed at the thought. Darby was far too dangerously beautiful himself. Who would ever want to consider such a man as a husband?

Imogen was still deep in the fantasy she was weaving. "You'd be married to a duke by now, Henrietta, with nothing to do but go to grand balls and dance with your husband. Perhaps with Mr. Darby!"

"Darby is not a duke," Henrietta objected. "Moreover, I shouldn't wish to fall in love with a man who cares more for his lace neck cloth than his little sister."

Imogen shrugged. "He's a London gentleman, Henrietta. He's not a homebody like you. Just imagine if you *had* debuted, then married Darby. Those children would be yours to care for!"

Henrietta's heart almost turned over at the thought. Children—and without risking her life to have them. Little bald Anabel and scowling Josie.

"Rumor is that he doesn't have a penny to fly with," Imogen continued. "At least, he won't if Lady Rawlings has a boy, because then he'll lose his uncle's inheritance. At the moment he's just an heir apparent."

"I dislike that sort of gossip," the dowager countess said.

"He's not exactly dressed in rags," Henrietta observed.

"I must look my best," Imogen announced. "Just think how marvelous it would be if he paid me notice. Sylvia Farley would expire of jealousy. Do you think that I should ask Crace to curl my hair?" The sisters shared a lady's maid, Crace.

"Why on earth would you do that?" Henrietta said. "Your hair curls beautifully on its own."

Imogen looked at herself in the glass and frowned. "It's

not very regular. Sylvia's hair lies in the most marvelous ringlets, rows of them right down her back. She said that her maid did it with a hot iron."

"I wouldn't bother. We have to leave in twenty minutes or so, and Crace gets frightfully bad-tempered when she's rushed. I may not have debuted," Henrietta said with an impish smile, "but you will be doing so this spring, Imogen. Perhaps Darby will fall in love with *you* and marry you out of hand."

Imogen looked surprised. "It's all very well to dance with the man, and I should like a compliment that would bring me into fashion. But I wouldn't want to marry him."

"Why on earth not?" Henrietta asked, picturing Darby's elegant physique and broad shoulders.

"He's too *old*. Why, the man must be well over thirty—perhaps even forty! Mother's age, not mine. In fact, he probably has to retire to his chamber directly after supper." She cast a darkling look at her mother, who had committed the unforgivable crime of dragging Imogen away from Lady Whippleseer's gala before light dawned in the east.

"He didn't seem very old to me," Henrietta said. But thinking of his practiced gallantry, she added: "I think you're right. He's far too much of a—a *rake* to be a good marriage prospect. He says farewell by kissing just the very tips of one's fingers."

"Wait till he meets Selina," Imogen said with a happy gleam of mischief in her eye. "She'll bust her seams if he kisses her fingertips!"

"Imogen!" said her mama. "Behave yourself!"

Imogen only giggled.

Lady Rawlings Hosts an Evening at Home

The first person Esme saw when she walked into her drawing room that evening was her nephew, Darby, being entertained by one of the local matrons, Selina Davenport. Mrs. Davenport was holding court before the great windows at the end of the room, throwing her head back in such a way that her breasts practically fell out of her gown and made themselves a present to Darby.

"Oh Lord," she moaned.

"Mrs. Davenport made a beeline for him," Helene murmured with a little chuckle. "I gather that she is determined to snare the fine gentleman who opportunely strayed into our midst."

To Esme's irritation, Darby looked engrossed. He couldn't be finding Selina's conversation so absorbing. Selina seemed to have only two topics: herself and her prowess at various activities. Some of which even occurred outside the bedchamber.

"Darby!" Esme said, approaching him from behind.

He turned with a start and bowed, kissing her hand. "My dear aunt," he murmured.

His voice was cool. Helene is right, Esme thought to herself. He *did* come to see if I'm carrying a bastard.

Selina swept a curtsy that exposed her breasts to the whole world. Never mind the fact that Esme herself was prone to magnificent displays of her chest. That was before she embarked on her career as a circus elephant.

"My goodness," Selina said with an arch smile. "I hope you don't mind my mentioning, my dear Lady Rawlings, that you are simply growing more"—she hesitated—"more beauteous every day."

Esme smiled at her, a dagger keen smile honed by swimming the dangerous currents of London society for eight years. "That is *so* kind of you," she cooed, "especially given that you undoubtedly met so many beautiful women in the years before I made my debut."

Selina's smile snapped shut like a fan.

Esme turned back to her nephew. "Darby, shall we take a turn around the room? I am hoping that you can make a long stay with me, and this is a perfect occasion to introduce you to some of my local acquaintances."

They walked toward the other side of the room.

"Lady Rawlings, I trust we do not intrude," Darby said. "I hoped that the children would be the better for country air, but we needn't rely on your hospitality."

"Oh please, do call me Esme," she said. "We are far away from the formalities of London, and we are family, after all."

He looked a little taken aback at that. "Of course," he murmured. "And you must call me Simon."

"How is little Josie? Miles told me that she had a particularly difficult time accepting your stepmother's death, poor little thing."

"He did?" Darby looked faintly surprised.

"Well, yes," Esme said. "He was quite distressed to think of the difficulties you would face becoming an unexpected parent. I only hope I can do as well as you, given that I must raise this little one without Miles."

Darby looked down at Lady Rawlings's hand, resting on the great mound of her stomach.

She was pregnant, all right. He'd never seen anyone so pregnant in his entire life. The elegant leader of the *ton* was swollen up like someone about to give birth in a day or two. It must be an illegitimate child. Miles certainly hadn't slept with his wife before going to that blasted house party in July.

Something must have shown in his face because she led him into the hall and from there into the library.

"Why are you here, Simon?" Esme said, sitting down on a velvet couch. He just looked down at her for a second, non-plussed by the change in his aunt's appearance. He remembered her as a sensual goddess, all luscious curves and glossy black curls. Now she looked bloated and tired and altogether unattractive.

Suddenly before he could speak, she said: "I *am* carrying Miles's child."

Darby bowed. "I never doubted it for a moment."

"Yes, you did." Her eyes twinkled, and for a moment Darby felt the pull of the glorious woman whom all London had called the Aphrodite when she debuted. "I don't blame you. But I am carrying Miles's child. He wanted an heir, you know."

"I know that," Darby said.

"So we agreed to a rapprochement," she said, unconsciously echoing his words to Gerard Bunge. "But I had no idea—no idea!—that Miles's heart was so frail." She looked up at him, and her eyes were suddenly brimming with tears. "You have to believe me. I would never have agreed to . . . to heir-making if I thought it would endanger his health."

Darby blinked. Perhaps he was wrong, and the child was legitimate.

His aunt was still talking. "Even if the child is male, I shall not disinherit you. We'll get around the entail somehow. Miles would not have wished it."

Darby suddenly saw through the aura of sensuality that his aunt had always carried around her like a suit of armor. He saw her anxious eyes, heard her words, and realized that he knew nothing of his uncle and aunt's marriage. The chilling truth was that her child likely was his uncle's own babe.

He sat down and said, flatly, "I owe you an apology, Lady Rawlings. Shamefully, I did come because I questioned whether Miles could be the child's father. I am deeply sorry that I ever doubted you."

"*Please* call me Esme," she said, putting her hand on his. "I completely understand your suspicions. I would have doubted myself. The fact is that it was a very recent arrangement between Miles and myself. And I simply can't understand why he didn't tell me about his heart. I know that we were estranged, but to risk his life in that fashion—"

"He wanted a child desperately," Darby put in. "If Miles thought there was a way to secure an heir, he would not have considered the risk too high."

Esme's hand tightened around his. Her eyes were painfully earnest and, Darby noticed with alarm, still swimming with tears. "Do you really think so? I can't stop thinking that if he had simply told me about his heart condition, he would be here at this very moment." Tears welled up and spilled over.

Darby patted her shoulder. "It's all right," he said.

"No, it's not all right," she replied in a strangled voice. "It's *not* all right! I am quite certain that he strained his heart that evening, and that's why it failed when, when—"

"It is unfortunate that Marquess Bonnington mistook your chamber and entered the room. The shock seems to have precipitated a heart attack. But Miles himself told me that the doctor had given him an ultimatum—"

"I know!" she wailed. "I went to the doctor after Miles died, and he said that Miles was not supposed to—to have—

to have—but Miles didn't tell me!" She collapsed against Darby's shoulder.

It was decidedly odd to feel her huge ball of a stomach pressing against his side. "Even if he had told you, it wouldn't have made any difference. The doctor had only given him until the end of the summer."

"The doctor told me as well. I simply cannot believe that Miles didn't tell me—*that*."

"Not Miles," Darby said. "He disliked making people sad. He didn't tell you because he didn't want to make you unhappy."

That brought on a fresh onslaught of tears. Her voice was falling to pieces now, and he could only catch tangled bits of language, about how Miles was too good for her, truly, and she would never, ever—something—and. . . .

He stroked her shoulder silently. He would have unequivocally stated that his aunt and uncle had no marriage at all, that they barely spoke and couldn't tolerate each other's company. But he was clearly wrong.

Esme was grieving for Miles, even if they hadn't lived together in the common way of things. And even if she had flirted with every attractive man in London. And even if Miles's affair with Lady Childe was public knowledge.

After another moment of patting his aunt's shoulder, his mind wandered to the woman who rescued Josie and Anabel, Lady Henrietta Maclellan. To the best of his knowledge, he'd never seen her in London. Perhaps her father decided she was too needle-tongued for marriage. She had certainly summed him up as beneath her notice in a mere breath. He had never seen such a dismissive expression on a woman in his entire life.

But he'd never seen such a beautiful smile either. When she smiled good-bye, she turned exquisite, in a way that made his heart stop: like a bird in flight, delicate and fine boned.

Beside him, Esme straightened up and mopped the last of her tears with a handkerchief. "I'm sa-sa-sorry," she said, hiccupping a little. "I'm afraid I'm terribly emotional these days, and I do miss Miles, and it's just so—so—"

"I know just what you mean," Darby said quickly, seeing the blue eyes fill up with tears again. "Shall I call your maid? I fear that your guests may begin to wonder where you are."

Esme blinked. "Oh dear. I suppose more rice powder is in order. I do have to spend a great deal of my time covering up evidence of my deranged spirits. You can have no idea."

For a moment they just looked at each other, an impeccably groomed gentleman with a damp shoulder, and a frowzled-looking, very pregnant gentlewoman with reddened eyes, and then they both broke into laughter.

"When your own wife is increasing, Simon, you'll grow to see how weepy a condition it is."

"I look forward to it with bated breath," he said gravely, kissing the very tips of her fingers.

~ 8 ~

A Light Supper Is Served in the Rose Salon

By taking great care, Henrietta managed to walk without limping to a small table in the Rose Salon, where a light supper was being served. The room was a graceful rectangle, with beautiful arched windows that looked into a conservatory. Those windows lent the conservatory just enough countenance that it was deemed adequately chaperoned, and thus became a pleasant trysting spot for amorous couples. Lady Rawlings had arranged for tables to be spread about the room in charming disarray, while a sideboard at the far end was piled with dainties. Henrietta joined her stepmother and her stepmother's bosom friend, Lady Winifred Thompson.

When Mr. Darby finally sauntered into the room, they all instinctively paused in their conversation. If he had been elegant in the Golden Hind, he was magnificent in evening clothing. He wore a velvet suit of a dark red color, with a complicated lace neck cloth and lace falling over his hands. To Henrietta's eyes, he looked terrifyingly expensive.

"Oh, my goodness," Lady Winifred said in a faint voice. "I remember my father wearing great lace cuffs that buttoned onto his shirt. But one never sees men wearing that sort of thing anymore. You'd think it would look old-fashioned, but it doesn't at all, does it? I expect my husband will think it rather effeminate." She giggled. "My husband is *so* unobservant."

Henrietta agreed. Lace on Mr. Darby looked anything but effeminate. For years she had welcomed home young ladies from their debut season, girls who returned engaged to marry or not, but universally replete with tales of how exquisite London dandies were, how dazzlingly proper, how gloriously unlike the country bumpkins of Wiltshire. Henrietta had always thought those tales must be exaggerated.

She had mentally produced pictures of foppish, delicate men, mincing about London cobblestones in their high-heeled shoes. But the truth was far from it. She never thought there were such men in the world, men with hair that gleamed in the candlelight, and cheekbones higher than her own, and a languid elegance that spoke of leashed power. Of maleness.

Mr. Darby's clothes were obviously made in London. But he inhabited them with male grace, and he wasn't overly fastidious. He wasn't wearing gloves, for instance. And his hair was much longer than men wore it in Wiltshire and tied at his neck with a ribbon.

Lady Winifred was ogling the man shamelessly. "Lady Rawlings's nephew, isn't he? I do believe I met him in London last season. You know, Darby was Rawlings's heir, at least until Lady Rawlings showed signs of increasing. I doubt not but that he's come to the country to wait out her confinement."

"An unpleasant interpretation of his visit," Henrietta said flatly, as a whole flock of matrons descended on Darby.

A woman with a towering arrangement of hair, only to be outdone by a nose that dominated her face, plumped herself into his way like an iceberg before a ship. "I am Mrs. Barret-Ducrorq of Barret Park," she announced. "I believe we met last season at Mrs. Crawshay's musicale."

Darby bowed. "I am afraid not, madam, as I do not have the pleasure of Mrs. Crawshay's acquaintance."

"Well, it must have been somewhere!" she shrilled. "Perhaps it was Bessie's house—Lady Panton, that is."

The woman couldn't know Elizabeth Panton. Lady Panton was so formal that she wore a feathered headdress to a simple musicale; it was impossible to imagine her responding to a name like Bessie. But what was the point of protesting?

"You are likely right," he murmured, kissing her hand. "I must remind—ah, Bessie—next time I see her."

Mrs. Barret-Ducrorq burst into an excited medley of speech, overjoyed at having established her friendship with a leader of the *ton.* Darby let it wash over him, simply nodding at appropriate intervals and surreptitiously gazing around the room. Stout squires and their flounce-trimmed wives sat about fanning themselves vigorously. The only young women he could see were sallow types with slumping shoulders and damp noses. And the lascivious matron whom he'd met on entering the house, Mrs. Davenport. Or rather, Selina, since she insisted within a minute of their meeting that he address her intimately.

Finally, he spied his acquaintance of the afternoon. Even from here he could tell that Lady Henrietta was as poorly gowned as she had been in the afternoon. The color of her gown seemed to be giving her hair an odd greenish tint. Still, he felt a sort of mild interest in making her further acquaintance.

Mrs. Barret-Ducrorq was summoning various ladies, in the manner of one auctioning a prize guinea fowl, and introducing him as her bosom friend: Mrs. Colville, Mrs. Cable (where did she get that grotesque tippet?), Mrs. Gower. Soon Darby was surrounded by a circle of matrons asking him about "events" of the town, and the newest styles. Unfortunately, his reputation as an arbiter of fashion had preceded him to the country.

"I'm afraid that I have no particular opinion of pearls,"

Darby said, bowing for the hundredth time or so. "Boots? Well, ladies' boots . . . yes they certainly do match the pelisse this season."

Just then Selina Davenport managed to push her way into the circle and leaned toward him in such a way that her breasts bounded slightly into the air.

"Mr. Darby, I am simply longing to be told some tattle from London," she said roguishly. "Due to illnesses and death in my family, I shall be visiting London this spring for the first time in years." She fanned herself vigorously, her eyes making an unspoken invitation over the edge of her fan.

"I'm sure that you could tell us some fascinating tittle-tattle about Rees Holland, Earl Godwin, for example." She leaned forward, and her breasts almost escaped and brushed his coat. "Is it quite true that he has installed an opera singer in his house?"

"Rees and I are such old friends that we are utterly uninteresting to each other," Darby said. "I have never asked him."

"His wife is here." Selina nodded across the room. Sure enough, the countess was seated at the pianoforte. "I *insist* that you share the truth about his domestic situation. But we should move away from this area, so as not to upset the countess, should she hear us." She took his arm firmly and led him away from the goggling matrons.

Damn it all, the last thing he wanted to do was wander about with a lascivious woman who offered an affair, not marriage, given that he had almost decided to seek a wife.

Not thinking too hard, he led Mrs. Davenport directly to the table where Lady Henrietta was seated. "What a pleasure to meet again," he said, bowing.

"Indeed," Henrietta said. "How are your stepsisters?"

"They are safe in the hands of Lady Rawlings's nanny, who appears to be most competent, and unlikely to leave Anabel in wet clothing. I knew you would appreciate that, Lady Henrietta."

He was right. She had a truly remarkable smile.

"We are just taking a stroll," Selina said with a roguish smile. "Mr. Darby has promised to tell me London gossip."

"Perhaps you should introduce him to the conservatory," Lady Henrietta said. "Likely Mr. Darby has never seen such exceptional roses at this time of year."

His eyes narrowed. She was throwing him to the hounds, the little vixen. She gazed at him with limpidly innocent eyes and the faintest smile and yet—and yet. She had quite interesting eyes. They tipped up slightly at the edges, and they were fringed with the longest lashes he'd ever seen. And he'd seen plenty.

He turned to Selina and took a quick glance at her truly magnificent bosom. The woman was wearing a girlish little gown but it suited her. The cotton looked frail, as if it were about to collapse under the weight of those glorious breasts. Darby felt a stirring in the region of his loins. Selina Davenport was beautiful, luscious, and clearly available. Lady Henrietta's gown was indeed a muddy green crape that dulled her hair. Moreover, it not only didn't display her bosom, but the neckline was so prim that ruffles almost brushed her ears.

He bowed over her hand. "Your servant," he murmured.

The expression in her eye was as effective as an icy shower. She was amused. No two words about it. She knew precisely what his reaction would be to Selma Davenport's bosom, had cataloged it and expected it, and was now showing pleasure that the little dog had jumped through the appropriate hoop.

Darby's teeth involuntarily snapped together.

"I believe I have more familiarity with exceptional beauty than you believe, Lady Henrietta," he said with a wolfish grin. "I should wish nothing more than a stroll in the conservatory with Mrs. Davenport." And he walked away.

Henrietta was disappointed. No two ways about it. For

whatever reason, she thought Darby would react with slightly more sophistication to Selina's obvious ploys. But the moment Selina Davenport sauntered toward him, he turned to her like a bee drawn to a flower. If you could imagine a fleshy flower made up of a creamy pair of breasts, precariously bound in violet ribbon. It seemed that even the exquisite London breed of men were turned into jelly by swelling mounds of exposed female chest.

Darby didn't reappear in the Rose Salon for well over twenty minutes and when he did, he didn't even glance in her direction. He appeared to be deep in conversation with a gray-haired gentleman, although of course she didn't watch him all the time. Then, quite suddenly, he raised his head and met her eyes. Swift heat raced down her body. At first she thought it was embarrassment—after all, she'd been caught peeking. But the heat didn't melt away. He kept looking at her, and there was something in his eyes that made her feel a bit dizzy. If she'd been standing, her leg would surely have given way.

Even as she watched he courteously disengaged himself from the gentleman he was speaking to and walked straight toward her. It was as if she called him, she thought numbly.

As if she—*she*—had Selina's power. She almost glanced down at her gown, but she knew full well that her breasts were exactly what they had been that morning. Quite nice in their own way, but nothing like the bovine-like exuberance of Selina's.

He must not know about her hip. Her common sense filled in the rest for her. If he was a bee, he'd picked the wrong flower.

This one had no pollen to give away.

9

Of Fox Hunts and ... Other Sorts of Hunts

"May I join you?"

"Naturally you must do whatever pleases you."

Darby was utterly stunned by the vision that jumped into his head in response to the question of pleasure. Surely not. He was used to being chased by women, not hankering after them. And certainly never after young—or youngish—virgins endowed with undoubted respectability and fierce temperaments.

It must be the accrued shocks of the day. He was deranged by the conversation with his aunt. He should retreat to his bedchamber and recline on the bed.

Although he would thereby pass up the attentions of at least fifteen country gentlemen with perfectly good daughters on the market. Daughters he ought by all rights to be assessing for their motherly qualities. Henrietta Maclellan wasn't a candidate for wifedom, given her propensity to throw water on small children. That particular trait reminded him of his own mother.

He sat down anyway.

It wasn't that Henrietta was unfriendly. She looked at him with a perfectly cheerful air, as if she had been joined by a maiden aunt. There was just a trace of irony in her gaze, a look that dared him to live up to her expectations of manhood. She *didn't* look at him with the slightly hungry awareness that he was used to.

Your comeuppance has arrived, Darby thought with some amusement.

"Are you enjoying Limpley Stoke?" she asked. Perhaps he thought her blue eyes were clear only because there wasn't even a hint of smoky awareness in them. Intelligent curiosity— and nothing more.

"The better for your company," Darby said, suddenly finding that he was enjoying himself very much.

"I suppose you find us countrified, if not worse."

"To some extent." The wallpaper was lined with bunches of posies, but none so jovial as the faces around them. Wiltshire society was a hearty, cheerful lot, interested in farming and hunting and, to a lesser extent, London and London matters. London matters covered a range of sins from Parliament to the Regent himself.

"Well, at least we're welcoming," Henrietta said, bristling at his bald agreement with her description. "From what I've heard, the city can be an unfriendly sort of place."

"Actually not everyone here has been welcoming," Darby said. "I haven't the faintest interest in drains and farmland, and I'm afraid that several worthy gentlemen have found me incomprehensible . . . even contemptible."

"That is surely too strong a word," Henrietta said with the strong suspicion that he was absolutely right.

"One Mr. Cable was particularly taken aback by my admiration of his waistcoat."

Henrietta smiled faintly. "Mr. Cable has jaundice, and I believe that sours his judgment. Moreover, his wife was recently converted to a rather vigorous form of Christianity by a traveling Methodist preacher, and lately she speaks primarily in Bible verses. I'm afraid his home life is rather uncomfortable at the moment."

"In the future, I will not mention a word about his sartorial efforts," Darby promised.

Henrietta was rather fascinated to find that the man had a way of laughing without even opening his mouth. The laughter was in his voice and his eyes.

"What can you expect if you wear lace around your neck?" she asked. For he didn't seem in the least perturbed by the slights dealt out by Wiltshire gentlemen. How could he be so confident and yet so out of place?

"I like lace," Darby said. She was right: he was unperturbed. "Lace has a symmetry, a perfection to it, that pleases me."

"Symmetry? I think of lace as girlish." There was no getting around the fact that lace didn't look the least girlish on him, however.

Darby shrugged. "It pleases me. Symmetry is a quality of beauty, Lady Henrietta. Now you . . . you are quite pleasingly symmetrical. Your eyes are perfectly spaced in relation to your nose. Did you realize that beauty is intricately connected to the space between one's eyes?"

"No, I didn't," Henrietta said. Somewhat to Darby's annoyance, she didn't seem to have even realized that he was offering a flirtation. Instead of giggling in delighted appreciation, her brows knit.

"There is a milkmaid in the village with one blue and one green eye, Mr. Darby. And she is considered quite lovely. In fact, all the village lads are striving mightily to gain her attention. Wouldn't that fact suggest that you are wrong about the underlying attractiveness of physical symmetry?"

"I believe not. There an opposite theorem might take precedence. Luck is generally attached to matters of dissymmetry, as it is to a four-leafed clover."

"A four-leaf clover is quite symmetrical," she pointed out.

"As is a three-leaf clover. But in the case of a four-leafed clover, its uniqueness makes it unsymmetrical."

"Your theorem is unreliable. My milkmaid is beautiful by right of being unsymmetrical, but only when the word is twisted to mean unusual."

"Let's return to your personal symmetry," he said silkily.

But she changed the subject as if he hadn't spoken. "Mr. Darby, I have been wishing to apologize for assuming that Josie and Anabel were your children and acting on that assumption. I should never have spoken to you in such a forthright manner."

"Please do not give it a second thought. Your advice was admirable. The employment office in Bath is sending me two nurses for review tomorrow morning, and I shall be sure to ask them their views on wet clothing."

She leaned forward, her eyes alive with interest. "Josie needs a particularly kindly woman, Mr. Darby. I'm sure you realize this, but perhaps you could find someone who knew of loss herself."

"Josie—" He broke off.

"She appears to be suffering mightily from grief for her mother."

"Josie hardly knew her mother. I much doubt that my stepmother did more than greet her at Christmastime, and perhaps on her birthday—although I rather doubt that, because Josie's birthday falls at a most inconvenient time of year."

At Henrietta's inquiring look, he said, "April 16, just at the beginning of the season. Josie presumably met her mother some four or five times in her life, and several of those when she was too small to have a perfect understanding of the occasion."

"Then why is she so despondent?"

"The devil if I know. Perhaps it is the shock of moving to London after my stepmother died."

Darby looked down and realized he was drumming his fingers on the table. He did need to find a wife. Perhaps a widow with children of her own who would know why Josie behaved like a wild animal. Lady Henrietta didn't seem to know any more about children than he did.

"I suppose it is possible that Josie is simply responding to change. May I say again how very, very sorry I am to have behaved so outrageously? I only hope that I didn't cause Josie any lasting distress."

Darby grinned. "There's no need to worry about that. Josie has had the time of her life regaling the servants with details about her interesting encounter. Luckily, she didn't quite catch your name and is describing you as Lady Hebby, so you won't be reviled in the neighborhood."

The annoying thing was that Henrietta's lips were outrageously sensual: a deep rose color that owed everything to nature. Moreover, they were full, and soft, and looked ripe for kissing. And kissing them was what he wanted to do. Lean across the table and forget the irritating problem presented by his sisters by tasting Lady Henrietta.

He did need a wife, so why not Henrietta? She seemed quite engaged by the children, even if she didn't know much about caring for them, and she was remarkably lovely.

It was a rather terrifying thought for some reason. True, he needed a wife. But he had always thought of a wife as a decorative appendage he might acquire at some point in the future. She had to be beautiful, of course. And of good birth. But other than that, he supposed his only requirement was that she have little temper. He'd seen enough in his early years to be wary of shrieking women.

And one could hardly say that Henrietta had no temper, he thought, remembering the look of surprise on Josie's face when water cascaded over her head. As a matter of fact, that was just the sort of thing his own mother might have done.

"Josie will mature and join the rest of the human race in a short time," he said. "I imagine the country air is already doing her good. May I bring you something to eat?"

"But Mr. Darby—"

"Lady Henrietta, I have been inexcusably rude. I owe you enough for rescuing Josie and Anabel this morning. I should not bore you with my family exigencies."

She blinked at his crisp refusal to continue their discussion, but she seemed to take no obvious offense. In his experience, women bristled when a topic of conversation was dismissed. Henrietta Maclellan gazed at him in just as friendly a manner as ever. But then she looked over his shoulder.

"Oh dear, I see Mrs. Cable approaching. We are organizing the church bazaar, sir, and have much to discuss. And I must not monopolize your company." She gave him that utterly beautiful smile, the one that lit up her eyes. And then she turned away to greet Mrs. Cable.

Dismissed, he had no choice but to rise and walk away.

Young ladies in London would have come near to fainting if he had bestowed a compliment on them. *There*, everyone knew that he considered symmetry in nature to be the greatest gift.

It isn't a question of vanity, he told himself. Just misplaced attraction on his part.

The stout matron who had claimed friendship with Lady Panton appeared at his elbow. "Mr. Darby!" she thrilled. "I have been longing to introduce you to my own dear, dear niece, Miss Aiken." She took his elbow and then led him away, saying in a whisper, "My sister married for love, sir, for *love*."

Obviously Mrs. Barret-Ducrorq's sister had married beneath her.

"My dear sister passed away only last year, and so the

happy burden of presenting her daughter to society has fallen to my shoulders," she continued in a piercing undertone. "She is the sweetest, most biddable girl; you simply can't imagine. And her father"—she lowered her voice—"well, he was in trade, although he now leaves business matters to his partners. But he *is* worth near a million of floating disposable assets."

Darby bowed in front of the young woman. She had fair skin, dotted with pale little spots that might have been freckles before they were attacked by assiduous applications of lemon juice. Her rusty-colored hair was made up into fat sausage rolls that advertised their origins in a curling iron. In all, she looked like a person doing her best to make herself a marketable piece of goods.

She looked at him with a properly coy glance. But from behind her fan and her fluttering eyelashes he quite clearly glimpsed a calculating female assessment of his worth and his goods.

"My niece just *loves* children," Mrs. Barret-Ducrorq was saying. "She absolutely adores them, don't you, Lucy?"

"I'm quite fond of them," Miss Aiken agreed.

That response annoyed Mrs. Barret-Ducrorq, who obviously wanted a gushing response to the beautiful fish she had snared for her niece. She gave Miss Aiken a fierce glance, and added, "And she just adores dancing."

Miss Aiken was still gazing at him from behind her fan. Unless he was very much mistaken, the heiress of a million floating assets was tempted by thoughts of making a purchase.

"Lucy's seat on a horse—"

But the advertisement was interrupted. "I am quite certain that Mr. Darby has no interest in my equestrian skills, dear aunt," the heiress said, throwing Darby a rather feverish smile. She had pointed little shiny teeth. "I understand that you have, most lamentably, become the guardian of your wee sisters. How adorable they must be! You must, simply *must*, introduce them to me. I do adore children."

"I would be enchanted to do so," Darby said. A pleasant vision of Anabel vomiting down the front of Miss Aiken's peach satin and chewing on her half wreath of roses popped into his mind.

"I think you'll find that my niece has some wonderful advice regarding your young sisters," Mrs. Barret-Ducrorq put in.

"I should be delighted to discuss them. I am certainly in need of advice. Would you care to adjourn to the salon and allow me to bring you some refreshments, Miss Aiken?"

It was clear before they progressed more than ten steps into the salon that this particular heiress was ready to trade her assets on the open marketplace. She fluttered her sandy eyelashes in a way that indicated her physical and material goods were his for the asking.

Darby knew he had to marry. Everyone said so. *He* said so. How could he possibly raise two small girls without female guidance? He cast a glance at Miss Aiken and was met by a burning look of admiration.

There were no open tables in the salon. His aunt looked up with a smile, and would clearly have welcomed him at her table, but he perversely made his way back to Lady Henrietta, who had been joined by two middle-aged ladies chattering like a pair of nutcrackers. Presumably they were talking of the church bazaar.

Lucy Aiken, thankfully, did not seem adverse to joining Lady Henrietta. She dropped into a chair and joined the conversation about the bazaar. Darby headed gloomily to the other side of the room to collect some food. He gathered up two plates. Lady Henrietta had nothing in front of her but a glass of wine, and she needed fattening up.

Miss Aiken greeted his return with glittering eyes that reminded him of an exulting fox spying a succulent pullet.

Lady Henrietta accepted his plate of partridge with a surprised, "Thank you!" and one of those smiles of hers, and returned to a lively discussion of the advisability of running an apple-bobbing stand at the bazaar.

Darby listened for a while, and then decided to find out more about his possible wife. After all, if he was going to spend the rest of his life with the chit, he needed to know what she did when not giggling. "How does one amuse oneself in the country, Miss Aiken?"

She fluttered her fan so violently that a strand of Henrietta's hair rose in the air and fell against her cheek. It was a delicious color, like honey warmed in the sun.

"Just—just with everything, Mr. Darby! I truly am a cheerful type of soul, at least that's what all my friends say! Why, I am perfectly happy sitting about in the conservatory plucking petals off roses—the wilted ones, you understand."

"Salutary," Darby murmured.

"But *you*, sir, what of *you*? I know, of course, that you are a London gentleman, and you do whatever it is"—she tittered madly—"that gentlemen do in London."

Could she be suggesting some sort of lascivious activities? Surely not.

"Do you *box*?" she asked breathlessly.

"No, I don't," Darby replied. "I'm afraid I never took to the art of pummeling my fellow creatures."

"Oh." She was visibly disappointed but rebounded quickly. "I have read about gentlemen boxing with Gentleman Jackson himself, but I expect you spend your time in an equally diverting fashion."

"Not really," he said dampeningly.

Just then Lady Henrietta's two companions bustled off. Miss Aiken immediately turned to Henrietta and included her in their conversation. She did seem to have impeccable manners. In particular, she didn't show an ounce of the jealous possessiveness that most young women would exhibit in the presence of someone as beautiful as Henrietta Maclellan.

"You must be very excited by your debut, Lucy," Henrietta

said. It was rather pleasing to note that he was not the only one affected by Henrietta's smile. Miss Aiken instantly perked up and looked like a young girl at her birthday party.

"If you can imagine, Lady Henrietta, my presentation frock is all sewn with gems. And I'm to wear three white plumes. Imagine that: three."

Darby moodily drank some Madeira.

"We move to the city on the first of February. Will you be in London for the opening of the season?" Miss Aiken asked him.

"Almost certainly," he said. He drank some more Madeira.

Her eyes sharpened. She had beady black eyes, and her hair was definitely reddish. Precisely like a fox, Darby thought to himself.

"Aren't you excited about the season, sir?"

"Truthfully, no."

"Goodness, why not? It sounds like the most pleasant thing in the world to me!" Her hands were clasped in an ecstasy of anticipation. "Dancing at Almack's, riding in the park, Her Royal Majesty's *Drawing Room*!"

"I dislike pushing women around the room to a tuneless orchestra. And the only men who ride in the park are man-milliners," he drawled.

"The season is not a new experience for Mr. Darby as it is for you, Lucy dear," Henrietta said, jumping into the rather awkward silence that ensued.

Miss Aiken was clearly rethinking her initial buyer's lust. "Goodness me," she trilled. "I *must* find my dear aunt. She'll be wondering whatever became of me!" And she tripped away, but not before casting a glance over her shoulder at Darby that made it quite clear that if he wished to trot after her, like a little pony on a string, she wouldn't be averse to keeping him. She would, in fact, overlook his exhibition of churlishness and lack of enthusiasm for the season.

He stayed where he was.

"Now *that* was foolish," Henrietta Maclellan said in a clear voice.

"What?"

"Blowing Lucy Aiken down the wind," she said promptly. "Lucy is a remarkably sweet girl who would be quite a good mother to your sisters. She has a passion for London, and will be easily satisfied by living there and riding in the Row a few times a week. You couldn't do better than marry her."

He blinked. Didn't she know that young ladies did not discuss other ladies' marriageable prospects in polite company? In other words, in the presence of a man?

Before he thought it through, he said, "I believe I am not quite used to the idea of assessing women as marriageable commodities." That made him sound insufferably conceited, so he added: "Of course, the assessment occurs on both sides."

"Perhaps your dismay is due to your gender. We women are, by necessity, quite familiar with the concept of the marriage market. I suspect that the problem is not that you didn't see yourself as part of that market previously. It's that you are used to being an object of great worth, and now your aunt's happy condition has made you slightly—but only *slightly*, Mr. Darby—more affordable."

There was nothing mocking in her eyes, actually. And it made sense that she thought he needed to marry an heiress.

"I suppose that's it," he said. He finished his Madeira. "You are remarkably frank, Lady Henrietta." He could never remember being labeled *affordable* in the past.

"I'm afraid it's a fault of mine," she agreed, looking utterly unrepentant. "Perhaps it's a facet of small-town life. One needn't obfuscate quite as much."

"Never having spent any time in the country," Darby said, "I can hardly disagree with you. I gather you heard the rumor that I have made this particular visit in order to wait out my aunt's confinement and determine whether I am my uncle's heir?"

"Is it true?"

Darby jiggled his wineglass, watching the last few drops of ruby liquid chase about the bottom. "I believe you would find my answer truly shocking, Lady Henrietta."

"I doubt it," she said tranquilly. "A small village contains just as much greed as a large city."

He looked up, a faint smile curling the edge of his mouth. "Now I am both affordable *and* greedy?"

"I did not say that. And I didn't mean it either." Something about her eyes looked trustworthy.

"I did visit my aunt to determine whether she was, in fact, carrying my uncle's child," he said, looking away. " 'Twas an ugly thought."

"Yes," she agreed.

"I was quite wrong. I believed my uncle and aunt to be estranged, but it seems I was wrong." He didn't understand his uncle's marriage, but there was no denying it had been a real one.

His companion said nothing, probably shocked to the bottom of her little country soul.

"Marriage is a strange business," Darby muttered. "Are you drinking champagne?"

"Yes, I am."

Darby signaled to a footman. "Would you like another?"

"No, thank you. I rarely drink more than one glass. I enjoy the bubbles, but not the effect."

As someone who had taken the unusual (for him) step of drinking himself under the table at least four times since inheriting small children, Darby did understand. Understood and didn't agree.

"Please bring me another Madeira," he told the footman, "and Lady Henrietta another glass of champagne. One more glass of champagne won't affect you in the slightest," he told her. "I shall use it for Dutch courage, myself, and perhaps even take your advice and approach Miss Aiken again." He didn't mean it for a moment.

"I think that if you approached Lucy again, you would find her quite pleased to talk to you," Henrietta replied. "She doesn't really see you as a commodity, Mr. Darby. Lucy is merely young. But I think she was quite taken with your symmetry."

He looked at her sharply, and there was just a trace of laughter in her eyes.

The wine was set down before him and he took a sip, rolled it like potent fire on his tongue. Since she was bold in her speech, she presumably would not be shocked by the same bluntness.

"So why are you not on the market, Lady Henrietta Maclellan?" he asked deliberately. "I have watched you talk to old ladies, and young ladies, but no gentlemen."

"Not so!" she protested. "Lord Durgiss and I had a long conversation about his hedges, and—"

"Is that Lord Durgiss?" He nodded toward a stout peer dressed in a florid satin waistcoat. "The man wearing a violet waistcoat?"

"No, that is Lord Durgiss's son, Frederick. Frederick does have dreadful taste in waistcoats, does he not? You see, he fancies himself the next Lord Byron. He's been writing perfectly appalling verse to my sister Imogen for the last month or so."

"And why isn't he writing verse to you? You are far more symmetrical than is Lucy Aiken, for all her thousands." He leaned just a trifle closer and held her eyes for a moment before she dropped them. "You are quite exquisite. Your hair is truly out of the ordinary, and yet here you are, in a rural backwater."

Deliberately he reached out and picked up her hand. It was

tiny, dwarfed by his own. In the back of his mind he realized that his heart was pounding, a ridiculous response to nothing more than a beautiful face and a fringe of black lashes.

She swallowed. Her throat rippled. God, she even had a lovely throat.

"Because I am not symmetrical," she said finally. She took a drink from her glass of champagne, looking at the bubbles rather than at him.

"What do you mean?"

"I cannot have children." She raised her head and looked at him. Her eyes were a navy blue color and perfectly set apart. She was like the most gorgeous mathematical theorem he had ever seen: devastatingly simple on the outside and fascinatingly complicated on the inside.

He hadn't really listened to what she said. "You can't— what?"

"Have children," she said painstakingly, just as if this was the kind of conversation that one often had with a person one has just met.

What the devil was he supposed to say to that? He had never heard a gentlewoman discuss her plumbing in company.

Her eyes were still on his face, and they had that slightly mocking edge in them again. She drew her hand away. "I apologize if I horrified you by my bluntness, Mr. Darby. I'm afraid that everyone is aware that you have to marry an heiress in order to support those lovely sisters of yours. As it happens, I *am* an heiress but, under the circumstances, I am not active in the marketplace."

He literally had no idea what she meant.

She finished her champagne and put it down with a little click. Her smile was kind. "I would not wish you to labor under the misapprehension that I might join the fray and purchase you myself."

He didn't even laugh until some time after she walked away.

10

Henrietta At Home,
After Leaving Esme's At-Home

It was unusual for Henrietta to feel restless once she retired to her bedchamber. Usually she tossed her braid over her shoulder, said her prayers, and went peacefully to sleep. Oh, there were nights when her hip hurt. And occasional nights when the idea of a childless, husbandless life seemed too much to bear, and she wept into her pillow.

But she had friends, and she felt valued, and most of the time she liked her life tremendously. Over the years, Henrietta had quietly taken over many of her stepmother's duties, to their mutual satisfaction. She spent her days visiting the ill and making certain that new families were adequately housed, meeting with the vicar when needed, and planning the various celebrations that marked a country year.

Except for the moments when some foolish person got their back up because she, Henrietta, had spoken rather more frankly than was advisable, she was quite happy. It didn't bother her tremendously that she had never had a season. What would have been the point?

But tonight she couldn't seem to relax. She drifted about

her room picking up this or that book of poetry and putting it down again.

She'd seen etchings of Greek statues in *The Ladies Journal*, and he resembled a god only in profile. From the front he was far too intelligent. His cheekbones were purely English, as were his eyes.

It was a shame that she had to tell him about her hip, although if he kept paying her so much attention, someone undoubtedly would have dropped a hint in his ear. She could see as well as anyone that there was a speculative light in his eye when she offered to help him find a nursemaid, and he could easily have discovered that she was an heiress. How nice for him: an heiress and a mother, all in one package. Of course she was right to disabuse him. She didn't want to start gossip.

His attentions *were* quite marked. She couldn't help grinning at the delicious memory of how he turned and walked straight to her table. And the way he returned with Lucy Aiken in tow. The way he brought her a plate of pheasant. The way he held her hand.

She had watched women and men flirt for years. But she had never realized how pleasurable it was to meet a man's eyes across the room and know that he desired you. Especially when he was the first London gentleman to appear in Wiltshire for over a year, since Lord Fastlebinder stayed for a month and seduced Mrs. Pidcock's downstairs maid. Fastlebinder was overly plump and not attractive, to her mind. But Darby cast all the local men into the shade.

Mrs. Pidcock herself had bustled over to her last night and asked in a piercing whisper, "What *was* Mr. Darby talking to you about, Lady Henrietta? I should not like you to have your expectations raised by a London fortune hunter. Because he *is*." Which was a slightly oblique way of reminding Henrietta that Darby didn't know about her inability to have children or he wouldn't waste his time wooing her.

Henrietta had patted her on the arm and told her, in the strictest confidence, that she rather fancied Mr. Darby had his eye on Lucy Aiken.

But Henrietta herself couldn't stop smiling over the fact that Darby had actually considered her as a potential wife. Otherwise, why the compliments? Why dally at her table? Why talk of her hair, and her symmetry, and hold her hand? Why look at her with that slow and easy grin, as if he was thinking—

For a moment she felt the pulsing wash of despair that used to attack her when she was younger, a numbing longing to be normal. To be a girl like any other girl, free to marry and have children without making her life the payment.

But she was skilled at pushing away thoughts of that nature, and she did so now. That was not the point. The point was that she had met a truly attractive man who didn't know about her disability—and he contemplated wooing her. Since she had spent her entire life in Limpley Stoke, where everyone knew her to be unmarriageable, it was a new experience. And new experiences, Henrietta told herself primly, are always advantageous.

She wandered over to the window, but the manicured lawns of Holkham House were hidden in the night. If Darby truly wooed someone, what a lucky woman she would be. He had lovely eyes. They even tried to tell *her* things, except she didn't believe any of that nonsense. If he were really wooing her . . .

Over the years various of her friends had received love letters, usually the precursor to a formal request for her hand in marriage. A letter written by Mr. Darby would be far smoother and more sophisticated than the bumbling missives of a Wiltshire gentleman. He'd write a letter that would be sweet, and eager, and—

No. He was too beautiful, and he was clearly used to having women fall all over themselves begging for attention. He'd write a love letter that would be arrogant and assertive, and expectant.

Except he hadn't really looked at her that way: as if he expected her to be his wife. It was more as if he thought there was something so delicious about *her*, about her lips or her nose or—she couldn't even say. It was a sort of look that made a woman feel a squirming sort of warmth.

Not the sort of feeling that she, Lady Henrietta Maclellan, ever felt. Ever.

Feelings aside, Darby would write a letter that would make a woman feel desired. Beautiful, even though she was lame. Desirable, even though she couldn't have children. Wanted. He had that lazy, calculating grin that told a woman she was beautiful. Even thinking of it gave Henrietta the oddest little shiver down her back.

She drifted over to her writing desk and sat down. She could almost see the letter in her head.

"*My dearest Henrietta*," she wrote, and then stopped and chewed on the end of her quill for a moment. From what she'd read, quoting poetry in love letters was *de rigueur*.

"*Shall I compare thee to a summer's day?*" Not that Shakespeare was her favorite poet. Henrietta had a secret passion for John Donne. Moreover, Darby was far too vain to adopt Shakespeare's self-deprecating attitude. He would never assume that his beloved thought he was too old or not beautiful enough. She balled up the paper and threw it to the side.

Darby would only write a letter if he were forced to part from the woman he loved. Otherwise, he would just kiss her.

She started over with a fresh sheet of paper, thinking of her favorite poem by John Donne. "*I do not go, for weariness of thee. Nor in the hope the world can show a fitter love for me.*" Her eyes dreamy, she stopped and blotted her quill. Time to move from Donne's to her own words. Or rather, to Darby's words.

> *"Never will I find anyone I adore as much as you. Although fate has cruelly separated us, I shall treasure the memory of you in my heart. I would throw away the stars and the moon only to spend one night in your arms—"*

She hesitated. The letter would have true poignancy if Darby had to leave her after spending the night together. When Cecily Waite ran away with Toby Dittlesby and they weren't found by her papa until the next morning, it was generally recognized as a tragedy.

She squeezed in a word so that the line read, *"I would throw away the stars and the moon only to spend one more night in your arms. I shall never sigh—"* Die? These letters were harder to write than she would have thought. She sent a silent apology to the gentlemen whose literary efforts she had ridiculed in the past.

> *"I shall never meet another woman with starlit hair like your own, my dearest Henrietta. The dangerous beauty of your hair will stay in my heart forever."*

She stared at her head in the mirror for a moment. Her hair was obviously her best feature. Except possibly her bosom. Not that she ever wore dresses akin to Selina Davenport's, but she privately thought that her chest was almost as bountiful, particularly if she jockeyed herself into a pair of stays like those Selina wore.

She dipped her pen into the ink again. If she wrote herself another letter she'd have to get some green ink. Colored ink was so elegant.

Time to finish the letter.

I never knew love until I met you; I never saw beauty until I saw you; I never knew happiness until I tasted your lips.

In different circumstances, she would have loved having a season, and receiving love letters. And writing them, she thought with a wicked little thrill. Replying to a gentleman's missive was considered unforgivably fast, but surely if you were engaged to be married, you might exchange a letter or two.

Without you, there is no reason for living. Perhaps that was a little too overwrought. Oh well, it was just a pretense, after all.

Without you, I will never marry. Since you cannot marry me, darling Henrietta, I shall never marry. Children mean nothing to me; I have a superfluity as it is. All I want is you.
    For this life and beyond.

Tears prickled Henrietta's eyes. It was all so sad. Imagine Darby returning to London and living alone for the rest of his life, never marrying for love of her. She shivered as a draft from the window kissed her neck.

Then her common sense resurrected itself, and a little giggle escaped her lips. An image of the cool, reserved Darby floated in her mind's eye. That champagne must have gone to her head! The man would collapse with shock if he knew about her letter.

It would serve him right. You could tell with one glance that Mr. Darby of Londontown would never fall in love. He was far too self-absorbed to love a woman the way she wanted to be loved: with devotion.

Henrietta was absolutely certain that one day she would meet a man who didn't care about children. Who would love her so much that it didn't matter. Not a fortune hunter like

Darby. A man who would love her for herself, so much that all that children business wouldn't matter.

Her hands stilled, folding up the letter she wrote to herself. It was a shame about Darby. He was perfect for her, in that he had the children she so desperately wanted. But he would never love her the way she deserved to be loved. His mouth literally fell open when she told him she couldn't have children. It was rather pleasant, in a way, to befuddle an elegant Londoner.

He would probably marry Lucy Aiken, or some other heiress since he seemed to have taken Lucy in dislike. Lucy would have been kind enough to Josie and Anabel, although she would have likely left them in the country under the care of a nurse and governess.

Henrietta's eyes prickled again when she remembered the sweet way Anabel said *mama* into her neck. Perhaps Anabel's new nurse would make her wear wet clothing and she would get influenza and die. She shook herself.

That was absurd: naturally Darby wouldn't hire another nurse with a propensity for leaving Anabel in wet dresses. And it wasn't as if she were much better herself—tossing water onto little Josie! Even thinking about her lack of control made her feel ill. After all the time she had spent reading books on child rearing, and all the time she had spent in the village school.

What she could do was assist Mr. Darby in selecting a nursemaid tomorrow morning. He wasn't fit to do it. Anyone could tell that he knew nothing about children. And since he knew about her hip, he wouldn't judge her offer as too forward. She wrote:

Dear Mr. Darby,

I write to renew my offer to assist you in employing a nursemaid for Anabel and Josie. I would be more than happy to join you in interviewing nursemaids. If you do not wish to accept my assistance, I, of course, completely understand.

Yours in sincerity,
Lady Henrietta Maclellan

Henrietta folded up the letter and put it to the side, where a groom could deliver it the next morning. She couldn't help a little smile at the thought of how different the two letters she had written that night were. She probably should discard the love letter. Except that it was likely the only such letter she would ever receive. She left it on her dressing table instead. She could show it to Imogen, and they could have a laugh over it.

~ 11 ~

A Midwinter's Night's Dream

Esme was having a dream. He'd come up behind her, quite silently, and put his hands on her shoulders. She knew who he was, of course, and she knew that they were alone in Lady Troubridge's sitting room. After all, she'd had this dream many times before.

And the reality once.

They were beautiful hands, large and graceful. It would be lovely simply to lean back against his chest, to allow his hands to slip forward and round her breasts. But she had to *tell* him. This time at least.

She turned around, and his hands fell from her shoulders.

"You are not available, my lord. You are, in fact, engaged to my closest friend."

"Only nominally," he answered, unperturbed. "Gina has fallen in love with her husband. Even I can see that. I expect she will tell me tomorrow that she has decided not to annul her marriage."

"I must also point out that *I* am not available."

"No?" Marquess Bonnington caught one of her hands in

his and brought the palm to his mouth. She trembled even at that mild caress.

Damn him for his beauty, for the emotion in his eyes, for the way his hands made her shudder with longing. "As it happens, I too am returning to my husband's bed," she said briskly. "So I am afraid that you have missed your opportunity. Strumpet today, wife tomorrow."

His eyes narrowed. "*Returning* does not imply immediate action." He paused.

She said nothing.

"Do I understand that you are not yet reconciled with the estimable Lord Rawlings?"

At her small nod, he reached behind her and locked the door. "Then I would be a fool to miss the small opportunity that I have, would I not?"

His hands glided down her arms, leaving a trail of fire in their wake. She'd forgotten something, forgotten to tell him something. But he had already taken off his clothes. Sometimes in this dream she watched him disrobe, and sometimes he would suddenly be there, naked amidst all the elegant furniture.

"Aren't you going to undress?" he asked. His voice was husky. He had a big body, a rider's body, which made her feel weak with desire just to look at it.

"Sebastian," she said, and paused. She was experiencing the dream on two levels: her dream-self living it as if it were truly happening again, and her real self struggling to warn Sebastian. To tell him that she was returning to her husband's bed the *very next night.* So he mustn't come to her bed, ever. He mustn't think that this . . . this encounter was for more than an evening.

He kissed her neck, and she felt his tongue touch her skin for an instant. His hair caught a golden sheen from the candles.

She looked up into his stern, familiar, beloved face. Kissing him was like drinking water after a long thirst. His mouth was so sweet, and so fierce, and she had longed for him forever.

She slid her hands up muscled arms, dusted with golden hair, to broad shoulders.

"May I act as your lady's maid?" he asked.

She laid her face against his chest for a moment, savoring the beauty of the moment, the slight roughness of his chest against her skin. He smelled sun-dusted, as if he'd been riding. He smelled like male skin, like Sebastian.

He began nimbly unbuttoning her gown, his fingers slipping little caresses between buttons.

"Doesn't it bother you that this is the first time you have done this?" she asked, with some curiosity.

He paused for a second in his nimble unbuttoning. "No. The process seems simple for most men, so why would it not be so for me? The action required of me does not seem complicated or difficult." A smile played at the corner of his mouth. "I am reputed quite an athlete, Esme. I trust I shall not fail you in the field."

The dream Esme noted his incredible arrogance. Had the man no lack of confidence?

But the real Esme had been in Lady Troubridge's sitting room before and *knew* that he wouldn't fail her. That his prowess was greater, even on that very first try, than that of any man with whom she'd been intimate.

He slipped her gown from her shoulders, leaving her in nothing more than a few French scraps of lace, held together with little ties and bows that delicately begged to be undone.

His eyes had darkened to black. "You're exquisite."

She walked away from him, enjoying the swing of her hip, the fact that she could hear him breathing quickly. Reaching up, she pulled pins from her hair until it fell in a gentle swoosh to her pantalettes. Then she sank backward onto the couch with an exquisite feeling of abandon. And held out her hand.

"Will you join me, my lord?"

He was there before she took a breath. He didn't seem to appreciate her French lace, because he pulled it off until she was quite naked, curling her toes into the carpet.

And then he just looked at her.

When he spoke, his voice made her jump. "I love you, Esme." He pulled her forward, up and into his arms.

In some part of her mind, the real Esme knew that her dream had taken a curve, a turn from the truth. Sebastian didn't love her.

But the dream Esme said, "As much as I love you, Sebastian?"

He smoothed the long line of her hip and thigh so that their bodies clung together.

"What about Gina?" she asked, feverishly aware that Gina was her best friend *and* his fiancée.

"Gina is in love with her husband. She will dismiss me," he said, kissing her shoulder and drifting south. It was pure discovery for him, since Sebastian Bonnington had never understood the folly that leads to setting up a mistress, and had never met a woman who tempted him into foolish behavior. Until he met Esme, that is.

"You can't . . ." She faltered. "You mustn't . . ." The real Esme was trying very hard to remember what she had to tell him.

But he was licking an exuberant trail from her collarbone down . . . he was kneeling. And what he was doing with his mouth—

Her knees went to water, but collapsing on the couch seemed to be exactly what he wished.

"I've desired you from the moment I saw you. God, you

are so *beautiful*, Esme. Every . . . every inch of you." His voice was husky.

Her body trembled. Those hands had never touched another woman's body, but they seemed to know exactly what to do. They stroked past her knees with a touch like wildfire.

"I have to tell you something," she gasped.

"Not now," he said, lowering his head again. Fire surged through her body, pleasure darting to her very fingertips.

"Seb—Sebastian."

He didn't even answer, and the dream Esme was utterly lost, curling forward to put her hands on his large body, to show him things he knew of but had never felt, heard of, but never experienced. Her breath was caught in her chest, unable to form itself into coherent words.

But Esme herself, Esme Rawlings, widow of Miles Rawlings, was twisting and turning in her bed and it wasn't from passion. She was caught in the dream, desperately trying to tell her dreaming self something—make her—

She woke up.

Woke up back in her body, not the lithe, sensual body that Sebastian Bonnington had been caressing, but her rotund, very pregnant self. Once again she had woken up before she could tell him.

A tear leaked down her cheek. She knew well enough why she kept dreaming about a certain evening last June, over and over and over again. Well, there were many reasons. One was that the child in her belly might well be the fruit of the night.

The second was that the child might well *not* be Sebastian's, because the following night she and her husband had shared a bed for the first time in years, precisely in hopes of creating an heir.

Her hands restlessly soothed her lump of a tummy. The child seemed to be asleep as well. No little bumps tumbled against the sides of her belly to make Esme feel less alone.

It was so mortifying that while dreaming she always told

Sebastian that she loved him, but she never told him to avoid her bedchamber the next night. She never managed to inform him that their affair must begin and end in that one night.

Because Sebastian *had* come to her room the next night. Startled them awake and led her husband to think he was a thief. And when Miles jumped on the intruder, his heart had given out.

They were familiar tears. They were familiar as the taste of bread, these grieving, guilty tears.

If only she hadn't succumbed to Sebastian and betrayed her husband. If only she'd walked out of the sitting room when he started disrobing. If she hadn't given in to the longing—

She sat in her bed and let sobs wrench her body as if she could physically expel her sense of responsibility.

It wasn't as if she hadn't been punished. Widowed. Pregnant. Not certain whose child she carried.

Alone.

She always kept a pile of handkerchiefs beside her bed, so her tears were appropriately mopped up. Dispatched and accounted for, understood.

She had loved Miles, in the same mild way that he loved her, with full awareness of each other's foibles. They hadn't lived together for ten years, but they were fond of each other. So missing him was part of the tears.

Guilt at being party to his death—ah, that was a greater part. She just kept wishing that she'd told Sebastian that the reconciliation with Miles was imminent. Of course he assumed it was happening at an unknown point in the future. It only made sense: every person at Lady Troubridge's house party knew that Miles and Lady Randolph Childe had adjoining rooms.

Who would ever think that Miles and she would reconcile for the sole purpose of making a child? That Miles would wish to do so immediately? Sebastian probably thought she meant that they would reconcile when they were back in London.

If only, if only, if only, if only. It beat in her head with every breath of air she took.

More tears, so hard-won that her chest hurt with every gasp. And all those tears couldn't mask a feeling that she was ashamed to be having.

She missed Sebastian.

Not due to their one night, either. She missed him for his sturdy, commonsensical, aristocratic self. For all the annoying things that drove her friend Gina to distraction when she was engaged to him: his honor, his rigidity, his strength of character and mind. The way he saw straight to the heart of a problem. The way he was always controlled and practical, except—Esme thought with mingled pleasure and guilt—except when it came to herself. Only in her presence was he consumed with passion, and only for her did he discard society's strictures.

Because Sebastian was gone. He had left for Europe in the wake of a howling scandal. He had told everyone he had mistaken the room when he entered Esme's chamber, that he thought he was entering the room of his supposed wife: Gina.

Except he wasn't even truly married to Gina, that he had tried to hoodwink the Duchess of Girton with a false marriage certificate because he wanted to bed her and not wed her.

It was just like her darling, honorable Sebastian: in one blow, he saved her reputation and allowed Gina to return to the husband she really wanted. Gina sailed to Greece with her beloved Cam, and Esme retired to the country to mourn. And Sebastian, rigid, proper, honorable Sebastian, sailed to Europe, his reputation in shreds. All England believed him unmasked as an arch villain, so desperate to bed the duchess that he tricked her into believing he had a special license.

The *ton* dined out for months on the duchess's lucky escape: why, if Sebastian Bonnington hadn't mistook the Duchess of Girton's bedchamber and ended up in the bedchamber of Lord and Lady Rawlings, why . . . he would have succeeded in bedding the duchess without the benefit of marriage.

That was the irony of it. Esme was the loose one, the one whose reputation deserved to be ruined, who should be living on the Continent, exiled and alone.

But Sebastian had sacrificed himself and his reputation, and made himself a pariah in the eyes of his countrymen. So now Sebastian was somewhere in the world, alone.

Or perhaps not alone. Now that he knew desire, and he knew pleasure, surely he would find a beautiful woman to marry. A woman who would understand immediately that he was honorable, and understand why he created the story about the wedding license, the one that sent him into exile.

That woman would probably rejoice, in fact, because the scandal brought him to her.

And if Sebastian had a thought for the infamous Esme Rawlings, it would only be with a moue of distaste at his own stupidity, for by seducing her, he had ruined his life.

These tears were bitter, and they tasted of heartbreak.

~ 12 ~

The Next Morning
Tears and Secrets Are the Best of Friends

Lady Rawlings's morning parlor was utterly charming, and by all rights occupants should feel frolicsome, if not joyous. Henrietta paused for a moment and savored the way the sun danced through rose gauze curtains and sent rosy streaks of light across the floor.

That was before she took a look at Lady Rawlings herself. The elegant leader of the *ton* had a pallid complexion and shadows under her eyes, neither of which were complemented by lemony yellow wallpaper.

"I have chosen the wrong moment to pay you a visit," Henrietta said. "I had offered to help Mr. Darby choose a nursemaid, but I could easily—"

"Absolutely not!" Her hostess tried to smile and failed. "Please do sit down, Lady Henrietta. I'm certain Simon will be down directly. May I offer you some tea?"

Henrietta sat down beside her hostess and watched as a tear rolled off Lady Rawlings's beautifully shaped nose.

"When Mrs. Raddle in the village was *enceinte*," she said in a conversational sort of way, "her husband swore that he would never allow her to have another child. She screamed at him like a fishwife the entire time."

"Truly?" Lady Rawlings handed her a cup of tea and mopped up the fugitive tear with a soggy handkerchief.

"I heard her myself," Henrietta said. "Poor Mr. Raddle was a bit stout, and first his wife called him a gammon-faced glutton, and then she accused him of being hog-buttocked. It was some six years ago, but I've never forgotten the magnificent phrase *hog-buttocked*." She put down her tea. Tears were falling faster and faster down Lady Rawlings's face.

"Oh dear." Her hostess smiled in a miserable sort of way. "I'm afraid if Mrs. Raddle is a fishwife, I'm a wet blanket. To be honest, I cry most of the time. My nanny says I'll hurt the babe."

Henrietta reached in her pocket and took out a clean handkerchief, which she used to wipe Lady Rawlings's face. Then she said: "I haven't the faintest idea about crying while in a delicate condition, although I think it is extremely unlikely that it would hurt your child. I do think that crying is not the best choice for the morning though."

"Why . . . why *not*? What could possibly be a better choice?" Lady Rawlings was clearly not herself.

"Tears will make your tea salty. Here, drink this." Henrietta had found that activity had a tendency to curb hysteria.

Esme Rawlings drank some tea, but it didn't seem to stem the tears.

"I expect you miss your husband dreadfully," Henrietta said. "I'm so sorry."

She gulped and said, "Of course, I miss . . . I miss my husband Miles, of *course* I do."

There was something odd about her tone. Henrietta was as aware as anyone that Miles and Esme Rawlings hadn't lived together for years. Moreover, having lived in Limpley Stoke all her life, she had quite frequently encountered Lord Rawlings in company with one Lady Childe. Everyone knew about that connection. But then, last night Darby had implied that his uncle and aunt had reconciled before Lord Rawlings died.

"They say the pain eases with time," she said rather awkwardly.

"It's just difficult, bearing a child under these circumstances. And now that Darby and children are here, I feel so . . . so . . ." Her voice trailed off.

"Perhaps if you think about your baby, it will make you feel better."

"I can't *imagine*," Lady Rawlings said, and there really was an edge of hysteria in her voice. "I don't know what my baby will look like!"

"Well, no one ever does, do they? But it doesn't seem to matter. I can assure you that you will be pleased by its looks no matter how unaesthetic. Mrs. Raddle's son is as plump as a parsnip, and yet she has never called him a gammon-faced glutton. Which he *is*, I assure you. He won a pie-eating contest last spring and he's barely seven!"

Esme Rawlings said, in one long wail, "You don't understand. I don't . . . I don't. . . . I'm not certain what my baby will look like!"

Henrietta blinked. "But, Lady Rawlings—"

"Don't call me that, *please* just don't call me that name!"

Esme was clearly descending into a state of hysteria. Henrietta looked around. Hartshorn or strong spirits were supposed to cure this sort of thing. She never carried a vinaigrette herself.

Luckily Lady Rawlings didn't appear in imminent danger of a thrashing fit. "My name is *Esme*," she said rather fiercely, taking a spoonful of sugar and placing it in her tea. "Please call me Esme. The fact of the matter—"

She raised the delicate teacup to her lips and met Henrietta's eyes over the rim of it. "The fact of the matter is that I am uncertain who fathered this babe."

By a strong exertion of will, Henrietta managed to show no sign of shock. She picked up her own teacup and took a sip. "Ah, is the—are there many candidates?"

"You sound like my friend Gina. The Duchess of Girton. That is just the sort of thing that *she* would say. She's so practical. Gina would never find herself in this situation." Esme started crying again. "I've been a terrible friend to her."

Henrietta tried to think of more practical, bracing things to say. And couldn't since she didn't really have any idea what Lady Rawlings was talking about.

"You see, Gina was going to marry Lord Bonnington but didn't," Esme gulped. "And I'm afraid that *he* might be the father of this babe."

Henrietta's eyes grew round. She knew, of course, about the perfidious marquess, and his rapscallion attempt to trick the Duchess of Girton. "The same marquess who tried to force the duchess—to—"

"No, no. That whole story was naught but a tarradiddle. He entered my room because he was looking for me. Because— he *was* looking for me."

"And he found your husband instead," Henrietta said. "That was bad luck." And there was something so gentle about her voice that Esme felt imperceptibly soothed and even forgiven.

"Henrietta—do you mind if I call you Henrietta?" At her smile, Esme continued. "I'm a miserable excuse for a human being. But I do love him, and it's just so impossible!"

Henrietta was trying to work it all out. "You love Lord Bonnington—"

"I truly am not a loose woman, for all my reputation," Esme interrupted. "I spent one night with Sebastian, *only one*. But it happened to be the night before Miles and I reconciled due to our decision to have a child. My husband said he needed to speak to Lady Childe first—" She peered at Henrietta through swollen eyes. "Do you know about Lady Childe?"

At Henrietta's nod, she said, "You must think that we're a most degenerate group of people. But we're *not*, truly. Miles and I married in error, and then years later he found some happiness with Lady Childe. Except that he desperately wanted an heir, and so obviously he had to inform her . . ." She trailed off.

"And the previous night you and the marquess, ah—"

"Exactly," Esme said miserably.

"The marquess has left for the Continent, has he not?" Henrietta had a vague memory of Imogen excitedly recounting the entire sordid tale of the Bonnington scandal as culled from *The Daily Recorder*'s News from Town.

"Yes. And I don't know whether the baby is his, or whether the baby is Miles's."

"Then you do not have a problem at all," Henrietta said, smiling brilliantly at Esme. "Because this baby is *yours*, not anyone else's."

"Well, I suppose that is true, but—"

Henrietta put a hand on her arm. "I truly mean it, Lady Rawlings—Esme. This child is *yours*. When he is born, he will be a blotchy little thing whom no one but yourself could love. Have you ever seen a newborn?"

Esme shook her head.

"They're quite homely. And from what I've heard, you have a devilish time getting them into the world, and then there they are, without a hair to their name, and all splotchy in the bargain. But he'll be *yours*. If you want him, that is."

Esme wrapped her arms around her stomach. "Oh, I do, I do! I want him. Or her."

"Then I fail to see the problem. The child is born under the aegis of your marriage."

"If it was just me, I wouldn't feel so hideously guilty," Esme said. "But there's Darby as well."

"Darby is a grown man," Henrietta said crisply.

"Yes, but you don't understand. Darby was quite wealthy until around a year ago. And then his father died, and Darby became the guardian of his two small sisters. But he was Miles's heir—"

"Heir *apparent*. I have very little sympathy for a perfectly healthy gentleman like Mr. Darby. His way is clear, and I have every expectation that he will take it. He needs must marry an heiress. Luckily enough for him, he has the face and figure to carry it off."

"But it's so unfair," Esme protested.

"I don't see anything unfair about it."

"But don't you see—"

"No. I would give anything to be Mr. Darby, with two beautiful children to raise. He can marry someone—anyone!"

There was a moment's silence. "I'm so sorry," Esme said. "I knew, of course, that you cannot have children of your own. But I didn't hesitate to burden you with my dismal tale. It was unforgivably rude of me."

Henrietta smiled at her a bit wanly. "There's nothing to forgive."

"Yes, there is. I've been nattering on about matters that must seem trivial in relation to your circumstances."

"It is true that I would love to be in your shoes."

A short laugh escaped Esme. "Don't you understand what sort of a scandal I'm in? What an awful wife to Miles I was? That I'm practically responsible for his *death*!"

"That seems an irrational conclusion. According to all accounts that I heard, Lord Rawlings's heart gave out. Unfortunately, his death could have occurred at any moment. As it is, he has the heir he wanted, and you are going to have a baby. You're going to have a beautiful, miraculous baby." She hesitated, and then said, "I wouldn't give a fig if I had no father for my child at all!"

Esme reached out and took Henrietta's delicate hand in hers. "Are you absolutely certain that you cannot bear a child?"

"Yes. But I should not want you to think that I feel heartache, for I do not, most of the time. However, if someone gave me a babe, I would not quibble too much over the circumstances of its birth."

"Well," Esme said thoughtfully, "I think you were probably the best person on earth to whom I could have confided my sordid little secret."

"I'm afraid that one of the things about having a condition such as I have is that one grows ruthless. I spend a great deal of time watching people, and it has caused me to become rather eccentric in my opinions. My sister complains constantly that I am becoming peculiar."

"Certainly most woman I know would regard me as a monster for what I have confessed to you," Esme said, looking curiously at Henrietta. "To be frank, I can't quite believe that I told you at all."

"I shan't tell a soul. And I do beg you not to give further thought to Mr. Darby's possible disinheritance. He is a grown man, after all."

"*You* should marry him," Esme said suddenly. "He has the children you want, and you—you are remarkably beautiful, Henrietta, which is of paramount importance to him."

"Now why would I want to marry a man with lace cuffs and an obsession with beauty?"

Now that Esme was paying attention, she saw that Henrietta's smile was astonishingly lovely. "He really isn't like that. I know he has a reputation for being finicky, and he does dress carefully. But Darby is quite sensible. Please at least consider marrying him!"

"He hasn't asked me," Henrietta pointed out. "And he won't. Men want their own children. I shall not marry."

"Not Darby! Darby loathes children. You should have heard him on the subject before he took responsibility for his sisters. Can you imagine Darby being truly interested in one of those spotty, hairless objects, as you described them?"

"It is difficult to imagine," Henrietta said with a chuckle.

Esme turned her head quickly. "And here he comes! Darby, do tell me what you think of children?"

In the morning light Darby was actually more elegant than he had been the night before, if that was possible. His waist-coat had embroidery all down the front and smooth scallops of lace adorned his wrists.

He paused and bowed. Even his smallest gesture had a studied elegance. "If I inform you that this is my second suit of clothing of the day, due to Anabel's unfortunate propensity to spray her breakfast in all directions, would that suffice to answer your inquiry? Good day to you, Lady Henrietta." He bowed before Esme, and Henrietta saw him register her tear-stained face.

"Perhaps if Anabel were your own daughter, you wouldn't feel the same," Esme suggested.

Darby shuddered. "I believe not. I want neither the responsibility nor the drudgery associated with children." He looked truly pained.

Henrietta couldn't help smiling. "Children needn't be such hard work. Most fathers rarely see their offspring and have no qualms about their upbringing."

"No," he said firmly. "I am quite happy to say that I have no interest in reproducing myself."

If he didn't have such a clearly defined chin, Henrietta would have thought he was nothing but a fribble. As it was, she felt a prickly awareness of the leashed strength of his legs. Trousers didn't look that handsome on Wiltshire gentlemen!

Esme started to rise, and Darby immediately moved to her side and helped her up. "Are you feeling quite well?" he asked.

Esme looked a little embarrassed. "I'm afraid I've been pouring my tedious tale into Henrietta's ear. And I did the same to you last night. I did warn you." She gave Darby a lopsided smile. "I'm a terrible wet blanket these days."

He had a sweet smile, to Henrietta's mind.

Esme was fussing about with her shawl. "I believe I shall visit my chambers for a moment. No, please do not bother to accompany me. I shall return directly because we are expecting the nursemaids within minutes, are we not? Not only that, but the employment agency promised to send along at least one candidate for gardener as well. Please excuse me, Henrietta. I shall leave you unchaperoned for only a minute or two." Then she bent down and whispered in her ear. "You see? No children!" And she left.

"May I offer you some tea, sir? I'm afraid this might have cooled."

Darby sat down opposite Henrietta and eyed her clothing. "No, thank you. Was that gown made up in the village?"

"Yes, it was," she said. "Was your clothing made up in London?"

"By exiled Parisians," he said.

"In that case I won't bother to give you Mrs. Pinnock's direction. I expect you would find her French inadequate."

He grinned. "Either that or her needle. I am truly grateful to you, Lady Henrietta, for assisting me with this project. I feel woefully unsuited to choosing a nursemaid."

Lady Rawlings's butler, Slope, entered and announced, "The nursemaids are here, Mr. Darby. Shall I show them in one at a time?"

Darby looked at Henrietta. "Better than seeing them all at once, don't you think?"

"Absolutely."

Slope bowed and returned with a stocky woman with a

prominent nose and a chest like a ledge. She was dressed severely in unrelieved black. Darby's charming greeting seemed to make her nervous; she took a good hard appraisal of his lace cuffs, sniffed loudly, and thereafter directed her remarks to Henrietta.

Henrietta knew on first glance that Mrs. Bramble was absolutely not the right person, and so she only listened with half an ear until she realized that the nurse was saying, "So you see, madam, I believe that a child's life must be organized and run by the best Christian principles. In fact, as a member of one of Upper Glimpton's best Methodist families, I can assure you, madam . . ."

Henrietta turned pink as she realized that Mrs. Bramble had fallen into the misperception that she was married to Mr. Darby. She must have assumed that "Lady Henrietta" signified "Mrs. Darby" had retained a family title after her marriage. Of course she assumed that. No young unmarried woman would be with Mr. Darby unchaperoned.

Darby shot her a quick look. His eyes were full of laughter. "Ah," he said, "you sound precisely the kind of woman I have been seeking for my children, Mrs. Bramble. You see our recent nurse had *popish* tendencies."

Mrs. Bramble drew in her breath.

"Yes, indeed," he said with gloomy emphasis. "I truly feared for the souls of my children."

Henrietta hastily intervened. "Mrs. Bramble, one of the children, Josie, is having a difficult time overcoming her grief at the death of her mother. Have you encountered this sort of situation before?"

"Indeed I have. Indeed I have. In fact, I am mourning the death of my own dear mama, as you can tell by my attire." Her face softened, and for the first time Henrietta thought that perhaps Mrs. Bramble wasn't as rigid as she appeared.

"I know full well how distressing the loss of a parent can be." She smiled in a melancholy sort of way. "I think I can say without reservation that I will be the best of all helps for the poor mite. We can share our sorrow."

"I am so sorry to hear of your loss," Henrietta said. "When did your mother die?"

"It will be five years and a fortnight, next Tuesday." Mrs. Bramble smoothed out the stiff black bombazine of her skirt and said, as if it were all settled, "I could move in Saturday, madam, and very pleased I will be, to take care of a poor, grieving child. We shall take our comfort in the Lord."

"Mrs. Bramble," Darby said, rising and helping her to her feet, "this has been a rare pleasure."

Slope returned two minutes later with a sharp-featured young woman who seemed just out of the schoolroom. She was wearing a dress of printed muslin, with five or six layers of flounces around the bottom and a few flounces around the shoulder for good measure.

This time Darby was much more explicit in outlining his relation to the children, and the fact that Henrietta was merely aiding him in selecting a nursemaid. But Miss Penelope Eckersall wasn't terribly concerned about their relationship.

She explained in a determined, rather shrill voice, that although she found the house terribly nice, she hadn't been prepared for how long it took to drive from Bath, where the employment agency was located, to the house. "I simply couldn't live so far from town," she said earnestly.

"Limpley Stoke is only a matter of a mile from here," Henrietta said.

"Well, as to that," Miss Eckersall said, "we did drive through the village on the way. It's very small, isn't it? Just a High Street and an inn, that's all. If there were a military encampment, or something that brought, well, some *liveliness* to the region, but all we saw on the way here in the coach were cows, and that's a fact!"

"It is a farming community," Henrietta agreed, "but—"

She was about to point out that Darby lived in London, but

he intervened. "I agree you would find it tedious. After all, a young woman likes a spot of excitement now and then."

"That's it exactly," said Miss Eckersall. When she nodded, the three rows of flounces at her shoulders all trembled in agreement. "I told my mum that I'd like to find employment in London. That's what I'd truly wish. But my mum won't allow that, not on any account. So she won't allow me to answer advertisements for the city."

"What a shame," Darby said sympathetically.

Like Mrs. Bramble, Miss Eckersall didn't seem overly impressed by his attire. She kept sneaking glances at his cuffs and looking away as if she'd seen something embarrassing.

Without responding to Darby she turned to Henrietta, and said, "Because a young lady does need to make friends now and then, as I'm sure you'll understand." She bounced out of her seat. "I'm very sorry to have wasted your time, I truly am. But I am quite certain that this post is not the right one for me."

As Darby pulled the bell for the butler, Miss Eckersall turned toward Henrietta and said, "May I speak to you for a moment, my lady?"

Darby bowed and strolled to the far end of the sitting room as Henrietta stood up, nodding encouragingly to the nursemaid.

Miss Eckersall whispered loudly, "Don't let him hire the other lady that traveled with me, my lady. That Mrs. Bramble, or so she calls herself."

"Oh," said Henrietta, rather discomforted by this advice.

"You know I don't want the position, so I'm not saying it for my benefit. That Mrs. Bramble told me that she has her mother's hand preserved and sitting on her mantelpiece! On her mantelpiece!" the girl repeated in a thrilled whisper. "I didn't believe her, and she said it's the hand with her mother's wedding ring—isn't that the oddest thing you ever heard?" And she turned and ruffled her way to the door.

Darby showed her gravely from the room and then came

back to Henrietta. "I would guess that neither of those candidates passes muster with you, Lady Henrietta." His eyes crinkled at the corners, and those crinkles made her feel simmering in her belly, even though she knew full well that he was naught but a fribble.

"Confession is good for the soul," he went on. "Was Miss Eckersall warning you about me?"

Henrietta blinked. "About you?"

He grinned. "From her censorious looks at my attire, I thought she might have decided to warn you away from gentlemen of my type."

Henrietta deliberately glanced from his head to his foot. "Are you wearing lace?" she asked sweetly. "I didn't notice. And no, I must disappoint you by confessing that she had nothing to say of you. Are you quite, quite certain that she even noticed your attire? I am afraid to tell you, sir, that outside London people do not take sartorial matters as seriously as you seem to."

He burst out laughing, and that made the simmering in Henrietta's stomach spread down her legs.

"Hoist by my own petard, am I? I think you are good for my vanity, Lady Henrietta." He picked up her hand and brushed her palm against his lips. "You consider me nothing more than a peacock."

She couldn't resist smiling at him. "Perhaps not a *peacock*, but—"

"A buck? A swell?"

"I'm not assured in my use of town slang, sir, given that I have never traveled to London. Could I mean a Tulip?"

He groaned. "Do you see me in cherry-colored stockings, Lady Henrietta? How can you wound me to the bone in such a fashion?"

She raised one delicate eyebrow. "They do say that self-knowledge is a virtue. You *are* an Exquisite, are you not?"

"Alas, my shoulders are not sufficiently padded, nor are my heels high enough."

"How padded *are* your shoulders?" she asked with some interest, peering at his coat as if it were obvious to all that his physique were not his own.

Darby smiled faintly. "While I would be more than pleased to satisfy your curiosity as to my padding, Lady Henrietta, I fear that your request is rather too intimate given that the gardener might join us at any moment. I assure you that I would never refuse such a request in private."

She didn't even blink. "I entirely understand that you feel more comfortable in intimate circles," she said. Damn it, she made it sound as if he were fit for nothing but bedroom matters. "But I have no great interest in your padding. It was simply a passing fancy. One hears so much about London fribbles, if I may use the word without insulting you, Mr. Darby. And yet one so rarely gets to see a fribble up close." She gazed at him rather as if he were a caged lizard with a slightly disgusting skin condition.

Darby felt an inexplicable stab of pleasure. He didn't know whether her sharp-tongued remarks or her exquisite face appealed to him more. Every time Henrietta lowered her eyes, he almost felt dazzled by the delicate shape of her face and the plump kissability of her lower lip. But then she would look at him and pin him to the board like an insect.

"I assure you that most people approve of my apparel," he told her. What a dim-witted comment. Damn it, she was close to making him into a stuttering idiot!

She shook her head. "I am no one to judge your clothing." She glanced down at her sturdy walking dress. It had a border embroidered with ears of corn. She glanced back up at him, a twinkle in her eye. "Now if you would just put yourself into the hands of Mrs. Pinnock, you might actually gain the label of Tulip."

"I shall keep that in mind," he said gravely. "Is Mrs. Pinnock responsible for your gloves?"

She glanced down, puzzled. "Of course. Mrs. Pinnock is good enough to deliver everything that embellishes a suit of clothing. That way, one needn't think at all before dressing."

He shuddered visibly and began peeling the wheat-colored glove off her right hand.

"What are you doing?" Henrietta asked, watching as her hand appeared. "Slope is sure to appear with the gardener in a moment. Although perhaps we should ask him to summon Lady Rawlings first. I can't imagine that she wishes us to interview her gardener."

"She asked me to speak to the fellow," Darby said. "Meanwhile, I am just checking to make certain that your fingers were not gravely thickened by illness. The shape of your gloves made me concerned for your health." He caressed one slender finger. "Swollen fingers are indicative of serious illness."

He was definitely flirting with her. With *her*, even though she told him flatly that she couldn't have children. Henrietta didn't know what to make of it. He stood there before her, large and male and beautiful, holding her bare hand.

"You see," he said gravely. "Beautiful. Slender fingers—" He touched her second finger lightly.

"Symmetrical?" she put in, with a lifted eyebrow.

"I think we can agree on that. You wear no rings?"

"I am not very interested in decoration."

"What a pity," he said sweetly. "I serve as such lovely decoration, myself."

Did he mean what she thought he might? That he—himself—was? She must have misunderstood. He drew his finger down to her fingertip, leaving a tingling path in its wake, and then put his palm to hers. "You see," he said gravely, "there are moments when a woman's fingers are bettered by addition of a male hand."

Her palm was tingling, which was absurd. She drew her hand away before he could touch it again, and said, "Mr. Darby, my glove, if you please."

But Darby didn't give her the glove back. Instead he looked at her with those golden brown eyes, and there was a wicked, laughing light in them. "There are moments—hours, really—when a woman's lips are better by the same addition, Henrietta."

She blinked. By what right did he address her—

He bent his head.

His mouth was hot. That was the first shock. She stood rigidly, wondering what she was supposed to be doing while he put his mouth on hers. Clearly, she was being kissed. The very realization was a second shock. He seemed to be enjoying himself. A large hand curled around the back of her neck and pulled her gently closer. Henrietta's thoughts had slid into a frantic race. Was she enjoying herself? This might be her only kiss—should she be enjoying herself *more*?

She probably should push him away. His lips were moving on hers, and it was—it felt almost—

He pulled back. "Was that your first kiss?" he said.

"Yes, it was." She hesitated. But in the past Darby had seemed undisturbed by her peculiar brand of frankness.

"Kissing is rather overglorified, isn't it?" She smiled at him. "I don't mean to impugn your skills in the least, Mr. Darby. I myself have never been very good at physical sports."

He seemed to be silenced by that. She could only hope that he wasn't famed for his kissing abilities as well as his sartorial opinions. "May I have my glove back, please?"

He handed it to her.

"Thank you so much."

Henrietta had barely drawn it on when Slope pushed open the door and said, "The gardener, Mr. Darby. His name is Baring."

Darby didn't even turn around. He just watched her, with a

half smile, half-inquiring expression that made Henrietta feel agitated. Her agitation was likely due to the unusual circumstance of a gentleman paying her such unusual attention. There was no reason to feel one's heart tripping along at a raised pace. To find one wondering if he would try to take off both her gloves. Or . . . kiss her again.

She turned away and greeted Baring. He was a big man, as tall as Darby. And he was good-looking in an outdoors kind of way. He had golden curls and bright blue eyes, and if he hadn't had a rather stupid expression, she would have thought him capable of raising himself to a better position.

Darby turned around and saw the gardener and for a moment his whole body froze. It happened so quickly that Henrietta wondered if she had imagined it, because the next moment he was saying easily, "Baring, is it? Lady Henrietta, do sit down, and we'll all discuss whether Baring has any experience in the garden."

It seemed an odd question to Henrietta. Of course the man must be handy in the garden. But what did she know about interviewing outside staff, after all? Her stepmother always left such hiring to her man of business, since she was only interested in hiring her personal maid.

Darby helped Henrietta to the settee and sat down just next to her. He leaned back casually and flung an arm over the back of the settee. Henrietta sat upright in her usual manner. He was sitting so close that his shoulder actually touched hers. She edged away.

"I expect the employment agency informed you that we are looking for an expert with roses?" Darby said.

"That they did," Baring replied. "I've been around roses since I was a wee child."

To Henrietta's mind, Lady Rawlings was sadly negligent as a chaperone. It was interesting to find that the whole chaperoning business actually had its merits. Clearly men were driven to kiss whatever female wandered within their arm's length.

Luckily, she didn't seem to be affected by those kisses. She'd heard plenty of talk from other girls about kissing. Molly Maplethorpe swore that when her husband Harold first kissed her, she melted into a bowl of vanilla pudding. Henrietta had puzzled over that image for a while before deciding that Molly was remarkably creative in her language. But other girls had said much the same sort of thing.

Still, it wasn't hard to feel pleased, even though she had felt no such liquefaction. She'd been kissed! Now when girls shared confidences she didn't have to feel like an old maid.

Darby was questioning the gardener about soil-tilling techniques. Where on earth did he learn those things? She had the distinct impression that he lived in London for the entire year. Well, for all she knew they grew roses in London, although it didn't seem possible, what with all the coal smoke.

"And how will you cure rust?" Darby was asking, with an amused tone in his voice, as if he were about to burst into laughter. What a strange man he was.

She stopped listening and went back to thinking about kissing. To the point: why did Darby kiss her? She'd made it quite clear that she couldn't have children, but that fact didn't seem to have warned him off.

In fact, his attentions had only grown more marked. Perhaps, she thought confusedly, he really *doesn't* want to have children.

Darby and the gardener had finished their conversation. The man bobbed his head farewell and left with Slope.

"Do you think that Lady Rawlings is quite all right?" she said, gathering her reticule. "Will you give my regrets to her, please, Mr. Darby? It's a shame that neither of the nursemaids was appropriate. Perhaps we should send an urgent message to the employment agency, asking for more candidates? I'm afraid that I have an appointment in the village and shall have to leave now."

"Don't worry about the nursemaids. We're lucky enough

to have Esme's nanny already at the house. And we did hire a gardener, so the morning wasn't entirely a loss." The smile in his eyes when he said that made Henrietta feel almost dizzy.

"Is your appointment in Limpley Stoke?" Darby continued. "I will accompany you, Lady Henrietta, if you would be so kind as to take me up in your carriage. It seemed to be a charming little village. Perhaps I should ascertain whether Miss Eckersall was correct in her assessment of its lack of liveliness."

"Were you thinking of making a long stay in the country?" Henrietta asked, unable to stop herself.

"No, I wasn't," Darby said thoughtfully. He looked at her in—oh, such a way! Henrietta didn't know what to make of it. For a moment she thought of asking him why on earth he was flirting with her. But even though she'd spent her adult life trying to be direct whenever possible . . . this didn't seem the right moment.

⤙ 13 ⤚

In Which Lady Rawlings
Interviews Her New Gardener

Esme only wandered down the stairs when she observed from an upstairs window that her new friend Henrietta and her nephew Darby had left the house together. She came down humming and feeling rather more cheerful than she had in weeks.

Something about Henrietta's calm acceptance of her unfortunate situation was immeasurably consoling. Henrietta was right to insist that Esme's babe belonged to no man.

After all, Sebastian had only offered to marry her due to a punctilious sense that he was responsible for her husband's death. And Miles was hardly a model husband, either, given that he had resided with Lady Childe for the past three or four years. Why should she feel so guilty about either of them?

If Sebastian had bothered to say good-bye to her after seducing her in a drawing room, he would have discovered that she and Miles were reconciling the very next night. Instead, he treated her like the doxy he clearly believed her to be, and simply visited her room the next night as if she were at home to all callers.

A flame of anger lit in her chest. Why *had* she wasted so

many tears on the man? Sebastian Bonnington was a reprobate who didn't even ask her before he strode into her room in the middle of the night. What did he think she was? A lightskirt, someone available for an easy romp whenever he wished? More fool he. She was not that type of woman. True, she hadn't been faithful to her marriage vows, but neither had Miles. That didn't mean she was a courtesan. She hadn't taken a lover for years, not until the one evening with Sebastian.

And nothing—*nothing*—in that encounter gave Sebastian the right to assume that her bedchamber was his territory.

She reflexively rubbed her tummy as she stared out the back window onto the flower garden. From now on, no more tears. No more talking about disinheriting her child, either. Henrietta was right. She would never be able to tell whose baby she carried.

Instead, she'd make certain that Henrietta married Darby, thereby ensuring Darby an inheritance more than equal to Miles's. Mrs. Pidcock had nattered on and on last night about the estate Henrietta inherited from her father, a clear twenty thousand pounds a year unentailed. Of course, Mrs. Pidcock had also blathered on about how Henrietta couldn't ever marry, given her inability to have children, but Esme thought that was a foolish conclusion. Such things may not be known in the country, but she was well aware of couples who had eschewed having offspring, after turning out the requisite heir-and-a-spare. She herself, before being caught off guard by Sebastian Bonnington, had never risked pregnancy.

There were ways . . . and she would simply ensure that Henrietta knew those ways. One could surmise that Darby was an old hand himself.

There was a large man moving about the bottom of the garden, which suggested that Darby had hired the gardener sent by the employment agency. Presumably the man could do something with the rose arbor. The old man who had been in charge of the gardens had clearly relinquished control to nature long ago. When she arrived last summer, each rose-bush had at most one or two roses. Buds started, but they mildewed without opening, in a distressing way.

She watched the man some more. He was behaving rather oddly. He was definitely doing something to the plants, but what was it? Perhaps he had a cure for whatever it was ailed them.

It took her a good half hour to dress herself warmly and set off down the hill. The lawns at Shanthill House stretched down a gentle slope, and the rose arbor was set at the very bottom. It was Esme's favorite spot. Some long-ago Raw-lings had arched white lath in a long line and then trained roses up the beams. When she and Miles first married, ten years ago, the roses used to crowd together, thick and plump, their wild perfume intoxicating anyone who sat in the arbor. Of course, in the midst of winter the arbor was nothing more than a scraggly tunnel of rose branches and thorns. So what on earth could he be doing to the roses?

She made it down the hill without twisting her ankle and paused at the bottom to catch her breath. Carrying this babe around was far more exercise than she would have thought. Before pregnancy, she had the vague idea that one "carried" the babe until it decided to be born . . . and that was that. No one warned her of the hysterical crying fits, the swollen ankles, or the inability to walk without rolling slightly from side to side.

The man was about halfway down the arbor. He had his back to her, but she could see what he was doing. He was reading a book.

How very peculiar.

She'd never heard of a literate gardener. In fact, Moses, the man who used to be in charge of the gardens, made it very clear that he didn't hold with book learning.

But this gardener was glancing from the rosebushes to his book, and back again.

"Excuse me," Esme said in her nicest lady-of-the-manor tone of voice. "I simply wanted to—"

But her voice died away.

His skin had turned amber brown. He wasn't dressed with his usual impeccable finesse. He wasn't sleek and well-groomed and marquesslike.

But there was no mistaking the man known to his intimates as Bonnington, and to the rest of the world as Marquess Bonnington.

And to her as Sebastian.

Whether Sebastian's friends would have recognized him as quickly as she did was an open question. He was wearing a rough work shirt, open at the throat, and a thick leather apron. He looked more muscular, more vital, and more alive than she'd ever seen him.

Esme recognized him effortlessly. "I'm having a hallucination," she said in a pleasant, conversational voice, staring at the apparition.

"Please forgive me for startling you."

The moment she heard that rational voice the blood drained from her head, and Esme's vision blurred. She swayed and instinctively put out a hand to prevent herself from falling. Her hand brushed a warm body. He was already there, scooping her into his arms, cradling her against his chest. A second later he sat down on the wrought-iron bench with her in his arms.

Esme had never fainted in her life. It simply wasn't in her nature to avoid conflict. Even in the most distressing moments of her bitter marriage, when it would have been marvelous to stage an elegant faint, she could never manage to do so.

But Sebastian clearly thought she had swooned. He was patting her cheek, and uttering witless commands like "Wake up, if you please."

She decided to keep her eyes closed. What on earth was

Sebastian doing in her rose arbor? She needed to think, even though every instinct told her to snuggle into the strength of his arms and pretend for a moment that the world wasn't a cold place in which she was a widow with a child.

"Esme!" His tone was getting more urgent. The blunderhead.

She opened her eyes to find his face just above hers. It was lowering to discover that he had just as much power to overset her as he used to. Something about passionate blue eyes and guinea gold hair made her heart beat quickly, shallow female that she was. Just as something about that rigid expression he always wore, and the punctilious manners he practiced, made her long to rip off his clothing and. . . .

Even when he was her best friend's fiancé. Even then. And even now.

A dismaying thought occurred to her. When Sebastian saw her last, she was a lissome woman. True, she had curves. She'd never been a wisp of a girl like her friend Gina. But those curves had *curved* in. Now she was just one round ball, all curves and no waist.

The thought brought her fully to her senses.

"What are you doing here?" she snapped, sitting up. He had pushed back the hood of her pelisse in an effort to wake her from her supposed faint, and she drew it back around her face. It was her opinion that white fur detracted from the fact that her face was as round as a peach. Perhaps she should get off his lap before he realized just how heavy she had become.

"I came to see you, of course. Ah, God, Esme. I missed you." He put cold hands on her cheeks and kissed her simply. Sweetly. As if he really cared for her.

Esme blinked. "I told you that I never wanted to see you again," she pointed out, rather lamely.

"You don't have to see me. If you stay in the house, I'll

make certain you never encounter me again. I know you hate me because of Miles's death. I have no expectation that you'll ever change your feelings."

A rueful smile touched the corner of his mouth. "It's just that I found myself in the grip of a similarly unchangeable feeling."

She stared at him. "I thought you had gone to Italy."

"I did."

"Well, why—"

"I had to see you."

"Here I am," she said pettishly, resisting the impulse to pull her pelisse even closer around her. She would make sure he never saw her again. At least not until she had this baby and returned to her normal shape. "So why don't you return to Italy and we'll both think no more of it."

"I don't wish to live in Italy, not while you live here."

"What you desire is not important compared to the fact that if anyone discovered you were in this part of the country, it would be disastrous for my reputation."

"No one will find out," he said. The statement had the calm confidence of all of Sebastian's pronouncements. He seemed to know precisely the way the world was ordered—and generally it was in favor of Sebastian, Marquess Bonnington.

"I don't see the reason for your being here." She frowned. "How could you possibly keep up a pretense as a gardener? What do you know of gardening?"

"Very little. I'm learning, thanks to an inestimable monograph on roses by Henry Andrews." His tone was cheerful, but his eyes didn't look happy.

"I just don't see why you're here," she said mulishly. "I'm *not* going to change my mind and marry you."

He was looking at her so intently she felt as if her skin was burning. "I am in love with you, Esme. I think I've been in love with you since the first moment I met you."

"You're cracked!"

He shook his head. "Unfortunately, I'm not the sort of man who does things by half measures."

"You can't be in love with me. You are—were—engaged to Gina. We simply shared an unfortunate. . . ." Her voice trailed off. She wasn't quite certain how to explain the evening they spent in Lady Troubridge's drawing room.

"I am in love with you," he said in his calmly assertive voice. "*You*, Esme, not Gina. I do not feel that sort of love for Gina, lovely though she is. And she knew it. I'm fond of her, but I love you." He bent closer until she could feel his breath against her cheek. "And I want you, Esme, not any other woman. You. I realized while living in Italy that I should have just stolen you away from your husband. But I was too attached to my pride and my position. Now I know that pride is hollow and worthless."

He must be deranged by guilt, Esme thought. That's why he thinks he's in love with me. He lost his reason after Miles died.

She cleared her throat. "There is something we should discuss, my lord."

"You called me Sebastian in the past."

"That was the past," she snapped.

By floundering slightly she managed to get her feet on the ground and stand up. He seemed to let go of her reluctantly, although surely he was grateful to have such a great weight off his legs.

There was something so Sebastian-like about the way he sprang to his feet when she stood up that tears almost came to her eyes. Even in gardener's clothing, Sebastian had the most graceful manners of any man she'd met.

She sat down on the wrought-iron chair opposite and looked in the vicinity of his shoulder. "The doctor tells me that Miles could have died at any time," she said without preamble. "I know that you must be blaming yourself for his death. I would have written you, but I did not have your direction."

"Thank you for telling me." Did he sound relieved? Perhaps he'd already learned about Miles's weak heart from someone else.

"I was wrong to blame you for my husband's death," she said in an offhand way, as if she were excusing herself for a negligible misstep. But the bitter words she flung at Sebastian the last time she saw him echoed in her head: *You think I would marry you? The man who killed my husband? I wouldn't take your hand in marriage even if you weren't a stodgy—boring—virgin!*

"I should not have accused you of killing my husband," she said again. "Miles could have died at any moment. Apparently he'd had two small attacks that week already."

Sebastian was silent. Finally, she risked looking at his face, but she couldn't read the expression there. He was staring at his hands.

Then he raised his eyes and looked at her, and a shock ran through her body. "I would have killed him," he said quietly. "I would have killed him in a second, if I thought I could marry you."

The words hung between them in the chilly air.

Esme's mouth formed a small arc of surprise. "You were engaged to Gina," she whispered.

"I could have killed him for the way he dallied with Lady Childe in front of you."

"But we didn't—he didn't—"

"Did you think no one noticed? I know you cared, Esme." His voice was low and fierce. "I saw you flinch when he kissed Lady Childe's cheek in public. I watched the way you avoided him, the pain in your eyes when you saw him with her."

"We had an agreement, and it was quite mutual, I assure you," Esme said, stumbling over the words. "If anyone, he was the offended party. I left him, not the other way around."

But she wasn't certain that he even heard her. "Rawlings used to call you over to join him when he was sitting with his mistress, as if you had no feelings at all."

Esme swallowed, remembering. "It hurt only because Lady Childe had children and I didn't," she whispered. "I was simply being a foolish, jealous—"

"I don't care. I could have killed him for wounding you in such a way. For not treasuring you as he should."

There was a moment of silence, and then Esme smiled, a crooked little smile. "I'm glad you didn't kill him."

He nodded. "So am I. But I cannot pretend to an immaculate conscience either."

"Darby—Darby told me that Miles knew he would be dead by fall," Esme said. Her face crumpled. "He never told me, Sebastian. He never told me!"

"Ah don't, love, don't." He was there, and she was in his arms and against his chest again, crying as if her heart would break and groping toward the pocket of her pelisse for a handkerchief. But he pressed one into her hand, a large linen one with a crest that didn't look at all like the possession of a gardener.

"Don't mind me," she finally said, in a crumpled kind of way. "It's just the way I am these days, that's all."

He didn't answer, and she finally wiped her eyes and hiccupped once more and looked up.

He had the oddest expression on his face. And—she realized a second later—he had a hand on her stomach.

"Jesus," he whispered.

Esme tried to think of something light to say, but failed.

"You're pregnant!"

Speed Is a Glorious Addiction

Henrietta regretted allowing Darby to accompany her the moment they left the house. How could she have forgotten that she had driven her racing curricle? No one liked to ride with her in the curricle, not even Imogen.

"I'm so sorry," she said, turning to Darby. "I drove quite the wrong vehicle this morning."

His eyes widened as a groom brought out Henrietta's prancing grays, hitched to a gorgeous little racing curricle, complete with high wheels and a small seat that would just barely accommodate two persons. It had a little perch for her groom, but otherwise made no concession to its female driver whatsoever.

"What do you think of my grays?" Henrietta asked, caressing the nose of her right leader, who was tossing his head and stamping his feet and generally indicating that he was full of spice and vinegar. "This is Parsnip, and the other is Parsley." Parsley snorted when he heard his name, and danced just enough to make his harness chime. "Aren't they lovely? Unfortunately, I have had to cure them of a lamentable tendency to bolt, which is why everyone in my family declines to accompany me."

"Are they brothers?"

"Yes, from China Blue by way of Miracle, if you are interested in that sort of thing."

"I'm not, particularly." But a smile curled the edge of Darby's mouth. The wheels on Henrietta's curricle were painted scarlet and picked out in dark blue. The body was scarlet with silver accents. "Did you buy your curricle from Birch?"

"I did."

"As it happens, I acquired precisely the same vehicle last summer. If I recall, you could have chosen scarlet cloth with a fringe." Instead, the seat was lined in a serviceable brown.

"I thought the effect was overly grand." Her eyes were twinkling. "Did you choose the scarlet, Mr. Darby?"

"With gold lace *and* a fringe." He grinned at her.

"Are you fond of curricles?"

"Will you think me sadly unsportsmanlike if I repeat, 'not particularly'?"

"Decidedly," Henrietta laughed. "Those worthy gentlemen who spoke to you last night about drains would not approve." She shouldn't have made the mistake of meeting his eyes. They were so full of devilment that she momentarily forgot that she was holding Parsnip's bridle. The horse immediately took advantage, throwing his head up and pawing the air like the ill-mannered beast he was.

Darby was remarkably swift for someone who appeared to be lazily contemplating her vehicle. He wrenched the horse down in a second, earning an approving smile from Jem.

"If I've told you once, I've told you a hundred times," Jem scolded Henrietta, with the familiarity of a longtime servant. "These here horses are too tetchy to be stroked like barnyard cats."

"You're absolutely right," she said apologetically. "I'm afraid that I was so taken by showing off Parsnip that I forgot his temperament." She walked around the horse toward the small perch of the curricle. Darby noticed with surprise that she had a slight but distinct limp. Had her gait been uneven when they first met? He couldn't remember seeing her walk before this moment.

"May I help you into your vehicle?" he asked.

"No, thank you," she said. "Jem and I have been driving together since the days of my first pony cart, and he is quite used to assisting me."

Jem picked up his small mistress and placed her in the driver's seat, handing her a long whip once she had her skirts in order.

"These horses are on the fast side, Mr. Darby. I trust that you are not distressed by speed?"

Darby clambered into the curricle. "Not at all."

A moment later he felt a little less confident. The horses were either extraordinarily fresh or they were friends with Old Scratch himself. They tore off down the drive from Shantill House with a matched toss of their heads.

No wonder Henrietta had a limp. It was a miracle she hadn't been killed rather than just lamed. She seemed unbothered by the fact her horses were out of control, slipping them around the corner into the high road as if she were driving a pony cart.

It was only when they were tearing along the high road that Darby realized that he was grinning like a fool. His hat was threatening to blow off, so he removed it. His hair had whipped out of the ribbon that held it at his neck, and he was braced for what he considered a likely spill in the ditch, but he was grinning. And Lady Henrietta Maclellan? Well, she was sitting bolt upright in that prim manner of hers, but as he watched she cracked her whip and caught the tip, as adroit as any Corinthian with a stolen mail coach and a bet on the books at White's.

"Where the devil did you learn to drive like this?" he shouted over the wind.

Lady Henrietta turned her head and smiled at him as she adroitly feathered the curricle around the very edge of a curve in the road. "My father was a member of the Four-in-Hand Club. Since he had no son, he taught me to drive."

"Most unusual," Darby commented.

She slowed down just a trifle to give a plodding landau an inch or two on the left. The driver waved, clearly used to seeing Lady Henrietta driving herself. "My father was one of those who bribed public coach drivers to let them careen madly down the road, terrifying all the passengers, I have no doubt. He had a great love of speed." She smiled apologetically at Darby. "I'm afraid that I inherited it. My family considers me to be dangerously prone to taking risks."

Darby laughed again. She was such a prim bundle of womanhood, a petite little female with her bonnet and gloves.

Henrietta pulled the horses to a walk. "We're nearing Limpley Stoke," she explained, "and I do try not to put anyone out of consequence in the village. Some of the villagers are so limited in their thinking about what a woman should and shouldn't do. I generally leave Jem outside the village with my equipment."

"I thought you said that you were not good at physical sports, Lady Henrietta," Darby observed, wishing she would look at him.

They had reached the outskirts of the village, where the road narrowed and turned to cobblestones. Henrietta pulled the curricle to a halt as a traveling carriage lumbered down the middle of the road. "I am not good at games, I assure you."

"Have you ever tried archery?"

She nodded, smiling. "I can't shoot straight. You'd fear for your life if you were near me."

"That suggests that I'm not in fear of my life now," he said with a crooked grin.

The curricle was at a stop, as the traveling carriage was followed by a succession of vehicles loaded down with trunks and boxes. Darby glanced back at Henrietta's groom, Jem, and jerked his head.

Jem blinked at him, and said, "Shall I get the horses' heads, miss?"

At her nod, Darby jumped out and walked around to Henrietta's side of the curricle. He reached up his arms. "May I?"

That was a devilish smile he had, to Henrietta's mind. He stood in a patch of sunlight, golden brown hair tumbling around his face, and the look in his eyes!

But there was nothing for it; she certainly couldn't scramble down from the high perch herself. Jem or some other man must lift her down.

She leaned forward and put her hands lightly on his shoulders. "This is very kind of you, sir," she said.

His face was just before hers now. He put his large hands on her waist and Henrietta shivered. There was something intoxicating about the way his eyes crinkled at the corners when he grinned at her.

"What do you mean by it?" she asked involuntarily. The second she said it, she longed to have the question back, but a lifetime's practice saying precisely what she was thinking had tripped her up.

He let her down to the ground rather slowly, but his hands didn't move. They lingered in an appallingly brash fashion. Even through her pelisse she could feel his fingers shaping the curve of her waist.

"Mean by what?" he asked.

"Mean by the way you look at me."

"I suppose," he said, and his voice was husky and dark,

"that I am considering your prowess at physical sports, Lady Henrietta."

"Oh," Henrietta gasped. His remark was well out of her usual conversational bounds. And moreover, she'd figured out exactly how he was looking at her.

As if he were hungry.

Starving, in fact.

She saw his head coming toward hers, and by all rights she should have moved away. But she simply stood there, still as a stone, and let his lips touch hers again.

This time it was a little harder to think clearly. His hands were still on her waist for one thing. They seemed to have settled at the curve where her hip flared, as if she were his possession.

And his mouth was harder than it had been earlier, less gentle, less respectful. And his *tongue!* She was definitely thinking about protesting, just as soon as her head cleared a little.

Darby never bothered to formulate thoughts or words when he was in the grip of desire, and so he suffered no such confusion. God knows why he was compelled to kiss a rackety female who drove like a fiend down the country roads and uttered whatever unsuitable comment jumped into her head.

But there you are. The compulsion was damn near unconquerable.

She was small, confused, and smelled like meadow flowers. And innocence. He pressed his hard mouth to her soft one as if he could plunder that innocence and replace it with his cynicism.

Her lower lip was plump and sweetly curved. He licked it, and she shuddered. Darby felt the tiny ripple move through her body. So he pulled her closer and licked that lip again, pulled her so close that he could feel her breasts pressing against his chest.

The thought drifted into his head that Lady Henrietta

Maclellan had a body that was made for sport. The hell she wasn't good at physical games.

It was true that she was an impressively bad kisser. Her lips were clamped together like a steel gate. He ran his tongue along her lips again, tempting her—nay, begging her—to open up. He tried teasing. He tried caressing. He tried slanting his lips across hers in a hard caress that had made previous companions melt at the knees and sag into his arms.

The only person his techniques seemed to affect was he himself. His heart was pounding and his groin—well, that would scandalize Henrietta, were she to glance down.

"Henrietta," he said, chagrined to find that his voice was a husky whisper.

"Yes, Mr. Darby?"

He opened his eyes to find her looking cheerfully into his face, seemingly not a whit affected.

The only thing that gave him a glimmer of hope was the wild rose blush high on her cheeks. That, and the fact he had felt a tremor move through her slender body.

"Did you enjoy your second kiss?"

"Oh, yes," she said readily, "I certainly did because—"

That was just what he was waiting for. Simon Darby wasn't above using nefarious tactics to get what he wanted.

He bent his head, captured her words, and drank the innocence from her mouth. He forgot that Jem was standing twenty yards away holding Parsnip and Parsley, forgot the fact that he was making an exhibition of the two of them on the side of the public road.

He forgot everything. She gasped as he plundered her mouth and wonder of wonders, her rigid body relaxed a trifle. A few moments later, one slender arm crept around his neck.

As it turned out, Henrietta Maclellan took to kissing like a duck to water. Far from holding her mouth closed as if to protect the crown jewels, her tongue began tangling with his in a slow dance that made the blood burn through Darby's veins.

The surprise he could almost taste in her mouth disappeared, replaced by an eager little pant, a sense of breath coming from a chest tight with desire.

When he pulled his mouth away, thinking to taste her cheek, her eyes didn't fly open. There was no cheery little comment. Instead she made a little sound that spoke of disappointment, and so he swooped back to the sweetness she offered, to the delicious plump curves of her mouth.

It was Darby who looked . . . looked at the long lashes against Henrietta's cheek, as delicate as a fringe of finest silk. At the clear shape of her forehead, the cream of her skin, the one dimple in her right cheek. In the shadow of the curricle, his hand drifted onto a sweetly rounded bottom, and even though he immediately moved his hand back to her waist, she sighed into his mouth, and he felt another shiver move through her body.

Some distant part of his brain had heard a coach rumble by, the occupants of which were undoubtedly intrigued by the spectacle they were presenting. A native thread of caution wandered into his brain, reminding him that he was kissing a gently born maiden—the daughter of an earl—on the side of the high road.

As if she could sense that wisp of chilly weather, Henrietta let her arm slip from the back of his neck and opened her eyes. She had eyes the color of a summer night, a beautiful dark blue. She looked at him silently for a moment. Her lips were swollen from his kisses. But it was her eyes that were surprising.

Where was the prim Lady Henrietta, the sharp-tongued spinster with untried advice about child rearing and a tendency to speak her mind?

The woman who stood before Darby looked utterly abandoned to desire, as sultry as any round-heeled wench outside the opera house. The new Henrietta swayed toward him without words and he caught her up, caught her squarely against his body, held her as tightly as he was capable.

It wasn't until she started kissing him back that Darby put two and two together. What he put together was one pounding heart (his), one set of shaking limbs (his), one sweet mouth (hers).

Those three things combined with a growing conviction—never felt by him in the thirty-some years of his life—that he had to bed the woman he was holding in his arms. Or die trying.

Two and two added up.

To marriage.

This was his future wife, and if he wasn't careful, he was going to deflower her against the side of her brand-new curricle.

⌒ 15 ⌒

Caught in the Act

One of the first things one learns as a member of the polite world is that proposals of marriage do not take place against the side of a curricle with a groom looking on and any number of carriages passing by. Just about the second thing a man learns is that relatives of females do not like to discover their daughters in just such a situation.

Darby had no sooner come to the realization that he was kissing his future wife than he felt a prickling in his shoulder blades and looked about to meet the blazing eyes of his future mother-in-law.

"Lady Holkham, how splendid to see you," he said, reluctantly stepping back from Henrietta.

"Mr. Darby," she snapped. *"Henrietta!"*

Darby noticed with a great deal of personal satisfaction that Henrietta had a rather dazed look, quite at odds with her competent self.

"My goodness," she said faintly. "I didn't know you were coming to the village, Millicent."

"I am aware of that fact," her stepmother replied, rather grimly. "I am just on my way home."

"I would accompany you, but I have a meeting with Miss Pettigrew at the school."

Henrietta didn't meet Darby's eye. He himself had a sense of swelling joy in his chest. Alarming joy. He'd never felt anything like it in his life. All he knew was that the woman who stood before him, with her spun gold hair pushed back on her shoulders from his hands, and a wild rose flush on her cheeks from his kisses—this gorgeous bit of nature was going to be *his*.

Moreover, she was going to be his, although she didn't know or give a damn about his power in the *ton*. She knew nothing of his wealth, and thought he was a pauper, in fact. How could one choose a better wife? She would marry him for his kisses, and nothing else.

He looked at her, and he was pretty certain that everything he was thinking was written there because she turned even pinker and looked adorably confused.

"Mr. Darby," Lady Holkham said in a piercing command, "I would request that you accompany me to my house, if you please."

"Of course," he said. "And I shall meet you when—in a half hour?" His eyes were on Henrietta.

Only the very corners of her mouth turned up. "I generally speak to Miss Pettigrew for an hour at the most, sir. It would be very kind of you to accompany me home."

"Not to mention brave," he said, casting a look at the curricle.

Her smile made heat lick through his middle section. "Brave as well," she agreed, and turned away.

"Mr. Darby!" He turned with a start to find Lady Holkham regarding him with all the affection of a rat-catcher eyeing his prey.

"Lady Holkham," he said, "I would have requested an interview with you the very moment I left Henrietta at the school."

Her mouth tightened at his use of her daughter's first name. "I should like to speak to you, Mr. Darby. Meet me at Holkham House in twenty minutes, if you would be so kind." She set off down the High Street without another word.

He stared after her, nonplussed. Surely Lady Holkham must be happy to find that a suitor had appeared who cared nothing for Henrietta's inability to have children? Then he realized that perhaps she thought he didn't know that fact.

Of course, once she knew that he didn't want children, she would welcome his suit.

An ironic smile curled his mouth. He had told Rees that he would find a wife in the wilds of Wiltshire, and that was precisely what he'd done.

He walked over to the Golden Hind and obtained a piece of foolscap from Mr. Gyfford. Then he scribbled a note to Rees:

Found a wife. Marrying her out of hand. Thought you'd be pleased to be the first to know.

Darby stared at it for a moment and then scrawled a postscript. "She's an heiress." He addressed it to Rees Holland, Earl Godwin, and handed it over to Gyfford for the mail coach when it came through.

Then he set off, whistling, for Holkham House. All he had to do was clear up this little issue with Henrietta's stepmother and he could go back to the schoolhouse and find his future bride. Ask her to marry him, and linger to steal a kiss or two.

Talking to the headmistress of the village school—an appointment Henrietta normally welcomed with pleasure—was proving itself difficult. For one thing, she kept smiling at the most inappropriate moments.

Miss Pettigrew said something about little Rachel Pander, and Henrietta smiled in response, only to find Miss Pettigrew looking at her perplexedly. But try as she might, Henrietta had no idea what the subject of conversation was. And when it became clear that Rachel's hair was home to several species of lively creatures, there was no explanation for Henrietta's grin.

"I'm quite sorry, Miss Pettigrew," she finally said. "I'm not entirely myself today."

Miss Pettigrew had clear gray eyes that effectively quelled the most rambunctious of students. "That's quite all right, Lady Henrietta," Miss Pettigrew announced. Henrietta shivered and said a silent prayer of thanks that she was no longer of school age.

But she still couldn't make herself pay attention. Darby had kissed her in just the way that her friends had described as the threshold to a proposal. In fact, she couldn't think of a friend who had been kissed like that and not received a proposal directly afterward.

What's more, when Molly Maplethorpe had described kissing as melting into a bowl of pudding, she wasn't exaggerating. In fact, Molly had diminished the experience. Just to think about Darby's kisses made Henrietta's knees feel dangerously puddinglike.

Miss Pettigrew looked at her curiously, but kept going over the lesson plan for the following week. Henrietta contributed not a single comment. She simply couldn't bring herself to care about whether the students were learning their numbers. All she could think was that Darby would meet her outside the schoolhouse in a matter of an hour, and then he would ask her to marry him.

He meant to do it. She knew that as well as she'd known anything in her entire life. She'd bet her life he almost asked her right there next to her curricle, except that Millicent happened to come along the street.

Perhaps he would wait until the evening. Or perhaps she

ought to drive them to a romantic spot in her curricle. Except how could she suggest such a thing? And where on earth could they go that would be romantic at any rate, given the chilly weather that was brewing?

Henrietta kept looking out the schoolroom window, and unless she was very mistaken, a snowstorm would descend on them within an hour or so. Finally, she used the storm as an excuse to escape.

Funny—she'd always like Miss Pettigrew. Honored her for her commitment to children's learning. But today Miss Pettigrew seemed like a lonely, unclaimed spinster, dressed in gray with a high collar and her hair all in braids, with her clipped way of speaking and little humorous asides. *She* had never been kissed. She didn't understand the way the world looked, gray if Henrietta considered the days before Darby arrived in Limpley Stoke, and shot with color yesterday and today.

The liquid warmth inside Henrietta's belly spread a little further as she walked outside the schoolhouse and looked casually down the street. Darby was nowhere to be seen, but of course, she had told him she might be an hour. Her heart thumped, thinking of him. He was so beautiful. It was astounding to imagine that he cared for her at all. That he wanted to kiss her.

Best of all was the fact that he didn't mind marrying her, even though they couldn't have children. Just as soon as he asked her to marry him, she would dash up to Esme's nursery and start getting to know Josie and Anabel—as their *mother*. Because that's what she was going to be: a wife and a mother.

Her heart sang with the happiness of it all.

~ 16 ~

Biology Is Not a Polite Subject of Conversation

"Mr. Darby, I must share some very unfortunate information with you," Lady Holkham said bluntly.

"I am well aware that Henrietta cannot bear children," he said soothingly. "I assure you that it is not of the slightest concern to me. I have never wished for offspring, and besides, I have two small sisters to raise. I am certain that Henrietta will be a wonderful mother to Josie and Anabel."

"You don't understand," Lady Holkham replied. "Lady Henrietta is not *merely* unable to bear children." She stopped.

He frowned, unable to guess what she was implying. She sat bolt upright, looking at him as if she had imparted something of great import.

"She is not merely unable to bear children," he repeated.

"Yes!" she snapped.

"I'm sorry," he finally said. "I am not following your train of thought, my lady." The issue was clearly one that the dowager countess would rather not say aloud.

She cleared her throat. "Henrietta cannot carry a child."

"Yes, I know."

"I do not mean that she would be unable to conceive that child," she finally said painstakingly. "I mean that in the event that she became quick with child, the child would kill her. And it is entirely likely that the child would die as well. It is a miracle that Henrietta herself survived birth; her mother was not so fortunate."

He swallowed. "How on earth can you predict such an event? Her mother's story is unfortunate, but not unusual."

"Surely you have noticed that Henrietta limps?"

He nodded.

"Her mother had precisely the same condition. It was that hip misplacement that made Henrietta's mother unable to give birth to the child she carried. Every doctor we have consulted has predicted that Henrietta will encounter the same problem."

"Have you seen doctors in London?"

"Not in London, but several good men in this area. And they all agreed. This is partly my fault," Lady Holkham continued. "Henrietta knows, of course, that she should not bear children. However, I only realized today that she may not realize the ramifications of her condition. In other words, your disinclination to have children seemed to solve the problem. She does not realize that marriage brings with it certain responsibilities." She said the word *responsibilities* with a bleak distaste that said volumes.

She meant intercourse, clearly. With one part of his brain Darby noted that Lady Holkham's distaste for the marital act had probably led to a lack of clarity in her conversations with Henrietta.

But the other part of his mind was reeling in shock and unwilling to accept the implications of the conversation.

"What you are saying is that Henrietta has no idea that impregnation follows intercourse," he said.

Lady Holkham visibly bridled at his unrefined language. "Precisely." She rose. "I am sorry to deliver such disappointing news, Mr. Darby." She looked down her nose at him. "I think you will find there are other heiresses in the vicinity, should you wish to remain in Limpley Stoke."

Darby bowed. What had just happened was part and parcel of his life in the last year or so. Naturally, when he met a woman whom he could contemplate marrying, she was ineligible. Naturally. The instance was in tune with the death of his parents, the death of his uncle, and his unexpected guardianship of two small girls.

"I trust you can give my apologies to Lady Henrietta? I find that I have forgotten an appointment and I cannot meet her this afternoon."

"I will."

The woman's eyes were shining with tears, but Darby didn't give a damn. What he really wanted was one stiff brandy.

Or five.

From that realization it was a matter of an hour before he found himself in The Trout, surrounded by men discoursing on precisely the correct subject: wives.

"It's not that I don't *like* her," the man next to him was saying painstakingly. He was a fresh-faced young fellow with a laborer's body and a tolerance for alcohol that amazed even Darby. "I do like her. But she hit me with a skillet. Who could forgive such a thing?"

Darby nodded. "No one," he said, swallowing the last of his glass of brandy. He forgot what number it was.

"No man could forgive her for such a thing," the lad said, sounding as if he needed to be convinced.

"At least you *had* her," Darby mumbled.

"What'd you say, man?"

"Nothing." There was no point to discussing it, and a gentleman never discussed such things anyway, especially when in the company of people who beat each other with kitchen implements.

17

Marital Intimacy, Sometimes Referred to as Marital Congress, And Sometimes As Unnecessary

Miss Pettigrew came out of the door of the schoolroom, pulling on warm gloves. Then she turned around and locked the schoolhouse door.

She looked a little surprised to see Henrietta standing on the stoop, as well she might since Henrietta had pleaded fear of the storm as a reason to cut their meeting short, and that a good ten minutes ago.

Henrietta watched Miss Pettigrew march away, back stiff, movements crisp, and felt a curling sense of relief. She had never let herself feel how reluctant she was to remain unmarried. What was the point of reading books about raising children, with the pretext of aiding at school, when all she really wanted was to raise her own children? But if she admitted the truth, she loathed the idea of a life without children and without a husband.

Which was a deplorable thought, she told herself. Miss Pettigrew had flatly told her, when they first met, that she saw no use in husbands. "They take an unwarranted control over a woman's personal circumstances," she had said. "My own sister—" But she pressed her lips together and didn't continue.

Henrietta had nodded and agreed, trying to find fellowship in the company of like-minded women. Except that she wasn't entirely like-minded. She wanted Darby, with his warm brown eyes and angular cheekbones, his lace and exquisite clothing. She giggled to herself, thinking of his curricle trimmed in gold lace and a fringe.

By fifteen minutes later she was growing very cold, and somewhat concerned. Big snowflakes had begun to drift lazily from an oily gray sky. It was surely coming on to snow, and Jem was still waiting for her on the edge of the village. He must be getting annoyed at keeping the horses out in such weather. She bit her lip and waited another five minutes. The snow was thickening, and even though the drive home was a mere half mile, she couldn't afford to wait. Parsnip and Parsley weren't plow horses, used to being abroad in all weather. They needed to be snug in the barn, with a hot mash and plenty of hay.

Finally, she started off down the street, walking slowly in case Darby came running down the street. The very idea was ridiculous—Darby running?

The sensations that rolled over her at the mere thought of Darby made her stepmother's announcement all the more difficult to understand.

"What on earth do you mean?"

Millicent was normally a calm and rather placid person. But she kept twisting her hands in her lap, and there were traces of tears around her eyes.

"I mean," she began. As she had began three or four times. "I mean that you can't—can't be married—"

"Darby doesn't want children, Millicent," Henrietta repeated patiently. "He doesn't care a bit about my inability to have children. He told me himself that he considers them an egregious nuisance."

"Oh, this is all my fault!" Millicent cried. "I should have discussed this with you long ago! It's my stupid reluctance to be straightforward."

Henrietta stilled. An empty feeling settled in the pit of her stomach. She clenched her hands in her lap and said, as calmly as she could, "Is there a further reason why I mustn't marry?"

"Yes. Well, yes and no," Millicent said miserably.

Millicent seemed to be utterly unable to clarify herself. A new, rather horrible idea occurred to Henrietta.

"Did Darby tell you that he didn't wish to marry me? That he found me objectionable in some way?"

Millicent shook her head.

Henrietta blinked with relief. "Then you must tell me why I cannot marry someone, even if he doesn't wish for children."

"I can't!"

"Yes you *can*."

"It's because of—of marital congress. Do you . . . do you have any idea what that means?"

She narrowed her eyes. "Are you talking about marital intimacy?"

Millicent nodded.

"I understand that," she said, to Millicent's enormous relief. Of course, Henrietta with her capable nature, *would* know that sort of detail. It was only noodleheads like Millicent who came to their wedding night ignorant and were subsequently horrified.

But then Henrietta paused. "At least, I suppose I do. Is there some reason I couldn't perform those duties as well as the next woman? My hip may occasionally ache, but it appears to be the same general shape as yours."

"You are correct. But that intimacy leads to children.

Frankly, that's why women agree to the procedure at all. I should have explained it to you long ago."

Henrietta blinked and said slowly, "Of course, what you're saying makes absolute sense, given what I know of barnyard matters."

Millicent colored and looked at her hands. She was so embarrassed by the topic of conversation it was as if someone had poured boiling water down her neck.

"I would have explained it to you in the event of your marriage. That is, I will explain it to Imogen on the eve of her wedding, and—"

"Then—then—you mean that Darby refuses to marry if he can't have that particular intimacy?" There was a bleak note in Henrietta's voice that her stepmother hated to hear. "Even though he doesn't wish to have children?"

Millicent nodded, unable to speak. Her throat was suddenly choked with tears. Why did her beautiful, sweethearted stepdaughter have to face such a terrible truth?

"Men are swine. *Swine!*" Henrietta cried. "Molly—Molly Maplethorpe—referred to the whole event as rather unpleasant and painful too."

"But it is necessary in order to have children."

"Darby has withdrawn his proposal because I am unable to be intimate with him, even though I would find it painful under the best of circumstances?"

"Men feel differently than do women," Millicent said. "They find enjoyment in it, truly."

"Swine," Henrietta said flatly.

Millicent had gone back to twisting her hands. "I haven't explained it very well, I'm afraid. Most women see it for precisely what it is: a rather distasteful procedure that is necessary in order to produce children. It's only painful for a time or two. After that it is merely a nuisance, truly. And oh, children *are* worth anything, Henrietta! After Imogen was born, I realized that—" She broke off, realizing that the subject was hardly a kind one to bring up.

Henrietta shrugged. "I know, of course, that men enjoy that side of life. But to be blunt, don't they maintain mistresses for precisely that reason?"

"Hen-rietta!"

Her stepdaughter looked unrepentant. "They do have mistresses, Millicent. You know they do."

"We don't speak of that."

But Henrietta had never been much good at not saying whatever came into her head. "Why can't Darby simply do the same?" She stared at Millicent. "Why? Why can't Darby take a mistress for that particular duty?"

"Men like to have that intimacy with their wives," Millicent said miserably. "Your father—" She stopped. "This is very difficult."

Henrietta's eyes were fierce enough to force a confession from a spy.

"Your father had a mistress. If you remember, he was rarely home on Tuesday evenings. And sometimes other nights as well. But that didn't affect your father's and my relationship. He married me because he enjoyed my—my appearance."

"I remember. He came up to the nursery and said he'd met the prettiest girl in five counties, and he meant to bring her home and make her my mama. I thought you looked just like a fairy princess, Millicent, truly."

"Thank you, dear," she said a little mistily. "At any rate, when a man takes a wife, he wants to—he want to—it's simply part of the bargain, Henrietta. I can't be more clear than that, I simply can't!"

There was a moment of silence in the room, broken only by the soft hush of wind blowing snow around the corners of the house.

"I believe I understand you. A man marries because he

finds a woman attractive." In her mind, she heard Darby's voice, husky and low, telling her that she had beautiful hair. "And therefore he expects this marital intimacy, whether the woman wishes it or not. Well, I think it's idiotic!"

"What is idiotic?"

"Why couldn't a couple be pleased with each other and yet avoid that particular event?"

"Men are driven. I can't explain it better than that."

Henrietta's eyes were narrow. "What *exactly* did Darby say after you informed him that I was unable to—satisfy him in this regard?"

"He looked quite saddened, my dear. I think he has a genuine regard for you. It is a shame."

"But what did he *say*?"

"He said that he had forgotten a previous appointment, and asked me to give you his excuses for not meeting you outside the schoolhouse."

"It was that easy?" Henrietta said, stunned. "He gave up that easily?"

There was no solace in her stepmother's eyes. "I am truly sorry if I ever gave you the impression that a man might— might overlook your condition."

"It's so stupid of me not to realize that the two things were connected. I thought there would be a man who didn't want children," Henrietta whispered. The desolate note in her voice wrung Millicent's heart.

"Oh don't, love, don't cry," she said, sitting down next to Henrietta on the settee and winding her arms about her.

"I'm not crying." And she wasn't, although her face was white and strained.

"Darby is a fool to let you go for such a reason," Millicent said. "You're right, men are fools."

"Not a fool," Henrietta said bleakly. "A lecher, it seems. Because that is what's meant by lechery, isn't it?" She twisted about to meet Millicent's eyes and found her answer there. "A man isn't content with debauching a mistress; he must have his wife as well." There was a moment of silence, broken only by the sound of the rising wind.

"Oh, this would all have been so much easier if I had known years ago!" It seemed wrenched from Henrietta's heart.

Millicent fumbled for a handkerchief, but it was she, rather than Henrietta, who used it.

"I know that Darby must have seemed a reasonable *parti*," the dowager said, a few moments later. "After all, he apparently dislikes the idea of having children, and his sisters are motherless."

"It's quite all right," Henrietta said. She didn't turn her head toward Millicent. "I shall do very well without a husband. And I hardly know Darby, after all. Miss Pettigrew has pointed out what a detriment a husband is in a woman's life."

"And for all we know, Mr. Darby is a criminal. Would you like to speak to Mr. Fetcham about this?"

Henrietta blinked. "*Mr. Fetcham?* Why on earth would I wish to speak to the vicar about marriage? Unless I were getting married, I mean?"

"Perhaps he could help you reconcile your misfortune."

"No amount of talk about God's will is likely to reconcile me to the future I see before me." Her voice was hard and to the point. "Stupidly, it seems, I had quite hoped to marry at some point."

"I didn't know," her stepmother whispered.

"I thought to find a widower or someone who didn't want children or already had offspring of his own. I hoped that such a man would fall in love with me . . . a love match." She almost laughed at how stupid it sounded out loud.

"There's nothing to say that a truly noble man won't happen along, someone less in thrall to his baser nature."

"I'll keep it in mind," Henrietta said flatly.

"I am glad that Darby moved so quickly to announce his

intentions. This way, you had very little time to become attached to the notion."

"Yes, of course." It was amazing how quickly she had built up the idea of marrying Darby. Truly, she knew almost nothing about him except for his penchant for lace. What if she grew disgusted by a man who likely had a house filled with fringes and gold lace? And he was a fortune hunter, which is a dubious basis for marriage at the best of times.

"You'll be better off this way. You found out his true nature very quickly."

"Yes."

"You see," Millicent went on, having a desperate wish to prove her point and simply *make* that look go away from Henrietta's face, "Darby must be quite a—a *lustful* man, my dear. Because he kissed you in such a way—and in a public spot!"

"Indeed," Henrietta said dully.

"He would have been a most uncomfortable husband." Millicent was on sure ground now. "He—he might even have wished to engage your company more than once a week, my dear. And that would be truly tiresome, as the years passed. You'll simply have to take my word for it."

Henrietta rose and kissed her stepmother on the cheek. "I think I shall go take a long hot bath. And I promise, we'll have no more talk of Mr. Darby."

Millicent discovered that looking at Henrietta through teary eyes turned her stepdaughter's hair to pure gold. "I'm just so *sorry* to tell you unpleasant news. It breaks my heart that you cannot marry and have children." Tears welled up again. "You're so beautiful, and you would have exquisite children, and . . ."

Henrietta leaned over her and wiped the tears away. "It's all for the best, Millie," she said, using her childhood name for her stepmother. "I would never suit Mr. Darby in the long run. He's far too elegant, and I'm too bluntly spoken. I would probably become annoyed with him, and we would fight bitterly."

"I hope it won't be uncomfortable for you to see him again."

At that, Henrietta smiled, and the smile only wavered a little. "Why should it be? We hardly know each other, after all." She walked out of the drawing room with her head held high.

She walked into her room, thinking that this was the time to cry, if ever. But her common sense stopped her from flinging herself on the bed in a fit of tears. She hardly knew the man. Why on earth would she cry over him?

What she primarily felt, she realized, was embarrassment that she had no idea she was ineligible for marriage. It was humiliating to think about how she pressed her body to Darby's. No wonder he thought that she was ripe for debauching, if that was the proper terminology.

Although thinking of the experience made her wonder about Millicent's understanding of intimacy. It seemed to her that Darby could make marital intimacy not quite so objectionable. Surely he, if anyone, would make it pleasurable.

But he couldn't find that pleasure with her. She sat down in front of her dressing table. It was such a pity that she had inherited her mama's hair and face. If she were plain, even ugly, then Mr. Darby would have taken no notice of her at all.

That very fact showed up how shallow he was, a man only interested in her honey hair, to borrow his own words. Well, and perhaps a few other body parts, she thought, remembering how his hands had strayed about.

The worst thing was not losing Mr. Darby, if she were honest with herself. The thing that made her heart feel like a piece of iron in her chest was that no man would wish to marry her, not even a widower. No man would ever fall in love with her. The only love letter she would ever receive had been written by herself. All those dreams she'd had, of finding a man who didn't want children, were nothing more than dust.

She swallowed and willed herself not to cry. The letter she wrote to herself was folded on her dressing table. She touched it with the tip of her finger. Now she knew Darby much better than when she wrote the letter. If he wrote a love letter, it would be far more earthy, and yet more humorous. More fierce and tender, at the same time.

She almost reached toward her writing materials. But writing another letter would only prolong a fantasy of her own making for a few minutes. No amount of letters could make a man agree to marry her. It was time to give up her childhood idea that a knight in shining armor would rescue her. That wasn't going to happen.

One tear slid down Henrietta's cheek. She dashed it away and rang the bell for her maid.

In the bath she practiced an old ritual: counting her blessings. She was perfectly happy before Darby wandered into the village, and she would be again. She had dear friends, and she was needed, and she felt . . .

She felt another tear slide off the end of her nose, and then another.

18

*Esme Rawlings Discovers That Some Truths
Are Difficult to Conceal*

"It isn't your child," Esme said, getting to her feet with a slight lurch. "It's Miles's baby."

Sebastian stared at her without rising, which was a sign of how shocked he was. "Oh my God," he whispered. "You're with child."

"Miles's child," she repeated, trying to invest her voice with authority.

He said nothing so she unbuttoned the front of her pelisse. "Look!" She molded the fabric of her dress against her belly. He looked.

She waited for him to draw the obvious conclusion.

When he said nothing, she supplied the truth herself. "If the baby were yours, I would only be six months pregnant, Lord Bonnington. I would hardly be showing my condition at all."

He wrenched his eyes away and met hers. "We are on a first-name basis, Esme."

There was something in his eyes that she didn't like to contradict, at least not when it came to something so trivial.

"Sebastian," she said reluctantly. "At any rate, I am much farther in the pregnancy than six months."

"When will the babe be born?" he asked.

She tried to look casually uninterested. "Perhaps next month."

Suddenly he realized she was standing, and leaped to his feet. Without speaking, he looked at her from head to foot. Esme suffered it. She had realized that he might as well see how plump she had become. It would convince him that the baby was not his but Miles's. And that was essential, because—because—she wasn't sure why. And he would lose that lovesick look when he realized that she was no longer one of the most beautiful woman in the *ton*, but a plump, round woman with a propensity to cry and not a bit of common sense left in her head.

He didn't seem to be immediately revolted. Still without speaking, he reached out and took her shoulders in his hands and began a gentle circling of her shoulders that felt so good she almost sagged against him.

"Well," she said instead, "I had better return to the house. I have many things to do. The Ladies' Sewing Circle is coming tomorrow."

He gave a little snort of laughter. "*You* are hosting a ladies' sewing circle? You, Infamous Esme?"

"Don't call me that," she said scowling. "I'm a widow, and I'm being respectable, don't you see?"

"Are you good at sewing?"

She wouldn't have even answered him, but he seemed genuinely curious rather than sarcastic. "Not very," she admitted. "But all we do is hem sheets for the poor. The vicar stops by to offer encouragement."

"Sounds remarkably tedious," Sebastian commented.

"Mr. Fetcham is a sweet man, truly. And quite handsome," she said with just a trace of smugness in her voice.

His hands tightened on her back, but he looked down at

her as calmly as ever. "A vicar could never keep you in line, sweetheart."

"I don't need to be kept in line," she said indignantly. "At any rate, Sebastian Bonnington, my point is that I am busy and happy. And I would be quite grateful if you could take yourself back to Italy. Why, a number of people who know you are arriving for a dinner party next week." She stopped, thinking that it wasn't very polite to tell him about a gathering to which he was obviously not invited.

"You must give up this foolish idea of being a gardener," she said, looking around the rose arbor. Luckily old vines and branches were woven so thickly between the lath slats that it was unlikely anyone had glimpsed them standing in the arbor. And no one could think that she would set up an illicit meeting with the gardener amidst the roses. Not in the winter, anyway.

"If you leave, no one will know the worst. I'll write the employment agency in Bath for another gardener immediately."

"I won't be going anywhere," he said. His voice was almost casual, as if he lacked interest in the whole subject.

"Yes, you will!" Esme said, starting to feel a bit annoyed. "As I said, I'm having a *dinner party*, Sebastian. Carola is coming, and her husband Tuppy—you know Carola. Helene will be here."

"You could cancel the dinner." His hands had slid down her back and were making little caressing circles that felt so good she almost swayed at the knees.

"Absolutely not. Why on earth would I cancel my dinner because you decided to leave Italy and come reside in a place where you are not welcome?"

His hands had reached her waist—or where her waist used to be—and now he slowly brought them together in the front.

"This is quite improper," she pointed out. But she didn't move back or take his hand away.

"Ah, God, Esme," he whispered. "You're forty times more beautiful now, you know. Your body is entirely different."

"That's true," she said rather glumly, thinking about her formerly slender limbs.

"Motherhood suits you," he said. "*This* suits you." She looked down fleetingly and saw bronzed hands caressing her belly. It made her feel a treacherous wave of warmth in her knees, so she moved back sharply and buttoned up her pelisse.

"I would prefer that you found another position," she said sharply. "No! What I mean is, would you please return to Italy without further delay? You must see how embarrassing it is for me to have you here. My reputation is gravely compromised simply by having you on my land at all."

He stood there, hands at his sides, and smiled at her. "I can't leave, Esme," he said simply. "Now, more than ever, I can't leave."

"I told you," she said sharply. "This babe is Miles's!"

"I could never doubt it," he said. "I don't know much about these matters, of course, but you are close to the shape my cousin was when she birthed a child."

She nodded. "So, you see, you must leave." She swallowed and looked at him with her heart in her eyes. "I don't want to be Infamous Esme any longer, Sebastian. I just want to be plain Lady Rawlings, a widow raising a child. So please . . . *leave*."

He shook his head. "You needn't come to the garden and see me, but I will stay here."

"You'll ruin my reputation!" she said, her voice going rather shrill. "Someone from the dinner party will recognize you."

"I doubt it," he said calmly. "I shall make certain that no one approaches me. I can't say that I ever met a gardener outside those on my own estate."

She had to admit the justice of that statement.

"Good afternoon, Lady Rawlings." He even touched his

cap, the way a gardener would. And then he turned his back and returned to his book and rose branches.

Slope sprang to open the door as his mistress toiled her way up the slope from the rose arbor. Lady Rawlings was a great one for traipsing around the estate even when it appeared she might drop that babe at any moment. He politely averted his eyes when it became clear that she was once again suffering from a lowness of spirits.

Odd, that's what he called all those tears. In the ten years since Lord Rawlings married, his wife had visited the estate two or three times at the most. Instead Rawlings came with his fancy piece, which she was, for all one had to address her as lady. Lady Childe indeed. No better than she should be.

Under the circumstances, he wouldn't have expected the missus to show quite so many tears at the master's passing. More than Mrs. Slope will do, Slope thought gloomily. Probably dance on my grave, that wife of mine.

Mrs. Slope had incurred her husband's disapproval that very morning by announcing that she had joined a Ladies' Improvement Society started by Miss Pettigrew, the lady schoolteacher. Every red-blooded man in the village and thereabouts knew that the society was nothing more than an opportunity to stir up trouble.

Slope took his mistress's pelisse, handing her a freshly laundered handkerchief as he did so.

"Thank you, Slope," she said mistily.

"Will you be having tea in the drawing room, madam?"

"I believe I will visit the nursery, Slope."

"Perhaps you will find Lady Henrietta there as well," Slope said rather frigidly. It didn't suit his sense of decorum to find grown people frequenting the nursery. Children belonged in the nursery, and adults belonged in the drawing room. Mr. Darby had appeared to be a model of decorum when he first arrived at the house. But he had developed a distressing tendency to wander up to the nursery in an odd moment.

"Shall I request that the children join you for tea in the parlor, madam?" That was much more acceptable, to his mind.

"I shall ask them myself, Slope."

He shook his head as he watched Lady Rawlings make her way up the stairs. He didn't care for newfangled notions.

And visiting the nursery—well, if that wasn't newfangled, what was?

Besides the idea of Mrs. Slope improving herself, that is.

~ *19* ~

My Brother Simon

"I came to apologize to you, Josie."

Josie looked up, speechless. No one *ever* apologized to her. It was always the other way around.

But there was Lady Henrietta, hands clasped in front of her, looking quite anxious and guilty. If Josie had been able to visualize such a thing, the look on Lady Henrietta's face was quite close to that often seen on Josie's.

"I should never, ever have thrown that glass of water on your head. I lost my temper."

Josie knew all about losing her temper. That was what their old nursemaid, Nurse Peeves, used to do, and then she'd scold Josie for making her lose that temper. Moreover, Nurse Peeves said Josie herself had the temper of a devil, and a disposition to match. So Josie backed up, cautiously, in case Lady Henrietta felt like smacking her for being so naughty.

After a moment, Josie still hadn't said anything because she didn't understand what she was supposed to say.

Lady Henrietta bent down and said, "I know that I insulted you terribly, Josie. Will you forgive me?"

Josie thought about it. "I have a temper too," she offered, adding rather uncertainly, "my lady."

Lady Henrietta's smile made Josie feel warm all the way to the pit of her stomach. "How generous of you to tell me. Will you call me Henrietta? I do think that people who share terrible tempers should be on a first-name basis." She looked around the room, which was brightly painted with baby ducks. Esme had obviously had it refurbished in anticipation of her baby's birth. "This is a nice nursery, isn't it? Do you like it here?"

Josie nodded vigorously. Life had improved considerably for Miss Josephine Darby since her brother brought them to visit their aunt Esme.

"Nanny is lovely." Aunt Esme's nanny smelled like cinnamon toast a good deal, which was Josie's favorite smell. "She doesn't mind Anabel spitting up."

"That is a sign of true nobility, don't you think?" Henrietta agreed.

"And my brother Simon comes to visit. He never visited me when we lived in the country. This morning he played soldiers with me!"

Simon? Henrietta thought. I'd forgotten that Darby's first name was Simon.

Lady Henrietta looked a little odd, and Josie thought perhaps she didn't believe her. "He knelt just here," she said, pointing so that Lady Henrietta knew exactly where it happened, "and he showed me how to make battalions, and line up my soldiers. Then he got a little peevish—that was what Nanny called it—because the floor put streaks on his knees, but now I know how to make battalions on my own. Aunt Esme came to play as well, but she can't kneel because her stomach gets in the way."

Henrietta shook off a twinge of jealousy at the thought of Esme's belly and smiled at the little girl before her. It was uncanny how much she looked like her older brother. "Did you know that your hair is the exact color of the leaves in autumn, Josie?"

Josie didn't much care. "Would you like to see my soldiers, Lady Henrietta? I could show you the way my brother Simon ordered the battalions."

"Henrietta," she reminded her. In truth, she would rather not hear about *my brother Simon.* "I would rather not play with soldiers today. How would it be if I told you a story?"

Josie's heart sank a little. In truth, she was longing to engage her soldiers in fierce battle. Ladies generally told stories about kittens and mittens and sometimes ducklings, none of which interested Josie very much.

"Of course," she said politely. For when she was happy, she was a quite polite child.

"This is the story of a pair of little boots, made of the finest calf leather," Henrietta said, seating herself by the fire. "They had twelve little buttons up the front and the buttons were chocolate brown, just the color of your hair."

Well, at least the little boots weren't little kittens. Josie tucked herself onto a hassock at Henrietta's feet.

"I don't think you ever saw these boots, Josie, because they didn't belong to a girl. Nor did they belong to a boy. In fact, these boots didn't belong to anyone, because when this story starts, they were lost. Lost in a deep, dark, forest full of shadows and trees with spindly branches."

Josie drew in her breath. "How did they get there?"

"No one knows. One day they just found themselves in the midst of a dark, dark wood."

Josie shivered just to think about it.

"So the pair of boots wandered down a twisting path, crying—"

"Were they crying for their mama?" Josie was tremendously interested in the whole question of mamas.

"Yes," Lady Henrietta said. "How did you know? That is *precisely* what they were doing."

As the story went on, the boots got wet. They got cold. They were frightened by an owl. Finally, they found their mommy, although she turned out to be a cow, because the boots were made from the finest calf leather. But it was all right because it was winter, and the mommy cow could use some boots to wear, so everyone was happy.

By the time the cow danced off wearing beautiful new boots with twelve chocolate-colored buttons, Josie was leaning against Lady Henrietta's legs, quite overcome with the pleasure of the story.

"Again? Will you tell me that story again?"

"Not at this time," Lady Henrietta said. But she was smiling.

Aunt Esme walked into the nursery at that moment, and said, "You must come to tea tomorrow, and I shall invite the children to the parlor, Henrietta."

"Yes, do come," Josie said.

"I would be more than happy to visit the nursery. We needn't disrupt the children's schedules."

But Esme clearly felt just as Josie did. "Nonsense," she said briskly. "Tomorrow is the day that the Ladies' Sewing Circle is meeting. Did you forget? You promised to keep my stitches from wandering right off the bedsheet. Moreover, both Mr. Fetcham and Darby have promised to stop in and relieve our boredom."

At that, Lady Henrietta really looked as if she were going to refuse, and Josie's lip began to quiver. She was just warming up for a really terrific bout of tears, when Lady Henrietta gave in, and Josie danced around and around in circles instead.

~ 20 ~

The Garden of Earthly Delights

It was impossible not to think about the garden. It drew her like steel to the true north. Sebastian was down there in the gardens. Doing . . . whatever gardeners do. What did gardeners do in January?

It was simply irresistible: the idea of the proper, stuffy Marquess of Bonnington digging holes in the frosty sod, or tying up fruit branches. Esme had brooded over it for two days, wondering where Sebastian was living. Whether he had given up and left. The whole situation seemed so unlikely. Most of their conversations during the time he was engaged to Gina had led to his admonishing her for imprudent behavior. But what could be more imprudent than what he was doing now?

What happened to the measured, thoughtful marquess, who never made a decision without consulting his conscience? Perhaps, having his reputation ruined turned him into another man. It freed him from the burden of social opinion.

She was standing at her bedchamber window—she didn't want to think about how often she had found herself there, looking over the back gardens—when she caught a glimpse of a tall, broad-shouldered man making his way toward the orchard. She watched for as long as she could see him.

There was something utterly different about Sebastian. She could swear he was whistling, although she couldn't see his face or hear him. He walked differently, not with the rigidity of a marquess, but with freedom. It made her wonder about other sides of him. For example, would the kisses of a convention-bound marquess differ from the kisses of a gardener?

Not that she had disliked Sebastian's kisses . . . not at all. But one thought led to another: would it change the way he made love, if he were living in a gardener's hut rather than sleeping on fine linen sheets?

It still made her grin to think that she was the only woman in the world who knew how Sebastian Bonnington made love. That stiff morality of his had kept him a virgin.

Sebastian had reached the orchard and seemed to be cutting various branches. It was simply too tempting. She had to go see what he was doing. A mistress should definitely show proper concern for the state of her garden, after all.

She had to make her way carefully down the slope and past the rose arbor because there was a crackling frost on the dead grass. Her boots slipped more than once, and the only thing that stopped her from turning back was the realization that she probably needed someone's arm to get back *up* that slope.

He wasn't whistling. He was singing—and it wasn't even a hymn, which wouldn't have surprised her.

"My mistress is a nightingale, So sweetly can she sing." He paused and slashed off another branch of the apple tree he was pruning. He had a deep, rich baritone. *"She is as fair as Philomel, The daughter of a king."*

"That's lovely!" she said.

He swung around and a slow smile crept across his face. "My lady." He ducked his head in a laborer's greeting.

"Stop that," Esme said, grinning despite herself. "You forgot to tug your cap," she pointed out.

He raised an eyebrow. "*I* only tug my cap for the male members of the household, I do. I don't hold truck with women trying to interfere with my work."

"Oh hush," Esme said. "Do you know more of that song, Sebastian? It's lovely."

"It's not a song for a lady."

"Yes it is!" Esme had a good memory, and she sang it in a high, clear voice: "*She is as fair as Philomel, The daughter of a king.* Beautiful. Is that a song from the court of Henry VIII? It sounds a bit like one of those old ballads."

She never would have guessed that the very proper marquess could look so wicked. He was leaning back against the apple tree, arms crossed over his chest. His voice rolled out as smooth as honey, "*She is as fair as Philomel, The daughter of a king. And in the darksome night so thick, She loves to lean against a prick.*"

Esme gasped.

He grinned. "I would guess it's later than Henry VIII. I learned it in the pub down in the village. Would you like to hear another verse?" Without waiting for her answer, he sang, "*My mistress is the moon so bright; I wish that I could win her.*"

Esme covered her ears. "I don't even want to know," she moaned.

"*She never walks, But in the night . . .*" he left the apple tree and drifted closer, "*And bears a man within her.*"

"That's despicable!"

"What part?" he asked in a conversational kind of way. "The place where he says he wishes he could win his mistress, or the question of what she does at night?"

"The entire verse! Haven't you anything better to do than repeat ribald verses you learned in the pub? You never would have sung such a song before you became a gardener!" she accused.

His eyes were bright with laughter. "True enough. And you're right, my lady, I do have work to do." He tugged at his cap and turned his back to cut another branch.

"Are you supposed to be pruning in the middle of winter?" she asked suspiciously.

He shrugged. "No, but these trees haven't been pruned in so long that I don't think it will make much difference." He reached up to slice a branch above his head.

She watched him idly for a moment but discovered that what she was really looking at was the way his shoulders tapered down to his waist. And the way gaiters emphasized the power and strength of his thighs.

Her face grew hot as she realized, and she pulled up the hood of her pelisse, but in that instant the branch dropped to the ground and he turned.

Sebastian always could read her face. He moved slowly but with the assurance that marked every one of his movements. He reached out and his hands went to the small of her back and pulled her slowly toward him.

He stopped when the hard circle of her belly touched his body. Esme didn't look away from his eyes. She knew damn well that if she looked away, she would think about what— she didn't want to think.

He bent his head and his lips brushed hers as softly. His lips were hot and sweet. They demanded nothing.

One of his hands roamed down and touched her belly as lightly as a feather floats to the ground. "I wish this was our child, Esme," he said against her mouth.

"It's not," she said hastily.

But she didn't move and his mouth came back to hers, and just as always, even the brush of his lip made her weak. Made her moral resolutions melt.

She meant to move back. She really did. But somehow her mouth opened not because he demanded it, but because she remembered . . . And she remembered correctly. The taste of him was heaven and earth rolled into one.

Their tongues met and mated, and all her dreams came back to her in a rush. It wasn't as if they were truly lovers, but she had dreamed so many variations on the evening they spent together that it felt as if they'd been together for years. It was that easy. They kissed with the sweetness of familiarity, and the deep craving of lovers separated for months. He moved as if he knew every tingle in her body, as if years had attuned him to her cravings.

She trembled against his hard chest and one of his big hands drifted southward, slipped into her pelisse and clasped her breast. She arched forward, just a trifle, into his palm.

He didn't really say anything except her name, but his voice, usually so controlled and urbane, sounded thick and hoarse.

In that one strained syllable was a valuable lesson. Suddenly Esme realized that it wasn't necessarily all bad to gain so much weight. Of course, she had curves before carrying a child. And she had noticed in passing that her chest had expanded as generously as the rest of her. But it wasn't until she heard the rasp in Sebastian's voice, and saw the way he shuddered just from touching the heavy swell of her breast, that she saw a benefit in the situation.

She melted into him as if the baby in her belly didn't exist, as if they were kissing in a bedchamber. He was kissing her back, his mouth hard and possessive, and his fingers moved over her breast in a way that sent flames through her body and weakened her resolve even further. A craving, that's what she felt. A craving for him, for Sebastian, a thirst that had only grown in the six months they'd been separated.

"I've dreamed of this," he said, and his voice was smoky with desire. He pulled back. "I dreamed of you until I thought I was going insane, Esme. I came back because I decided it was better to return than endure any more of those dreams."

His words brought her back a measure of sanity. "We can't do this!" she gasped, pulling back so quickly that she almost fell over. He steadied her.

"Why not?"

She gaped at him. "What's happened to you, Sebastian Bonnington? I used to call you a Holy Willy when you were engaged to Gina. Sometimes I thought you lived for the moments when you could catch me in an indiscretion and read me a lecture!"

"I did," he said. "Because I wanted to talk to you, Esme. I wanted to watch that flush rise in your cheeks, and find your magnificent eyes focused only on me, not on other men. I didn't ever want to see you flirting with a simpleton like Bernie Burdett. I wanted you only looking at me."

"But you were engaged to Gina."

He shrugged. "We were friends for years, and it seemed an entirely reasonable marriage."

She scowled. "That's a foolish notion—a reasonable marriage."

"*You* were married," he said quietly.

"Yes, in a reasonable marriage."

"I think Gina and I would have been kinder to each other than you and Miles were. I genuinely love Gina and I respect her enormously."

"Miles loved me!"

He raised an eyebrow.

"Well, he was genuinely fond of me," she snapped.

"He didn't respect you."

She looked away with a careless shrug. "Well, who could? Early in our marriage, I behaved like a strumpet . . . But I loved Miles. It's true that I didn't love him in an amorous fashion, but there are very few love matches made these days."

"You were never a strumpet," Sebastian said, looking down at her.

She met his eyes. They were the cloudless blue of a summer's day. "I wouldn't wish you to misunderstand the life I've led, Sebastian, out of foolish romantic notions that you have nourished in Italy. You only slept with one woman in your life, but you were merely one of a list who entered my bed. True, the list is not terribly long, but you know as well as I do that there are only four kinds of women in the world: maiden, wife, widow, whore. I would say that I have the last two nicely covered."

He cupped her face in his hands. "Did you enjoy the first time you were unfaithful to your husband?"

She swallowed, and then raised her chin. "No, but I did it. And I enjoyed those who followed." She said it defiantly.

"If Miles had returned to your bed; if he had shown any distress at your blatant, public seductions; if he had shown any wish to pleasure you himself, would you have sought out those men?"

There was a moment of silence.

She raised her face, eyes shining with tears. "I would have sought out you, Sebastian."

He didn't say anything, just swept her into his arms and held her as tightly as she'd ever been held. He smelled like apple trees, and woodsmoke. He crushed her face against a coat rougher than anything a marquess ever put on his body, and she just clung to him.

After a few moments he tipped up her chin and pressed a kiss on her lips. She swallowed, hard. "I must go."

He nodded. "I am not saying this due to a lascivious impulse, but you can always find me in the gardener's hut at the bottom of the apple orchard, Esme."

"You're living in a hut? *You?*"

He nodded. "I'm enjoying it. But the important thing is that I'm there if you need me. For anything."

She couldn't smile straight because she was going to cry again. He looked down at her silently, and then he said, "I thank God I didn't marry Gina. Even if I had, I'd still be living at the bottom of your apple orchard. And what a scandal that would be."

She made it up the frosty slope by herself.

The Sewing Circle Meets at Lady Rawlings's House

The next afternoon came all too slowly. By four o'clock, Josie was so excited that she hardly knew what to do. She ran around the playroom with a little basket over her arm, trying to put all the soldiers in it so she could take them downstairs with her.

"Do you think my brother is in the drawing room already?" she kept shrieking. The idea was so exciting that she dashed around and around the room. That sort of unladylike behavior would have driven Nurse Peeves quite out of her mind, but Nanny just patted her head as she tore by, and asked if she wanted to use the chamber pot before going downstairs.

Her new friend Henrietta was sitting with Aunt Esme when they reached the parlor, and Josie was so excited that she ran in a little circle before she managed to drop two curtsies and say, "Good afternoon," just as she'd been taught.

Then Henrietta told her the story of the lost boots again, and Josie ate seven lemon tarts without feeling the least inclined toward sickness, so when Anabel had to go upstairs for a nap, Josie begged to stay. She sat quietly just in front of Henrietta, and started pulling the soldiers out of her basket, one by one, and organizing them into battle lines.

"Where did you find those toys?" Aunt Esme's voice was sharp, just like Nurse Peeves's when Anabel threw up on her.

Josie shot her a quick glance, nudged just an inch closer to Henrietta, and said, "They were upstairs. Nanny said it was all right to play with them."

Aunt Esme didn't say anything more, and after a moment Henrietta patted her head, and said, "Why don't you take your soldiers back to the nursery? I'm certain that Anabel is missing you."

Josie knew as well as anyone that Anabel was still taking a nap. She began putting her soldiers back in the basket one by one, very slowly. Then she looked over at the settee and saw that Aunt Esme was crying again.

The first time Josie saw her aunt crying it was baffling, almost frightening. But now she knew Aunt Esme well enough to know that she cried quite often, so Josie just put the last soldier into her basket in a long-suffering type of way, and curtsied to her aunt. But after she curtsied to Henrietta, she whispered, "Do you think you could visit me tomorrow? And tell me the story of the lost little boots again?"

And Henrietta smiled at her and said perhaps, and so Josie didn't mind going upstairs very much.

Which left Henrietta in the drawing room with Esme. She handed her a handkerchief. She had taken to carrying some extras in her reticule. Esme was in the stage of weeping in which she appeared to be having trouble breathing, but luckily Henrietta had seen at least two such attacks in the last week and had no fear of her extinction.

"I—I'm so-sorry," Esme said. "Those are my bro—my brother's soldiers, that's all. Nanny must have brought them with her. I haven't seen them in years."

"I didn't know you had a brother."

"His name was Benjamin."

Henrietta got up and sat next to Esme on the couch and put a comforting arm around her shoulders. "I'm so sorry."

"He died when he was fa-five. It was a long time ago. I shouldn't cry about it now. It was just seeing his tin soldiers again." And she dissolved into sobbing on Henrietta's shoulder. "I ne-ne-never *cry*," she wailed. "Never! I didn't even cry at the funeral, even though he was my own sweet Benjamin, my own-own poppet, and no one loved him the way I did. He was my very own."

"Oh, Esme, I'm so sorry," Henrietta repeated. Her own eyes felt prickly. "That's awful."

But Esme was pulling herself upright. "I am so tired of all this grief," she said in a wavery sort of way. "I truly haven't cried much in my life at all. I know you probably don't believe me, because we've only known each other a month, but it's true. I am *not* a wet blanket. At least, not in my normal state."

"There's nothing improper about crying at the memory of one's brother. Any child's death is heartbreaking."

Esme blew her nose, which was already rather red, and reached for a lemon tart, except Josie had eaten them all. Henrietta passed her a tray of jellies.

"I cry at everything. This morning I spilled my hot chocolate all over the bed and almost started crying over that. All I do is eat and cry. Thank goodness, at least I enjoy the former activity. I'm sorry, Henrietta. What were we discussing before this happened?"

"Nothing terribly important."

"Yes we were," Esme said. "I was trying to pry out of you what happened with Darby. Because you left the house last Monday, looking quite pleased with each other, but have you exchanged more than two words in the last few days?"

"Of course we have spoken on occasion," Henrietta said in her most reasonable voice. "We don't have a great deal to say to each other, but that is natural when people's interests are so very disparate."

"I simply can't understand it. I'm a fairly good judge of character. I truly thought you two were a certain match, if you don't mind my saying so."

Henrietta did mind. But what could she say about it? "Of course I don't," she hastened to say. "I think you simply misinterpreted our interest in each other."

"I may not be able to sew a straight seam to save my life, but I'm an expert at interpreting males," Esme said. "What's more, I know Darby. When I left the two of you in the drawing room, he had the look of a man about to steal a kiss. And, darling, having been in the *ton* for too many years to remember, and having kissed a huge number of men, *that* is one look that I recognize!"

Luckily (or unluckily, depending on how one looks at it), Henrietta didn't have to answer because the ladies of the sewing circle streamed into the room, all chattering at once. Esme heaved herself to her feet and waved at Slope to remove the empty plate that had once contained lemon tarts; Henrietta rose to greet Lady Winifred, Mrs. Barret-Ducrorq and, to her surprise, her stepmother, Millicent.

Henrietta knew immediately why Millicent had joined the sewing circle. Her stepmother never attended charity functions, having declared them boring as dust years ago. But Darby's presence in the house made it different. She undoubtedly wished to observe his behavior around Henrietta. Or vice versa.

Mrs. Cable bustled in a bit late, after the rest of the ladies were settled with a cup of tea. "Hello! Hello!" she shrilled, darting around the room and issuing kisses. She stopped short before Henrietta and said, "*Well*, Lady Henrietta!"

Henrietta curtsied. "How nice to see you, Mrs. Cable."

"I saw you but you didn't see me," Mrs. Cable said archly, shaking her finger at Henrietta.

Henrietta felt a sinking in her stomach.

"Oh yes," Mrs. Cable said, with the shrill pleasure of a woman holding a piece of ripe gossip. "I was *there*."

"There? Where?"

"Well, I was in my traveling carriage, actually," Mrs. Cable said. "We were going to visit my sister who lives a mere five miles away, but my husband always says to me, 'Mrs. Cable, make yourself comfortable whenever you wish.' So I had, my dear. I had taken the traveling carriage even for such a short distance."

When Henrietta still looked blank, she said, "I was in the traveling carriage. And if you don't mind my saying so, I truly think that you might well wish to be more circumspect, Lady Henrietta. As the Second Book of Titus says, a good woman is discreet, chaste, and keeps at home." There was an edge to the sentence. "I could have had a young child with me. One of my nieces, for instance."

"I'm afraid that I don't—" Henrietta began, but her stepmother interrupted.

"Mrs. Cable, I would hazard a guess that you witnessed the admiring kiss that Mr. Darby bestowed on my daughter?"

"Indeed," Mrs. Cable said, plumping herself into a chair. "That is exactly what I saw, my dear lady, but if I might say so, that kiss showed more than admiration!" She tittered.

Henrietta sat frozen on the settee, but Millicent had taken over. "The poor man offered for her hand, ladies."

Everyone looked at Henrietta and then glanced away as if she showed signs of the pox.

"Of course, Mr. Darby didn't understand the circumstances," Millicent finished.

Lady Winifred, who was seated next to Henrietta, patted

her hand. "That must have been very difficult for you, my dear. If only the old customs prevailed, and gentlemen had the decency to approach one's parents or guardians before expressing their feelings! In my day, this never would have happened."

"True, true," Mrs. Barret-Ducrorq said shrilly. "I have instructed dear Lucy that she is not to respond at all to an importunity from a gentleman unless he has spoken to me and I have given my assent."

Henrietta shaped her lips into what she hoped was the smile of someone importuned against her wishes. Now she knew why Millicent had joined the sewing circle. It wasn't so she could observe Henrietta conversing with Darby. It was so that she could defend Henrietta from the consequences of that scandalous kiss.

Esme joined the battle. "My nephew is simply devastated by the news," she said with a convincing catch in her voice. "I'm afraid that he truly lost his heart to Henrietta. He told me that it was the effect of being offered absolutely *no* encouragement, ladies. Now isn't that an improving tale for young women? I daresay you know that my nephew is quite authoritative in the *ton*. So many young ladies have tried to engage his interest. But it wasn't until he met Henrietta, and encountered her utter lack of interest in him, that he felt the wish to marry."

Millicent nodded. "I could tell that it was a tremendous blow, when I had to inform the poor gentleman of Henrietta's circumstances."

Everyone looked sympathetic.

"I daresay he'll recover," Esme said sadly. "But not for a good period of time. I only hope that I might see a grand-nephew or -niece during my lifetime."

That was overdoing it, to Henrietta's mind, but the ladies were nodding.

"It must have been a terrible disappointment," Mrs. Cable

murmured. "There, I could tell from the way he was—was holding Lady Henrietta that his heart was engaged. And all because you showed him no interest! 'Tis truly a pity that more young women don't have our dear Lady Henrietta's circumspection."

"I've had to tell my niece more than once to be more prudent in her behavior," Mrs. Barret-Ducrorq noted a bit sourly. "Mind you, Lucy gave Mr. Darby no encouragement. Said she thought he was not terribly nice. But there you go, we've always been a very perceptive family."

Darby sat in his small bedchamber and wrestled with his conscience. There was absolutely no reason to go downstairs for tea. What he ought to do was return to London. He came to Limpley Stoke to discover whether his aunt was carrying his uncle's child, which she was. Actually, he felt ashamed of his suspicions. The fact that Esme might well have a lover on the premises, given that Sebastian Bonnington seemed to be masquerading as a gardener, was none of his business. There was nothing to keep him here.

The problem was that he couldn't remember ever wanting something the way he wanted Henrietta Maclellan. In the past four days it seemed all he could think about was that he should have taken the reins of that absurd little curricle and driven them back to the house and then—and then—

Even thinking about her made his mouth dry. Thinking about the way she shivered when his hand swept down her back and clasped her bottom made his groin leap to full attention. Thinking of her throaty little cry when he pulled away from their kiss made him certain that if he could have maneuvered her into a bed, she would have been the partner of his life.

That was the hell of it. He'd never even considered another woman as a partner for life. As an exclusive occupant of his bed.

Never.

A gentleman never discussed such things, of course, but he knew that he and Rees were pretty much in agreement on the subject. They both liked wild and unruly women. In Rees's case, the women seemed to have big voices to match their big chests; in his case, they just had to have a keen sense of humor. A way of moving and wearing clothing that was sensual. And an eye that met his across the room and said, clear as daylight, *come to me.*

Henrietta had the sense of humor—but nothing else on that list. She wore silk as if it were sackcloth, and moved as if her body were made of wood.

Of course, he could come up with a new list, one that included a frank honesty that took his breath away. A passion that was genuine, but limited to sensual gestures and silky garments. A way of laughing at him that was tender and intelligent and made him feel as if he was admired for himself. Not for his power in the *ton*, nor his physical attributes. Himself.

The whole train of thought made Darby feel as if ants were crawling up his back. It wasn't that he hadn't thought about a wife. Of course he had. He wanted a wife as much as the next man: that is to say, in a fuzzy, future-bound sort of way. He had a dim idea that perhaps his marriage could be better than his parents' had been. It would be best to feel affection for one's spouse. And to be able to enjoy spending time in each other's company.

Yet until he met Henrietta, he had never visualized spending years of his life with one woman. He'd also never considered the pleasures of introducing a woman to sexual pleasure. He tended to bed seasoned women, as adroit in their bedroom affairs as they were in the management of household staff.

But with Henrietta . . . things could be different.

A sharp knock on the door brought Slope with a note from Esme.

You were seen kissing Henrietta; I think it would be best for all if you did not join us for tea today.

Best for all if I returned to London.

Best for Henrietta if I never saw her again.

Except how could such a sensual woman live her entire life without a man? A memory of the way her tongue danced around his made his body stiffen again.

But Esme's note settled the burning question of whether he should join the sewing circle downstairs. He would leave for London as soon as it could be arranged.

~ 22 ~

A Council of War

The ladies were gathering up their sewing baskets, as Slope carried off a smallish stack of hemmed sheets (there had been too much excitement for proper concentration on needlework). Henrietta gratefully rose to her feet, but Esme reached up and grasped her hand.

"May I borrow your stepdaughter for an hour or so?" she asked Lady Holkham.

Henrietta said, "No!" rather more forcefully than she meant to.

"Not for dinner," Esme said, sending an unspoken message to both women that Darby would be present at dinner. "My dear friend Lady Perwinkle and her husband are arriving for a brief visit, and I would be most grateful for Henrietta's help with preparations for a small dinner in their honor. Of course, this will be a very small, sedate dinner, since I'm in mourning."

Henrietta looked as if she were going to refuse again, so Esme put a hand on her belly. "It *is* difficult to find strength these days," she said sadly.

"Henrietta will help you however she is able," Millicent

assured her. "I will send the carriage back for her in an hour or so, shall I?"

"Well," Esme said as she closed the door behind them. "So you and Darby have nothing in common, hmmm?" Her eyes were sparkling with laughter.

"I can't marry anyone," Henrietta said awkwardly. She was afraid that she would burst into tears if she explained the situation.

"I've been meaning to speak to you about that," Esme said, plopping back heavily onto a couch. "I gather you can't be married because it is inadvisable to undergo conception of a child due to your hip, am I right?"

"Exactly," Henrietta said. A lowering depression seemed to be sitting in her chest. She shrugged. "After my stepmother explained the situation to Darby, he quite properly withdrew his proposal—if he had ever had the inclination to make it."

"Of course he had the inclination. Gentlemen—and Darby is a gentleman—do not plaster a woman against a carriage in the broad daylight unless they have matrimony in mind. At least, if the woman in question is a lady."

"Well," Henrietta said dully, "I suppose it is a coup that Darby thought to marry me."

Esme leaned forward. "I am going to be utterly frank, Henrietta."

Henrietta nodded.

"What I am going to say is absolutely unheard of in polite conversation, but believe it, it is practiced regularly. There are ways to limit one's offspring, and I don't merely mean abstaining from a shared bed."

"Really?"

"Various methods. Would you mind if I shock you further?"

At that, Henrietta smiled, if a bit shakily. "I haven't found you too shocking so far. I *have* seen women cry before you moved to Limpley Stoke, you know."

"Wretch! Well, the truth is that Sebastian Bonnington was not the first man in my bed—other than my husband, that is."

"Oh."

Esme felt a crawling embarrassment, but she barged ahead. "When Miles first left our house, I was enraged. I wanted his attention and tried to get that attention any way I could. I flirted with every gentleman in the *ton* who showed the inclination. I didn't bed them. But I gave every indication that I was doing so. Do you understand, Henrietta?"

"I think so. You were trying to make your husband angry. Did it succeed?"

"No," Esme said a little sadly. "No, it didn't. You see, we really weren't suited as a couple. My father insisted that I marry Miles, and Miles knew that I had been forced to do so. He was the most good-natured person in the world. My behavior only made him feel more guilty, and less as if he had a right to reprimand me for my wanton behavior. He was utterly pleasant, whenever we met."

"I expect that made you even angrier."

"Yes . . . I was very young and very foolish. Eventually I found myself in the bed of an older gentleman who was more experienced in such matters than I was. He provided himself with a means of preventing contraception."

Henrietta's eyes widened.

"By a year or so later, I tired of affairs. But during that period I used something called a sheath. It's very simple. Frankly, I think the advice you've received about not marrying is all foolishness. Given the existence of this and other methods that prevent pregnancy, your circumstances are no bar to marriage. I'm surprised that Darby didn't point that out to your aunt."

The hope that had flared in Henrietta's breast died again. "Darby must not have really wished to marry me. Surely he knows about these methods."

"Naturally he does. The fact is, the male brain is arranged

in a quite nonsensical fashion. I expect he thinks that a gentlewoman would never touch such an object. Or that a lady's sensibilities are too delicate even to hear of it. But I never had any hesitation to use the sheath, and I firmly suspect that other gentlewomen do the same. After all, how many women do you know who have produced no more than an heir and a spare? Clearly the method works. It certainly did for me."

"Then why did no one tell me about it before?"

Esme had a rueful look on her face. "Perhaps it takes a fallen woman to share such secrets. None of the ladies of the sewing circle would want to introduce the subject, Henrietta. It simply isn't a topic for polite conversation." She hesitated. "There is also an idea that women don't enjoy making love anyway, or shouldn't enjoy it."

"I know it is an uncomfortable procedure."

Esme suddenly laughed, a throaty little laugh that had made men crumple to their knees from London to Limpley Stoke. "I will leave it to my elegant nephew to change your mind about *that*, Henrietta. Believe me, there is discomfort and then there is pure pleasure. But, if ladies have been told that the act is supposed to be unpleasant, I expect it is difficult for them to admit that they engage in the act for reasons other than impregnation."

"That seems logical."

Esme laughed again. "I can't fathom that we are having this conversation! My close friends are married, but until recently none of them has been living with a husband, so we had no opportunity for such frankness."

"*None* of your friends live with a husband?"

"I wasn't living with Miles, obviously. And my friend Gina's husband actually left the country twelve years ago, when they first married. So not only was she not living with a husband, her marriage was never consummated." She paused and grinned. "Of course, that situation has changed. Gina and Cam returned from Greece together just before Christmas."

"Gina is the Duchess of Girton," Henrietta said, putting the stories together. "The woman who was engaged to your—to Marquess Bonnington."

"Exactly. And I told you already about Carola and her husband Tuppy. They are together now and will be arriving tomorrow for a short stay. You met Helene, Countess Godwin. Her husband is utterly dissolute," she said with a face. "Rees is now sharing the family home with a young opera singer. For a while, he had six Russian ballet dancers residing with him. Oh, and he's Darby's closest friend."

"Goodness," Henrietta said rather faintly. "Is Darby as flagrant in his personal life as his friend?"

"Oh no, Darby is discreet in everything he does. He and Rees have been friends since they were children. I do think you and Darby are very well suited. Since we are being quite frank, he needs your inheritance, and Josie needs you as a mother. I have to admit that I find that story you told Josie about little boots searching for their mama quite heartbreaking. I almost started crying in the midst of your tale."

"That would have been a change," Henrietta said with a touch of irony. "But as for marrying Darby, he'll never ask me. He must believe that I am too ladylike even to consider this sheath. And I can hardly announce my understanding to him!"

"The real question," Esme said, "is whether you wish to marry *him*." She folded her hands in her lap and waited.

Henrietta swallowed. "Of course I would like to be a mother to Josie and Anabel. Quite desperately, in fact."

There was real kindness in Esme's eyes, but she didn't say anything.

"And I do have a fortune," Henrietta said awkwardly.

"True. But marriage is difficult. Mentioning Carola and Helene reminded me of that fact. Are you quite certain that you would wish to marry Darby in particular? Because if you came to London for a season, we could find you a nice widower with children. In fact, I can already think of an inestimable gentleman, Mr. Shutts. He must have at least three small children, and—"

Henrietta discovered, to her dismay, that the very name Shutts put her teeth on edge, and so she stumbled into speech. "I should like to marry Darby. I would—I would quite like to marry your nephew."

Esme seemed unsurprised. A tiny smile played around her mouth. "In that case, we need a plan."

"What sort of a plan?"

"Men are fundamentally foolish and easily driven in the proper direction." Esme dismissed the thought of Sebastian, who had ignored her explicit demand that he return to the Continent.

"I remember that your friend Lady Perwinkle wooed her husband, but I cannot woo Darby. It wouldn't change the situation."

"No," Esme said with a dreamy expression in her eyes. "You may not be able to woo him, but we can think of something. Just give me a moment."

Henrietta waited.

Esme chewed on her lip. "The thing is," she said, "Darby is a born rescuer. Do you know what I mean? He never paid any attention to his little stepsisters—well, who would?— but when they were orphaned he instantly brought them into his household."

"Did he have any other choice?"

"Yes, certainly. There are various aunts and uncles who on the face of it would have provided a better home for the girls than would a single man living the rackety bachelor life in London. But Darby would not allow it."

"I don't see how he can rescue me," Henrietta objected.

"The only way a man can be forced to marry a woman is if he has ruined her reputation. So Darby has to ruin your reputation."

"But everyone knows, and even so—*why* would he want to

save my reputation when everyone knows I can't bear a child? The two things are connected!"

Esme shrugged. "Not really. Of course, everyone will be scandalized at the idea that you behaved indiscreetly with him, and by that I mean that you bedded him, Henrietta. But as long as you marry with extraordinary speed, it will be a nine days' wonder, and nothing more."

Henrietta swallowed. "How am I going to get him to—to bed me?" she whispered. "Another kiss, perhaps."

"Oh, we don't have to go as far as that," Esme said to Henrietta's great relief. "We simply have to arrange for your reputation to *be* ruined, if you see what I mean. Then Darby will step in and rescue you!" She smiled brilliantly.

"How on earth are we going to do that? I've heard of reputations ruined by indiscreet behavior, or evidence of some sort, but—"

"We'll present evidence," Esme said patiently. "Believe me, there's often very little connection between evidence and truth. If we present evidence that you and Darby spent the night together to Mrs. Colby, for example, she'll have the two of you married off before you even turn around, and it won't matter a smidgen to her that you are endangered by the whole childbearing issue. The important thing to her is that scandal is tied up in neat packages."

"I just don't see what could be offered as evidence, under the circumstances."

"Oh, a letter," Esme said carelessly, "a letter or a poem should do it. A poem would add an elegant rather Darby-ish touch, really."

Henrietta's eyes widened, and Esme caught the slight movement. "He wrote you!"

"No."

"But you have *something*, don't you? Something we could use as evidence?"

"Well . . ."

"What is it?" Esme demanded.

"It's embarrassing," Henrietta admitted.

"How embarrassing can it be? *I* just confessed to you the whole tale of my seamy past!"

Henrietta had to admit the truth of that statement. "I wrote myself a letter," she said. "From Darby, if you understand."

"You wrote *yourself* a letter? Why didn't you write a letter to Darby if you were in an epistolary mood?"

"I think I'd had too much champagne. I was thinking about love letters that friends of mine had received. And I— well, I'm unlikely to receive any love letters, am I?"

Esme's eyes grew misty. "That's so *sad.*"

"So I wrote one to myself!" Henrietta said brightly, before her friend could collapse in another fit of tears. "And believe me, it's better than any man could write me."

Esme, caught on the cusp of weeping, chuckled instead. "Isn't that the truth? I've received hundreds of letters, myself, and not a one of them worth the paper they were written on." Except perhaps that note she had upstairs under her pillow, the one written by the gardener. Which had not a word of love on it.

"I consider my letter to be a model of its type," Henrietta said, laughing as well. "I even quote poetry—"

"Who? Shakespeare?"

"John Donne."

"Donne's love sonnets? I am glad that I rusticated near you! I wouldn't have thought there was a soul in Limpley Stoke who had read Donne's early poems."

"Well, I have."

"And I'm quite certain that Darby has read them as well. I hope you did it properly and referenced a night you spent together?"

A blush edged Henrietta's cheeks. "I did."

"Good! This should be easy. We'll launch the plan at my dinner, naturally. The important thing is the guests, and where they sit."

She sat for a moment in silence.

"I'll invite the Cables," she said finally.

"Myrtle Cable?" Henrietta asked in disbelief. "You must be joking! Even my stepmother, who is the sweetest woman in the world, won't have her to an intimate meal. Every other word she says is a biblical passage, haven't you noticed?"

"Perfect," Esme said with satisfaction. "And I'll have the vicar too. We have a shortage of men, since Helene is returning tomorrow. As the head of the family, Darby will be at one end of the table, and that leaves you with no partner. The vicar can escort your stepmother. And he will surely frown on illicit goings-on within the parish."

"I doubt it," Henrietta said. "He's not the interfering sort of vicar."

"Pity," Esme said. "Still, I'm sure Mrs. Cable will more than make up for his reticence. As for the letter, Carola will be particularly useful. Now here's what we'll do . . ."

~ 23 ~

An Island, a Nymph, and Thou

There was the menu to plan. The chef had requested yet another conference, as he was unable to obtain sufficient trout, and the menu would have to be changed. She needed to discuss precedence with the butler, and dinner cards with the housekeeper. Why on earth had she asked even one guest to the house? She was supposed to be in retirement, not giving supper parties. But it was too late. Fired by loneliness in the first month after Miles's funeral, she had asked Carola to visit just as soon as the initial mourning period of six months was over.

Esme sighed and lay back on her bed again, looking at the list of guests. Perhaps there was time for just a short nap. After all, Carola wasn't arriving until tomorrow.

Her brain was so slow. She couldn't seem to think what to do about the fact that she'd received a note from Rees Holland, Helene's loathed husband. Darby must have invited him to stay, and that was a disaster, because Helene was arriving any moment. If Helene didn't want to stay at the house due to Darby's presence, Esme could just imagine how she'd feel when Rees himself made an appearance.

Perhaps she should wander down to the apple orchard. Marquess Bonnington was exquisitely aware of the intricacies of personalities and precedence. He was certainly the best person to consult about such matters. Unless he was busy digging a ditch, she thought with a drowsy chuckle.

He wasn't. Esme found the hut without any problem. It seemed snug enough, a little one-room structure at the very bottom of the gardens. It was made of rough-hewn wood, and smoke was wisping out of a little crooked chimney. She almost didn't knock. Lord knows, the mistress of the house was not supposed to visit a gardener in his home. It simply wasn't done.

An image of Sebastian's censorious face before he became a gardener flashed across her mind, and she pushed open the door without knocking.

He was sprawled on a rough bench to the side of the fire, head propped up on his arm, reading. The image of him caught in her mind: the comfort, and the ease in his long body. The intentness with which he was reading. The happiness that seemed to cling around him.

"A bucolic scene," she said mockingly.

He looked up and didn't instantly leap to his feet. Instead he sighed and put his book down, and then swung his feet to the floor in a leisurely sort of way. The proper marquess was well and truly gone, Esme thought with wonder.

With a broad-shouldered gardener on his feet, the hut was suddenly much smaller. She managed to stop herself from drifting forward to touch his chest and see if it was as muscled as it appeared in a work shirt.

"Esme. What a delightful surprise."

"What are you reading?" she asked, abandoning the idea of questioning him about precedence. Instead she strolled over to the bench and sat down. She would have reached for his book but there was no way around her stomach.

"*The Odyssey*," he said, adding another log to the fire.

"My God, Homer? Why on earth are you reading that old stuff?"

"It's not old stuff—merely the tale of a man trying to come home. But he keeps getting waylaid by strumpets."

She cast him a needle-eyed glance. Could he possibly mean the innuendo that she read into that phrase? No. That would verge on rudeness, and Marquess Bonnington was never rude.

"Strumpets?" she asked. "It's Odysseus, isn't it? Doesn't his ship run into a Cyclops? My impression was that the Cyclops was a one-eyed—and very male—monster."

"True enough. But I happen to be reading about the time he spent trapped on an island as the slave of the nymph Calypso." He didn't even look at her, just gazed into the fire. He put his arm up on the mantelpiece and Esme feasted on the strength of that arm. God, but he was beautiful.

"What was he doing on the island?" she asked, giving herself a short silent lecture on the sins of lust.

"Oh, it appears he was a slave to the nymph," Sebastian said dreamily. He looked at her now, and those eyes were absolutely wicked. "Obeyed her every command. And I gather from Homer that she relished his presence in bed. One can only imagine . . ."

"Yes," Esme said thoughtfully. "Lucky Calypso."

"Or lucky Odysseus. After all, she was his mistress, and he didn't have to worry about anything. His only task was to fulfill Calypso's wishes." His voice was threaded with laughter and something else. Something rougher and altogether more disturbing than laughter.

"Well, I'd better go now," she said brightly, standing up. "I just wanted to make sure you were comfortable and I can see—"

He stepped in front of her and the words died on her lips. "Is there anything you would command, *mistress*?"

Esme's mouth was dry. This beautiful barbarian was offering himself to her. One hand, rough with physical labor, touched her cheek with a caress as gentle as an evening breeze. Then he moved back and propped a shoulder against the wall and just waited.

"Sebastian—" she started, and stopped.

He turned and opened the door. It was dark outside. Inside the hut was all glowing warmth. The firelight threw licks of golden light around the rough-hewn walls and danced over the table, a bed in the corner, that bench, one chair. The huge body leaning against the wall.

Her finger seemed to rise of its own volition and trace the pattern of firelight on his chest.

Her breath caught. He felt like liquid gold under her fingertips.

"I must go!"

"I'll walk you to your door," he said serenely.

He touched her arm just as she turned to enter the house.

"Whatever you desire, nymph."

~ 24 ~

In Which Mrs. Cable Receives
an Invitation to Dinner

Mrs. Cable was having a lovely morning. She thought it was truly scandalous of Lady Rawlings to host a dinner party so soon after Lord Rawlings's death. As she reminded her bosom friend Mrs. Pidcock, Esme Rawlings was barely through her first mourning period. "When Mr. Cable dies," she assured Mrs. Pidcock, "I shall mourn for a decent period of time, and so I have assured him. I think I have a small reputation in the village for understanding propriety. Two years in black, I will be, and without a thought for hosting entertainments such as this."

Mrs. Pidcock had her own ideas about what Mrs. Cable would do when her husband expired. Probably dance a jig on his grave. But there was no arguing with Myrtle's sense of proper duty. She would dance in black ribbons, no doubt about it.

Naturally, Mrs. Cable's outrage was not sufficient to prevent her accepting Lady Rawlings's invitation. "I shall attend the dinner," she assured Mrs. Pidcock, "if only to verify that our dear Henrietta has not fallen prey to the wiles of that Mr.

Darby. The man's up to no good, if you ask me. I'll feel more comfortable when she's five years older, and that's a fact."

Mrs. Pidcock didn't share her anxiety. She had a hard-headed sense that no man would marry just for a pretty face when an heir could not result.

"Lady Henrietta has a good head on her shoulders," Mrs. Pidcock said. "She won't succumb to some fribble from London."

"But everyone says he's *desperate* for money. And you know Henrietta is remarkably well endowed in that respect."

"He's not so desperate that he'd marry a wife sure to leave him a widower. I know that man's a peacock. George is beside himself, muttering about Darby's lace cuffs. But he is not a fool. True, it was unfortunate that he kissed Henrietta in the village, where anyone might see. But now that Lady Holkham had informed him of the situation, I have no belief that he will continue his suit."

"I suppose you're right," Mrs. Cable said. "And Henrietta did say that he was wooing Lucy Aiken."

"Well, there you are then. Lady Henrietta is such a good-natured girl that she probably smoothed the way for Lucy— and you know, dear, I do believe that Lucy would love to marry just such a fribble as Mr. Darby."

Mrs. Cable was almost convinced. But she was still overjoyed to have a chance to keep an eye on Darby.

~ 25 ~

Lady Rawlings Receives Guests

"I can hardly believe it! You look so splendidly—maternal!" Carola Perwinkle cried. With her short golden curls and pointed little face, she looked a perfect cherub.

Esme laughed. "It's a good thing that I am so fond of you," she said, returning her kiss. She held out her hands to Carola's sweet-faced, quiet husband, Lord Perwinkle. "And how are you, sir? It's a pleasure to see you again."

He kissed her hand. "I gather that I have you to thank for Carola's return to my household, madam. May I say how very, very grateful I am?"

For all he was overabsorbed in fishing, and not very talkative, Tuppy Perwinkle had charming blue eyes. No wonder Carola was so in love with him. "It was my pleasure, sir," she said, dimpling at him.

Carola broke in, giggling. "I think it was *his* pleasure!"

Tuppy rolled his eyes. "I can't keep this baggage from making indiscreet remarks, Lady Rawlings. You must forgive us."

"Please, do call me Esme," she said. "Your wife and I are very old friends, you know."

"It would be an honor," he said.

"Go away, Tuppy, do," his wife said. "I must speak to Esme. Why don't you make certain that our bags are all removed to our chamber?"

Esme caught the smile he sent Carola and surprised herself by a deep flash of jealousy. There was something so enticing in the way their eyes met, and his held such a potent blend of love and attraction and lust. She swallowed down an attack of self-pity.

Carola dropped next to her on the settee as if such looks from her husband were not out of the ordinary, and stared at Esme's stomach.

Esme looked too. She was wearing a fashionable mourning gown of plain white satin cloth, trimmed around the bosom and sleeves with black lace points. Even though the gown looked entrancing when she chose the pattern, there was no getting around the fact that satin seemed to magnify her stomach. Sitting next to Carola, her stomach looked like a sparkling, shimmering mound claiming attention.

"Where on earth did that come from?" Carola said in a wondering voice.

Esme laughed. "If you don't know yet, I'm going to leave it up to your husband to explain."

"I didn't mean *that*! I meant that I just saw you a mere six months ago, and you were as thin as a—as a twig!" Carola said. "It was I who was whinging about my figure, do you remember?" Her eyes wandered up to Esme's bodice line.

"If I recall correctly, you thought your bosom was too large. Well, wait until you're carrying a child."

Carola blushed and leaned closer. "I have the most wonderful news—I *am*!"

"Oh, Carola," Esme said, kissing her on the cheek. "I'm so very happy for you, and for Tuppy as well."

"He doesn't know yet." Carola had a cat-in-the-cream type of smile. "I was only certain myself a few days ago, and I'm waiting for just the right moment to tell him. Perhaps after our next fight."

"Are you still fighting? I thought all was sunlight and roses now."

Carola shrugged. "How can anyone live with a man and not argue with him? The first quarrel we had after I moved back in the house, I was devastated. Terrified, really. I thought he might up and leave, or ask me to leave, and I simply wouldn't be able to bear it." Her voice trailed off.

Esme pressed her hand. "What happened?"

A smile teased the corner of Carola's mouth. "He had stamped off to the stables, and I was rushing about my sitting room, not really doing anything, but trying not to think. Because I was afraid that if I thought about it, I would have to leave him, you understand."

Esme nodded.

"Well, he came to me," she said simply. "We"—she lowered her voice— "we ended up making love in the sitting room—have ever heard of such an outrageous thing?"

Esme bit back a smile. "Yes," she said gravely.

"I suppose we weren't the first couple in the world to make love there, but it was a revelation to me." Her eyes were soft even thinking of it. "I think I conceived this child that very day." Her hand drifted over her perfectly flat stomach.

Esme let herself wonder for a moment whether sitting rooms were particularly conducive to conception, then pushed the thought away. Her baby was Miles's—or rather, her own.

"That's lovely," she said, straining to sound rational.

"I know," Carola said with a merry grimace, "I've become terribly boring since Tuppy and I reunited. I can't seem to think about anything but him."

"Well, I have a subject of interest for you," Esme said. "Do you remember our plan to effect that reunion with Tuppy? I have a friend, Henrietta, who needs similar help."

Carola's eyes sparkled with interest. "A bedtrick!" she cried. "I'm an *expert* on that subject!"

"Not quite," Esme said. "It's more complicated than that, although it's essentially the same thing. We need to convince a man that he has compromised Henrietta's virtue. We need to make it absolutely impossible for him to refuse marriage."

Carola's eyes grew round. "This man compromised your friend and is refusing to marry her? What a blackguard!"

"Not exactly," Esme said.

"What do you mean, not exactly? Either he did or he didn't."

"He didn't."

"Well, then, he'd have to be an awful fool," Carola said.

"There's another wrinkle," Esme said. "The man in question is my nephew Darby."

"Darby? *Simon* Darby? You have to be joking!"

"No, I'm not. We're going to arrange it so that he has to marry Henrietta. He needs her, but he simply doesn't understand that yet. For one thing, my child, if male, will disinherit him, and Henrietta has a fortune. And for another, she would be a wonderful mother to his two small sisters. Did you know that Darby is raising his sisters?"

"Well, of course," Carola said, "all of London knows that. But how on earth—"

"We've made up some evidence," Esme said serenely. "And if I say so myself, the evidence is fairly damning. All we have to do is present it, and everything will fall into place. Darby will have to marry her."

Carola was shaking her head, but at that moment Rees Holland walked up and bowed.

"Lady Rawlings," he said, putting an impatient kiss on her hand. "Very kind of you to put me up like this. Where is Darby?" He acknowledged Carola with a mere bend of his head.

"Lord Godwin, may I introduce Lady Perwinkle," Esme

said, overlooking Rees's extreme rudeness. After all, it wasn't pointed at her. He acted this way toward the world in general.

"Pleased to meet you," the earl growled, throwing a brief bow in Carola's direction. "Has Darby made an appearance yet?"

"Not yet," Esme said, controlling her irritability. No wonder Helene couldn't stay married to the man. He looked as if he were invited to a badger hunt. Oh, his coat was well made enough, and his shirt was white, but his hair was even longer than Darby's. Moreover, he had ink spots on his fingers.

"In that case, I'll go roust him from his chambers," Rees said, rough amusement in his voice. "The peacock is probably still gazing at the mirror and trying to decide which coat to wear." He walked off without further ado.

"Helene's husband is deplorably rude," Carola said crossly. "Honest to God, I've met the man at least six times, and each time he acts as if he had never seen me before."

"You can't take it personally," Esme observed. "The only reason he recognizes me is because I'm Darby's aunt."

"What on earth were you thinking, inviting him to the dinner?" Carola asked. "Helene is here, isn't she?"

"I didn't invite him," Esme protested. "He simply announced he was arriving. I assumed that Darby invited him to the house, but Darby swears he only wrote him a note and never invited him to join us."

Carola was looking around. "Is Helene downstairs yet? She's going to be angry about Rees's presence, you know. She is the calmest person in the world until she loses her temper."

Esme had painful memories of the one time Helene had lost her temper with her. "I know," she said glumly. "It's the way she looks at one." The moment when Helene confronted her with the fact that Esme had slept with Gina's fiancé was one of the worst memories of her life.

"Well, I'll try to protect you," Carola said, patting her hand. That was an absurd statement. Carola was as delightfully small as Esme was large.

"I think I can manage," Esme said. "I did send a note to Helene's room and warn her that her husband had arrived."

"Oh, that's all right then," Carola said. "I'm quite sure that she will choose to eat in her room."

"She can't," Esme said. "I need her for the plan."

Tuppy appeared at Carola's side. "I must change my gown," she told Esme.

"You will know exactly what I am talking about, Carola, when it happens," Esme said to her, with a meaningful frown.

Carola had clearly forgotten all about Esme's plan, since her husband seemed to be kissing her ear in public.

"Of course!" she said quickly. "You may count on me to support you."

"You mustn't be late for dinner," Esme said with a warning look.

"We won't!" Carola said, with such earnestness that it was clear she and her husband had retired early to their chamber a time or two.

~ 26 ~

A Man in Velvet and Lace

Two hours later Lady Holkham and her stepdaughter arrived
for dinner. Slope brought them to their hostess, who was
seated on a couch.

"Are you feeling quite all right?" Henrietta asked.

"I am simply taking a holiday from standing," Esme said,
smiling at them. "How beautiful your daughter looks tonight,
madam!"

Millicent looked back at Henrietta. "I should hope so," she
said rather crossly. "Generally I can count on Imogen holding up a party, but tonight Henrietta changed her dress at
least three times!"

Esme grinned at Henrietta. "The work was beneficial. You
look magnificent." Henrietta was wearing a gown of pale
green crape, embroidered around the neck.

Henrietta sat down next to Esme as Millicent went to greet
Mrs. Barret-Ducrorq.

"I don't think this was the right gown to wear. Darby is
so . . ." Henrietta's voice trailed off.

"One can't possibly compete with Darby," Esme said matter-of-factly. "Just to warn you, he's wearing brown velvet to-night. Ladies have fainted when he's worn that particular costume."

"This is impossible." Henrietta looked at Esme miserably. "I can't think why I ever thought it possible. He's a peacock, and I'm nothing more than a crow!"

"A crow?" Esme said, smiling. "I don't think so. Let's see." She looked Henrietta over from head to foot. "Wait, I have to remember all those turgid letters that have been sent to me. Your hair is the color of moonbeams—no, sunbeams, because it has honey-colored strands running around it. Your eyes are the color of pansies; your lips are the color of rubies; your cheeks are peaches and cream—need I go on? I'm running out of colors."

Henrietta rolled her eyes. "You know what I mean. I'm lame, Esme, *lame*. I can't have children. And I'm not accustomed to looking elegant, nor do I really wish to achieve such a thing. I saw Darby walking down High Street yesterday. The man is unlike anyone I have ever known."

"Darby is unlike anyone in London either," Esme said, waving her fan gently before her face. "Don't fool yourself, Henrietta. London is not full of men wearing lace and velvet. Look at Rees, for example." She nodded toward the edge of the room, where a man, whose neck cloth appeared to have been thrown around his neck and knotted in approximately two seconds, was tossing back a glass of something.

Henrietta looked a little blank, so Esme added, "Rees Holland, Earl Godwin, husband of my friend Helene. I think you met her, didn't you?"

"Oh, of course," Henrietta said. "She was charming."

"Well, he isn't," Esme said bluntly. "Of course, the messiness in his dress is nothing to the messiness in his private life."

"Still, you are suggesting that a man who wears a pink coat—"

"Pink?" Esme said with a chuckle. "Darby was wearing pink on High Street? I am sorry to have missed that."

"Pink. My stepmother complimented him on the color, and he said it was maiden's blush. How can I marry a man who knows that a certain pink is called maiden's blush, when I never spend more than twenty minutes dressing myself?"

Over Esme's shoulder Henrietta saw Darby wander into the room. Sure enough, he was resplendent. He would probably call the color of his coat topaz rather than brown because it had a golden undertone. What seemed more important to Henrietta was that the jacket fitted him like a glove, and what a body it clung to! Broad shoulders slimming to his waist, powerful legs, that elegant, negligible ease. He walked over to Rees, and it was Beauty and the Beast, with a masculine twist.

"You know why you should marry him?" Esme said, laughing. "Because your eyes just turned the smokiest dark blue I ever saw. And that, my dear, tells me that my nephew just entered the room." She looked over her shoulder. "There he is. As elegant in full dress as he undoubtedly is without clothing."

"Esse-me!" Henrietta said, shocked.

She just laughed. "Don't worry. I'm not trying to picture him. I don't want him; I never take up with intelligent men. And Darby is far too intelligent for me."

Henrietta rolled her eyes. "I gather you forgot to tell me that Marquess Bonnington is a lackwit."

"That's different," Esme said. "Put it down to the fact that my own wits have gone wandering. At any rate, it's time, my dear."

Henrietta looked at her imploringly. "This isn't going to work, Esme."

Esme ignored her. "Go sit over there in the corner, Henrietta," she said. "Just signal him to join you, all right?"

"I can't do that," Henrietta said desperately.

But Esme lurched to her feet. She wanted to have one last

word with Slope about the formation of the table. She had very carefully chosen the four people to each side of her. The vicar, Mr. Fetcham, to her right and Mr. Barret-Ducrorq to her left. Barret-Ducrorq looked just starchy enough to play a brilliant role in their little performance and do it without prompting. Carola next to Mr. Barret-Ducrorq, with her husband on the other side. Tuppy never said much, so she counted him as a benign presence, likely to back up his wife.

Then Henrietta was seated next to the vicar, with Darby on her other side. Helene was next to Tuppy, which put Rees opposite her, and Lady Holkham between Darby and Rees. Rees was a bit of a wild card—after all, a man who deserted his wife years before and lived with an opera singer could hardly be called a champion of propriety, nor was he likely to promote the state of marriage. But in the course of a misspent life she had discovered that sometimes the least stuffy people actually responded rigidly and vice versa. Look who was acting as her gardener, after all.

The only person missing was Sebastian. Oh how well he could have played it—at least the new Sebastian, with wit to laugh at himself. With his unbending propriety and strict observance of social conventions . . . well, it was a huge shame that he was out in the gardener's hut. Of course, he was likely far more comfortable than she, stretched out on his bench, drinking whiskey and reading his Homer.

She was longing to go to the water closet—only the fourteenth time she had had to go this evening—and feeling much more nervous about the plan than she let Henrietta know. Managing a plan of this magnitude was difficult. It was much easier to just send Carola into a bedtrick. Carola had to do the dirty work.

But this was truly a work of art.

She rose to her feet. "May I invite everyone to join me in the dining room?"

The play was about to begin.

～ 27 ～

Sartorial Splendor Cannot Solve All Problems

Darby was bored. Bored and irritable, as if his skin didn't fit. Which was ridiculous because by rights wearing a suit this magnificent should make his physical situation a happy one.

For one thing, he had to deal with Rees, who had hied his way to Limpley Stoke in response to Darby's note. *Not* that Darby had expressed the slightest wish for company, but as Rees laconically explained it, when a man announces the intention to marry, it behooves his friends to dissuade him. Well, he arrived too late to do any dissuading, marriage not being an option anymore.

For another thing, Darby was intolerably aware of Henrietta's presence in the room. She was adequately dressed this evening, although pale green did nothing for her hair. He brooded about that for a while and decided that ruby would probably look best.

The green gown fell straight to the floor, as if Henrietta didn't have a curve to her body, although he knew well that she did. The very thought made him drink a glass of wine far too hastily, drowning out images of honey hair sliding down a delicate, naked back. Slipping over a breast.

"I'll accompany you back to London tomorrow," he said abruptly to Rees. "I have to meet my man of business."

"Will you be traveling with the children?" Rees said, looking distinctly inclined to refuse.

"Esme offered to keep them here. I believe I'll hire a decent nurse in London and bring her back with me. Meanwhile they can stay under the care of Esme's nanny, who seems a good soul. Josie has developed a bloodthirsty streak with her tin soldiers, but she isn't throwing as many tantrums, thank God."

Rees got to his feet. "You can't get me out of here too early in the morning," he remarked. "Why didn't it occur to me that Helene might be here? Jesus."

Both of them looked to the other corner of the salon, where his wife was seated at the piano. Helene wasn't playing, just looking through the music. From this distance, she looked too slim for health, her cheekbones standing out in her face and an intricate set of braids surrounding her head.

"Perhaps she'll play for us later," Rees grumbled. "That'd be about the only thing that would better this affair." He looked contemptuously around the room.

"I haven't heard Helene play since she left your house," Darby said. "How do you know she still enjoys music?"

"Heard her last year, at Mrs. Kittlebliss's. I had just dropped in. At any rate, she plays even better than she did when we were married. Actually had to tear myself away, or I would have spoken to her." Rees looked faintly astonished.

"Nothing surprising about that. From my recollection, about the only time you two weren't quarreling was when you were making music together."

"There you're wrong," Rees said promptly. "We used to fight like cats and dogs over music as well. Those battles were rather fun, though. She always had some sort of criticism of my work." He looked truly astonished at that admission.

"*You?*" Darby said with derision. "She criticized the work of London's foremost writer of comic opera?"

"Shut your trap," Rees growled.

"So did she really criticize your work?"

Rees nodded. "Made it better, I'll say that for her. Helene has a perfect ear. She could tell instinctively when something was just a little off."

Henrietta had moved to a couch quite close to them, and Darby found himself watching the way she laughed.

"The devil about marriage is that you don't quite get over the woman," Rees said abruptly. "That's what I came up here to tell you. Marriages fall apart right and left, but what no one says is that your spouse is like a burr in your side. You just can't get rid of her."

"You've done a pretty good job," Darby said, pulling his attention away from Henrietta. "How long did you and Helene live together, a year or so?"

"Not quite," he grunted. "Doesn't matter. They get under your skins, wives. I *still* find myself wondering what she would think of this or that stave of music." He looked outraged.

"Hmmm," Darby said. "Why don't you go play her a stave or two then?" He walked off as if he was giving Rees permission to go, when what he wanted to do was walk over to Henrietta, which of course he wasn't going to do.

She was seated in a couch placed at an odd angle, almost stuck in the corner of the room. Earlier, it seemed to him that her limp was a bit more pronounced than normally. He thought about that and decided to amble over and ask in a neighborly kind of way about her status.

He wasn't quite sure that he would actually do it until she looked up. Without warning, she smiled at him.

Henrietta Maclellan might not have had much experience calling men to her side, but that didn't mean that she wasn't a god-given genius at it. Darby had been the subject of many a come-hither smile, and he enjoyed brilliance when he saw it.

Her eyes widened just a little bit, and then she smiled. She didn't even smile with her mouth. It was all with her eyes. Naturally, he walked over to her like a sailor to a siren.

Carola Perwinkle was seated next to Henrietta. He had always liked her, impudent little thing that she was, and he liked her even more when she got up as he approached, gave him a saucy smile, and pranced off to walk with her husband into the dining room.

He sat down, naturally. A bit closer to Henrietta than he needed to be. "How are you feeling, Lady Henrietta?" he asked, finally.

Henrietta had that look of utter calm, as if nothing that happened could shake her friendliness. "I am quite well, thank you," she said.

Looking closely, he could see that she was nervous. Still, she didn't edge away from him. He stretched out his leg so that it just touched hers. He didn't bother to think about why he was flirting with an ineligible woman. He just wanted to flirt with her, that's all. Actually, what he really wanted to do was run his tongue around her little shell of an ear. She was wearing her hair up with curls drifting into ringlets over her ears. He would brush those aside and find her ear like someone looking for blackberries in a thicket.

"What on earth are you thinking about?" she finally asked.

"Eating blackberries," he said lazily.

"Really?" She looked surprised.

"Finding them in a blackberry patch, when you have to reach in among the prickly branches. When you bite them they're sour as the devil if they're not ripe, and God's perfection if they're ripe."

She looked at him suspiciously.

"What I like to do," he said gently, "is roll one between my teeth. Did you know that that's the best way to test for . . .

ripeness?" He couldn't stop himself and reached out with one hand and casually touched her on the nape of the neck.

She shook her head.

"Just roll it between your teeth and curve your tongue around the berry. If it's perfectly ripe, it will bathe your mouth with sweetness."

She swallowed, which gave him untold satisfaction. "I don't think you're talking about berries," she said, finally.

He was caressing her ear, his fingers sliding down her slender neck. Thank goodness Henrietta's couch was at an angle to the rest of the company, and it looked as if they were all preparing to enter the dining room.

"May I escort you to the table?" he asked. His voice was a little strained, but that was only because this ineligible woman had caused an unsightly bulge in his pantaloons, merely by sitting next to him and allowing him to touch her neck.

She gave him her little crooked smile, the one that she gave when her leg hurt.

"There's something wrong," he said, eyes narrowing. "Did you injure your hip yesterday?"

"No, of course not."

Her eyes looked truthful enough. But there was that smile. She obviously had no idea how easy she was to read.

"What is it then?" She started to get up, but he let his hand slide down her back in an utterly inappropriate gesture. He looked around quickly. Everyone else had left the room. Slope had apparently not seen them, tucked away on the couch.

Oh, why not? He leaned forward and just tasted her. Just put his lips on hers. Just a touch.

But the touch . . . well, the touch had her arms around his neck and his hand sliding up her neck. The touch meant that he didn't hear Esme's butler Slope until the man loudly cleared his throat just behind the couch.

He would have expected Henrietta to pull back as if the furies were behind her, to gallop into the dining room. But she just stared at him, and then raised a hand to tuck a lock of hair behind his ear. And her lips curved in a different sort of smile.

I have to leave tomorrow, Darby thought numbly. I'm over my head.

"Lady Henrietta, Mr. Darby," Slope was saying. "I fear that the dinner party is awaiting your arrival." He had an oddly pleased look about him.

Darby rose and held his arm out for Henrietta. Then he thought again and helped her to her feet.

Her little blush deepened when he did that.

"Thank you," she said.

Slope had turned his back and was pacing majestically toward the door.

"Steady," Darby said, holding back. "Ready to make an entrance?"

She nodded, eyes on his.

An entrance didn't even cover what ensued. Normally, Darby rather liked being the center of attention. He always thought that the more attention he received, the more time his lace received in the fashion columns. One thing leads to another.

But he had never walked into a dining room and had clinking glasses freeze, and heard a roomful of shrill voices come to an utter standstill.

Slope was obviously enjoying himself as he majestically paced about the table. "Lady Henrietta, if you please," he said. "Mr. Darby."

He was seated next to her. Darby sat down and realized that he was in a frenzy of sexual attention such as he hadn't suffered through since he was a schoolboy and fell in love with the third housemaid, Molly. Then he would lurk in the hallways until he saw her, living for the moment when she would brush past him with a muttered, "Excuse me, Master Simon."

It was precisely the same now. He edged his chair over to Henrietta's so slowly that no one could see him. By the time the first course was served, he'd managed to put a leg against hers. When she turned startled eyes on him, he moved his leg, but a moment later he touched her arm with his.

And that flush—that flush on her cheekbones deepened. Oh, she felt it too. I'm leaving tomorrow, Darby thought recklessly. Leaving tomorrow, and I won't come back.

She was smiling again. Smiling with her eyes. Smiling with a promise. Every glance to his left told him that he wasn't wrong when he thought Henrietta was exquisite.

Henrietta's lips curved in a smile that might—just might—be sarcastic. But that faint curve on rosy lips had heat pounding in his groin in a way that another woman's licking smile could not.

～ 28 ～

The Pleasure of Good Deeds

Mrs. Cable was delighted to find that Lady Rawlings had seated her next to Rees Holland, Earl Godwin. He was likely the most scandalous earl in the entire aristocracy, which meant that she could dine out on this encounter for years. Not to mention the fact that she might be able to help the poor man into a better understanding of the errors of his ways.

She waited until the soup course had been served before she addressed the subject. "Lord Godwin, it is a pleasure to see you and your dear wife at the same event," she said, conscious of her own rashness. But after all, if one is to take the Lord's work seriously, one must work boldly. Not like the vicar, Mr. Fetcham, who was talking to Lady Holkham as if he hadn't a care in the world. Even though he was positively surrounded by sinners.

Rees Holland turned and looked at her for the first time. So far, he had been rather annoyingly ignoring her presence. He had shocking black eyes, the earl did. No wonder everyone called him degenerate. He looked it, with those fierce eyebrows. "Should I say the same to you, Mrs.—Mrs.—"

He hesitated, having obviously forgotten her name. No more than she would have expected.

"I am Mrs. Cable, sir. And Mr. Cable accompanies me to all events," she informed him.

"A brave man," he drawled. "I am always amazed by the courage people show in their daily lives." Then he turned his eyes away and swallowed some more soup.

Mrs. Cable was pretty sure that she'd been insulted. Either she or Mr. Cable. "It's a sin—" she said rather shrilly, and then recalled where she was and lowered her voice. "It's a sin to forsake the matrimonial bed."

Godwin looked her over. His eyes were dreadfully cold. "Bed? You wish to discuss beds? You amaze me, Mrs. Cable."

But sinners and their wicked jokes were of no interest to Myrtle Cable. "Paul's letter to the Colossians counsels men to love their wives," she announced.

"He also says that women should submit themselves to their husbands," Godwin said. He looked bored and irritated, but Mrs. Cable paid that no mind. The devil quotes scriptures for his benefit, she reminded herself, and returned to the attack.

"A man may have business outside the house, but he returns at night to his wife. Psalm 104," she snapped.

He paused for a moment, spoon halfway to his lap. "Almost, I would enjoy sparring with you, Mrs. Cable," he said mockingly, "but not if you alter your text. Psalm 104: *Man goeth forth unto his work, and to his labour until the evening.* It says nothing in that text about his wife."

"*You* know the psalms?" she asked, studying him more closely. He looked like nothing more than an indolent, spoiled aristocrat, although he was distinctly less elegant than the normal breed of Londoners. His hair was unattractively long, and he had stubble on his chin.

"I set 104 to music," he said. "Glorious words there: *The*

Lord makes the clouds his chariot, and walks on the wings of the wind. Who could forget those lines?"

Mrs. Cable was impressed. A fallen angel, perhaps. Something about his careless arrogance rankled. "Therefore shall a man leave his father and his mother, and shall cleave unto his wife: and they shall be one flesh," she said primly. "Genesis."

"Proverbs: It is better to dwell in the wilderness, than with a contentious and an angry woman," he said. They both instinctively looked to his wife, seated across from them.

To Mrs. Cable's mind, the countess didn't look like a contentious woman at all. Naturally Mrs. Cable didn't value fashion much, since it was clearly the devil's lure. But she wasn't blind either. The countess was wearing a lovely crape robe with a border of shells around the bosom. It was elegant but restrained, without the low bodices that women affected these days. Moreover, the countess's hair was bound in smooth braids with just a pearl ornament. That too was more proper than most women wore these days.

"She looks like a true countess," she told Lord Godwin. "Virtuous, not like so many gentlewomen these days."

He took a bite of fish and said, "Oh, she's virtuous all right."

Mrs. Cable was feeling uncertain. She had made her point. How much could she emphasize? Perhaps she should just let the seeds of God's love work in his barren heart. One more dash of wisdom wouldn't hurt.

"Who can find a virtuous woman? For her price is far above rubies," she commented.

Lord Godwin looked her square in the face, and Mrs. Cable felt an odd tingle in her midsection.

She turned promptly to her other dinner partner. He was a dangerous man, Lord Godwin, for all he looked too messy to be attractive to young girls. No wonder he had such a desperate reputation. He probably *did* live with an opera singer, just as the gossip said.

* * *

Slope played his part to perfection. Esme waited until after the soup had come and gone, and fish had been eaten. She kept a sharp eye to make certain that Helene and Rees weren't going to explode in a cloud of black smoke, because then she would have to improvise a bit, but besides the fact that Helene was going to get a stiff neck from looking so sharply away from her husband, they were both behaving well.

The roast arrived, and Esme sent Slope for more wine. She wanted to make certain that her part of the table was holding enough liquor to respond instinctively. Mr. Barret-Ducrorq was ruddy in the face, and saying bombastic things about the Regent, so she thought he was well primed. Henrietta was pale but hadn't fled the room, and Darby showed every sign of being utterly desirous of Henrietta. Esme smiled a little to herself.

Just as she requested, Slope entered holding a silver salver. Speaking just loud enough to catch attention of the entire table, he said, "Please excuse me, my lady, but I discovered this letter. It is marked urgent, and feeling some concern that I might have inadvertently delayed the delivery of an important missive, I thought I would deliver it immediately."

A little overdone, to Esme's mind. Obviously Slope was an amateur thespian. She took the note and slit it open.

"Oh, but Slope!" she cried, "This letter is not addressed to me!"

"There was no name on the envelope," Slope said, "so I naturally assumed it was addressed to you, my lady. Shall I redirect the missive?" He hovered at her side.

She had better take over the reins of the performance. Her butler was threatening to upstage her.

"That will be quite all right, Slope," she said. Then she looked up with a glimmering smile. "It doesn't seem to be addressed to anyone. Which means we can read it." She gave a girlish giggle. "I *adore* reading private epistles!"

Only Rees looked utterly bored and kept eating his roast beef.

"*I do not go for weariness of thee,*" Esme said in a dulcet tone, "*Nor in the hope the world can show a fitter love for me.* It's a love poem, isn't that sweet?"

"John Donne," Darby said, "and missing the first two words. The poem begins, "*Sweetest love, I do not go for weariness of thee.*"

Esme had trouble restraining her glee. She could not have imagined a comment more indicative of Darby's own authorship. He actually knew the poem in question! She didn't dare look at Henrietta. It was hard enough pretending that she was the slowest reader in all Limpley Stoke.

"*Never will I find anyone I adore as much as you. Although fate has cruelly separated us, I shall treasure the memory of you in my heart.*"

"I do not believe that this epistle should be read out loud," Mrs. Cable said, "if it truly is an epistle. Perhaps it's just a poem?"

"Do go ahead," Rees said. He appeared to have developed an active dislike of his dinner companion. "I'd like to hear the whole thing. Unless perhaps the missive was addressed to *you*, Mrs. Cable?"

She bridled. "I believe not."

"If not, why on earth would you care whether a piece of lackluster poetry was read aloud?"

She pressed her lips together.

Esme continued dreamily, "*I would throw away the stars and the moon only to spend one more night—*" She gasped, broke off, and folded up the note, praying that she wasn't overacting.

"Well?" Mrs. Cable said.

"Aren't you going to finish?" Mr. Barret-Ducrorq said in his beery voice. "I was just thinking perhaps I should read some of this John Donne myself. Although not if his work is unfit for the ladies, of course," he added quickly.

"I believe not," Esme said, letting the letter fall gently to her left, in front of Mr. Barret-Ducrorq.

"I'll do it for you!" he said jovially. "Let's see. *I would throw away the stars and the moon only to spend one more night in your arms.*" He paused. "Sizzling poetry, this Donne. I quite like it."

"That is no longer John Donne speaking," Darby remarked. "The author is now extemporizing."

"Hmmm," Mr. Barret-Ducrorq said.

"Did that letter refer to a night *in your arms*?" Mrs. Cable asked, quite as if she didn't know exactly what she had heard.

"I fear so," Esme said with a sigh.

"Then we shall hear no more of this letter," Mrs. Cable said stoutly, cutting off Mr. Barret-Ducrorq as he was about to read another line.

"Ah, hum, exactly, exactly," he agreed.

Esme looked at Carola, who turned to Mr. Barret-Ducrorq and sweetly plucked the sheet from his stubby fingers. "I think this sounds precisely like the kind of note that my dear, dear husband would send me," she said, her tone as smooth as honey and her eyes resolutely fixed on the page, rather than on her husband. "In fact, I'm quite certain that he wrote me this note, and it simply went astray."

Esme could see that Mrs. Cable was about to burst out of her stays. Henrietta was deadly pale but hadn't run from the room. Tuppy Perwinkle was torn between laughter and dismay. Darby looked mildly interested and Rees not interested at all.

Helene raised her head. She had spent most of the meal staring at her plate. "Do read your husband's letter, Carola," she said. "I think it's always so interesting to learn that there are husbands who acknowledge their wives' existence."

Esme winced, but Rees just shoveled another forkful of beef into his mouth.

Carola obediently read, "*I shall never meet another woman with starlit hair like your own, my dearest Henri—*" She broke off.

All eyes turned to Henrietta.

"I'm sorry! It just slipped out!" Carola squealed. "I truly thought the letter must be from my husband."

Henrietta maintained an admirable calm, although a hectic rose-colored flush had replaced the chilly white of her skin.

To her enormous satisfaction, Esme saw that Darby was looking absolutely livid.

Mrs. Cable said, "Who signed that letter?"

Carola didn't say anything.

Mrs. Cable repeated, "*Who* signed that letter?"

There was an icy moment of silence.

Esme said gently, "I'm afraid it's too late for prevarication, Carola. We must look to dearest Henrietta's future now."

Mrs. Cable nodded.

"It is signed 'Simon,' " Carola said, looking straight at him. "Simon Darby, of course. It's a quite poetic letter, Mr. Darby. I particularly like the ending, if you'll forgive me for saying so."

"Read it," Lady Holkham said in an implacable voice.

"*Without you, I will never marry. Since you cannot marry me, darling Henrietta, I shall never marry. Children mean nothing to me; I have a superfluity as it is. All I want is you. For this life and beyond.*" Carola sighed. "How romantic!"

Then Henrietta did something that Esme had not anticipated, and which was absolutely the best of all possible actions.

She slid slowly to the right and collapsed directly into Darby's arms.

She fainted.

~ 29 ~

The Fruits of Sin

In the years that followed, Darby was never able to think of the ensuing half hour without shivering.

Henrietta's faint was immediately accepted as a sign of guilt. The fact that she fainted to the right—in other words, directly into Darby's lap—was another signifier, obviously.

Darby barely got his mouth shut when Henrietta's step-mother turned to him and smacked him on the cheek so hard that his head snapped back.

"That's because my husband isn't here to do it for me!" Millicent shouted.

Darby privately doubted that her husband could have done much better. His entire jaw ached.

"I gather you did this abominable act *before* I told you about Henrietta's condition and this was your idea of a good-bye letter to her?"

He just stared at her.

"Seducer of young women!" she said fiercely. "You *will* marry Henrietta now. You will. And your punishment will be that you will have neither heir nor child."

Darby felt as if he were facing Medusa. A woman he had

thought a sweet-faced motherly type had metamorphosed into a gorgon. She glared at him like the avenging mothers of Greek tragedy.

Luckily Henrietta blinked her eyes and appeared to be recovering from her swoon. Darby still hadn't said a word, hadn't denied writing the letter nor denied spending the night with her. It was as if his brain had frozen.

The dowager countess swung her attention to her step-daughter. "How could you do this, Henrietta," she hissed. Suddenly Lady Holkham appeared to realize that seventeen fascinated pairs of eyes were watching her. She rose from her chair and drew herself up to her full height.

"Ladies and gentlemen, I am happy to announce the engagement of my beloved daughter Lady Henrietta, to Mr. Simon Darby," she said. Her gaze flashed around the table, leaving scorch marks in its path.

Esme was feeling all the pleasure of a successful stage manager and so she didn't hesitate to back up the leading lady. She clapped her hands and gestured to Slope, who immediately began uncorking champagne and sending his underlings around the table with brimming glasses.

Millicent gave Darby one last measured stare that promised to remove his manly parts if he didn't dance to her bidding, then sat back into her chair, her chest heaving.

Darby felt as if he were watching everything without really participating, and if he was correct, Henrietta was in something of the same state. He didn't believe for a moment that she had genuinely fainted. Not unless she could faint while simultaneously keeping her back rigid.

He leaned over. "What do you want me to do?" he asked in a low voice.

She just looked at him, seemingly struck dumb.

"As God's my witness, I didn't write that letter." For some reason it seemed important that she know that he would never have wantonly destroyed her reputation.

She nodded.

"Well, all we have to do is find out who wrote it," he said, with an awkward feeling of gratitude. Henrietta obviously believed him without hesitation. It would be impossible for those blue eyes of hers to conceal anything. "There's nothing to worry about. Of course your stepmother will naturally retract her demand once she understands that you and I have had nothing to do with each other. I would suggest that we retire to the drawing room and discuss this with a modicum of privacy. But do you have any idea who wrote it?"

She nodded again.

"Who?"

"I did," she whispered.

~ 30 ~

Confessions Are a Private Affair

"You wrote the love letter to yourself?"

"Yes," she said. "I was lonely." She twisted her hands in her lap. "I never had a debut, obviously. There wasn't any reason to, under the circumstances. But it meant that I never made any friends, so we aren't invited to house parties and things of that nature. I just wanted—"

"A letter."

"No. A love letter. I didn't think I would ever receive such a letter, so I wrote one to myself."

He couldn't fault her for that. It was heartbreaking, but hardly corrupt.

"But I wrote the letter for myself," Henrietta insisted. "How could I know that it would go astray? It was just a pretense."

"That pretense has ruined my life," Darby pointed out.

Henrietta swallowed. "Surely your life isn't *ruined*," she said. "Don't you think that's a bit harsh? True, you will have a wife, but most men do take a wife at some point in their lives."

He raised his head and looked at her. The warm brown of

his eyes had darkened almost to black. A clear little voice in the back of her head cataloged the color change and thought: that's a warning sign.

"Ruined seems a strong description," she persisted.

"I disagree. I fully intended to marry at some point in the future, but I would rather chose that date myself."

"Well, is it so bad to marry now rather than later?" She fixed her eyes pleadingly on his. She had never felt quite so sick to her stomach.

He gave a short laugh, more like a bark than a laugh. "I meant to marry—" he ran a hand through his hair. "I meant to marry someone I could bed."

Color rose in her cheeks.

"Do you understand what I'm saying?"

She nodded.

"What the hell am I to do with a wife I can't bed? Believe it or not, I thought of myself as someone who would be faithful to a wife, once I had one. But this is impossible."

"I'm sorry," she said. "I wrote the letter before I knew. Before I completely understood that side of marriage." She thought desperately about how she could bring up the sheath, but it simply wasn't a decent topic of conversation. "You must continue to engage yourself outside of our marriage. That is the only tenable solution."

He laughed, a brutal humorless noise. "A tenable solution, is it? So you want me to keep a mistress?"

"I can't see that it matters one way or the other. Had we married in the normal course of things, I expect it wouldn't have been much different. Many men—" She hesitated. "Many men have mistresses."

"Oh, yes," he said. "But I didn't fancy myself joining their ranks."

It seemed a petty trifle to her. Perhaps he was afraid that his wife would cause an unpleasant scene, the way Lady

Witherspoon did at the Regent's ball last spring. "I would never make a fuss over such a thing," she said in her most consoling tone. "I promise you, I truly am a very sensible person."

"Sensible? *You?*"

She colored. "I am very sensible in person. And I will be a good mother to your little sisters. I would never say a word about your mistress—"

"Even if I flaunt her before your eyes? What if I take a woman from your circle of acquaintances? What if I dance with her before I dance with you?"

"I can't dance. And I promise you, I won't turn a hair whatever you do. I truly apologize for writing the letter. But it never occurred to me that anyone would see it except me. Even so, it may be the best for all of us."

He looked at her sweet oval face, framed by silken hair, and longed to shake her. "You understand nothing," he said savagely. "Nothing!"

"What don't I understand? I do realize that you're disappointed—"

"There is no such thing as a chaste marriage. I cannot live with you under those circumstances, Henrietta."

As he watched, her eyes grew hazy with tears. She swallowed, but not one tear slid down her cheek.

"My stepmother explained to me that gentlemen have expectations about that intimacy," she said, finally.

"I cannot imagine living with you without being able to bed you," he said fiercely.

"I see." She was biting her lip hard, but still she didn't cry. Her very self-control made him feel insane, made him want to destroy her composure.

He wasn't sure where his own equilibrium had gone. It was swallowed into the dizzying prospect of marrying Henrietta—of not bedding Henrietta—of bedding Henrietta—

"Why didn't you think when you entangled me in your ridiculous set of lies?" he snarled, with all the force of his confusion. "Did you think of anyone but yourself?"

She blinked. "Of course I didn't. It was *my* letter, after all. I had no expectation that anyone other than myself would read it."

"When Lady Rawlings brought it up in the dining room, you could have confessed," he said. "You could have saved me from this—this travesty of a marriage!"

"You're absolutely right," she said steadily. "I didn't because I was greedy. I have never had anyone for myself, you see."

"I know," he said, feeling tired. "So you took me and my sisters."

He saw that her little hands were clenched tight inside her gloves.

"I am not sorry that I wrote the letter, and I am not even sorry that it found its way to a public forum. I will love your sisters. I will love them as if they were my very own children. No one could love them more than I will."

Her tone was fierce. Now her eyes were passionate. Now—when it was a matter of the children, and not him.

"I see no reason for further discussion," he said slowly. "I suppose I would summarize our future life thus: you act as a nursemaid to my sisters. I carry on amorous relationships outside the house. We occasionally meet in the hallways or at dinner."

"You are very cruel," she said.

"Practicality is the bane of my family."

"I see no reason why we cannot be friends."

"Friends?"

"I should like to be your friend, Mr. Darby. I would like to be more than a nursemaid in your house."

"I am never friends with those who have stolen from me," he said.

Somewhere Henrietta found a pulse of anger stealing up her spine. "It seems to me that you are taking a great deal of umbrage for this. After all, if I am a nursemaid, you will pay my salary with *my* inheritance. Unless I am mistaken, you desperately need my dowry in order to support your sisters. At least, that was my understanding."

She waited, shaken. Would he explode with rage, or, or—

Instead the corner of his mouth twisted in a wry smile.

She continued. "You knew there is a fair chance that Lady Rawlings's child will be a male. It may be only gossip, but people say that your father's estate was not . . ."

"Was not profitable," he said. "The gossip is truthful as regards my father's gambling debts."

"You would have had to marry," she said, looking at him. "You would have had no choice."

"Had I decided to hunt a fortune, I should have liked to chose my own heiress."

"English gentlemen frequently marry to extract themselves from debt," she said, with that wry strain of irony that characterized her observances. "You likely would have had to marry a woman whose father was a merchant."

He shrugged. "You're absolutely right, my lady. I might have had to marry someone from another class. But at least I could have bedded her."

That silenced Henrietta.

"The primary point on which your gossip went astray concerns my financial situation," he remarked. "I am worth approximately double your father's estate."

She stared at him, mouth open.

"I own lace in this country," he said gently. "Had you ordered gold lace on your new curricle, the lace would have been supplied by me. The lace on your fichu was undoubtedly imported by me, and the lace on your stepmother's reticule was made in a factory in Kent. My factory, as it happens."

"No one knows—Esme doesn't know that!"

Her observation didn't seem pertinent, but he nodded. "You are correct. I never saw any advantage to advertising my wealth. People assumed that my uncle was making me an allowance. In fact, I supported my uncle for the past five years."

"In that case, everything is different," she said slowly. Her chin rose even higher in the air. "I shall inform my step-mother that I am uncompromised, and I shall tell her that I wrote the letter myself. You are right: she will immediately withdraw her demand that you marry me."

He said nothing for a moment, just looked at her little pointed face. How could someone who looked so delicate be so intrepid? He'd met women who looked like army ser-geants, and were as weak as kittens. It was oddly erotic to face a woman who looked like a kitten but had the ruthless-ness of a corporal.

She rose. "I shall inform her immediately. I offer my apologies, Mr. Darby."

He didn't bother to rise, just reached up and pulled her back down on the settee. "You are likely right," he said. "I am infuriated—but I shall get over it."

"That is not relevant. It would be an adequate bargain if you had need of my fortune, and I had need of your children. But there is no reason in the world why you should continue with the marriage if you have no need of a fortune. You may find a mother for Josie and Anabel as soon as the season be-gins, if not sooner. And then, as you say, you may bed your wife."

"I will strike you another bargain," he said. "My children for—"

"I have nothing to offer," Henrietta said quietly. Her hands were clenched in her lap. "I cannot accept an offer in which you would lose so many things you hold important."

All of a sudden her heart started thudding against her ribs.

His eyes had darkened again. Danger, she thought. Danger. But it was danger of a different flavor.

Darby reached out one finger, let it run down the clear plane of her forehead, the elegant nose—stopped. Stopped at her lips.

"I think," he said, and his voice had lost its expressionless quality, "I would go mad married to you, Henrietta."

She shivered.

His finger moved, a bit unsteadily, over the curve of her lower lip.

"Do you see what I mean?"

She gave a little gasp. The finger tipped up her chin, forced her to meet his eyes. She felt a dark shiver down her spine.

"You can't feel that—for me," she said rashly.

"Oh? Why not?"

The finger burned its way down her neck.

"I think you mean to say that I ought not to feel *that*. And indeed, I ought not." But he leaned closer. She could smell him, a clean, male scent. Suddenly his hand left her neck and curved around the back of her head.

"You think I should not—why?"

Henrietta's mouth was open and she spoke breathily, in a way she detested. "Because . . . Because I am lame."

"True enough." She was exquisite, untouched, pure.

He had to leave her that way.

She was going to be his nursemaid, for God's sake. He'd never approached a servant.

A weak defense.

She had the most beautiful lips he'd ever seen: curved and plump and begging to be kissed. In fact, the whole of her was begging to be kissed. The devil of it was that he'd just tied himself to her for a century of longing. Actually, centuries of watching his wife, his own wife, with that heightened sense of erotic desire that almost burned as it ran through his veins.

And without further thought, he bent his head and put his lips on her mouth.

For a moment, his rational abilities stayed with him. He tasted surprise on her lips. She held herself very still, the way she did when she was afraid that she would fall over and embarrass herself.

So, purely in order to relax her, he ran his hand down her back. She had a back like a bird's wing: slender, fragile, speaking of willowy bones and exquisitely delicate shapes. He kept his hand there, a great still hand that could almost encompass her entire back in one grasp. So she couldn't fly away, his little bird.

Then he turned his head and began to kiss her in earnest. And forgot about his rational thoughts.

She opened her mouth and welcomed him in. He meant to teach her a lesson. But she opened her mouth as if *she* craved him, as if she felt even half of the surging roaring waves of lust that made his life miserable when he saw her.

Her tongue met his. Heat roared down his spine.

She gasped against him. Heat pooled in his loins, thundered in his ears. He took her small mouth as if it were a world to be conquered. And she let him . . . how she let him! She moaned. He tasted the moan on his tongue.

She gasped; he stole her breath with his own.

He melted into a simmering, driven lust, a fierce desire to taste her, to touch her. He spread his hand on her back. She had not swayed toward him, the way women normally did during such a kiss. She still sat as upright as a statue.

Her breath was coming quickly, in little pants. She had her eyes closed. And yet she sat without touching him. She had not even moved her hands from her lap.

"Henrietta," he said.

Her eyes slowly opened. They were the color of the evening sky, dazed pools of desire.

"Put your hands around my neck."

She blinked and looked down at her hands as if she'd forgotten they were there.

"Of course," she murmured. And lifted her arms around his neck, as commanded. Her back was so narrow that he could feel every movement.

Then she just looked at him.

This was damnable. He'd never wanted anyone as much. Even now, he could catalog her face without hesitation: slim nose, the most intelligent eyes he'd ever seen in a woman, eyebrows that bent delicately, lips that were a deep red.

Normally her skin was porcelain white. Now there was a little bloom in each cheek.

"I have a—" she blurted out and stopped.

He kissed her nose, let his lips slide to her eyes. "You ravish me," he said quietly. "That's the damnable thing, Henrietta. I'm damned with you, and damned without you."

"Esme told me about an object called a sheath," she said in one breath.

He stopped for just a second, and then went back to kissing her cheekbone.

"It prevents conception," Henrietta whispered, drunk with kisses and mortified by the very words that were falling from her mouth.

"I've heard of them," he said neutrally. Inside, his mind was racing. Henrietta—his own prim and proper Henrietta—was raising the issue that he had intended to save for marriage. For the right moment on their wedding night, even if he had beg her to try it on hands and knees.

"She—" Henrietta gasped. He seemed to be licking her neck so she forgot what she was saying.

"Do you have a sheath?" he said, sometime later. "Do you know how to use it?"

She blushed even brighter red. "Esme will explain its use."

"Infamous Esme," he said.

"She is *not* infamous," Henrietta said sharply.

"Mmmm." His fingers played with the neck of her gown and then very slowly, looking directly into her eyes, he pulled it down. For a moment Henrietta thought about protesting, but every inch of her body was celebrating the fact that he seemed to be giving in.

Perhaps he *would* marry her.

A large hand curved around her breast. His lips followed his fingers, slipped below the line of her bodice.

Henrietta was too busy trying to decide whether she should allow him to make this sacrifice to pay much attention. Not that she wasn't aware of his big hands roaming around her body, but her mind was still spinning with the implications of his lace empire. He didn't need her money. He didn't need her. He could find a mother—a nanny— anywhere. And the woman he married would be able to bear him children.

Misery threatened to swallow her, but there was an insistent, sweet ache that she hadn't really noticed.

There was a lot she hadn't really noticed.

Darby had pushed her bodice so low that her breast—her naked breast—was visible. And he had his hand cupped around it, holding it as if it were some sweet fruit he meant to devour.

As she watched, so shocked that she couldn't even summon a response, he lowered his head and lips drifted across the creamy surface of her breast, rubbed across the nipple, drifted to the other side.

Henrietta's entire body went rigid. A sharp wave of pleasure shot through her midsection.

He brushed his mouth back and scraped gently over her nipple again.

Henrietta found she was going light-headed from not breathing, but when she let out her breath, it sounded awful, a hoarse noise, as if she were getting ill.

The sound just seemed to encourage him. He cast her a glance, a wicked, laughing glance, and then brushed his head back and stayed . . . stayed at her nipple, sucked, stroked, nipped, and Henrietta couldn't catch her breath at all. She couldn't move either. She just sat there, trying to catch her breath, and feeling as if pleasure jolted through her body with every move of his lips, with every touch of his hands.

And Darby feasted on her. Discovered that her breasts had a curve as exquisite as he'd seen in his life, that she was as delicious as he had imagined. Listened, in the back of his mind, to a small voice saying: this is what you want. Relief bloomed in some remote part of his heart.

"I want you," he said against the smooth cream of her breast. "Damn it, Henrietta, I even like you."

At that, a tiny smile grew in those beautiful eyes.

"I'll marry you," he said, and his voice had a little rasp. "Oh yes, I'll marry you."

⌒ 31 ⌒

Motherhood Is An Ideal State... Sometimes

Henrietta hadn't seen her husband-to-be since Esme's dinner party, five days earlier. The following morning she had received a note saying that he would obtain a special license from the Bishop of Salisbury; Darby hadn't been seen since.

"Darby is adjusting to the shock," Esme advised. "Men can be foolish when their routine is upset. Just remember that once you're married you need to keep him on his toes by changing your mind—and plans—once a week or so. You don't want to nurture this type of impoliteness."

Henrietta lay awake at night thinking about how devastated Millicent's face had been when she realized that her stepdaughter had done such a loathsome thing as bed a gentleman without the benefit of marriage.

Her stepmother hadn't said much about it since. In the carriage on the way home, she said, "I am sure you are aware of how disappointed I am, Henrietta. We need not refine upon the subject."

Henrietta tossed and turned in her bed, thinking that she would tell her stepmother, that she *had* to tell the truth. But Millicent had a firm grasp of morality, and Henrietta was quite certain that her stepmother would feel it necessary to inform Darby about Esme's deliberate revelation of the letter. It was one thing to admit to Darby that she, Henrietta, wrote that letter. But it was another to admit that she was part of a plot to force him into a marriage proposal. As it was, he had assumed that the letter had been mixed up with the note she sent him about hiring a nursemaid.

Was it terrible to start a marriage with such a falsehood? But what if she told the truth, and he denounced her as a scheming woman and refused to go through with the marriage?

The problem was that she desperately wanted to marry him. Desperately. With every inch of her body, and it didn't have that much to do with Josie and Anabel either. She had to face that cold truth in the middle of the night. She was manipulating a man into marrying her because she coveted him, and that was a despicable thing to know about oneself.

He desires me, she thought, but she knew it was a weak defense. Darby—the elegant fashion leader of the *ton*—would never marry a mere nobody from the country if he weren't forced to do so. If only he weren't so rich! She had little problem with the ethics of the plan when she and Esme thought that Darby had no money, and that he needed her inheritance. She had even thought, rather smugly, that he must marry so that Anabel and Josie would have dowries. But Darby didn't need her inheritance. He didn't need *her*.

She had overheard a conversation between Darby and his friend Rees Holland that confirmed her assessment. It was after the dinner party, when everyone was putting on their wraps and preparing to return home. She was kissing Esme good-bye when Holland's bellow floated from the drawing room: "Why in God's name would you marry the woman if you haven't even tupped her yet?" She couldn't hear Darby's reply.

But the earl hadn't stopped there. "Don't do it merely because the woman has a bloody fortune. I shall dower Josie. The baby as well."

Henrietta paused in the very act of pulling on her gloves. Esme raised her eyebrows but they both stayed absolutely still.

"The devil you will." Darby's voice sounded calmly uninterested to Henrietta.

"Didn't say I *can*," Rees retorted. "Said I shall. Got more than enough blunt for myself, don't I? And since my wife is unlikely to give me an heir—"

"Their dowries do not present a problem."

"Wasn't Rawlings's estate entailed?"

"Undoubtedly."

"Then . . . You can?"

"Fallen into the common belief that I'm good for nothing but clothing, Rees?" He said it gently, but there was an edge there. Henrietta could just imagine the look in Darby's eyes.

"Don't be an ass," Rees snapped back. "I think you are exactly what you've appeared to be since we were both in short-coats. A dandified nib with a pretty face and a prettier way with the rapier. Don't tell me you've been making music on the 'Change? I would have heard about it."

"The lace, Rees, the lace."

"I thought the lace was nought more than a hobby. And didn't you import most of that from France? Must be impossible these days."

"Since the war cut off supplies from France, I've become the foremost importer of lace from Belgium. In the last five years, I've extended my reach. I own Madame Franchon's on Bond Street. Madame de Lac's in Lumley—"

"Franchon's," he interrupted. "You own that place that sells lingerie? Purveyed your lace cuffs into a fortune, have you?"

"Precisely."

"Hell, the way women spend money on clothes, you must be worth more than I am. You, the very glass of fashion, dabbling in trade."

"Money would have naught to do with my decision to marry," Darby said, and silence fell in the library.

Esme had looked at Henrietta, eyes alight with laughter. "Rees is probably contemplating murder, merely to save Darby from himself," she whispered. "Lord, but the man hates marriage!"

"I don't think Darby thinks much more of it," Henrietta had mumbled.

"I wouldn't be too sure," Esme had replied.

But Henrietta knew the truth of it. Darby was getting a bad bargain in this marriage. No children. And no money, because he didn't need it.

Approximately fourteen times a day Henrietta resolved to write Darby a letter and break off their engagement, if one could call it that.

And fourteen times she changed her mind, metaphorically bared her teeth at the future, and thought: I *will* take what I want. It's hard enough that I can't have children; I deserve to have Josie and Anabel. She longed for them with an ache that sank into her very bones. She couldn't help dreaming of teaching Josie how to read, or singing Anabel a lullaby before she slept. They need me, she told herself.

That proved to be a soothing thought. Josie and Anabel did need a mother. And she was quite sure that no one else would love them the way she would, because another woman would likely have children of her own. And then that woman might neglect Josie and Anabel, or favor her own children over them.

The very thought made Henrietta shudder. Having been lucky enough to grow up with a loving stepmother didn't blind her to the possibilities.

She went every day to Esme's nursery and played with the girls. Anabel was a perfect cherub, always toddling around with her arms stretched out for a hug.

Josie was not a cherub by even the most generous assessment, but she was interesting. She divided the day between screaming tantrums and playing with the tin soldiers that had belonged to Esme's brother.

The problem was that while Josie and Anabel needed a mother, Henrietta herself was beginning to lose confidence in her own mothering abilities. Oh, she hadn't thrown any more water on Josie. But that wasn't saying that she hadn't had the impulse. She had. And it was a terrible thing to contemplate. Would Josie be better with a different mother?

Esme's nanny had a placid way of simply patting Josie on the shoulder whenever she started shrieking, and saying, "I'll speak to you when you feel a wee bit calmer, my duckling."

Henrietta tried to copy her. But she could feel her teeth starting to clench whenever Josie broke into the "I'm a little motherless girl" routine. What if she actually turned out to be a *bad* mother to Josie?

She frantically leafed through Bartholomew Batt's advice about governing children in their younger years, but it was disconcerting to find how useless his advice seemed to be in the face of Josie's tantrums. Who cared if Mr. Batt believed that wet nurses had a tendency to drink too much, thereby passing on alcoholic tendencies to children? She wasn't nursing Josie, but spending time with her was likely to drive her to drink.

Josie did like it when she told fairy stories. Perhaps it was just a matter of their growing accustomed to each other.

On the fifth afternoon following the dinner party, Henrietta was seated on a short stool, surrounded by tin soldiers in battalions, trying to fight off the excursions of an enemy spy who kept sneaking over the battlements (her skirts) and attacking her troops, when Darby walked into the room.

He was wearing a single-breasted sage-colored morning coat with double-gilt buttons, and his pantaloons were of a pale, clinging fawn. His waistcoat was of dark green striped silk, and he was carrying an amber-headed cane that was the precise color of his pantaloons.

Josie leaped up and shrieked, "Simon!" She dashed across the nursery. Darby looked enormously relieved and gratified as she skidded to a halt a mere inch from his pantaloons.

"Thank you very much, Josie," he said, stooping down. "I appreciate your forbearance."

She scowled, not seeming to know what to do next.

With a sigh, Darby reached down and scooped her up, carefully avoiding his pale trousers. His sister seemed to be taller than she had been last week, if that was possible. A lanky leg dangled in front of him, one little pointed boot dangerously close to his crotch.

She stared directly into his eyes in a most disconcerting fashion. "You're my brother Simon," she announced.

"We are both aware of that." Darby looked over at Henrietta. Why wasn't she coming to rescue him? What was he doing, holding a child? He disliked children. In fact, what was he doing in the nursery?

"I'm a poor motherless—"

"I know that too," he said, interrupting her.

Josie's lower lip quivered.

"Why do you need a mother?" he demanded. "You have a brother."

Her forehead crinkled as she tried to figure out whether that made any difference. He could see that it didn't.

"Fine. Lady Henrietta will become your mother. How does that sound?"

Josie twisted her head to see Henrietta, who was still seated on the little stool, looking rather taken aback. Though what Henrietta had to be surprised about, Darby didn't know. The concept was hardly a revelation.

"Lady Henny threw water on me," Josie reminded him. Then she leaned closer to his ear and whispered noisily, "I'm not sure that Anabel likes her very much."

Darby considered Anabel's propensity to kiss total

strangers and address them as Mama. "Anabel will get used to her," he advised Josie.

"She *did* throw water on me, Simon. Don't you remember?"

"You deserved it."

"Why don't you make Aunt Esme my mother?" Josie whispered loudly. "Nurse says she's going to have a baby. Then we'd have a new baby in the nursery. One that doesn't throw up!" She gave Anabel a baleful stare.

Anabel was headed toward Darby in a staggering kind of way. She looked clean enough, but one never knew. His valet was pessimistic about the removal of vomit stains from boots.

"Well," he said briskly, "I must go." He placed Josie back on her feet. "Good afternoon, children. Lady Henrietta, may I have a word with you?"

Henrietta followed him reluctantly. He escorted her downstairs to the sitting room, and all she thought of as they made their way down the stairs was whether her leg was dragging. He held her arm as if he didn't notice the roll in her step. The moment they entered the sitting room, he said, without ceremony, "I have obtained a special license. We can have the ceremony whenever you wish."

But Henrietta had known the moment he walked into the nursery that she couldn't go through with it.

He was too beautiful. Simply too beautiful. He looked like some sort of Greek statue, and she was nothing more than a short country girl with a limp. Just his cheekbones, and the way his cheeks hollowed beneath them, were simply too much for her. Too beautiful, too golden, too perfect. There wasn't a trace of a limp, or anything deformed about him at all.

He needed to find a flawless person, just like himself. Someone who would bear him children who shared his elegant, lean form and deep eyes.

She sat bolt upright on the settee and ignored the pain shooting through her hip. It had been a mistake to sit on a stool in order to play with Josie. But the pain lent her a certain clarity of mind. She was deformed. He was not. That very fact spoke for itself. She had to set him free to find someone as perfect as himself.

"I am going to tell my stepmother the truth," she said. She cut off the rest of her statement because her tone had an unbecoming edge to it.

He didn't seem to notice. "That would be pleasant. I shall feel much easier if my mother-in-law didn't growl at me each time we met."

"I mean to say, I will tell her the truth, and that will remove the reason for this marriage."

His brows knit. "We have an arrangement. I have obtained a special license. Why are you reneging on your word, Lady Henrietta?"

"Because you don't deserve this."

He was standing in the last rays of the afternoon sun as it crept through the windows. Henrietta didn't want to think about his beauty. She really didn't. He was tiresomely attractive; well, he could go off to London and find himself someone who would suit.

"I fail to see what you mean," he remarked. He lifted his amber-topped cane and examined the top, seemingly looking for scratches. There were none.

"We will not suit," Henrietta said.

"I believe we shall."

What was she to say to that? She said nothing.

He strolled over to her, a model of self-possession. "You made a bargain, Henrietta. I expect you to live up to it." He jerked his head toward the ceiling. "Those two little creatures are yours, from the day we rattle off our vows. You said you want them: you've got them."

"You might want children of your own someday."

"I believe I am the best judge of that. I have decided that I rather like the relationship you sketched out. It seems to me that we both have a good deal to gain. Appearances to the contrary, I am quite fond of my stepsisters." He hesitated.

"I can see that."

"We shall, I suspect, learn to be frank with each other," he said. "My mother had a devil of a temper, Henrietta. She was most famous for an attack of choler while dining at Buxton, in the company of the Regent, you understand." He paused as if she would surely know the incident to which he referred.

Henrietta tried to look inquiring but not overly curious.

"She threw a piece of roast beef across the table at my father. Unfortunately it had been scraped with horseradish," Darby said unemotionally. "The horseradish flew into the right eye of a gentleman named Cole, a younger son of Archbishop Cole. His vision was severely hampered for some time after."

"Ah," Henrietta said.

He rocked back on the heels of his boots. "My mother was a remarkably uncomfortable person to live with. She could not moderate her temper, and threw objects around the room on a regular basis. Apparently this did not disturb my father, as shortly after my mother's death he married yet another bad-tempered woman with a strong arm. The last Christmas season of my stepmother's life was enlivened by her throwing a tureen at the vicar. I am worried about Josie in that respect. She is in a fair way to growing into her mother's temperament."

Henrietta swallowed. "Recall, sir, that I am the person who dropped water on Josie's head. I very much doubt that I will be able to teach docility."

"On the contrary. You seem to maintain a sense of decorum without problem. You might simply teach Josie some more restrained ways to achieve what she desires. Witness your graceful faint at dinner, for example." He gave her that slow smile that made her insides melt.

She blushed. "It seemed appropriate at the time."

"Teach Josie a few noiseless techniques. I will be grateful if I only have to hear the *poor motherless child* refrain once or twice a year."

"I can try." Luckily Bartholomew Batt had just published a new book, and she meant to order it the very moment she could. Perhaps this one would be a bit more informative when it came to fits of temper.

"Good." His expression brightened so quickly that Henrietta suddenly wondered if he was, indeed, as uncaring as he appeared.

She was still trying to sort out the justice in the situation. "Are you quite certain that you wish to marry me, Mr. Darby? It doesn't seem fair to you. After all, by marrying you, I gain the children. But I'm quite certain that you could hire a nursemaid to teach your sisters manners, and she would likely do a better job than I." She looked down at her hands. "I have quite a temper too."

He sat down on the couch beside her. From the corner of her eye she could see the way the cloth of his trousers strained over powerful thigh muscles. "Ah, but I gain something from this marriage too," he said. "You are exquisitely beautiful, intelligent, and I even like that brutal honesty you display at times. You should call me Simon, don't you think?"

When he said nothing further, she finally had to look at him.

His eyes had such a wicked glint in them that a wave of heat rushed up her neck. How could he want her? No one wanted—

He kissed her as gently as a dandelion blows on the wind, but it made her feel scorched.

He wanted her.

～ 32 ～

Honey . . . the Nectar of the Gods

There was no getting around it. Esme was not going to be able to sleep. The bed had never seemed larger, or lonelier. And she was hungry. She was hungry all the time, so that wasn't a great surprise. But this was the sort of gnawing hunger that settled in at her backbone and told her that she wouldn't be able to sleep until she ate buttered toast.

Of course, she could ring a bell, and that would wake up some poor servant who would have to traipse up here and then straggle back down to the kitchen and make her toast. She'd never been that kind of mistress, though.

Why she was even bothering to argue with herself, she didn't know.

She had a slave, after all, didn't she?

She was the nymph Calypso, and out in that tiny island of the gardener's hut . . . well, the gardener could make her a piece of toast. *He* couldn't complain if she woke him up, or say that she was a harsh taskmaster, behind her back. *He* could be kicked off the island if he misbehaved.

It took a moment to find her pelisse by the light of one candle, but Esme managed. It was even harder to get on her boots—she had taken to allowing her maid to button them, since she couldn't reach her feet anymore, but she managed that too, by leaving all the buttons undone.

Finally, she crept from her room. The house was large and echoing at night. She walked down the corridor into the front hall. The black-and-white marble shone ghostly white in the moonlight. She eyed the front door but Slope had it bolted for the night. She turned and went through the Rose Salon, slipped out the side door through the conservatory with no more ado than a mouse traveling its familiar path.

It wasn't quite dark outside, because the moon shone like a misshapen lemon. The lawn stretched away from her, down the slope toward the rose arbor, looking quite strange and magical in the moonlight. Somewhere a bird was singing a rather raspy song, stopping and starting again as if he'd lost track of the point.

Esme started down the slope, her shoes leaving little dark trails in the dew.

The hut was pitch-dark, of course. For a moment she felt a pulse of guilt. Sebastian was probably not used to putting in a full day's labor as a gardener. He needed his sleep. But she hadn't come this far to leave without buttered toast.

She walked up to the door and knocked. There was no answer. Of course, he was asleep. She knocked again. Still no answer.

Was he in the village? But the pub had closed its doors hours before. What could he be doing? She narrowed her eyes. Perhaps he had found some slattern who was broadening his education.

Without further ado, she pushed open the door and walked in.

It was rather alarming to realize how relieved she felt to see a large mound of body under the blankets in the corner. Moonlight streamed in the open door over her shoulder, and she could see a patch of his tousled white-blond hair over the rough blanket, and his copy of *The Odyssey* splay-backed next to the bed.

She walked forward, not bothering to tiptoe. "Sebastian," she said. "Oh, Sebastian."

The blankets rustled, but he slumped back into sleep.

So she touched his shoulder. "Sebastian! Wake up, I'm hungry!"

"Mumph," was all he said.

She rocked his shoulder. Really, this was worse than waking up a child. "Sebastian, wake up!"

Finally, he sat up, blinking in the moonlight. He was sleeping without a nightshirt, and the moonlight picked out a chest of perfectly defined muscles. She froze, staring at him.

For his part, he blinked at her and then reached out one arm and pulled her to him. "Oh, good," he said sleepily. And with no further ado, he hoisted her, great stomach and all, up on the bed, leaned over her, and his tongue slid into her mouth before she even took a breath.

Her unbuttoned boots fell off. One plopped to the floor. She wound an arm around his neck.

Of course she didn't want buttered toast. She wanted him, the smoky male taste of him, that broad chest pressing against her breasts, the callused hands moving over her body as if they couldn't get enough. He kissed her until she writhed against him, until her body was drenched with desire, every nerve singing with a wish to be closer to him.

Then he pulled back and looked down at her. He looked serious, of course. For a moment she thought he was going to say something about propriety, or impropriety, but this was the Sebastian of the garden, not the marquess.

"I need to remove your pelisse," he said. "I am going to hold you, Esme." His gaze was fierce, and she felt a lick of fire in her legs. "I am going to kiss you. All of you." He had her pelisse off in a moment.

She was wearing one of the lovely nightgowns that Helene brought her from London, a generous fall of the palest pink silk. He didn't seem to notice, just began pulling it up, as if to take it over her head.

Esme promptly returned to her senses. "What are you doing?" she demanded. There was no way in heaven that she would allow Sebastian to see her body in its current condition. She held the silk tightly at her hip level to make certain that he couldn't unclothe her cumbersome body.

He stopped pulling. "I have to see you, Esme." His voice was hoarse. "I have to . . ." His voice died away. He was looking down at her breasts, sharply outlined by the silk. Esme felt a pulse of embarrassment. Pregnancy made her nipples stand out like little rocks, rather than blending into her skin the way they used to.

And her breasts looked sloppy. Not gracefully curved like the breasts that she used to exhibit in low-necked ball gowns. Then, even a glimpse of her pale pink nipples was guaranteed to drive a man into a frenzy. But now her nipples were dark red and swollen, and stuck out from cowlike breasts. She would never be able to contain them in the flimsy bodices she was accustomed to wearing.

Esme swallowed. What on earth was she doing in the gardener's hut? Had she lost her mind? This was so embarrassing. She started to hoist herself upright, but he stopped her with one of those powerful hands.

"Sebastian," she said as firmly as possible, "I'm very sorry, but you have misinterpreted my visit."

"Hush."

Esme was not a woman who liked to be silenced. She started to struggle. But he had smoothed the silk against her breast again, and now he lowered his mouth, without even paying heed to her obvious wish to rise from the bed.

Despite herself, Esme shivered. His mouth closed on her nipple, sucked, and she let out a startled squeak. He raised his head and grinned at her, smoothed the silk across her nipple again. It was wet now, a dark blotch showing against the faint pink shimmer. The wet made a bolt of heat shoot down her legs. He rubbed a thumb, lazily, across her breast, still looking into her eyes.

She opened her mouth, but couldn't remember what to say.

"Esme?" he asked gently. "Was there something?"

He was rubbing wet fabric back and forth over her breast, making her feel as if steam must be rising from her skin. Before she could formulate a response, he bent his head again and sucked her nipple back into his mouth.

The sensation was exquisite. He was suckling her, and the sense of his mouth, and the rough suction, combined with the wet sliding silk against her nipple drove her mad. She cried out, hoarse with pleasure, and pressed up against him.

"I want to kiss you without the nightgown, Esme," he said, and she dimly noticed that his voice was husky.

She didn't want to think, so she willed herself not to notice that her nightgown was inching up, past those legs that used to be slim and now were sturdy and mottled in various places, past her great stomach, with the silvery white marks that had appeared a few weeks ago.

By the time the nightgown went over her head she was rigid with humiliation and embarrassment. *Never* had she felt this way before a man. For all her reputation, she hadn't had very many affairs, but in every encounter, whether with her husband, or another man, her body had been a luscious present she offered for his appreciation. She had always been supremely aware of the fact that she had reduced the man in question to incoherent awe.

Except, now she thought of it, perhaps with Sebastian, because he was so terribly beautiful himself.

He still was, of course. He was on his knees on the bed,

gazing down at her body, no doubt in the throes of regret that he found himself in bed with a whale. Esme swallowed and looked at his body so she wouldn't have to think about it. There wasn't an extra ounce of flesh on his body anywhere, not that massive, masculine body, every inch of it powerful and sleek.

He wasn't even moving. Perhaps he was so horrified he was trying to think how to leave the room. Esme cast a desperate look to the side. Where had her nightgown fallen? She could pull it on, and leave silently, and spare both of them the distress of even discussing this incident.

She would have sat up, but his hands descended on her belly. There was something fascinating about great male hands touching that stomach.

"It's beautiful, Esme." His voice was quiet, reverent. "*You're* beautiful."

"No, I'm not," she said crossly, but she was pleased. Even in her current loathing of her body, she was secretly fond of her great stomach.

"You are. These look like falling stars, like streaks of moonlight." He traced the silver rays across her stomach. "Do you mind my touch?"

"Of course not," she said, quite resigned now. Of course the great seduction would turn into an anatomy lesson. What did she expect? No man in his right mind could think sensually about a woman in her condition.

His hands slipped to her belly, and her skin, pulled tight by the baby, tingled in his wake, left little whispers floating toward the juncture of her legs that told her that *she* wouldn't mind doing something, even in her condition. He was stroking her gently when a little bump appeared, just under his hand.

The look of shock on his face was so comical that Esme laughed out loud. "That's the baby," she said.

"I understand," he said, and in his voice was such a gathering of awe and joy that it almost made up for the fact he wasn't attracted to her body anymore.

"Where did he go?"

"That was just a kick," she said, enjoying telling him. After all, this was all new to her as well, and so far Helene had been her only confidante. "But it means the babe is awake, and perhaps—"

She could feel the next kick better than usual because his hands were against her. They lay there for perhaps fifteen minutes, the three of them, with Sebastian sweeping lazy circles over her belly and trying to entice the babe to kick him again.

"He's not kicking *you*, silly," Esme chortled. "He or she just seems to be an active sort of person."

Finally, the baby stopped kicking, lulled (if you listened to Sebastian) by his gentle rubs. He removed his hands reluctantly and looked at her.

Quite suddenly, there was a look of bedevilment in his eyes. "Now," he said, and his voice was deep as dark honey, "where were we before this baby woke up?"

"Oh no," she shook her head. "We weren't anywhere." Somewhere in the last fifteen minutes she'd lost all embarrassment before him, so she just lay there with her puffy breasts and plump thighs.

His hand descended on her breast, claimed it and shaped it as a rough thumb rubbed across her nipple. Her mind felt instantly drunk with desire, which must explain why she didn't simply rise and put on her nightgown.

Desire had never deserted Sebastian; he was in the same burning, desperate condition he always found himself in around Esme. His own, beautiful Esme.

"I want you, Esme," he whispered.

He licked her ear, made his way over her cheek to her lush lips, laid siege to her body with his hands. He knew from the way their tongues lazily tumbled over each other that she was *his*. Once again, and for this moment, but the moment was good enough.

That was a lesson he'd learned as a gardener and a pariah.

Her fingers ran through his hair and pulled him closer. Finally, he trailed kisses down her neck and made his way toward her lavish breasts. He couldn't help rising up on his knees to see them better, to feast on their beauty. "You look different," he said achingly, just before his mouth claimed possession. For a few minutes he was intoxicated, drunk with their creamy smoothness, with the dark rosebuds begging for his attention, with the broken pants coming from her lips.

His hands fell lower, shaped her lovely hips, found a sweet curve of bottom that a man could hang on to while he sunk between a woman's thighs. Just one thought managed to fight through the haze in his brain, but it was an important one. How was he to sink into her without putting pressure on her belly?

A man in this sort of extremity can usually think of something. He shaped the round fullness of her lovely bottom in his hands and lifted her slightly, pulled her toward the end of his bed, and then returned to her side. He wasn't ready to bypass the feast and go for dessert. His hand trailed up her legs, slipped between, and now he wasn't so sure that he could stand up anyway. His blood was pounding through his veins. Telling him to stand up and bury himself between those gorgeous legs, over and over until they both cried for mercy.

He had a mouth on her breast, and a hand between her legs, his breath was like fire in his chest, and his loins were clamoring for attention, and yet . . . and yet. A niggling worry had entered his mind. She wasn't herself, not his imperious, lusty Esme, the Esme who walked over to a sofa wearing only a French corset and then gave him a look that brought him to his knees.

She wasn't the same Esme who told him where to place his hands, and taught him how to move and how to touch, and then, by touching him, taught him how to beg. She wasn't watching their bodies together with that frank enjoyment she showed last time. She had her eyes closed, and even though her breath was catching in her throat, and her body moved urgently under his touch, as if it longed for him, she wasn't doing much more than trailing her hands over his chest.

He hovered over her, uncertain for a moment what to do.

Then he rolled to his side, propped his head on his elbow, and waited for her to open her eyes. After a startled moment, she did. She looked up blindly at the ceiling, and then over to the side where he lay. He smiled, the lazy smile of a hunting animal.

"Sebastian?" He was enormously pleased to hear a rasp in her voice.

"I need to know your pleasure, O Nymph," he said gravely.

She blinked in a puzzled sort of way.

"I live for your pleasure." His voice was dark with suggestion, his eyes heavy-lidded and just a glimmer of a smile around his lips. "To hear is to obey."

Esme smiled and rose up on her elbow, but as she did so she felt the heavy weight of her breast shift and felt another flash of embarrassment.

And yet he obviously wasn't undesirous. The sweep of his great male body lay like a tiger's next to her. Her eyes roamed along those strong legs, caught at his thighs. God almighty, she'd forgotten *that* about Sebastian.

"You may touch, Nymph," he said, and there was something more urgent about his voice this time. "I am your slave. My body is yours." The words hung on the night air.

She reached out. It seemed almost sacrilege, to pair a body as beautiful as his with hers.

But she reached out anyway, and he jumped when she

touched him. She ran her fingers over his nipples, and he made a low growling noise in his throat. Ran her hand down his flat stomach, and she heard the breath catch in his chest. Curled her hand around him . . . hot and smooth and male.

He was watching her, looking at her body, and she tried not to let it bother her.

"You are more beautiful than you were last summer." His hand delicately ran up her leg. His fingers played between her legs, teasingly danced in her curves.

Slowly she moved her hand, an unspoken thank-you.

His eyes closed in torment, lashes black against his cheek.

"Tell me more," she commanded.

His eyes opened. "You must have seen the changes in your breasts, Esme." In his eyes she saw the truth of it. To a man, the generosity of her chest didn't raise a query about flimsy bodices. It was cause for celebration. His eyes turned dusky blue as he watched creamy flesh swell around his fingers.

She arched her back, and a hoarse noise came from his throat. His fingers closed around the deep crimson of her nipples, and she moaned.

"More," she demanded.

"I need a better perspective," he said, rolling swiftly off the bed and standing at the end.

Looking at him, she felt a surge of her old siren power. Lazily she drew up one leg, and trailed her fingers down her thigh. Her skin felt satiny smooth . . . perfection. His eyes were black with hunger now.

"Well?" she prompted, letting her leg fall open just slightly.

"May I touch you, O Nymph?" His voice was thick.

"I think not." She trailed her fingers closer to the curls at the juncture of her legs, to the place that ached for him.

He disobeyed her, reached out and curved his hands

around her plump, firm bottom, pulled her a little closer to the end of the bed. "Don't tell me you'll lose these curves, Esme," he said hoarsely, his fingers burning into her flesh.

She filed away the fact that men didn't think a plump round bottom was a bad thing. Even though it would look awful in a high-waisted gown. He didn't seem to care. She let her leg slip a little further to the side as a present.

He seemed to be shaking.

Her fingers touched herself. "Some curves never change—" she whispered.

But strong hands pushed her legs apart, and a golden head of curls replaced her hand. She couldn't think, she couldn't breathe, she was only a body in flames.

In flames and in love.

Even as she entwined her hands in his curls and pulled him up, up so that his mouth came to hers, she knew.

He was making her heart sing by kissing her, and pulling her thighs apart, not gently. And then,

And then,

She arched to take him, to take all of him, because that was the only thing that mattered in the world. She was lost except for the choked sound of his voice saying her name, and his rhythm, God, for someone who hardly knew how—

But that thought slipped away in the rising heat and the way he was thrusting against her, his hands on her breasts now, and she was going to shriek, really shriek—she *never* shrieked; it wasn't ladylike.

Sometimes even a lady breaks the rules.

"All I wanted was buttered toast," she said sometime later, running a lazy finger over his stomach.

"To hear is to obey," he said, and the lazy pleasure in his voice made her shiver all over again.

He stoked the fire and made her toast without bothering

with his clothes, and that gave her the inestimable pleasure of watching him.

"Gardeners don't eat butter," he said, bringing back the toast.

She brightened. "Jam?"

"They can't afford such niceties. Why, the mistress of this house is a terribly hard taskmaster. Pays her workmen a pittance."

"What *do* gardeners eat on their bread?" she asked.

"Honey," he said, taking a little wooden ladle shaped like a spindle from a jar and raising it in the air over her bread so that a thin gold stream of honey curled in the air and fell on her toast.

They ate toast, tucked side by side on the edge of the bed. He kept a hand on her stomach, even though the babe was still sleeping, although how the child managed to sleep through the last hour, Esme had no idea.

"Why are you doing that?" she finally asked, deep in the comfort of a satisfied body and honey toast.

"I'm pretending he's mine," Sebastian said. He gave her a smile. "Don't worry: I know the child is Miles's. I'm just pretending." He bent and kissed her ear, just a brush with his lips.

Emotion choked her throat, and she could hardly finish her toast, but she managed, and then she had to think of a way to leave, or she would cry.

So, with her usual bad luck of the last few months, she was struck by an idea that achieved just the opposite effect.

She took his hand off her stomach and pushed him back on the bed. He went without protest, but with a surprised look in his eye.

And then she reached out for that little earthenware jar, the one with the tiny ladle in it, the ladle shaped like a spindle. And smiling her Infamous Esme smile, the smile that had seduced the most starched marquess in London, she held that little ladle up in the air.

Golden drops of honey clung to the spindle, dropped slowly, fell to something smooth, and hot, and male.

It was a good thing that she was always hungry.

Pregnancy does that to you.

The Remedy for Sin and Fornication

The wedding was to be a very quiet affair, held at Holkham House, which was graced with a very small fourteenth-century chapel that had a tiny altar and high-backed oak pews. It was a rather dim and damp sort of place, but Lady Holkham insisted.

"I won't have the villagers out gawking at you, which they would if we held it in St. Mary's," she said.

Millicent had not taken the story of the letter well, although she seemed relieved that her stepdaughter had not truly thrown all propriety to the winds. "Of course Darby must marry you," she had snapped. "It doesn't matter what the truth of the matter is: your reputation is ruined."

Henrietta didn't sleep more than an hour or two the night before her wedding. She lay awake in an agony of irresolution, certain that she was making the mistake of a lifetime. But finally dawn came, and with it a numb sense that she had no choices left.

The first thing she saw on walking into the chapel was Darby, speaking with Mr. Fetcham. Naturally he was a vision of elegance from head to foot. Henrietta looked down at her own gown. She was wearing a creamy satin gown with an overskirt pinned back over straw-colored silk. It was her best, although it had no pretensions to being a London gown.

Darby kissed her hand and then stood for a moment, looking down at her. Then he said, "Are you ready, Henrietta?"

She nodded, unable to speak for a moment.

"Are you certain you wish to accompany me to London directly after the service? I do need to return, but I don't want to wrench you away from your family."

"Not at all." A tiny part of her mind longed to go on one of those newfangled bridal tours that her sister told her about. But they weren't that sort of couple, and besides, she had made up her mind not to leave the girls until she found a trustworthy nursemaid.

"I had no idea that you shared a maid with your sister," Darby said, his brow creasing.

Henrietta bit back a smile. Obviously Darby would never share a manservant, the way she had always shared Crace with her sister.

"I had thought that your maid would travel with the children, since we are still without a nursemaid," Darby continued. "However, I will ask Lady Holkham if—"

"*I* shall travel with Josie and Anabel," Henrietta said firmly. "There's no need whatsoever to borrow one of my stepmother's servants."

"I know you mean to be a devoted mother to the children, Henrietta, and I honor you for it. But Anabel's stomach problems cause quite a pestilence in close quarters. And I'm afraid that traveling does Josie's temper no good whatsoever."

Henrietta lifted her chin. "They shall be my children."

His surly friend appeared. Henrietta curtsied. "Good morning, Lord Godwin."

"Morning," he muttered. Then he took Darby by the side and drew him toward the back of the chapel, and Henrietta distinctly heard him say, "It's not too late to . . ."

The wave of relief she felt on hearing Darby's laugh was quite terrifying.

The little chapel was growing crowded, even though Millicent had insisted that they invite no one. The children were seated in the right front pew, flanking Esme's nanny, and Lady Holkham with Imogen were opposite them. Helene and her husband Lord Godwin were, naturally enough, at opposite ends of the chapel. The vicar, Mr. Fetcham, nodded to her, and Henrietta walked into the little crypt off to the side. She was to wait for her cue before she emerged.

She leaned against a stone crypt and tried not to think about what was to come. The crypt was adorned with a statue of its occupant, lying on his back, rigidly poking his hands up in the air in an eternal gesture of prayer. The crypt was bitterly cold. Slowly the damp cold sank into Henrietta's bones, making her feel as rigid as the statue.

Finally, the door pushed open, and Lord Godwin stood in the doorway, waiting to escort her to the altar.

"Rees is my closest friend," Darby had told her. "Since your father is dead, I asked him to stand in."

Henrietta had the fleeting thought that perhaps Lord Godwin would tell *her* that it wasn't too late, but he simply held out his arm.

Everyone stood up as she began walking from the back of the chapel. The cold had done its work: she was limping badly. *Why* hadn't she thought about that walk to the altar? She'd be lucky if Darby didn't turn tail and run, given that she was almost lurching, in a moment that should be a woman's most graceful.

Mr. Fetcham looked as cheerful as if he weren't celebrating a marriage of sinners, which is surely what he must have thought she and Darby to be. "We are gathered here together to join this man and woman together in holy matrimony."

Henrietta could only hope that her family could hear the words of the marriage service over Josie's loud whispering.

She shifted her weight, wondering whether her leg would simply crumple, throwing her to the ground.

The vicar was pointing out that marriage was not to be taken in hand to satisfy men's carnal lusts and appetites, like brute beasts that have no understanding. She could see instantly why *those* particular lines were in the service. Not that her soon-to-be husband seemed to care that marriage was ordained as a remedy against sin and fornication. Actually, fornication was a good word for it: an ugly, sharp word.

The vicar droned on, but Henrietta stopped listening when he said that marriage was ordained for the procreation of children. The service seemed to have little to do with her, what with the fact she had advised her husband to take a mistress, not to mention the fact that they couldn't procreate. Instead, she tried to understand Josie's piercing commentary from the front row. She could just guess what the little girl was saying. Josie wanted Esme as her new mother, not Lady Henny who threw water on her. Henrietta tried not to feel hurt. Josie would learn to love her.

Her leg was sending bolts of pain all the way to her right knee. Darby must have noticed that she was shifting her weight, because he looked down with a small frown. Henrietta tried to still herself.

When they turned about from the altar, man and wife, one would be hard-pressed to say whether Josie or Rees looked more disgruntled. Only Esme looked delighted.

"Congratulations, Darby," Rees said, shaking his hand.

I suppose, Henrietta thought dispiritedly, now that it's too late to save his friend from an awful fate, Lord Godwin has decided to make the best of it.

"Are you quite convinced that you wish to travel with the children?" Darby asked her again, after they had accepted everyone's congratulations. "A coach is not the best place to further your acquaintance with Anabel, in particular."

"No," Henrietta said sturdily. "I do not wish the girls to be taken care of by strangers, and I had better begin as I mean to go on."

"In that case, perhaps I shall take Rees up in my barouche. I bought a traveling coach just before leaving London, so you and the children should be quite comfortable."

"Of course," Henrietta said with all the dignity she could muster. She suspected Rees would spend the trip counseling Darby on his horrible future as a married man, but she could hardly prevent that.

Henrietta gave the traveling coach a cursory glance, then walked forward to meet the horses. They were sturdy draft horses, suited to pulling a coach that looked big enough for a traveling theatrical troupe. "What are their names?" she asked Darby.

"Haven't the faintest idea," he replied. "I bought them just for this purpose." He was very cheerful, no doubt welcoming the male comfort of his barouche.

Josie was brought out clinging to Esme's nanny and yowling at the top of her lungs. "I don't *want* to go! I hate London, I hate London, I hate London." She caught sight of Darby and changed her tune slightly. "I hate Simon! I hate Simon!" Her little face was red and blotchy, and she appeared to be going hoarse.

"We'll go a bit faster than you on the road," Darby said, blithely ignoring his little sister. "Everything will be ready for you when you arrive at the Bear and Owl, our first stop."

"I have no doubt but that you will arrive before us." Henrietta eyed the powerful horses hitched to Rees's vehicle.

"You should be comfortable." Josie's howls could be heard emerging from the traveling coach. "Although you might want to make frequent stops as they seem to help settle Anabel's stomach. Henrietta—"

But she cut him off. "I shall travel with the children."

He bent and gave her a quick kiss on the cheek. "I am remarkably pleased with this situation."

"By 'situation' do you mean our marriage, or your traveling arrangements?" she asked with just a touch of acid in her tone.

"Our marriage, of course!" Then, with the nimbleness that all men show in times of narrowly averted crisis, he bowed once again. "I shall await you at the Bear and Owl."

Efficiently handed into the traveling coach by her husband, Henrietta sank onto a seat. Josie was lying in a heap on the floor between the seats, sobbing disconsolately. Henrietta could only make out a word every now and then, but *motherless* could be heard and that discouraged Henrietta from inquiring further.

Anabel, on the other hand, was quite happily sitting on the seat opposite Henrietta. Her little legs were sticking out straight in front of her, and she was eating a meat pasty with some relish. Her face was covered with filling. Esme's nanny put an enormous covered basket on the floor between the seats and turned to Henrietta, who was alarmed to see distinct sympathy in her eyes. "You've a nice hamper of food here, my lady."

She lowered her voice. "After Miss Anabel loses her luncheon, she'll probably take a wee nap. And then she does get hungry. There's toweling in the basket, plenty of nappies, and two changes of clothing for the babe."

"*Two?*"

"Mr. Darby did say that she lost her stomach many times on the way from London, my lady. Of course, he may well have been exaggerating, men being what they are." She gave her an encouraging smile. "It's a true shame you don't have a nurse for the children yet."

Bartholomew Batt said, above all, one must approach children in a resolute, firm, and loving manner. That being the case, Henrietta should do something about the sodden heap of little girl lying on the floor between the seats.

The coach lurched and began to rumble up the gravel road. It was moving even slower than Henrietta could have imagined. She had an idea that the horses weren't even trotting. They were merely ambling.

Showing remarkable endurance, Josie kept sobbing. Henrietta leaned over. "Would you like to sit next to me?"

Josie raised a tear-stained face and said in a scratchy sort of way, "I want—I want—I wanta go back! I wanta go back to the nursery. I love Nanny. I wanta stay there."

"I'm sorry. I liked Esme's nanny too, very much. Shall we find you a nurse just like her?"

Josie gave her a look of withering scorn. "Aunt Esme said that she was one of a kind." Tears spilled down her cheeks again. "I hate traveling. And I was ha—ha—happy at Aunt Esme's. I hate Simon for moving us. I want to go home!"

Henrietta didn't even know where home was. Probably Esme's nursery, given that the poor little thing could hardly be talking about her own mother's nursery, since the loathed Nurse Peeves of the wet garments had been in charge there.

"Please sit next to me, Josie," she said as coaxingly as she could.

Josie just sobbed.

Henrietta wondered what Batt would do. Unfortunately, the maids had packed his *Rules and Directions* somewhere in the trunks. But she already knew that he didn't say a useful thing about temper tantrums. Lord knows she'd looked hard enough.

She leaned down and tried to guide Josie up on the seat, but her small body proved to be wiry and resistant. Josie wailed louder.

Finally Henrietta managed to grasp Josie and haul her up on the seat. Unfortunately, she had to brace her legs against the floor, which sent such a jolt of pain down her leg that she gasped. She did keep hold of Josie, though. The little girl seemed to be losing steam, as well she might after a half hour of crying.

"I know you're worried about finding a kind nanny," Henrietta said soothingly. "I can assure you that your brother and I will do everything we can—"

"I don't like you," Josie said, in a wretched tone. "I don't like you, and I don't want you to be my mother."

The coach swayed along at its gentle pace while Henrietta held on to Josie and wondered what to do next. Josie solved that problem by wrenching her way out of Henrietta's arms and crawling onto the opposite seat. Henrietta put up her chin and tried not to care.

She turned to Anabel just in time to notice that the baby was looking a bit white. Sure enough, Anabel made that funny dry coughing sound Henrietta recognized and, without further ado, threw up the remains of a meat pie all over the floor of the coach and Henrietta's shoes.

As if on cue, Josie regained her strength. "I don't want you for a mother!" she shrieked. "And neither does Anabel!"

~ 34 ~

Of Babies in Baskets and Families in Carriages

Darby and Rees arrived at the Bear and Owl around three in the afternoon. Rees spent the trip bundled up in a corner, tunelessly humming fragments of music over and over. It was enough to drive a man to drink. And the moment the carriage drew to a halt, he strode off down the street, muttering something about an organ and the village church.

Darby arranged for rooms, found a woman to care for Anabel and Josie for the night, then strolled back outside and looked down the road they had traveled. He'd had a creeping sense of guilt for the past hour or so.

He'd mishandled the trip. The truth was that his feelings were hurt by Henrietta's emphasis on their marriage as a convenience by which she acquired his stepsisters, as if they were an inheritance he brought with him. Still, it wasn't right to leave his bride alone in a carriage with two children, no matter how much she talked about wanting to be a mother.

A seasoned nursemaid had been unable to cope with Anabel's weak stomach and Josie's tantrums. The trip from London had been hell; there was no reason to expect that the trip back would be different. With a sigh he turned to the innkeeper and began negotiating to hire a hack. Five minutes later he was trotting back down the road.

A half hour later he caught sight of his traveling carriage. It was swaying gently along, looking like precisely what it was: a carriage containing a man's family. He waved it over, tied his hack behind, and climbed in with a sense of dread intensified by the odor that greeted him. The first thing he saw was a large basket between the seats, holding a pile of crumpled linens and children's clothing. Clearly, Anabel was no longer in the clothing she wore that morning. But all in all, it was a remarkably peaceful scene that met his eyes.

Henrietta was tucked into a corner, Anabel against her chest, both of them fast asleep. From the way Anabel's eyes looked swollen even in her sleep, he guessed she'd probably wailed up a storm before napping. Josie was sitting on the other seat, one leg curled beneath her, sucking her thumb. As soon as she saw him, she took out her thumb and said, "Shhh! Anabel is sleeping!"

"I see that," Darby said, sitting down next to her and nodding to the footman, who closed the door. The carriage resumed its slow, lumbering journey. "I thought I would join you, in case Henrietta needed some assistance. Have you had a pleasant journey?"

Something about the dedicated way that Josie was sucking her thumb and staring at her boots made him suspicious. "You have had an easy journey, haven't you?"

She didn't answer. "Josie?"

Finally his little sister took her thumb out of her mouth and said, "I can call her Henrietta, because she married my brother."

Darby blinked. "Good."

"She has a temper," Josie said in an offhand sort of way. "Look." She pointed to one of the little lamps that was attached to the carriage walls. It seemed fine to Darby, but Josie stared at it with satisfaction. Presumably the shade had suffered some sort of abuse.

Well, Darby thought, my mother threw roast beef. I suppose I could prepare myself for flying lampshades. Josie didn't seem perturbed. In fact, displays of temper probably made her feel quite at home. He had a vague sense that she had been present the Christmas before last—well, obviously Josie had been summoned downstairs at some point, but was she downstairs when his stepmother launched a tureen at the vicar? All his father had said was, "Damme if you haven't bent the edge."

I can cultivate the same lassitude, Darby told himself. Now he had been in the carriage a few moments, he could hardly smell an unpleasant odor at all. What's more, Henrietta's hair was falling out of its snood, and she looked unusually disheveled, which made him remember that every journey had its end—and this one would be his wedding night.

Josie's eyes were looking heavy, and Darby guessed that she would be asleep in a moment. He hesitated a moment, then picked up Anabel and plopped her into the half-empty basket on the floor. It could have been designed just for the purpose; the child barely shifted in her sleep. Then Darby sat down next to his wife and pulled her against his shoulder.

She opened her eyes briefly, looked at him in a dazed sort of way, and said, "I warned you!" and went back to sleep.

So Darby propped himself into the corner and watched Josie drift to sleep. By the time her eyes closed, he had decided to please himself and remove that little netting that Henrietta used to keep her hair in place. Slowly, slowly, he began removing just as many of his wife's hairpins as he could reach without waking her up. No wonder her hair seemed so docile. She wore far more pins than he would have guessed a woman needed. Finally, he managed to ease the little net she wore on top of her head off and toss it to the side. No wife of his was going to dress like a grand-mother.

Two minutes later, he knew precisely why Henrietta Maclellan resorted to a hairnet and more hairpins than one normally saw in a mercer's shop. Her hair tumbled down her shoulder like a lion's mane, streaked and shot with gold and amber. It didn't curl: the word *curl* brought to mind ringlets, and little girls. It leaped with fire, unruly and ungoverned, all the way to her waist. His fingers ran through great masses of rough silk.

Naturally she was wearing a traveling gown constructed with no regard to the female body. It was thick, and the seams didn't even lie flat in places. Darby ran an experimen-tal hand down Henrietta's front, but he couldn't feel anything other than poor seamsmanship. Well, there were bumps that likely hid her breasts, but damned if he could feel their shape. Not that he needed touch to remind him, he thought a bit grimly. The swell of her breasts in his hand haunted his dreams. His fingers traced the sturdy wool of her bodice. Un-der this wool, her breasts were the color of the finest cream lace, yet far softer. And from cream bloomed a nipple as dusky as a late rose.

Josie snorted in her sleep and Darby froze. It was not very gentlemanly to feel his wife's chest in the presence of chil-dren, even sleeping children. He left his hand on the warm curve of Henrietta's right breast, or at least on the rumpled broadcloth presumably covering her breast, while he thought about it. Then he stopped thinking and began feeling the shape of her body with his hand again. It was rather like try-ing to guess the shape of a fruit in the dark.

Except that all he could feel were her garments. He could feel each separate bone in her corset, which meant that his bride was wearing undergarments as restrictive and as heavy as those his grandmother presumably had worn. He idly traced each up-and-down spear, feeling through the layers of rumpled wool. No wonder Henrietta kept her back rigid. She didn't have a choice.

For her part, Henrietta was enjoying herself far too much to open her eyes. It was oddly soothing to wake from sleep to find Darby's long fingers dancing over her breasts, sweeping down her sides. She almost shivered, it felt so good, except that would give her away. Even through layers of wool and corset and linen, her body knew his hand was there.

He seemed to be feeling her corset now. Henrietta's eyelids trembled and almost opened, tense with the desire to demand what he was doing. It was intoxicating, the sense that his fingers were gliding over her breasts. The very thought made her heart thud in her ribs, made a tremor of feeling quake down, down between her legs. It was as if he skimmed the surface of water, and she were just below. Longing for him to break the surface. Her breasts tingled and almost begged for his touch.

She opened her eyes with a little gasp. His fingers stopped instantly, relaxed as if he were doing nothing more than prop up his sleeping wife, and had happened to drape his hand on her chest.

For a second his eyes burned down at her. Then she saw, deep in their depths, a glint of laughter. He knew she wasn't asleep. He'd guessed somehow. She never could keep a secret.

"Enjoying yourself, darling?" he whispered, bending his neck so that his breath stirred the curls on her forehead.

She should deny it . . . she should claim sleep . . . she should act like a lady. She sat up and thought about what she wanted to do next.

"Are you comfortable?" he asked, and his husky, almost sleepy voice made her feel like sagging back against his shoulder. It was as if he heard her thoughts. "Why don't you lean back, Henrietta?"

She never, ever leaned, or sagged. "Keep your back straight and your deformity will be less noticeable," one doctor had advised. Henrietta had never forgotten that advice.

Suddenly she leaped up. "The children!" she gasped.

"They're both asleep," he said, pulling her back against him. She lost her balance and fell directly onto his lap. His breath caressed her neck.

"What on earth has happened to my coiffure?" As she twisted to the side to recapture the heavy fall of hair, she heard the oddest, almost stifled noise from Darby.

"Is something the matter?"

Darby had to think about how to answer that. The cruel gods who had designed corsets had forgotten to cover Henrietta's curving little bottom with whalebone. It rounded into the juncture of his legs, intoxicatingly round, soft and tender. She probably had no idea what was jutting between his legs.

But she sure as hell noticed something. She kept wriggling, trying to find a comfortable spot.

He put his hands on her waist and placed her next to him on the seat. His wife was looking about, obviously wondering where her little hairnet had gone.

Then her eyes widened as she noticed something else was missing. "Where's Anabel?"

"Here," Darby said, lifting the top of the picnic basket proudly. It was an admirable baby carrier, if he said so himself.

"You put Anabel in a picnic basket? And then you put a—a top on the basket!"

"She couldn't suffocate," Darby pointed out. "The basket is made of woven reed, and there's plenty of air."

Henrietta stared at him, mouth open, and Darby was fairly

sure that had there been a side of roast beef in the area, it would now be sailing through the air in his direction. So he moved first.

No gentleman's kiss, this.

It was a warning, an advisory, a precursor to the evening. If she didn't know why his lap had turned into such a lumpy seat, Darby certainly did. For some unknown reason, his drably dressed little wife had him aching with lust in a way he hadn't experienced even when he was infatuated with the third housemaid. It was a deep, hungry need that he felt, one as primitive as anger or grief.

His tongue invaded her mouth in the way that the Cossacks invaded small villages: invasion first, questions after. It was a kiss that spoke of nakedness, of breasts without corsets, and laps without trousers.

And his wife, his little rigid-backed wife, understood the message all right. She braced her hands against his shoulders and said something incoherent. An admonishment, surely. But he could taste her . . . could taste the passion in her, even as she pushed at his shoulders. He merely grabbed her and pulled her across his lap again, a flare of fire searing his groin as her bottom settled on his legs. Then he took her mouth, fell into a dipping stroke, his hands holding her close.

Quite suddenly her tongue met his, shyly perhaps, willingly for certain. The raw lust that swept his body was a revelation.

Simon Darby never lost his composure. Never. Early in his life, he formed the opinion that raw emotion was inadvisable and unattractive. He had watched his stepmother burst into an ecstasy of rage while his father, still enthralled with his beautiful wife, hardly complained. Later Darby watched his father succumb to a gambling fever, unable to stop bidding higher and higher, even on cards of no value. Darby had early succeeded in curbing his own responses to appropriate measures.

But now, in the inner recesses of his mind, Darby was aware that his own wife might prove his undoing. He was trembling—literally trembling. He'd never shook while holding a woman in his life. It was mortifying.

He had to talk to her, explain that he wasn't—

"What are you doing to Henrietta?" said a small voice from the other side of the carriage, with some interest.

His wife made a hoarse sound in her throat and tore away from him so quickly that she nearly pitched to the carriage floor.

Darby straightened and stared at his sister. How long had Josie been awake? She sat on the opposite seat, thumb in her mouth, looking at them with an inquiring expression.

"I was greeting Henrietta," he said.

Josie's eyes narrowed. "You never greet me like that," she said.

"You are not my wife."

Josie's mouth instantly thinned to a mutinous line. Darby braced himself for an explosion of mamaless cries and shrieks, but Henrietta cut off the shriek as it was about to appear.

"Remember what I told you, dear," she said, nodding at the lampshade.

To his immense surprise, Josie blinked and stilled. Clearly there was some ferocious threat attached to the lampshade.

"Mr. Darby does not mean to be sharp," Henrietta continued. She was twisting up her great rope of hair as she spoke, winding it briskly, although how she thought to get it to stay on the top of her head without the hairnet (now snugly stowed in Darby's pocket) he couldn't say.

Luckily the carriage seemed to be rumbling over cobblestones, a sure sign that they had finally reached the Bear and Owl.

"Your brother and I were merely exchanging greetings," Henrietta said. She gave up the effort to rearrange her hair and simply crammed her bonnet on over it. "Married persons do greet each other with a kiss when they meet unexpectedly."

Josie looked unconvinced, but Henrietta serenely suggested that she replace her own bonnet, as they had undoubtedly reached the inn.

Darby was as unconvinced as his sister. He glanced down at his lap. If this was a mere greeting, what would his wife think of the night?

He looked at Henrietta and was gratified to see a flush of color high in her cheeks, a fullness to her bottom lip that spoke of his ravaging kisses.

Little flakes of snow were beginning to drift past the carriage as Darby stepped to the ground. It was only early evening, but the sky was dark and lowering, promising to storm. Henrietta handed him a barely awake Anabel. He looked around for a footman, but the only one available to carry the baby looked like a clumsy brute who might drop her. So to his surprise, he found himself carrying the child toward the inn. She woke up, gave him one of those toothless grins of hers, and called him mama. She was a snug little bundle of person, especially when she didn't smell too markedly.

Small flakes of snow were falling into the fiery mass of Henrietta's hair. They disappeared instantly, scorched, no doubt.

"I shouldn't think we'll be able to travel tomorrow," he said, catching up with his wife as she led Josie toward the inn.

"Oh dear," Henrietta said, looking at the sky.

He surrendered to a sweet temptation. "We may have to spend the day in bed," he said, bending near her ear. "Just to keep our warmth, of course."

She looked up at him, lips swollen from his kisses, and surprised him again. There was a flickering smile in her eyes, even curling the edge of those deep rose lips. Snowflakes flecked her hair and her eyelashes, but she was no snow maiden, frozen to the core.

He silently followed her into the inn door because he literally didn't know what to say. The idea that a mere smile could cause heat to sweep his body like a fierce plague was frightening.

~ 35 ~

Dinner for Three

"Did you find the village organ of interest, Lord Godwin?" Henrietta said, resolutely trying to ignore her new husband. He was acting in the most foolish manner, pressing his leg against hers and smiling at her as if—as if—She wrenched her mind away from that thought.

The innkeeper bustled in and himself supervised the remove of fillets of turbot with a harrico of mutton.

"It wasn't terrible." If Lord Godwin didn't precisely grunt, he sounded as if he had. Henrietta was beginning to feel indignant. She had been sitting here for nearly thirty minutes, doing her best to make pleasant conversation to the man who claimed to be her husband's closest friend, and he was being abominably rude. That was the only word for it.

Even now, he was showing not a particle of interest in continuing their conversation, but just poking at his mutton as if it were undercooked. She took a sip of burgundy, cautioning herself not to fly into an extravagant comment. It was none of her business if the man was taciturn, and surly, and altogether—

She'd give him one more chance.

"Lord Godwin, what did you think of Napoleon's exile to Elba? Do you believe that he'll remain on the island?"

"Don't give a hang either way."

Henrietta spared her husband a glance.

"I wouldn't even bother," he advised her. "Rees hasn't had a conversation with a respectable woman in so long that he doesn't remember the language."

But Henrietta was known for her persistence. "Wasn't this past year tremendously interesting for France, Lord Godwin?"

"For Austria, perhaps."

"Austria?"

"Beethoven's opera *Fidelio* was performed for the delegates at the Congress of Vienna in autumn," Rees said with perfect indifference. "Mrs. Darby, if you are trying to impress your husband by exhibiting your profound knowledge of international relations, could you please save the demonstration for your private quarters?" He drained his glass and set it down with a thump. "I assure you that I am sufficiently impressed by your abilities as demonstrated by your current marital status."

Henrietta narrowed her eyes. The man clearly wanted to lure her into a demonstration of temper, likely to prove some moronic point he made to Darby about women's temperament. She knew that all-male carriage ride was going to incite trouble.

She thought about it for a second, then threw Rees a melting look from under her eyelashes. "What a pleasure, Lord Godwin, to see you become so unexpectedly verbal."

He gave her a guarded look. He probably thought she was making advances to him. Rees is your husband's closest friend, she told herself. Be kind to the man.

"I'm afraid I hadn't realized until Darby told me just now that it was quite so taxing for you to speak to married women. Although I did notice that you had some difficulty making conversation to dear Mrs. Cable during Lady Rawl-ings's dinner." She gave him a kindly smile. "We will make this as uncomplicated as possible. I certainly wouldn't want to disconcert you, especially now that I realize your topics of conversation are so limited."

Beside her, Darby choked.

"I am certain that speaking to a respectable woman can be quite a strain. What could we discuss that would make you feel more comfortable? Let's see . . . I gather that your latest houseguest is an opera singer. How very interesting that must be! Do you two discuss Beethoven on a regular basis?"

Rees Godwin kept chewing his meat, but she could see that she had his attention. Henrietta stifled a grin. She was feeling a rush of exuberance.

"She is indeed an opera singer," Godwin finally replied. Just as Henrietta glimpsed a calculating glint in his eye, he added, scandalously: "With a lamentable tendency to sing in bed."

"That must be due to her extreme youth," Henrietta replied serenely. "There was a time when I was quite given to singing when I first awoke. I believe that 'Peter Peter Pump-kin Eater' was my favorite. But let me see . . . what *is* the sec-ond line of 'Diddle Diddle Dumpling, My Son John'?"

"Something to do with going to bed missing articles of clothing, isn't it?" said her husband. His voice was ripe with laughter. "*Went to bed with his stocking on*—or no, I think he had his stockings off. I can't quite remember."

"I expect that's a complaint suffered by Lord Godwin's *friend* as well. Ah, what a pleasure it was to be young enough to wake with a song!"

"She's not that young!" Godwin growled, but Henrietta could see a gleam—just a gleam—of appreciation at the back of those sullen eyes of his.

"There's no need to make excuses," she said soothingly.

"For someone who suffers so mightily during a conversation with a grown woman, I would guess that the separation in your ages is quite reassuring. You must be thirty years older than your companion, no? Children are so diverting."

"There isn't thirty years between us!" Godwin roared. "I'm in my thirties myself!"

Henrietta put a hand to her heart. She was enjoying herself mightily. "Goodness, I hope I have not insulted you!" She eyed him head to foot. He was as messy as he ever was, hair curling around his shoulders and his shirt all spotted with ink. "You're absolutely right: I see now that you're not *so* old." She paused, as if doubting her own assessment.

"At any rate, time does have a way of solving this sort of problem, my lord! Just think: in a matter of what? Five years or so? Your lady friend will reach the age of majority and you will be able to ease into this whole difficult business of *conversation*."

She took a sip of her wine and offered him a glinting smile full of the pleasure she was feeling. It was such a pleasure to be eating with two grown men, rather than with her stepsister and stepmother. She'd never, ever thought that she would be exchanging delicately insinuating barbs with men. The way Darby's best friend was gaping at her was almost enough to make her laugh aloud.

"I'm afraid that Lord Godwin is having some difficulty even with this little chat," she said, turning to her husband. "Darby, shall we model polite discourse for the poor man? Now, Lord Godwin, do listen carefully, and perhaps we can explain the Treaty of Paris to you."

But Rees interrupted. "Damn it if you haven't done yourself a favor, Darby," he said with a bark of laughter. Then he leaned across the table and took Henrietta's hand. While she watched in some amazement, he lifted it to his lips in as gallant an expression of courtesy as she'd ever seen. "You've surprised me. You'd better call me Rees, by the way. I can't stand the title."

She took her hand away and laid it over her heart. "Darby, do revive me in case I swoon. I can feel myself growing younger by the second. The earl is speaking to me. I do believe that I just entered the honorary ranks of courtesan!"

Darby leaned close to her shoulder. "I don't believe you can truly achieve that title until after this evening, my dear."

His deep voice pulled her straight from improper humor to a kind of reeling, overheated flush. In fact, she could feel pink stealing up her cheeks as she looked into his eyes. They were wicked. Purely wicked.

On the other side of the table, Rees chuckled. "Damned if I'm not almost envious of you, Darby."

"Hmmm-hum," Darby said. He had Henrietta's hand in his, and raised it to his lips. Funny—when Rees kissed her hand, she felt nothing but a cheerful pleasure, but all Darby had to do was brush his lips across her knuckles and her stomach clenched in a confused, overheated muddle. "Shall we retire, lady wife?"

Henrietta pulled her hand away. "Certainly not! We haven't even—there's another course arriving," she said, in some relief. The innkeeper pushed open the door, waving in footmen carrying a jelly, some apple puffs, and a plate of rout drop cakes.

Rees laughed again but thankfully didn't comment. Once the door closed behind the footmen, he said, "I suppose politeness dictates that I should begin a subject of conversation."

Henrietta gave him an approving smile. "You see how easy it grows to be!"

He snorted. "How did you survive in the carriage, then? I must say, the idea of traveling with wee Anabel makes my stomach churn. I visited the nursery just after the girls moved to London, and she upchucked on my boots by way of greeting."

"Oh, it was lovely—" Henrietta said, and stopped. There

really wasn't any point to prevarication. "Actually, it was quite desperately horrible." She cut her apple puff into four precise pieces. "Josie screamed like a demented person, to the point at which I thought she might crack a lung, if that is possible."

Darby's warm hand touched her back. "She's an ungrateful little beast," he said.

"No, she's not," Henrietta said. "She's just quite—quite miserable. And I don't know how to help her."

"I thought Anabel's stomach was the problem," Rees said. "What did Josephine scream about, then?"

Henrietta tried not to think about the warmth of Darby's hand on her back. "She cried and reminded me that she is a motherless child."

"So? Tell her you're her mother now," Rees said.

"But I'm not her mother," Henrietta pointed out. "I have informed her that since I've married her brother, I will *act* as her mother. Mr. Bartholomew Batt, a noted expert on child rearing, says that children should not be prevaricated to."

"That's rubbish," Darby said. "I heard far too much truth from my own mother. Just tell Josie you're her mother, and the end with it."

Henrietta looked at him with a little frown, but he didn't say anything further.

"I agree," Rees said. "And then tell the girl to stop throwing up a fuss because she'll never catch a husband at that rate. Nothing a man hates worse than a squalling wife."

"Oh my, yes. I must tell her *that*. Husbands are such an enviable possession, after all. Just look at you, my lord."

Rees gave his bark of laughter and pushed back from the table, standing up. He surprised her with a swooping bow. For a moment he looked almost handsome, his forbidding face relaxed into a grin. "Lady Henrietta, it has been indeed a pleasure. Darby, I take back everything I said in the carriage."

The moment he left the room, Henrietta turned to Darby.

"I knew he was telling you dreadful things in that carriage!"

Her husband drew her to her feet before answering. "I didn't listen," he said, looking down into her eyes. Henrietta was suddenly aware that she was alone with him. That they didn't need a chaperone. That they were married.

"I was thinking of other things."

~ 36 ~

A Wedding Night

Wedding nights are many things to many people: terrifying to the unwilling, too quickly finished to the eager.

Henrietta had read enough poetry, especially all those poems anticipating the night, to understand that some women were eager. Look at Juliet, going on and on about Romeo lying on her, like snow on a raven's back. Of course, Juliet said that *before* Romeo climbed up to her room—which was the important distinction, to Henrietta's mind. Juliet didn't know what the marital act entailed, whereas she, Henrietta, did.

The problem was that she, Henrietta, knew far too much about the whole procedure to look forward to it. In fact, were there a rope ladder dangling from her window, she'd be down it herself in an instant. Never mind the fact that rope ladders were undoubtedly difficult to negotiate. She looked longingly out the window, but there was nothing to be seen but a brick wall with snow blowing over it.

"Just lie still," Millicent had told her that very morning. "It's over faster if you simply lie still. Think about something useful. I often cataloged the linen in my head. That way, one doesn't feel as irritated by the event." Then she added practical, if rather nauseating details about how to deal with leakage—none of which Henrietta really understood. It sounded as if the procedure were almost as messy as one's monthly, which happened to be Henrietta's least favorite time of month. In fact, had she any idea that marital intimacies required one to pad oneself with rags the next day, she would never have agreed to the marriage.

But then, Anabel had called her mama when she said good night. And Josie had only one small bout of tears before bed, and it was inspired by Anabel spewing on her nightgown. Henrietta considered throw-up a justifiable reason for temper. Now both children were fast asleep, with a likable girl named Jenny watching over them. Even better, Jenny had agreed to accompany them to London.

All of which left a newly married Henrietta Darby in the largest bedchamber the Bear and Owl could offer. By herself.

Henrietta couldn't decide whether to disrobe or not. She had no maid until they reached London and could engage one, and so she was wearing a simple traveling dress that she could easily unfasten by herself. In the end she bathed (to remove the reminders of Anabel's supper) and pulled on her night rail with a dressing gown over it.

She was sitting by the window gloomily thinking about Rapunzel's ability to turn her hair into a ladder, when the door opened and Darby appeared.

"Good evening!" he said. He was holding a bottle of wine and two glasses. Henrietta looked at him rather bitterly. It was due to his inconvenient lust that she was sitting here awaiting such an unpleasant event.

The fact that he was so elegant made the whole procedure seem more embarrassing than ever. It had been a long day, but he was impeccably attired. His hair was tousled in a manner that looked coiffured, and his fingers were long and elegant as they wrestled the cork out of the bottle. Why did *she* have to endure leakages and pain and blood when he would doubtless remain as exquisite and polished as he always was?

Darby handed her a glass and she took a sip. Despite herself, she was rather curious to see her husband without clothes. An improper thought, no doubt.

"I've been downstairs, and the innkeeper confirms that we're snowed in," he said, with what seemed to her unnecessary emphasis.

She drank some more wine.

"How's your hip feeling?" he asked, sitting down across from her.

She felt the beginnings of a blush. Was this married life? A husband mentioning body parts to you with no shame?

"Precisely as customary," she said, inviting no further commentary.

Darby looked at his new wife and wondered how the devil he should proceed. Virgins did not come into his area of expertise, given that Molly, the third housemaid, resisted his blandishments. Henrietta was sitting as upright as a marionette. Her back was perfectly aligned with the straight-backed chair on which she sat, her head poised atop her body like the marble ball at the bottom of a staircase.

He should have guessed that her stepmother would feed her a load of tripe about the wedding night. Lady Holkham had made her distaste for the act clear enough. If he followed his own inclination and simply pulled off her nightgown and tossed Henrietta on the bed, she would freeze.

But then, Henrietta was no Lady Holkham. She desired him. He fancied that her eyes lingered on him, even now. He stood up. "I dismissed my valet for the night," he said, trying for a careless tone. He hadn't exactly expected her to leap to her feet and offer to help him, but she didn't even make a comment. Instead she just watched him suspiciously, as if he were likely to rip off his clothes.

"Care to begin your wifely duties?" he asked. Despite her obvious distress, he couldn't help thinking this was great fun. Probably the best fun he'd had since a certain Madame Bellini decided to show him all seven pleasures of Aphrodite. Henrietta was such a bundle of contradictions: her wild lioness hair (now tidily braided in an arrangement that he intended to undo as quickly as possible), her delicate little face, the steely resolve in her eyes and chin. The passion that lay under that rigid little body of hers. She was presumably not wearing a corset, but she was just as stiff as if she had one on beneath her night rail.

A small fraction of his soul felt sorry for her, but the truth was that she desired him. He had felt that desire coursing through her body. She simply didn't understand her body yet. Or his body, for that matter.

"Wifely duties," she said slowly. "I understand."

She stood up and took off her dressing gown. But before Darby did more than glimpse an enticingly unsteady swing of breast through her night rail, she turned, climbed into bed and pulled up the sheet. For a moment, he just stood in the center of the room, dumbfounded.

Then he strode over to the bed and looked at his wife. She was rather white, lying as if ready for a coffin fitting, sheets up to her chin.

"Henrietta," he asked, "what are you doing?"

Her eyes opened. "I'm ready to perform my duty, Darby. You may proceed." She closed her eyes again.

"Ready," he said, savoring it. This was too delicious. She looked like an early Roman martyr. He reached out a hand and let his finger trail down her white neck, down to the edge of the sheet. Then he sat down on the edge of the bed, nudging her over a bit. And spread his hand and curled it around her breast. It was all he could do to simply leave his hand there. But he did. Waited for her, willing himself not to move, pretending not to notice that he was holding one of the most perfectly shaped breasts he had ever held.

She had backbone, his Henrietta. It seemed to take forever for her to open her eyes again and look at him.

He swallowed his grin at her bewildered look. Still, to reward her, he let his thumb wander over her nipple. And again. *And* again, until the pulse in Henrietta's throat quickened, and he was humming with the urge to kiss her. Then he stopped.

She blinked. He didn't move, didn't say anything. He was betting that Henrietta would be unable to resist commentary, given that devastating honesty of hers.

She had to steady her voice first, which pleased him immeasurably. "Is there something I should be doing?" she inquired. "I was under the impression that you would simply . . . ah . . . proceed."

"You need to help."

She frowned. Clearly she thought that having to provide aid in something so distasteful to herself was not quite fair. "What would you like me to do?" she said resignedly.

"Help me undress," he said, with just the right touch of pathos. She cast him a suspicious look, but she did climb out of bed. Given the way she thrashed about under the sheets for a moment, he'd guess that her stepmother had instructed her to pull her nightgown to her waist. He'd bet the woman had also told her that a husband would leap on her like a wild beast.

"You see, Henrietta," he said in a discursive tone, "men can't perform their marital duties without some participation."

She blinked. "Why not?" she asked, bending her lovely head over his cuff links. "I thought this sort of thing was—was—" She stopped and amended the statement. "Men always find pleasure in this activity." Being Henrietta, she didn't bother to hide the hint of scorn in her tone.

"Not every man," he said. "Why would I take pleasure in giving my new wife pain?" The look on her face encouraged him. "Do you think I wish to cause you embarrassment? Or discomfort?"

"No, of course not!" she said, clearly relieved. "I knew that Millicent must be wrong about your intentions, Darby." A huge glimmering smile spread across her face. "I tried to tell her that you weren't as—" she paused, uncertain of the word—"as debauched as she seemed to think."

"Won't you call me Simon?" he asked, ignoring the growling beast in his loins that suggested he fulfill her stepmother's directions. "I have asked you before."

She turned a bit pink. "I'm sorry. My stepmother addressed my father by his title until his death. Such informality seems unnatural."

"You can call me Darby in public, if you wish," he said.

"So what shall we do instead of *that*?" Henrietta asked. She had clearly jumped to the conclusion that he was too much of a gentleman to require marital intercourse. Her face was glowing with happiness.

Darby sternly warned himself not to laugh. "If you could help me remove my clothing," he said gravely, "I could prepare for bed. I won't ask you for this assistance every night, naturally. It is only because I dismissed my valet."

But Henrietta was obviously so pleased to be relieved of her marital duties that she would have emptied the chamber pot, if he asked. "I'm afraid that the current fashion demands that I wear very tight-fitting coats," he said.

She was at his side immediately, biting her beautiful little rosy lip with concentration. "My valet simply wrenches it off," he explained. He started slowly—so slowly—to peel off one arm. Her eager little hands were instantly on his sleeves, helping him slide the broadcloth down his arms. He pretended to be outrageously inept, brushing against her breasts as he struggled to free himself from the jacket.

"Ow!" he cried, once she was folding his jacket.

"What happened?"

"I must have been injured by a button," he moaned. "We'll have to remove my shirt in order to have a look. If you could . . ." He let his fingers slip apathetically from his buttons. She had to stand very close to undo his shirt placket. He could smell just a faint trace of spicy rose perfume. It nearly did him in, but he managed to rein in his lust and stand quietly as she discovered that he didn't pad his coats because he didn't have to. She seemed to be unbuttoning slowly, her fingers brushing his chest, so he stared at the other wall as if he had gone into a trance.

As soon as she finished unbuttoning, he pulled the shirt over his head and tossed it to the side.

"Where does it hurt?" she asked, staring at his chest.

"I'm not sure. Perhaps if you touch me all over, I could tell you when it hurts."

She looked at him. "Why on earth would I be able to locate an injury on your chest that you could not? It must not be very painful."

He sighed, giving up the idea of her fingers brushing over his chest. Instead he directed her toward his trousers. Her eyes widened, but she obediently started tugging at his waist. Her slender fingers brushed his stomach, and he shivered. Pink mounted in her cheeks, but she seemed determined to continue. Likely she thought that if she didn't undress him, he might change his mind and demand marital satisfaction.

Darby almost groaned as she struggled to free his trousers from an unexpected obstruction between his legs. He stared down at her bent head, wondering if she had any idea what that lump in his smalls represented. Since her blush had turned fiery red, he could only assume that she did. She managed to wrestle his trousers to the floor though, and rose, with an air of having done all that she could to satisfy her husband.

He watched her place his trousers over a chair. He could just see the long, slender line of her thigh through her thin nightgown.

"Henrietta," he said gently, "I sleep without clothing."

She narrowed her eyes. "That is a vastly improper habit."

Darby had to admit that if he had a grain of conscience in his body he might almost—almost—feel sorry for her. He shrugged.

She chewed her lip a bit more, and then yanked his smalls down so fast that he winced and lurched forward. "Damnation!" he said, grabbing the family jewels. "Watch yourself there."

His sweet little wife was clearly working herself into a temper, fired (Darby hoped) by lust. "Those who are incapable of undressing themselves must expect inconveniences," she snapped.

He laughed at that, couldn't help himself. Then he unwrapped his fist, slowly, so she wouldn't miss anything. Her eyes widened.

"How was I to know that you—that part of you would be sticking out in such a fashion?" she asked.

"It's the same as this part of you," he said. His hand seemed to curve naturally around her breast, his thumb leaping to rub her nipple again. And it was already swollen, waiting for him. For a moment there wasn't a sound in the room except for the gentle swish of his thumb across her nipple.

"You're seducing me, aren't you?" Henrietta sounded surprised. But any idiot could see that she couldn't take her eyes off him. Part of him, that is. The good part.

"Absolutely," he agreed, giving her breast a bit of a squeeze. It was so luscious that if he didn't have it in his mouth soon, there was no saying what would happen.

She shivered all over, and he gathered her into his arms.

She fit as if they were made for each other, all the delicate, smooth parts of her, and the hard maleness of him. He bent his head and licked her ear, its delicate little whorls and beautiful curves, and she trembled.

"You *are* going to do that, aren't you?" she said, surprising him as always with her directness.

"What if you like it?" His breath was hot against her ear. He let his lips slide down her slender neck. His fingers danced over her breasts, visiting and revisiting the heavy curve next to her arms.

"Impossible," she said in a strained sort of way.

"I promise not to do anything that you don't explicitly request," he promised.

"Why would any woman request that? I simply don't understand the point of it, except from the point of view of having children, naturally."

He had discovered a tender curve under her jaw. "Pleasure," he said rather thickly. "Women can find pleasure in it, Henrietta."

There was silence for a moment as he kissed his way to the corner of her mouth, little kisses, as light as tiny feathers. Oh, she knew of pleasure, his Henrietta. She simply didn't realize that she knew. Because when his lips came to hers, teasingly light, she opened the sweetness of her mouth to him without hesitation, proving that she'd been waiting for his kiss.

She sighed into his mouth, and her tongue met his. He plunged in, taking possession, turning a groan into a dark possession. And she was with him. She didn't pull back when he pulled her slender body against him and ran a demanding hand down her back, molding every curve to his hardness. Then he made a demanding undulation against her body, one that spoke of his intention and made clear his dominion.

"Would you mind if we went to bed now, Henrietta?" The question came out half-strangled.

"Well, no, I wouldn't mind," she said in a considering sort of way that told him that she wasn't yet completely comfortable. In fact, she was still thinking too much. It's hard to grin when you're gathering a bundle of fragrant womanhood in your arms, but he managed it.

He put her down on the bed. The first thing that had to go was her braid. Setting free her hair took time though, since her braid went almost to her waist. Darby could see that she was thinking, so he helped her out by standing between her legs so that she had plenty of contact with him.

"You won't do anything I don't request?" she said, finally.

He raised his head from her braid. He pressed a kiss onto each eyelid. "I promise," he said huskily. "If you don't ask me, I won't do it."

"I will *never* ask you to—to—" she stopped, clearly uncertain how to convey the idea of intercourse.

"I understand. But just in case you do ask, have you brought the sheath that Esme gave you?"

She turned even pinker. "I needn't because it's my first time," she whispered.

"Are you quite certain?"

She nodded. "Esme said no woman becomes pregnant during her first night. And I might not—apparently there's some obstruction there." Her words trailed off, clearly mortified by the topic of conversation.

Darby thought quickly. Presumably the sheath wouldn't fit due to her virginity. But they probably should have a frank talk before things became too heated for discussion.

He waited until he had finished undoing her braid, and then let his fingers run through the rough silk of her hair once or twice, just for pleasure. God, but she was beautiful. In the candlelight, her hair looked like gleaming gold, as soft and slippery as butter.

Then he rose and grabbed a small bottle from his bag. He held it up. Henrietta took the blue glass bottle and looked at him inquiringly. "This is an herb called pennyrub. Apparently it is a remedy for childbearing," he told her.

"What on earth do you mean?"

"Should you become pregnant, even using Esme's sheath, all you have to do is drink this medicine, and no pregnancy would result. It's security, Henrietta."

A flicker of a frown crossed her face. "I could never do such a thing."

"We needn't think about it," he said soothingly.

"It's not easy to become pregnant if we don't do that—*thing*, Darby."

Now that he could believe.

He took the bottle and stuck it on the bedside table. "I simply didn't want you to be fearful of intimacy due to pregnancy, Henrietta."

"Oh, I'm not. I'm not fearful." She paused. "I'm simply disinclined. I do not like untidiness, Darby."

She used that term before, with reference to her hip, he thought dimly. He gently pushed her to her back, lifted her voluminous nightgown and without further ado, slipped his head under it. Instantly her fingers descended on his shoulders to shove him away, but his lips found her breast before she could get leverage. Delectable it was. She had perfect breasts, gloriously weighty, rounded with that unsteady softness that made a man's loins explode.

He could hear her protesting, but it was too late. The marauder had entered the village. He was in the dim tent of her nightgown, feasting on her body. He moved from one breast to the other and back again. Her nipples were swollen dark rose. His hands shaped and danced on her skin, and in a few moments she had stopped pushing him away and began twisting up to offer him her breast. There were no more protests, only whimpers flying into the candlelight.

He smiled. Screw Aphrodite's seven pleasures—or fourteen of them, for that matter. There was nowhere he'd rather be than hidden under a cumbersome nightgown, listening to his own little Henrietta discover that her body was not untidy, but pleasurable.

Darby's presence under her nightgown was one of the most bewildering experiences of Henrietta's life. When he first ducked under her gown, she felt a quick ripple of terror and violation. Millicent had said her husband would effect his messy work under the covers, but had never mentioned a thing about him gazing at one's body or—or putting his mouth to it! Surely this was some new London perversion, known only to rakes.

But when his mouth descended on her breast, she lost her logical faculties. His rough suckling made her feel whimpery, and soft, and unable to move. And the longer he stayed there, the more weak she became, until her legs and middle section were liquid, and she could hardly breathe. She was quivering in the most embarrassing way.

The result was that when he ducked out from her gown and began to pull it up, inch by inch, running a strong hand up her legs, she didn't even protest. She let him expose her legs to the air because she was too busy trying to grapple with the rising fire in her belly, with the shameful impulses that crowded on her. Far from wanting to recite laundry lists, she wanted to—to touch him. Worse, to put her mouth to him, to lick his golden skin.

It took all her fortitude not to descend in the very depths of depravity. To hold her hands at her sides although she positively longed to—

"They look exactly the same, don't they?" he said.

Henrietta raised her head and discovered that her nightgown was gone, over her head and tossed away. Her husband was on his knees over her, muscled brown legs straddling her white legs. He was caressing her right hip with his fingers, soothing it as if to make any pain go away.

She couldn't seem to think clearly. His fingers were brushing her skin over and over, which was a simple enough action except that it created a gaping sense of openness between her legs. A melting, languid inability to move. So she just lay and let him . . . well, do the things he did. Touch her shoulder, and then press kisses into her ribs, and trail his tongue over her belly. Run a hand inquiringly up her leg and even in her dazed state she knew exactly what he was asking, because she'd been longing to do it.

She let her legs fall open to his hand, and barely registered his murmured, "Good girl," because he was touching her—*there*—and it felt so good that she found herself arching toward his hand, panting and moaning out loud, deep in her throat.

But he left . . . he left. He seemed to be fascinated by her hair. He was using it to caress her breasts, dragging a few locks across her nipples until she shivered all over and cried out for a firmer touch. He left her breast with one last rough stroke.

"You *can't*—" she managed, shocked, but he already had. The sensation was rough, and soft, and unbearably exciting between her legs, especially when he suddenly bent his head and he was licking her and then rubbing—

She had her knees up now, where he'd pushed them, and she didn't even think about whether her hip hurt (it didn't), just stayed exactly where he bid her.

"Simon," she moaned, not even realizing it was the first time she used his first name. "Simon, please, please . . ." There was an aching emptiness between her legs, and his kisses were stoking that fire, not curing it. In fact the hunger was so great she opened her eyes and wound her arms around his neck. He was braced on his hands, leaning over her, and she was just able to notice that he didn't look composed— not at all. His hair was standing straight off his head, and his eyes looked wild.

"My wife," he said hoarsely. She didn't listen because she was too busy rubbing against him, again and again, like a cat, trying to cure some itch she never knew she had.

"Henrietta, ask me," he said, and the ache in his voice sank through to her.

She took her hands off his chest, and said, "Yes?" It didn't even sound like her own voice.

"Ask me, Henrietta!" His eyes were black, and he drove forward just slightly. She clutched his arms and arched forward, following the sensation.

"Please," she said hopelessly, "Oh God, please."

"Please what?"

Henrietta Maclellan had considerable courage. She faced the world with her injured hip every day of her life. She had faced down scornful ladies and once, a drunken man in the village. But nothing compared to the moment when she removed her hands from their fierce grip around her husband's neck and reached down between his legs. "Bring me *this*, Simon," she said, and her voice broke with longing. He throbbed, hot and smooth in her small hand. She kissed his chin and the edge of his shoulder and arched up against him. "Bring me yourself."

Her hand slipped away and Darby lowered his head for one last agonizingly sweet kiss. Then, when she was quivering all over, he entered with one long, smooth stroke, praying for control. But she was a virgin, all right. He hit a barrier and stopped.

He bent down and kissed that sweet mouth, all swollen from his kisses. "This part is going to hurt," he whispered.

She whimpered in response, but it wasn't from pain. She was clutching his forearms so hard that he'd likely have bruises.

"How does it feel, Henrietta?" he whispered. He'd never cared much how any of his other partners felt, as long as they seemed appropriately gratified, but he couldn't stop watching Henrietta's face: the way she looked at him with sheer longing. When it came to his wife, he wanted to know everything about her.

She opened her eyes and what he saw there drenched him with lust. He drove forward without waiting for an answer, caught her cry with his mouth, answered it with a groan of his own.

There was a momentary pause in their conversation, if you could call it that, while Darby tried to adjust to the sweetest, tightest experience of his entire life.

"Oh God, Henrietta, you feel so good," he said thickly.

"You don't." He almost laughed at her honesty. "But—" she wiggled a little, and the breath caught in the back of his throat—"perhaps . . ."

He withdrew and slid smoothly back to her core.

"Do you like that?" he whispered, placing feather-light kisses on the edge of her mouth.

He was teaching her something. Henrietta knew it dimly. All she could do was try to chase the feeling that raced through her body when he moved. It was nothing that she would have described as pleasure. It was too fiery for that, too all-encompassing, too much. It made her feel anguished with longing.

"Do it again," she cried. She had been holding on to his forearms, but it didn't feel enough—none of it felt enough. She let her hands run down his back, over lovely muscles and then—what was a pair of buttocks compared to what she had already touched? They were muscled and tight and she clutched them and said something fierce, something to make her husband move in, closer to her, all the way.

He shuddered the moment she touched him. Dimly Henrietta realized that she could make him groan, make him burn as she was.

So she pulled him closer, and arched up until she could

feel every inch of him, until that empty, craving space inside her was filled with him, and her arms were filled with him, and her heart—

Well, that too.

~ 37 ~

In Which Lady Rawlings Remembers That Propriety, Decency, and Honor Rule English Society

He was sitting by the fire, sharpening a set of garden implements. He sprang up when she entered. "Esme."

"Did you know that my friend Henrietta married Simon Darby?" she said without preamble, sitting down on the rough-hewn bench across from him.

He picked up the tool again, his eyes guarded. "There was talk of the wedding in the village."

"Have you heard the marriage service lately, Sebastian? It's so beautiful." She caught her voice before it shook. "I don't think I listened when I married Miles. There was a part—I don't have it just right, but the vicar said that marriage was a remedy against sin, and to avoid, to avoid fornication."

"You are no longer married, Esme."

"I never honored him in marriage," she said, and a tear escaped down her cheek. "It's the least I can do to behave with propriety after his death."

Sebastian put the tool aside. He knelt beside the bench with utter unself-consciousness. "Marry me, Esme. *Please*. Honor me. I will honor you as your husband never did. Our marriage would be a remedy against sin, if anyone could ever call it a sin to love you."

She just shook her head, her throat thick with tears. "I can't. I dreamed of Miles last night," she said, trying to explain. "In my dream, he was so happy about the baby. And he was alive and well."

"I can't say that I wish he were alive, but I am sorry that his memory causes you grief."

"It's not his memory, or not entirely. I hate myself for what we are doing *to* his memory. I am still in mourning. In mourning! And yet here we are . . . I hate myself!"

"Why hate yourself?"

"I am betraying Miles, my husband."

"I don't agree," he said, and all the stiffness was in his tone that used to accompany pronouncements by the Marquess Bonnington. "Lord Rawlings is dead. You have no husband. You are widowed, and I am unmarried. While our interaction was unconventional, I do not see how it could be construed as betraying a dead man."

"He is still alive in my heart," Esme said slowly. "I can't stop thinking about him. And the baby. I keep thinking about the baby too."

"I am grievously sorry about your husband's death. But we did not kill him, Esme. He had a weak heart. He could have died at any time. You yourself told me that he had had two attacks that week alone, and that the doctor had given him until the end of the summer."

"That's not it, Sebastian. I cannot do this. I cannot *be* this kind of person."

He opened his mouth, but she forestalled him.

"Last summer, at Lady Troubridge's house party, you walked into my bedchamber as if I were a courtesan, available for all callers." She didn't say it with anger, simply as a fact. "You came because I acted like a whore."

"No!"

But she stopped him again. "Like a whore," she repeated calmly. "Falling into your arms in the drawing room. It's no wonder that you thought to enter my bedchamber without warning and that you expected I would greet you with open arms. I made myself into a convenient woman." Wonder of wonders, she wasn't even crying. Her pain was too deep for tears.

"Please leave, Sebastian. Go back to Italy. I bewhored myself for you twice now; please don't make me do it again."

"Don't *ever* say that about yourself," he said. His eyes had the fierce rage of an eagle.

"I only say the truth," she said. "That will be the world's assessment if they find out what truly happened between us. Your presence here, on my estate, threatens to make that truth known to all. And that name—whore—will ruin this child's future."

His eyes were blue-black, burning into hers, but she could see that he was listening to her.

"When Miles and I agree to reconcile, that was the one thing he asked. He said that we had to live together, and we had to be discreet. Because it was important for the child's sake. I keep dreaming that he's there and that he's asking me—begging me, really—to be a good mother."

She looked down at Sebastian, kneeling by her side. Miles wasn't the only one in her heart.

"Do it for Miles, if not for me," Esme said, and there was a catch in her voice. "You owe his child that much."

He put his head down on her arm, the first time that Esme had ever seen him show despair.

She put her hand on his head, and a gold tendril curled around her finger as if to keep her there. She walked out the door without looking back.

38

Food Fights Are Not Limited to the Young

The snowstorm lasted three days. Anabel's stomach rejected several meals. Josie had a tantrum in which she began a fierce and familiar refrain—"I'm a poor, motherless child"— but then broke off because she realized that Henrietta was telling Anabel a story and she might miss it. It was her favorite tale, about the angry little lampshade who traveled all the way to Paris. Henrietta pretended not to notice what almost happened, and simply welcomed Josie on her lap.

In fact, Josie was almost startlingly good. The low point was when she threw a spoonful of mashed potatoes at her sister, but then she wasn't the only one playing with her food during the three days they spent in the Bear and Owl.

For example, the second evening, Henrietta and Darby ate supper in their private chamber. Without a moment's warning, he coolly tipped a spoon of trifle down the low neck of her gown.

Henrietta just sat for a moment, mouth open, staring at him while the icy trifle slithered between her breasts and caught on the top of her corset.

He got up just as elegant and sophisticated as he always

was. "Have you suffered an accident, my dear? Here, do let me help." And he started nimbly undoing the fastenings to her gown while she wondered whether she had misunderstood. Perhaps the trifle flew out of his spoon—but no.

It wasn't until he had her standing and was briskly unlacing her corset that she caught a good glimpse of his face. His silky brown gold hair was falling out of its tie at his neck. He was wicked—wicked! His hands teased as they untied, tracing the sticky chill of the trifle.

"What a pity," he said, "I believe you'll have to travel without your corset."

She narrowed her eyes at him. "I have others, sir."

"But this monstrosity"—he held it up in the air—"is what has been making you resemble a marionette, and has been making your gowns hang on you as if these luscious pieces of you didn't exist." His fingers left trails of fire across her breasts.

"You cannot make me into a person like yourself," she said.

"What sort of person?" he asked silkily.

"Elegant," Henrietta said bluntly. "Dresses will never look their best on me. I limp and I am short besides."

He laughed and there was genuine amusement in his voice. "Clothes exist so that a man can see through them and imagine an unclothed woman. Height has nothing to do with it, and neither does your weak hip."

"Darby, clothes exist to decently cover the body," she observed.

"You called me Simon last night," was all he said, pulling off her chemise.

She blushed, even thinking of the previous evening. "I was not myself."

He smiled at her, a sinful mischief in his face. "One says many things in the heat of passion that should not be aired in the morning."

He had found the very beginning of the sticky trail of

sweetness, at her collarbone, and he was licking it. Down and down he went, and his wife said not a word even when he was on his knees before her, still lapping the trail of the trifle. Lower—lower than where the errant piece of cake traveled. When her knees folded and she said, "Simon! We're not in a bedchamber!" he merely rose, threw the bolt on the door, and then returned.

But she had taken advantage of his absence to pull a plate from the table. He turned around and found her standing there, laughing, all her glorious hair tumbling over her shoulders, her gown, corset and chemise in a heap on the floor. She was naked but for pale blue slippers and delicate stockings tied in tidy bows at her knees. Naked, she was the most elegant woman he ever saw. She was holding a plate of trifle in her hand, but he hardly noticed that.

"You take my breath," he said slowly. "I cannot believe that you were still there for me to find. Even the dullards of Limpley Stoke must have seen how exquisite you are."

She grinned at that—who wouldn't? She put her plate down for a moment and undid his neck cloth and put it neatly to the side. Then she pulled out his shirt at the neck and plopped a spoonful of trifle down his neck before he had time to think.

It was a terrible shock to find that his retaliation was ruthless: cold fingers, holding a bit of sugary cold sweetness, cupped over the warmest place in her body.

And that induced a dizzy, light-headed feeling . . . enough to make one lie on the floor.

It wasn't until they traveled back to London and started to settle into Darby's town house, that she realized what marriage was really like. It was about peeling back all the layers of clothing that covered one, and she didn't mean only those made of cloth either. All her privacies were breached. She was truly naked to Darby.

Her husband liked to stride around the matrimonial bed-chamber unclothed—who would have guessed? He, who was generally properly dressed in silk and lace, felt most happy without a stitch on his body. But he didn't merely wish to be undressed. He wished *her* to join him in that naked state. And the whole business of the sheath stripped off another layer of privacy.

They discussed it, for one thing. She never would have imagined such a thing. When they first arrived in London, Henrietta would retreat upstairs after dinner, discreetly soak her sheath in vinegar and insert it. She didn't like it. But she didn't hate it either. In a way, she was fond of the sheath since it gave her the chance to engage in such wonderful intimacies with Darby.

But then one night he delayed her at dinner and she ended up on his lap. She was wearing an evening dress and no corset, as her husband had taken to sabotaging undergarments of which he did not approve. It was a bit odd for Henrietta to find that she was wax in the hands of her husband. He only had to look at her with those laughing brown eyes of his and she—she, who was running a household *and* a school by the time she was seventeen years old—would give in to whatever outrageous demand he levied.

At any rate, he was whispering wicked suggestions about drawing up her gown and sitting on his lap, and she was almost befuddled enough by his hands to do it, when she suddenly remembered and pushed his hand away.

"No, Simon! My sheath!"

He swept her up in his arms and carried her upstairs. Then he laid her on the bed and said, "Let me do it tonight."

She blinked at him, truly shocked. "Absolutely not!"

"Why not?" he coaxed. His fingers were everywhere, her gown at her waist. "I'm quite certain that I can place it correctly."

Given where his fingers were, he probably could. She gave a little involuntary moan. "No," she breathed. "It's private."

"Your body is my body," he said, leaning over her. His lashes were so long they cast shadows on his cheek. "We're married, Henrietta, remember? Weren't you listening to the marriage service? I have to admit that I found it rather riveting, especially the bit where the vicar talked about men loving their wives as their own bodies."

She stared up at him, dumbstuck.

Darby had a little smile, wry and expectant at once. *"He that loveth his wife loveth himself: for no man ever yet hated his own flesh, but nourisheth and cherisheth it."*

He didn't wait for a reply. He stood up and went over to the little table where her new lady's maid had left a little glass of vinegar, and her sheath.

"I don't think this is what is meant by the marriage vows!" she managed. "Is there to be no privacy?"

"None!" He was back at her side. One of his hands was on her breast, making it difficult to speak. And his other hand . . . well, he did know her anatomy as well as he boasted.

Later they lay together in a heap of tangled limbs. He traced a figure on her creamy flank. "Does your hip hurt when we make love?"

She shook her head.

"What makes it hurt? You were in pain this afternoon, weren't you?"

"Only a trifle," she said, surprised. She was certain that she had concealed it. "I was tired."

"You should have told me. Madame Humphries is so overjoyed to be dressing you that she would have kept you standing all afternoon."

Henrietta smiled. She still didn't care two pins for clothing, but it was rather astounding to discover how differently she looked in clothing not designed and sewn by Mrs. Pinnock.

"I find it interesting that your lame hip looks precisely the same as the other," Darby said. "I don't understand why doctors believe that you would be unable to bear a child, Henrietta. There's no difference between this hip"—he caressed it again—"and that of other women."

Henrietta frowned. She didn't like to think about other women's hips in relation to *her* husband.

He knew, of course. "Not that I plan to compare your luscious hip to anyone else's," he said into her ear. "Why don't we visit a London doctor, Henrietta? There's a famous physician on St. James's Street who is also an *accoucheur*. Ortolon, I believe his name is."

"Whether you can see the problem or not, it exists. Truly, it was a miracle that I survived," she said earnestly. "And my mother was not so lucky."

"Were people cruel when you were growing up?"

"Not cruel," she said slowly. "It was more that the reality of it was cruel. Because I grew up in a very small village, there was nothing unexpected about anyone's future. Billy Lent was the bad boy in the grammar school, and everyone said he was bound for the Assizes. Sure enough, he was sent there before he reached eighteen. I was lame, and everyone said I would never marry."

She looked at him with a glimmering smile. "I would have seen it as a crueler fate if I had imagined someone like you walking down the High Street of Limpley Stoke." Warm brown hair tumbled past his perfectly shaped ear. The drape of linen sheet over his hip turned him into a Roman senator.

"Did you never dream of marriage, then? You must have!"

"Of course I did. But I thought I would find an older man, someday, perhaps a widower with children. Someone who would wish for a companion, not—"

He raised his mouth from her breast. "Not a bedmate."

"I didn't quite understand that," Henrietta said.

"That's right. You hadn't put together marital pleasure and babies, did you?"

She shook her head, and then added, teasingly, "And I still can't countenance why it's so important to gentlemen!"

"Probably wouldn't have been important to the kind of doddering old stick you thought of marrying."

"I didn't imagine doddering. But what other choice did I have?"

"I was just lucky enough to be the first gentleman to walk into that village, Henrietta. There's not a man among my friends who wouldn't have leaped at you, hip or no hip."

"Rees wouldn't have," she pointed out.

"Ah, but he would. As a matter of fact, he's having a difficult time accepting the fact that he finds you amusing, and intelligent, and beautiful," Darby said, his lips leaving scorching little trails on her skin. "Thrown his world into a spin, you have."

"He isn't!" Henrietta gasped.

"Poor sod. He's too late. You're mine." He pulled her closer, under his body.

She clutched his forearms. "But what about children? Wouldn't all those London gentlemen have wanted children?"

"Not unless they were firstborn," Darby said, his mind obviously elsewhere. "I don't have an entailed estate trailing behind me like the wag on a dog. There's a fair number of us out there just like myself, you know. Now, if you'll excuse me, love—"

But she managed to gasp, even as he eased between her legs and that familiar melting ache spread down her body, "I still think they would have wanted children."

The muscles in his shoulders bulged. Henrietta flicked one with her tongue.

"They wouldn't give a damn," Darby said. "They wouldn't give a damn if they could just be here with you." He looked down at her so fiercely that she knew he spoke the truth—

as he saw it, anyway. "But they can't," he said against her mouth. "No one will ever have you but me. You're mine, Henrietta."

There was nothing to do but smile.

39

Knowing One's Enemy

"That's not the proper way to advance your troops," Josie said uncompromisingly, reaching out her hand and stopping Henrietta's contingent of tin soldiers. One fell on his face, and she carefully set him back in formation. "If you bring them around the turn of the hill there, you'll be seen by my sentry. You mustn't be seen. That's a rule."

Henrietta blinked. She didn't remember games with her sister being quite so fraught with rules. "You should let me play my part, even if I do make a mistake," she pointed out. "You'll win all the faster." Josie's troops always won, since Henrietta spent most of her time trying to figure out how quickly she could sacrifice her own men and escape the battle.

"It wouldn't be any fun that way. If you bring your men around to the west, they can try to attack from the rear of the castle."

Henrietta sighed and started moving her troops all the way around the little crimson hassock to the "west" for a rear attack. It was tedious enough to make her look hopefully toward Anabel's crib. Surely her afternoon nap was almost over.

The tin soldiers were looking rather more worn than they

had a few months ago, when Josie found them in Esme's nursery. The red soldiers could only be identified by a faint rosy tint that hung around their belts; all the rest of their paint had worn away. The blue soldiers were doing better, as Josie didn't like them nearly as much. Some of them even had faint uniforms left. They weren't given daily baths, after all, and they didn't have to sleep with their commander, the way the red soldiers did. Henrietta had grown accustomed to feeling around Josie's sleeping little body at night for hard metal lumps of male soldiery. As far as Henrietta knew, Josie never inquired how her troops managed the nightly climb from bed to bedside table.

"If you make a rear attack," Josie said now, busily lining up her men on the battlements of the castle (alias the red hassock), "I am likely to pour boiling oil on you." She looked up earnestly. "That's not to discourage you, but I thought perhaps you should be warned."

"What a bloodthirsty idea!" Henrietta said. "Where on earth did you learn about that revolting custom?"

"My brother Simon told me. He never makes a rear attack for that very reason. But then, he's knows a great deal about everything." Josie cast Henrietta a pitying look.

"Hmmm," Henrietta said. "And just when did brother Simon teach you about the fascinating practice of boiling one's enemies?"

"This very morning," said a deep voice, just over her head.

Henrietta looked up with a start. "I wouldn't have thought you knew anything about battle strategies," she said, resisting a wayward impulse to throw herself into her husband's arms and kiss him senseless.

"There are many things you don't know about me," Darby said, crouching down next to his stepsister. "Why have you placed these men in a double rank, Josie? If a flaming arrow comes over the battlements *here*, you'll lose all the men at one blow."

Josie stared for a moment. "I'll put them behind a pillar," she said, pointing to empty space.

"Good idea," Darby said, and Josie began carefully moving her soldiers.

"Couldn't you construct these poor men some clothing?" Henrietta said idly to her husband. She held up a blue soldier. "The poor man is quite naked."

"Fancy him in a nice lace shift, do you?" Darby said. "He's a man of battle, for God's sake, woman. Besides, I don't fashion clothing."

"Better lace than nothing," Henrietta pointed out.

"I've had a note from Rees asking me if we'd like to attend the opening of his new opera. That's a compliment for you. He's never once asked me to attend an opening night."

"How marvelous! When is it?"

"Tonight," he said with a grin. "I have the feeling we're an afterthought."

Henrietta's face fell. "Tonight? I'm not certain that I can attend."

Darby raised an eyebrow. "Surely Madame Humphries delivered at least one evening gown amongst all those garments?"

"Henrietta's leg hurts today," Josie put in matter-of-factly. "She couldn't come on our walk. The oil is boiling now."

Which was an unsubtle call to come-and-be-boiled. Henrietta obediently began moving her soldiers into range of flaming liquids from above.

A large hand helped the last of her sacrificial lambs into place. "I'm sorry that you're in pain," Darby said, under cover of Josie's war shrieks. Boiling oil was being delivered with howls of outrage.

"It's quite all right," Henrietta said, helping Josie knock over the last few of her men. "Josie, don't shriek too loudly. We don't want to wake Anabel from her nap."

Henrietta got to her feet with some help from Darby.

"Shall I ask Fanning to move dinner forward so that you can be there on time?"

"Do you think that I would go without you?" There was a curious testing in his voice.

She gave him a frown. "You must. An opening night is a very important occasion for Rees, especially if it is the very first to which you were invited."

"Do you believe that I wish to go anywhere without my wife?" He began kissing her fingertips.

"That is not the point," Henrietta said, trying to inject severity into her voice. "You must attend Rees's opening night, because otherwise I would feel even more invalidish than I already am."

It was Darby's turn to frown.

"You must," she said firmly. "I shall wait up until you return home to hear whether the opera is a success."

He leaned closer. "Not to worry if you fall asleep. I quite like to wake a sleeping woman." The smile in his eyes! Henrietta turned away quickly lest Josie see.

A few hours later Henrietta joined her husband in the drawing room. His only greeting was a profanity.

Henrietta looked down at herself with a tinge of anxiety. It was a formidable project to live up to her husband's magnificence, but in the safety of her chamber, she had quite thought that she had. "Don't you like the gown?" she asked.

His eyes moved from her head to her slippers. "I gather that is the fete dress we ordered from Madame Humphries?"

"Yes," she said. And then, because she saw something in his eyes that gave her courage, she turned in a circle. Her gown was quite short, over a white satin petticoat, and it showed her ankles beautifully when it moved. But unquestionably the best part of the gown was its bodice of pale blossom-colored crape. It laced tightly up the front, and was extremely low both before and behind.

"Damn," he said again.

"When I met you, I had no idea that your speech was so expressive." She readjusted her white kid gloves so they clung just so to her elbow. "What do you think of my veil? Madame Humphries assures me that it is made from your lace." Madame Humphries had used Darby's lace in each and every gown she designed for Henrietta. This particular gown had no lace trim, so she created a little veil that fell from the back of the head and was carried over the arm as drapery.

He walked toward her and there was something panther-like in his stride.

"Very nice. I like the pearl beads."

"It's quite unusual to find them in this leaf pattern, or so Madame Humphries said."

"I see the pattern is repeated on the sleeves."

"If you can call them sleeves," Henrietta said. "They're much smaller than anything I've worn before."

"The bodice is much tighter than any garment I've had the pleasure of seeing you wear."

Henrietta choked back a smile. "That's the lacing," she pointed out. "You see that the bodice laces in front."

He ran a finger over the lacing between her breasts. "I do see that."

"You seem to like the gown," Henrietta said, as his fingers lingered in that lacing. "So why the profanity when I entered?"

His head had been bent; suddenly he raised it and looked straight into her eyes. "This is not a gown that makes one wish to leave one's wife at home," he told her.

Her leg was throbbing with the exertion of standing up, and Darby seemed to know, because he scooped her up and carried her over to a chair by the window.

"I'm sorry," she said. There was no way to signify precisely how sorry she was to be so lame that she couldn't attend the opening of Rees's new comic opera. Or to tell her husband the jealous desperation in her heart when she thought of an opera house full of beautiful women. That jealousy had spurred her to wear a fete dress to a simple dinner with her spouse.

He sat down and she folded into his lap as if they were designed to be together. "I've been thinking about it, Henrietta, and I do believe that your hip dislikes it when I put your legs on my shoulders."

"You mustn't say such things aloud," she said, rather feebly. She was becoming accustomed to his blithe disregard for convention.

He shrugged. "This is our drawing room, my dear, and there isn't a footman in sight." His eyes had that wicked glint again. "There are many other positions just as delectable that we could try. Looking at you in that lacing, I'm just as glad that you're not accompanying me to the opera. I can't have every man in London dreaming of unlacing your gown."

"But I will never be as beautiful as you," she blurted out. Red surged into her cheeks. Would she never learn to keep her tongue silent?

"Why on earth would you say that?" His fingers stilled on her chest, and he looked at her with curiosity.

It irritated her. "You never seem to remember that I'm lame. Deformed. You are perfect. There's not the slightest thing wrong with your body."

"I see no disfigurement in yours either."

She swallowed. "Don't you understand, Darby? It's not just my hip. If a woman can't give birth, she's—she's nothing. Bartholomew Batt says that children are a woman's greatest accomplishment."

"I am beginning to dislike Bartholomew."

"Well, I agree with him. To be a mother is—is—" She couldn't even put into words what it meant.

"When my father lost the estate I grew up on," Darby said, dropping a kiss on her ear, "I couldn't imagine what I would do with myself. After all, I was only trained to run a large estate. That particular estate, to my mind: the one my great-grandfather established. And it was gone."

"Lost? How did your father lose it?"

"Gambling." Darby's lips dropped away from her skin, leaving an unwelcome coolness. "Gambling. He lost our house and land on the turn of a pair of dice. I still have them. He brought the pair home, swearing that he'd kill himself. He didn't do that, but he did wake me up, give me the dice, and tell me that they were all I'd ever inherit from him."

"How old were you?"

"Fourteen."

"Oh, Simon, that's awful." Henrietta twisted around and kissed him. She had taken to calling him Simon in intimate moments, although she still couldn't bring herself to do it in public.

"But now I have my own estate," he said. "It's not the one my grandfather lived on, but it is mine. And I am happy there. Are you happy in the nursery, Henrietta?"

She blinked at him.

"And how is that pestilent little child of yours today?" He dropped a kiss on her ear. "Did Anabel lose a meal on you, or just in your sight?"

She smiled wryly in acknowledgement of his point.

"Families are what we make them," Darby said. "I have two brothers, Henrietta, did you know that?"

She shook her head, fascinated. "I had no idea. Where are they now? And what are their names?"

"I didn't think you were the sort who had memorized *Debrett's Peerage*. Their names are Giles and Tobias. They are twins. But as to where they are . . . no one knows."

"What do you mean?" Henrietta asked. "Where could they be?"

"The world is a wide place." His fingers slipped over her shoulders and wandered down her back. "They left England when they were eighteen."

"But you must have some idea where they are!"

"None. My father put out inquiries every year, and I have continued the practice. My father was quite certain they had not been lost at sea. I am not so sanguine. It's one of the reasons that I decided not to have children. It has given me a sharp sense that no one knows what may happen on the morrow."

Henrietta slung an arm around his neck, and rubbed her cheek against his shoulder. "I'm so sorry. You must miss your brothers dreadfully. I do hope they weren't lost at sea."

"So do I," her husband said. "So do I."

They sat snugly together in the twilight while Henrietta thought about lost brothers and found children. And then she decided that a wife's role included cheering her husband in moments of despondency.

So she stood up, smiled down at Mr. Simon Darby, and began slowly, deliberately undoing the tight lacing that graced the front of Madame Humphries's fete dress.

In the end, Simon Darby missed his closest friend's debut as a composer of comic opera. The note he sent Rees the next day said that he'd come down with a sudden ailment that necessitated a few days confined to his chamber.

Rees read the note and snorted. One could only dream that Darby was covered with chicken pox. But he didn't hold out much hope that an invasion of small itchy spots was keeping Darby on his back.

~ 40 ~

Of Frost Fairies and Other Surprising Beings

Henrietta wasn't thinking in terms of routines. Cycles. Days of the month. But one morning she found herself lying sleepily in her bed, thinking about Millicent's marital advice and how sad it was, truly, that her stepmother had found the experience so unpleasant, and that Millicent thought of mess rather than of pleasure.

Thinking of messiness made her entire body rigid.

She'd had no flux. Feeling as if the breath were being squeezed from her body, she began to count backward. They had been married almost four weeks. That meant it had been over six weeks since she last had her monthly bleeding. She was late.

She lay back, arms and legs leaden, and tried to catch her breath. How could this have happened? She had followed Esme's instructions regarding the sheath faithfully. She kept counting and re-counting the days, as if that could make a difference. Her maid appeared with an offer of clothing. She waved her away. Why dress when you've received a death sentence?

It was one of the worst mornings of Henrietta's life. Darby

was meeting with his man of business. The children were up-stairs playing with a lively new nursemaid.

She had never felt more alone in her life. She spent the morning staring into the lace canopy over their bed. She didn't cry. She just tried to breathe.

Finally she rose and took off her night rail and looked at her body in the mirror. It looked precisely the same. No signs of a swelling in the belly. Her eyes stared back at her, ringed with dark circles. As far as she knew, her tummy might pop out at any moment. There were a few women in the village who seemed able to conceal a pregnancy for a matter of months, but the small ones like herself looked very large from the beginning.

She spread her hands over her tummy and thought danger-ous thoughts. Inside her, a little bud had started to grow. A baby. A child of her own. Perhaps a little girl with Darby's somber beauty. Her body shook with longing at the thought. If only . . .

But the moment her husband found out, he would inquire about that little bottle he gave her on their wedding night—the pennydub, or pennyroyal, whatever it was. And Darby would be right, she thought, trying to persuade herself. Everyone said it was a miracle that she herself survived. Would she give up her life, only to lose the baby's life in the process? What would be the good of that?

No good, beat her heart. No good. No good. No good.

Blood pounded through her body, telling her with every beat that she had no choice. She could hear it roaring in her ears. If Henrietta had been capable of it, she would have had a fit of the vapors. But instead her heart just keep beating, and her mind kept racing.

That night she requested privacy, pretending that she'd taken cold. Darby slept in another room. He asked what was wrong in such a sweet fashion that she almost told him—but telling him meant the end. She couldn't do it, not yet. Not take that bottle, and give up her little babe. Not yet.

An hour or so after he retired to the other room, she realized that when one's life might be counted in a matter of months, spending even one night alone was idiocy. She slid into bed beside him in an ecstasy of gratefulness for the familiarity of his roughened legs against hers, for the sleepy way he turned and drew her into his arms. For the way they lay together, she curled inside the circle of his arms as snug as a walnut in its shell.

She drifted into uneasy dreams. At first, she thought she was still in a dream. He was touching her gently and his strong hands rolled her to her back. Sleepily, she thought about protest, but there was something about her husband that made her allow him liberties. Her stepmother wouldn't approve. But then the realization of what he was doing sank in. Was there *no* privacy in married life?

"Simon Darby!" she snapped, sitting up in bed. "Just what do you think you're doing?"

He grinned at her. "I took care of that sheath, my dear. And now that we have that out of the way . . ." He picked her up and carried her over to the window overlooking the garden.

At that she really did protest. The room wasn't cold, due to a large fireplace with a still glowing fire, but it was winter and she was naked, thanks to someone removing her nightgown while she was sleeping.

But he ignored her, just brought her to the window seat, and said, "Look, Henrietta."

The back of the house had turned into a fairy landscape. The garden was usually a delicate stretch of trees and rosebushes. But now ice gleamed from every branch, even the tiniest twig. Moonlight skittered and danced from silver point to silver point. Even the window was decorated with hoary ferns and flowers of ice.

"Frost fairies have been here," Henrietta said, touching one with her finger. "Oh Simon, how beautiful."

"Mmmm," he said, kissing the delicate bone that topped her shoulder.

"It makes me want to cry," she whispered. The garden looked unearthly, like a wedding cake decorated for giants.

His warm body crowded behind her. She knew that hardness now and leaned back against him, welcomed it as a glutton does a feast.

"Crying seems to me an unnecessarily glum reaction to a chilly night," he said. His voice was shot through with desire, and his hands were on her breasts, so sure and knowing that her head fell back against his shoulder and a whimper escaped into the quiet night.

He rubbed his fingers against the icy window and then ran an icy trail around her nipple. She gasped and squirmed. It felt too good. He rubbed the window again and trailed ice down her tummy, down to her sleek folds, burning for him, bucking against his finger.

Where his fingers had melted the frost, the window turned black as pitch, reflecting only the long line of her flank back into the room. She knelt on the window seat, trying not to wake the whole house as his icy fingers slipped everywhere. He pressed his lips to the glass and then kissed her neck, laughing as she squirmed away.

Later, she heard no laughter, only the breath rasping in his chest, as hard warmth replaced chilly fingers. His strong body bowed behind hers. At some point she even bumped her cheek against the icy glass but it didn't matter because she was burning, her body consumed with the feeling of him, with the hundred points of liquid fire that flew throughout her body at his every stroke.

He carried her back to the warm nest of their bed, afterward. As she curled into his body, she felt him rise against her belly again. She reached down to touch him, to bring that strength and warmth to her.

He was kissing her, cupping her face in his hands, and kissing her eyes and her mouth and her cheeks.

"I love you," she gasped, in between his kisses. "I love you, Simon." His mouth took hers and stifled her voice, but her heart sang with the truth of it.

She dreamed that she had a child, a little boy. He had ringlets just like hers, and Anabel's high joyous laughter. She was having tea with the vicar, and ladies from the sewing circle kept wandering through the room carrying flowers for a funeral. Finally the vicar left and she went to retrieve her baby from the nursery, but the nanny hadn't seen him. And Henrietta couldn't remember leaving him there in the morning. She began running, searching through piles of old clothes, trying desperately to find him, but he was so small. She couldn't find him. Her heart thumped against her ribs. She was too frightened to weep, too breathless to scream.

She woke. Lack of air gripped her ribs.

She spent the morning staring at the lace canopy of her bed. When there was a little scratching noise at her door, she sat up wearily, expecting her new maid, Keyes, with a hot bath. But it wasn't Keyes. It was Josie.

"Hello," Josie whispered loudly, slipping into the room.

"Hello!" Henrietta said, smiling.

"Nurse Millie says you're ill. Are you going to lose your breakfast?" Josie said, hovering near the door.

Henrietta could understand Josie's reluctance to enter. In a mere month as Anabel's mother, she'd seen enough vomit for a lifetime.

"Not a chance of it," she said reassuringly, holding out her hand. "I just have a little cold. Come tell me what you two did yesterday."

Josie's smile warmed the corners of Henrietta's heart. "I came to visit you because Nurse is cleaning up after Anabel lost her breakfast milk." She clambered up on the bed.

Henrietta wound an arm around Josie's shoulders. "Do you think Anabel's stomach is getting stronger?"

"No," Josie said, after considering the issue for a moment.

"Well, she's bound to stop soon. I don't know any adults with her peculiar habits."

"I wouldn't be too sure," Josie said, with that solemn combination of adult behavior and a childish voice that always made Henrietta long to laugh.

Keyes scratched on the door and entered, followed by two footmen with hot water.

Josie pulled on Henrietta's sleeve. "May I stay? Please don't make me go back to the nursery."

"While I take a bath?"

Josie looked at her, lower lip thrusting forward. "I *am* a lady. Nurse Millie bathes Anabel and me together because we are both ladies."

But Henrietta had barely recovered from her husband's blithe invasion of her bath time. "I don't think that's a good idea, Josie," she said gently. "Very young ladies, like yourself and Anabel, may bathe together. But grown-up ladies bathe in private."

Henrietta ended up bathing Josie instead. There's something tantalizing about a steaming tub of hot water, after all, and once Keyes had swirled rose petal oil in the water, Josie started hopping on one foot and begging to get in.

She had a sturdy little body with just a hint of a toddler's tummy. Henrietta tried to wash her, but spent most of the time stemming floods of water as they sloshed over the sides of the tub. Josie talked the entire time, without pausing for breath. She showed Henrietta the scar on her knee from when she fell down the servants' steps in the back ("Nurse Peeves said it was my own fault because I wasn't supposed to go down those stairs"). She told her three times that she wanted a mama puppy for her birthday. Henrietta tried and failed to explain the dissonance between *mama* and *puppy*.

At some point, the nursemaid, Millie, appeared, having discovered the whereabouts of her missing charge. Henrietta sent her away with apologies. Josie stayed in the tub until the water was chilly and little bumps formed on her legs. She talked . . . and talked . . . and talked.

Even when Henrietta plucked Josie out of the bath and wrapped her in a piece of toweling, Josie still talked. She told Henrietta about the frog she had seen in the pond at the bottom of the garden last summer, and the ducks that were born there and decided to live in the stable. She told Henrietta all about the Christmas dinner during which her mother apparently threw a serving platter at the vicar. She told Henrietta that Anabel looked like a plucked chicken when she was born, and that her mother had sent the baby to the nursery, and said not to bring her back until she had more hair. Josie loved this story; Henrietta hated it.

It wasn't until Josie wound down, exhausted, that Henrietta knew exactly what she had to do. She would drink the blue bottle, because Josie and Anabel needed her. Because she loved them. She had responsibilities, and she couldn't let herself think about her own baby, she simply couldn't. There was nothing she could do for *that* baby.

Dying in labor wouldn't keep her child alive. It wouldn't, it wouldn't, it wouldn't. Perhaps if she said it a thousand more times, it would seem real.

"It's time to return to the nursery," she said to Josie, when she finished combing her hair.

Josie's lower lip trembled. "I don't want to."

"Anabel will be missing you."

"I don't care!"

By now, Henrietta knew all the warning signs. Sure enough, within thirty seconds Josie was crying so loudly she could probably be heard two streets over. And her refrain was remarkably consistent: "I'm a poor—" The sob that tore up from her chest stifled the *motherless* part, but Henrietta knew it was there.

Suddenly she bent over, picked up Josie and plumped her onto her bed. Enough was enough.

"Josephine Darby," she said, hands on her hips, "be quiet and listen to me." Josie never paid any attention to that sort of command and she didn't now. Her crying notched up a bit louder.

"I *am* your mother."

Josie kept wailing.

"*I am your mother!*" Henrietta shrieked.

Josie's eyes went as round as marbles, and she fell silent.

"Haven't you noticed, Josie?" Henrietta demanded. "You have a mother: *me*."

Josie blinked. And stared.

Henrietta knelt down in front of Josie and pushed her damp hair out of her face. "I love you, Josephine Darby. And I'm going to be your mother, whether you want me to or not."

Josie's pointed little face seemed to be frozen in shock. Henrietta took her hand and started walking toward the door. "I'm your mother, and Simon is going to be your father. You don't have to call me mama, but that's how I think of myself."

Josie still didn't say anything, and Henrietta made herself keep walking toward the nursery.

When they reached the third-floor hallway, Henrietta smelled toasting cheese and Josie suddenly twisted away and dashed into the nursery.

"Anabel!" she shrieked. "I've been downstairs and had a bath!" She ran around the nursery a few times just as if the whole conversation hadn't happened.

Henrietta stood in the doorway. What did she expect? That Josie would suddenly call her *mama* and all would be well? "I hope I didn't keep her too long, Millie," she said to the girls' nurse. "We had a lovely time."

"Not at all," Millie replied. "Miss Josephine is always trying to sneak out and find you. It stood to reason that she would succeed one day."

"Really?"

"Oh yes," the nurse said indulgently. "She runs circles around me, bothering me to death, she does. *I want to go see Mama! I want to go see Mama!* Oh my, don't we hear that often!" She managed to catch the tie on Josie's dress as she ran past. "Now you sit down, young lady, and show your mama that I'm teaching you proper manners."

The smile uncurling in Henrietta's heart was so large that there wasn't room for it in her body. "I must have my bath now, girls," she said. "Be good for Millie."

Josie looked up from where she was putting on a decent imitation of a proper young lady, seated on a stool before a small table. "Will you come kiss us good night?"

Henrietta grinned. "I always do."

"Story too?"

"Of course."

She went back to her room and rang for another bath. Soaping her arms and legs had a different feeling, now that Simon was her husband. *He* had kissed this elbow, and *he* adored her shoulders. She couldn't run a washcloth over her breasts without thinking about him.

Henrietta had always prided herself on her logical faculties. She could see to the bottom of a problem. But what was the bottom of this problem? There was something defective with the sheath, that was clear. Would she and Darby never make love again? Should she take the bottle without telling him? That seemed dishonest, not to mention useless. If the sheath didn't work, she would simply face the same problem again next month. And she could not do that without going mad.

Or Darby could take a mistress. They would return to the plan to which they originally agreed, in which she would act as a glorified nursemaid and he would take a mistress. Or mistresses. Even the thought of Darby with another woman made her stomach churn.

Yet a life of celibacy was not for Darby. He wasn't a man to live without a woman. He would grow to hate me, she thought. A pang of anguish struck her heart.

He had to take a mistress. He must. Because if he had a mistress, at least she would be able to see him, to live in the same house with him. And those crumbs would be enough—would keep her alive. If he hated her . . .

I'd rather die, Henrietta thought, and the thought made all the air disappear from the room.

It was just as well that she had discovered the sheath's defective qualities now, since she was about to be introduced to the *ton*. The season was not truly in full cry, but Darby had explained that London was already crowded, and most everyone would attend a ball being given by the Duchess of Savington this very evening.

But now Darby would likely want her to stay home. Surely a wife would intrude on his search for a mistress? Given the way he came to her night after night, even (she blushed to think) twice a night, her stepmother had been right. He was a man of fierce desires. He might well take two mistresses.

She tormented herself for a moment by imagining dainty female hands playing over Darby's smooth chest, touching—she wrenched her mind away.

～ 41 ～

Yet Another Love Letter

It was presumably a note saying good-bye. Saying good-bye and mentioning that he loved her. That was the problem with an unopened letter: it might say anything or nothing.

Esme turned it over and over and then took her time opening the envelope. Henrietta had mourned receiving only one love letter in her life—that written by herself. Esme had received many, perhaps even a hundred, and yet this one was the only one that had ever mattered. She had told him to go, yes. But she would treasure his letter until she died.

But even wishing can't slow down the process of opening an envelope. The letter was written on rough foolscap, the kind a gardener might use if he were lucky enough to be able to write. The writing was that of a marquess, confident and bold.

Esme, it said at the top. Her eyes caught there. No *Dear Esme*?

Esme,

Before I became a gardener, I found it difficult—nay, impossible—to deny a lady's request. One of the rea-

sons I never took a mistress was that I scorned my friends: if they submitted to outrageous requests, they were fools. If they did not, they were ungentlemanly. Now that I am no longer known as a marquess, I find this problem much easier to negotiate.

I am refusing your request, my lady. I shall not willingly leave your employment. I am aware that your reputation is endangered by my presence on your estate. My only excuse is that I have no reputation myself, and I am thereby well aware of its ephemeral value. Reputation is worthless.

I can't leave you, Esme. Perhaps if you were not with child . . . but you are. And I am not stupid, Esme. I remember every detail of the night we spent together in Lady Troubridge's house. You said that you had not yet reconciled with your husband; I took advantage of that fact.

The child you carry could be mine.

Were you to send your butler to terminate my employment, I shall build a willow cabin at your gates, as Viola threatens to do in Twelfth Night. That will cause a scandal, no doubt. Perhaps in the aftermath of the scandal you will allow me to whisk you and your baby away. We'll find Cerces' island, and live on pomegranates and bananas.

Your Sebastian

Esme drew a long breath. If one were to receive only one love letter in a lifetime, surely this was the letter to receive. A tiny smile blossomed in her heart. He refused to leave.

Sebastian refused to leave her.

She could hardly force him to return to Italy. I am a weak woman, she thought. Then she read the love letter—her first love letter—again.

~ 42 ~

Unwelcome Revelations at Supper

That evening Keyes put her in a chemise as light as a spider-web, trimmed with lace so fine that it tore with a fingernail. Henrietta wore no corset. Darby had thrown out all her corsets. Over her chemise went a white satin petticoat, made quite short and embroidered all around the bottom with silver spangles. The bodice was of figured silk adorned with the same spangles. Finally, she wore a robe of white lace on top that fell in easy folds to the ground, quite like a Grecian gown. The costume was exceedingly graceful. Everything that Henrietta wasn't. Even given her limp, the lace floated about her in such a way that she seemed to glide rather than walk.

Henrietta watched numbly as Keyes's nimble fingers gathered up all her hair. Rather than harnessing it to the top of her head, the way that Henrietta normally did, Keyes shaped it into a glittering stream down her back, held back from her face with a silver ornament that matched her spangles.

"Are you quite certain?" Henrietta asked dubiously, straining to see over her shoulder. "I thought that the current fashion was to tie up one's hair, leaving just one curl to the side."

"Madam has such lovely hair that she should ignore fashion."

Henrietta frowned at her reflection. To her mind, she looked like a puffy marigold.

Keyes leaned forward. "Your husband always ignores fashion when it comes to his lace, madam."

"Oh, all right then," Henrietta said, although she didn't really see that as a justification for marigold hair. But what did it matter anyway? She still couldn't imagine that Darby would want to display his limping wife to the public, given a pressing necessity to find a mistress. From now on, she would be little more than a nursemaid, after all. As he had said.

Recognizing that she was being childish didn't help. She could feel the pull of an overwhelming black mood, such as she hadn't experienced since she was a girl, and the reality of her situation became clear.

Darby preferred his butler, Fanning, to leave the room during the second course. After Fanning had taken a last eagle-eyed look at the table and left, Henrietta took a large swallow of claret. It was a far stronger wine than she usually drank and made her head swim. But tonight it gave her courage.

A black mood was pulling her into its embrace. There were days when she was a young girl when she raged against her fate all day long. When she could not tolerate the idea of an existence dictated by an error of nature. It was even more embittering now, when she knew what a delight it was to lie in Darby's arms.

"I need to tell you something," she said.

He was looking particularly handsome. The candles on the table between them emphasized the lean hollows in his cheeks and made him look rakish, almost Eastern, not like a fine upstanding English gentleman at all. He raised an eyebrow.

She loathed the fact that she could feel his gaze on her, as if he were the sun and she a violet. She took a deep breath. And another swallow of claret.

"I have been wanting to tell you something too, Henrietta. Last night you said you loved me."

In the cold morning's light, she wished she had kept that fact to herself. She needn't have stripped herself of every bit of dignity.

"I don't know very much about love. I doubt I love anyone, to be honest. I simply wasn't brought up to the emotion. But I do want you to know how very much I honor your feelings for me. How—how pleased I am by your affection."

Lovely, Henrietta thought. At least she didn't have to worry about her husband feeling heartbroken once she could no longer act as his partner in bed. He could find affection elsewhere. It was she who would wait out the nights of her life in an empty bed. The black well in her heart grew and spilled into anger.

"I'm carrying a child," she said bluntly.

He was fingering his wineglass and watching her with an impenetrable expression on his dark face, almost as if he were waiting for her to say something shocking—but not that.

"*What?*"

She spelled it out. "I have not experienced a flux since we married."

"We've been married three weeks."

"Four weeks tomorrow. And I am very regular in that respect."

There was a pause, then: "God damn it to hell."

That seemed to sum it up from Henrietta's point of view as well.

Darby stood up, walked the sideboard, and retrieved the bottle of claret. Then he poured them both another glass.

Henrietta's hand shook as she reached for her wineglass.

"Where is the remedy that I gave you?" Darby said. His voice was even, seemingly untouched by the news she had offered. The brief flash of rage he displayed was gone as if it had never been.

"On the mantel in my bedchamber."

He met her eyes and she was surprised at the deep sympathy she saw there. "I'm sorry, Henrietta. Given your love of children, this must be a hellish thought for you."

"I have no choice," she said fiercely, trying to make it sound real to her own ears. "I have made a commitment to Josie and Anabel. And isn't it a hellish thought for you as well?"

He blinked. "I dislike the idea of your distress, naturally."

"It's your child!" she said shrilly.

"I am not—" he stopped. "Henrietta, I have never pretended to be a family man. But I am well aware how much you wish to have a child. Why don't we visit a doctor before we make any decisions? Perhaps someone from the Royal College of Physicians. London has the best medical doctors in the world, or so they say."

"I have seen doctors," she spat. "They pried at my hip, and shook their heads. They heard the story of my mother's death, and they looked at me—with death in their eyes." Her voice was alarmingly shaky, so she stopped speaking.

He pushed away the plate before him. "Then I suggest we become foxed and skip the ball." The obvious subtext was that little blue bottle.

"No!" Hysteria rose in her chest. "I cannot drink an herb that would take away a child's life. I cannot do it. I would rather die myself. I have wanted this baby my entire life!"

"I will not—" He stopped and started again. "Perhaps we should discuss this in the morning."

"There are things we must discuss now."

He looked at her calmly. To Henrietta, losing her baby and never sleeping with Darby were mixed up together. The pain felt as if a tiger was tearing at her heart. But her husband looked unperturbed. Truly, men were a different species than women. "The sheath apparently provides inadequate protection," she stated.

"Your conclusion seems warranted by the circumstances."

"What are we going to do?" The question was wrung from her heart.

He was silent.

"Simon, what are we going to do?"

"I'm thinking." His tone was brusque.

A gentleman with as high a standard for mannerly behavior as Darby would dislike informing his wife that she was relegated to nursemaid status. "I don't think we have many choices to consider," she said. Her voice was high and rang as sharply as broken glass. "Obviously, we must immediately cease all activities that lead to procreation."

He swallowed a mouthful of wine. Still there was no hint on his face of emotion.

"You must avail yourself of a mistress," she said savagely.

"I could suggest other—"

But she cut him off. "I forced you into this marriage."

"I accepted the marriage with a clear understanding of its limitations," Darby said.

"You don't understand," she snapped. "I wrote that letter—" She stopped. Telling the truth was too awful. Even if he didn't love her, and merely honored her affection for him. What good would the truth do? If he wanted a mistress, he'd take one.

"I know that," he said patiently. "Believe me, Henrietta, I was well aware of the risks of marrying you when I did it."

She continued, driven by some sort of blind, destructive misery. "You do not understand what I am saying. I wrote that letter, and then Esme and I arranged for it to be revealed at her dinner." His expression didn't change. "Don't you see? I decided that I wished to marry you, and so I trapped you. You had no choice other than to marry me."

A leaden silence descended on the dining room, broken only by Fanning entering the room. Like all good servants, he knew instinctively that privacy was required and left without bringing the next course. Darby indicated with a jerk of his head that he would ring for him if desired.

Henrietta drank the remainder of her glass of wine. "I deliberately compromised you."

"Why did you go to such lengths to marry me?" he asked, finally.

"I wanted the children," Henrietta said. But it was too easy, and too untrue. "I wanted *you*," she said. She was absolutely filled with rage. Rage against fate, rage against her body, rage against her husband, most of all, herself. If she'd never done such a stupid, stupid thing as marry him, she wouldn't be contemplating that blue bottle.

"Ah," he said. "Why?" He sounded mildly interested.

"You were different from the men of Limpley Stoke," she snapped. "You kissed me. I wanted your children. You needed my inheritance." She shrugged. "Does it really matter?"

"I suppose not. May I ask how this rather unsavory revelation affects our future married life?"

If he was angry, she couldn't tell from his tone: there was no anger, merely distaste. A great, weary distaste.

She had a terrible feeling in the pit of her stomach, as if she were crushing something delicate and precious, as easily destroyed as the frost fairies on a window. But then—what did their married life matter, in proportion to what she would do by drinking that bottle?

"Immediately after Esme's dinner party, before we discussed the sheath, you suggested a marriage in which you would keep a mistress and I would act as something of a nursemaid to your children."

"As I recall, you were the one who raised the question of a mistress."

She ignored that. "We shall revert to that idea. I cannot ask you to sacrifice yourself, given that I brought this marriage upon you by fraudulent means."

She faced him, head high, tearless. "After tonight"—and she meant, after she drank that bottle—"we no longer share the same body, as you put it. My body will be mine own again." That was almost the worst of all. After experiencing Darby, after being part of Darby, there could be no returning to one's own skin without despair.

"You seem to be angry at me, Henrietta. And you are offering me reasons to be angry at you. Why?"

She looked at him and hated—*hated*—his calm. Why wasn't he angry with her for wrangling him into marriage? Because he didn't give a twig, that's why. Even without sleeping with her, he still had the nursemaid he needed.

Henrietta had always been a terrible liar. "I'm not angry at you." She could hear the rage in her own voice.

"My mother did her best to entice my father into displays of anger similar to hers. I will not show myself a lesser man than my father in this respect, Henrietta. I will not dance to your piping. If I have offended you in any respect, I would be happy to discuss the offense."

"Your mother was probably trying to force your father to show some reaction," Henrietta said rather shrilly.

"It always seemed to me that she was trying to dictate his feelings." His long fingers played with the stem of his wineglass.

There is no penetrating his calm, Henrietta thought. He must feel nothing for me. "I have no doubt but what we both regret this marriage," she said, hearing her own churlishness. "I certainly regret my—my rashness in writing that letter. But I will not make scenes, Darby. I will not behave like your mother, I assure you. I am perfectly prepared to recognize that you have other—that you have interests outside the house."

His eyes were black in the candlelight. "And what of your professed love for me? So quickly dismissed, is it, that you can watch me take a mistress with equanimity?"

"One says many things in the heat of passion that should not be aired in the morning. You said that yourself." Her voice was hard, and she spat it with all the rage she felt in her soul.

"True enough." He put down his glass. "Shall I summon the carriage? I expect you would like to powder your nose before we leave for the ball."

"The ball?"

"Naturally. We did send our acceptance."

"But I thought you would not wish me to go, given—"

"Given that I must needs find myself a mistress? Why no, my dear. I see no reason to deprive you of pleasure." He pulled out her chair, and if it had been anyone other than Darby, she'd have thought there was rage in the gesture.

Dancing Like a Fool

Lady Felicia Saville felt a mild glow of pleasure. By any reasonable assessment, she was the most important guest at the Duchess of Savington's ball. Of the seven patronesses of Almack's—the young matrons who could make or break a reputation—she was only one to be in London this early in the season.

It was up to her and her alone, to make or break the reputations of provincials who sought entry to the *ton*. So far, the ball had been disappointingly thin as regards such caterpillars. She had declined only one request for a voucher to Almack's, and that didn't involve a delicate weighing of negotiations and favors. Mrs. Selina Davenport had traded on their very small acquaintance, but Felicia felt no more than a fillip of interest when refusing her request for a voucher. The woman was virtually unclothed; what her fellow patronesses would make of Mrs. Davenport needed no intuition, and she would never be granted a second voucher even if Felicia had promised her one.

Her cousin pranced through the crowd toward her.

"Bunge," she said, holding out her hand. "It is *such* a pleasure." It wasn't really, but the Honorable Gerard Bunge generally had slanderous news to report and that fact made him a palatable companion.

"Felicia, my dear, Simon Darby has taken a wife!"

She waved her fan idly, as if the news were old to her. In fact she was riveted with interest. If seven young matrons controlled the female side of the *ton*, Simon Darby was their male counterpart. His physical beauty and exquisite sense of dress meant that his attention to a young woman (or lack thereof) was as sought after as Brummell's, and served the same purpose as Almack's vouchers.

"I admit surprise. I would have thought Darby had long ago decided against the marital state," she said languidly.

"Took my advice." Bunge's chest swelled out a little. "I told him to marry an heiress, and that's just what he did. Haven't seen her yet. Should be here tonight though."

"Of course!" Felicia said, belatedly putting two and two together. "I did hear of Lady Rawlings's happy condition."

"Exactly." Bunge twitched the seam of his crimson stockings straight. "Betting is seventy to one in White's that the child will be male."

"Ludicrous. Who can possibly know such a thing as the child's gender?"

"Betting on the child's father is a great deal more lively. Last I looked at the book, Rawlings himself was only leading by a faint margin, and that after he died in his wife's bedchamber!"

"I suppose Darby didn't have a difficult time finding himself an heiress," Felicia said. "What a pity he didn't wait until the season. It would have been *such* an interesting courtship to watch. Do you suppose that his new father-in-law is in trade?"

"I suggested the woolly breeder," Bunge said with an

eruption of giggles. "But no. He married a daughter of the late Earl of Holkham. The man apparently left her an unentailed estate in Wiltshire."

Felicia considered it a requisite part of her duties as a hostess of Almack's to memorize *Debrett's Peerage.* "Let's see," she said slowly, "that must be the elder daughter, unless Darby stole the younger girl from the schoolroom."

"Didn't hear anything about her age," said Bunge. "But it must be the elder because she inherited the estate."

"But that girl is deformed," Felicia said with a little gasp. "She was never brought to London for a debut, you know."

"Perhaps it was a love match," Bunge suggested. "Overlooked her deformity due to passion. Or if not passion . . . hard currency."

"Do stop tittering," Felicia said with all the freedom of a second cousin. "It is *such* an unattractive habit. I wish I could remember what was wrong with the elder daughter—"

But everyone was turning about and looking at the ballroom entrance, where the butler had just announced, "Lady Henrietta Darby and Mr. Darby."

"Nothing wrong that I can see," Bunge observed. "She's a ripe one." Lady Henrietta stood next to her husband wearing a gown whose panels floated about her like gossamer wings. Tendrils of gold curled gently around her face. Even from across the room, it was obvious that her eyes were a luscious blue. Bunge could taste the envy in his mouth. "Trust Darby to come up smelling like roses."

Lady Felicia had married early and well, and for a few years the *ton* had considered her to have made a good marriage. But now everyone knew that Henry Saville was stark raving mad. The tip-off was when he rode a horse up the steps of St. Paul's Cathedral, insisting that the horse was his brother and should be baptized without delay.

So Felicia watched the Darbys with her eyes narrowed. She didn't mind admitting that she found the company of ravishingly happy couples hard to bear. But after a few minutes of watching the Darbys, curiosity replaced her agitation.

"There's something odd there," she told Bunge.

"What? What?" Bunge was always eager for gossip but desperately unobservant, to her mind.

"The newlyweds," she said slowly. "Lady Henrietta doesn't seem—look! Darby just deserted her to dance with Mrs. Ravensclan. What a grotesque affront to his wife. I can hardly believe it." Felicia felt a growing sense of cheer. "Come along, Bunge," she said impatiently, "let's go befriend the poor woman."

Darby was finding it difficult to completely ignore his sharp-tongued little wife. He had something of a rudimentary plan when they arrived at the ball: he meant to desert her in the rudest fashion possible, then flirt extravagantly under her very nose. That would presumably make her feel an iota of the black misery that had engulfed him since dinner. How *dare* she believe him a man of so little honor that he would take a mistress, after what she had said . . . after what she had said. No one could talk of love and yet believe he was without honor.

She didn't know him after all. Or love him.

His jaw set.

It would do his wife good to realize that he was a power in the *ton*. He wasn't some country bumpkin, to be tricked into a contrived marriage. He was respected. His influence was felt throughout London, or the civilized world, which was the same thing.

He swung his partner through the motions of a country dance and looked back to feast on his wife's discomfort.

He swallowed a curse. Felicia Saville had appeared out of nowhere and was introducing Henrietta to that nitwit, Lord Bellington.

The dance ended. Perhaps he should return to Henrietta. There was no doubt but that his behavior would be noted by half the ballroom, given that Lady Saville was performing a role that should be his. His eyes narrowed. Henrietta was greeting Lord Bellington with that smile of hers, the one that melted a man's bones. He turned on his heel and found himself before the buxom Selina Davenport. She greeted him with the sloe-eyed desire that he wanted only from his wife.

An hour later, his wife was established as a roaring success. Acquaintance after acquaintance had congratulated him on her exquisite beauty, her wit, her sense of dress. Their eyes sparkled maliciously as they noted his absence from her side. They positively giggled in his face when he couldn't bring himself to answer urbanely to their little barbed comments.

Gerald Bunge was the worst, hovering at his side like an insect, buzzing about how he couldn't have found a better spouse. And all the time Bunge's little body trembled with lust to find out why he was on one side of the room and his wife on the other.

Darby could feel his reputation for urbane calm falling to shreds about his feet. She'd done it, by God. She'd turned him into someone akin to his mother. His self-command was paper thin.

At some point during the evening, he had started drinking. Heavily. Rees turned up at the ball around one in the morning and found Darby wandering through the ballroom, glass of whiskey in hand.

Having known Darby since he was breeched, Rees instantly put together the dazed misery in his friend's eyes with the fastidiously upright way he was prowling across the dance floor. Like a bloody savage he looked. Last time Rees remembered seeing Darby that way was when his mother—an outright bitch if there ever was one—scanned him from head to foot just before his first London ball, and then made a laughing remark about a popinjay to her husband before turning away.

That evening Darby had bowed so sharply that he almost

cut the air, and proceeded to get so drunk that the evening ended in the stables with Rees holding Darby's head. Of course, he was only fifteen then, as proud of his yellow pantaloons as he was resentful of his knife-edged mother. It always struck Rees as unfortunate that Darcy's mother died a few months after that episode.

No doubt it was again a woman that had put him in this state. "Where is she then?" Rees asked, hauling Darby off the ballroom floor.

"My wife?" Darby asked airily. "God knows."

Rees looked around.

"She's been talking to Henry Piddlerton for the last half hour," Darby said, revealing that he knew Henrietta's whereabouts precisely. "The poor old sod is staring into her eyes as if she were the holy grail. Down her gown too."

Rees sighed and towed him into a card room off the library. "What the hell is going on?" he said, leaning against the door in case Darby tried to make a run for it.

"It's all quite commonplace, really. I should have taken your advice and avoided matrimony," Darby said, not meeting his eyes. He ranged the room, picking up trinkets and putting them down with enough force to crack them. "Wives are devils."

Rees opened the door and sent a footman for a pot of strong coffee.

It took quite a while to pry the situation out of Darby. Only after drinking three cups of coffee did he become at all coherent.

"I tend to agree with you," Rees said slowly. "At the very least, an expert should examine her hip."

"She definitely wants the child. I believe that Henrietta's limp would not be an impediment to carrying a babe."

"You know nothing of midwifery," Rees objected.

"Her hip looks precisely like any other woman's. And who knows what happened during her mother's lying-in? A bunch of country doctors jumped to the conclusion that the tragedy resulted from that weak joint. I don't call that sufficient evidence. But she believes—she truly believes—what she's been told."

"Then you must tell her different."

"How? She expects me to take myself off and get a mistress. She's decided that future bedding is out of the question—and she doesn't seem to have any other use for me! She thinks I'm the kind of man who would betray her." Darby ground to a halt. He hadn't meant to tell Rees that particular truth.

"Bosh," Rees said, turning around from the mantelpiece and scowling at Darby. "You're a fool if you believe that tripe. You're as bad as she is. She's likely been told that men have to tup a woman every other hour or die trying, and she believes it; you believe that she doesn't care if you take a mistress. Fools, both of you." He paused for a moment. Then: "I never had the chance to have a marriage like yours. You know that."

Darby stared at his friend. Rees looked like a great, growling bear.

"I have no use for women. But if Henrietta was my wife—" Rees turned to the door and said it over his shoulder. "Don't—" He stopped, turned around, and looked his friend straight in the face.

"Don't lose her."

Darby emerged from the card room shaken. He'd known Rees for years and never seen him look like that. Almost . . . almost as if he were lonely.

It only took a minute to locate Henrietta. She was seated on a rounded settee in the corner of the ballroom, being entertained by two gentlemen.

She looked up when he approached. "May I request the pleasure of this dance?" he said, bowing with a flourish.

There was a collective little gasp amongst the men around her, and he remembered too late that Henrietta was lame.

That his wife couldn't dance. He never thought of her in those terms.

She threw up her fan but he could feel the anger glittering from behind it. "You must have misremembered," she cooed. "I do not dance. I suggest you find some other partner. I shall be quite happy here." She waved her fan and smiled brilliantly at the Honorable James Landow, seated to her left. The poor besotted fool smiled back as if she had promised him the moon. "We were just discussing the old-fashioned tradition in which a lady invites gentlemen into her boudoir to help her dress."

Henrietta in a rage was a revelation. Gone was the country mouse. She shone with a glittering, sensual wit that made every man within her orbit come to attention.

"Told Lady Henrietta I think it would be a charming habit to resurrect," Landow said, with a quick sideways glance at Darby.

"Oh, don't worry about my husband, dear sir," Henrietta said with a roguish smile. She tapped her closed fan on Darby's arm. "We have a thoroughly modern marriage. In fact, we hardly know a thing about each other. He *did* just ask me to dance!" Her laughter spilled out, but there wasn't a trace of humor in it.

The two gentlemen seated on either side of her laughed as well, although neither of them met Darby's eyes.

"Ah, my lady," Count Frescobaldi said, lowering his mustached face to kiss Henrietta's hand, "I am certain that your husband merely expressed his deepest wishes. As would I, if I had asked you to join me on the dance floor." His voice was deep and rich as chocolate.

Darby's fists clenched. But what was the point of hitting Frescobaldi? Henrietta looked a bit taken aback. Perhaps she grasped the implications of Frescobaldi's deepest wishes.

"I think you underestimate how well we know each other," Darby said to Henrietta through clenched teeth.

"In what respect, dear husband? Do enlighten us all."

Darby met the avid eyes of Frescobaldi and Landow and knew that his carefully nurtured reputation for exquisite calm was shattered. A muscle was beating in his cheek. He was near to roaring. And he didn't give a damn either.

"I think you underestimate your inability to dance." The musicians had just begun a waltz. Before his wife could move, he pulled her up and away from the gentlemen, into his arms, and onto the dance floor.

Henrietta was too shocked to react at first. He read it in her body, poised stiffly against him, and the way she held back. But he *knew* her. He knew her body as intimately as he did her own. She was hardly limping tonight. There was only the merest hesitation when she walked. She could dance, God damn it. She could dance with her husband.

He splayed his hand around her slender waist and swept her into the waltz. It was no more than walking, after all. Walking to great gorgeous sweeps of music, walking in a rhythm that reminded him of their bed.

For the first few minutes he didn't even look at her. He just carried them, thigh to thigh, circled and swept, drawn in circles down the room by the music. When he finally glanced down at his wife, her cheeks were pink and her eyes luminous—not with anger, but with awe.

"I'm dancing," she whispered, and that shaken little breath touched his heart.

He took her into a breathtaking series of circles as the music curled in the air around them.

"Oh Simon, I'm dancing!"

The music quieted to a languorous *One, Two, Three; One, Two Three*. "You have spent too much time believing what people tell you," he said. The truth of it put a fierceness into his voice. "You listened to people who said you'd never marry and said you'd never dance."

"I am married—"

"To *me*," he said, breaking in. "You're married to me. You

are mine, Henrietta. And I am yours. Do you understand what I'm saying?

"You cannot simply throw me back into the stream, like a trout you no longer want," he said, his voice rasping. "We are one, Henrietta. It's too late. Don't you see?"

He couldn't read her expression.

"I'm not—I'm not a man who would ever betray his wife," he said. "I wouldn't *do* that. I'm not—" And then suddenly he saw that her eyes were shining with tears.

"I'm a fool, Simon." Her hand touched his cheek. "Forgive me?"

He nodded. For a moment they drifted together, lapped in music so delicate that it sweetened the air around them.

"They said you would never marry, Henrietta. You are married."

She nodded, just a tremulous wobble of her chin.

"They said you would never dance. We are dancing."

There was a spark of hope in those blue eyes. He could see it.

"And they said you would never give birth. But I know you. I know you want this baby. We'll go to every doctor in England if we have to. We can find someone who will save the baby. And you."

"I feel as if you read my heart," she whispered.

He looked at her, dark hair tumbling over his brow, as beautiful a man as ever walked the earth. "Can't you read mine, then?"

She swallowed, caught by his eyes, afraid she didn't understand.

"I love you."

The music drew to a close, and they stopped dancing, although he kept his arms around her.

"I love my wife," her husband said, his eyes as urgent as his voice. "And, Henrietta—

"I love you," she said, her voice breaking with it.

Lady Felicia Saville happened to glance that way and paused. It was a pity that she had already offered Lady Henrietta a voucher for Almack's. Otherwise, she'd be sorely tempted to refuse. In truth she would. What sort of example was Lady Henrietta setting for young, impressionable maidens by allowing her husband to kiss her so publicly?

Yet there was something about the way Darby held his wife, so fiercely and yet so tenderly, as if she were infinitely precious and dearly beloved, that made Felicia's vision blur. She turned away with a little moue of disgust.

～ 44 ～

Expert Advice

Dr. Ortolon knew himself to be the finest *accoucheur* in London. Nay, in the private recesses of the night, he considered himself the finest in the world. He had a degree from Oxford and trained at the medical school in Edinburgh. He was the only *accoucheur* to be a member of the Royal College of Physicians. He rarely lost a patient: he wouldn't allow it.

He was quite aware that his imposing stomach, square jaw, and domed forehead (domed because it housed the superlative Ortolon brain) went a good way toward convincing others of his worth in the world. Moreover, he was blessed with a voice like a barking seal, which undoubtedly helped as well.

"Facts are facts," he barked at the couple before him. "Facts are the *only* thing to which I listen. I think of it as drawing scientific truths from the well of ignorance. Now, the facts here are slim. The most relevant one is that you, Lady Henrietta, are carrying a child. I think we may conclude such."

The lady nodded, obviously awed by the way his voice resonated through the ignorant air.

"The fact that your mother perished while giving birth may or may not be relevant to the issue at hand. She was greatly unfortunate, if you will forgive me for saying so, in that your late father did not bring her to London. Had your late mother been seen by myself, even in the very bloom of my youth, there might be quite a different outcome to her story. In short, she might be sitting by the fire at this very moment, surrounded by an adoring brood of children."

Ortolon cast a sharp eye on the lady's husband, who was exhibiting an unseemly tendency to grin. Still, he knew that nervousness sometimes showed itself in an unbecoming levity. He'd seen it in previous instances.

"A brood of children at her knee," he repeated, jutting his chin a bit further into the air. "The second fact worth noting is that you, Lady Henrietta, suffer from a weakness in the hip joint, as did your mother, although that is not necessarily relevant to the matter of her demise." He frowned thoughtfully and paced up and down a few steps.

"From my examination of your limbs, Lady Henrietta, I can state unequivacably that while you have weakness in your joint, there is no obvious malformation. I can see no reason why you should not birth this child, undergoing no more than precisely the same risks as any other woman."

He paused to make certain that his message was understood.

"It is my considered opinion that your mother's misfortune lay in the circumstances of her confinement, not in the organization of her limbs. In fact, I consider the relevant fact there to be that you, Lady Henrietta, were born in a breech position. I count myself among the very few physicians able to facilitate such a difficult birth, although I have attempted to share my knowledge in my recently published volume, *The Management of Pregnant Women, with a Treatise on Love, Marriage and Hereditary Descent.*"

Darby let his mind wonder. The old pudding-bag was

clearly going to take on Henrietta as a patient, and he seemed to have enough experience to know what he was talking about. Ortolon was curiously reassuring. In fact, Darby had the sense that the physician wouldn't allow any harm to come to Henrietta, for the simple reason that death might blunt the good doctor's reputation.

"Yes," Ortolon wound up, "if I supervise your confinement, Lady Henrietta, you shall suffer no ill effects whatsoever, and neither will the Darby heir." He beamed at them both with such an air of confident self-satisfaction that Darby almost applauded.

Henrietta's eyes were fixed on Ortolon's face as if he were the Oracle at Delphi. Darby guessed that Bartholomew Batt and his *Rules and Directions* had just been dethroned in the Darby household, replaced by Jeremy Ortolon and his *Management of Pregnant Women*. A grin crept over Darby's face. It wasn't that he wanted a child personally, but Henrietta wanted one. And fool in love that he was, he wanted Henrietta to be happy.

Darby wasn't quite so sanguine seven months later. As they neared the end of an entirely uneventful pregnancy, he grew more and more conscious of a growing unease. There was no clear reason for it. Ortolon's daily pronouncements on his wife's condition were pompously approving. The baby was in a proper position, and Ortolon expected no problems.

Their child might be born any moment. That is, if Darby didn't figure out some way to stop the whole thing.

To be blunt, Darby had realized too late that he had participated in the worst decision of his life. He should never have listened to Ortolon. He should have begged Henrietta to drink the blue bottle. Perhaps he should never have visited Limpley Stoke at all. If the idea of never knowing Henrietta was bleak, the idea of Henrietta losing her life was unbearable.

Unease wasn't the right word. It wasn't unease he felt, but

fear: gross, unpalatable, and ugly. Gentlemen didn't experience this sort of thing. Not as a gut-gripping emotion that made one wake up sweating and on the verge of shouting.

He felt as if he could burst with the desperation of his wish to turn back time. His nights were marked by dreams in which he found himself laying flowers on a grave and once, with particular horror, on two graves: one large and one small. In his sleep he constantly relived the moment when Henrietta told him she was carrying a child. Once he dreamed that she laughed, lightly, and said it was all a joke. He almost wept with relief.

He started to watch his wife as intently as an artist watches his subject, prowling in the hallway while she was dressing, watching her bathe, barely allowing her to make private trips to the water closet. He pretended that he stayed near her in order to help her from chairs and make certain that she didn't slip on the stairs. She saw through him—oh, he could see in her clear eyes that she saw through him. But she loved him, and so she said nothing about his absurdities.

As the birth drew nearer he began waking in the dark stretches of the night and lighting a candle so he could watch her sleeping. Henrietta was more lovely pregnant than he could have imagined. She shone with the pure, exquisite joy of a madonna, as if all the despairing longing of her youth had poured into thankfulness for the new life growing inside her. Every day she grew more serene, more confident that labor would present no problems.

In contrast, Darby couldn't sit for more than five minutes. He snarled and snapped at the household until maids scurried by him in the hallway with a look of terror. He didn't give a damn. This could be the last week—nay, the last day—of his wife's life, and no one else seemed to have noticed.

One evening he couldn't sleep at all. What had he been thinking? He had allowed Henrietta to sacrifice her life for a child who might not live. What would Josie do without his wife? The little girl's motherless state had turned to a fierce adoration of Henrietta. Anabel never made the mistake of calling strangers "Mama" anymore. She knew exactly who loved her best. Could the children survive the loss of another mother?

Finally he stopped trying to sleep and sat up. He breathed in the truth with the chill night air. Imagining a world without Henrietta was like thinking of a world without warmth. She lay beside him, looking leached of color by the gray light, her skin porcelain white as if—as if—

He touched her, softly, on the cheek. She was breathing. At his touch, a little smile curved her lips, and she nestled against his hand, in her sleep. That was Henrietta: so deeply loving of Josie, Anabel, himself, the unborn baby, that it seemed as if love shaped the current of life in her.

She opened her eyes and opened her mouth but stopped suddenly, the word dying before it was spoken.

Darby's eyes narrowed. "What just happened?" he said, surprised to hear that his own voice was even.

Henrietta smiled at him brightly. But she'd never been any good at keeping secrets.

"That was a labor pain," he said.

"Perhaps."

"I'll send for Ortolon," Darby snapped, swinging his legs out of bed.

Henrietta tried to grab his arm. "No, Simon, I want to wait. I barely felt anything at all. It was a mere twinge."

"Nonsense."

It turned out there was nothing Ortolon could do. In fact, he was wildly ineffective from Darby's point of view, only saying a few nonsensical things about how well things were going and heading back to his club.

Darby followed him to the door and took his arm in an ungentle grip. "I shouldn't drink anything at your club, Ortolon." He didn't care how rude he was being. He had half a mind not to let the physician leave the house at all.

Ortolon shook him off, and barked, "Pull yourself together!" and left.

Henrietta went back to bed. The pains didn't seem to bother her much.

"You know, Simon," she finally said rather sleepily, "I am used to living with a certain degree of discomfort." And to his utter shock, she fell asleep again.

He lay on his side, watching her face. She wasn't all that beautiful. She didn't have a classically beautiful Roman nose. But every pulse in his body was tied to hers: to her blunt little English nose, and to those blue eyes that couldn't hide a thought.

Every once in a while she frowned, and discomfort shot across her face. In the middle of the night, she woke and said his name, groggily.

"I'm here."

"What on earth are you doing awake?"

"Thinking about the poem you used in that absurd love letter."

"The John Donne poem," she said, smiling up at him. "How could I forget the poem I used to trap you into marriage?" She squeezed his hand rather hard. "Goodness, that seems to be—oh, it's gone."

"I'll send for Ortolon."

"There's nothing he can do, Simon. We simply have to wait. Why are you thinking about the Donne poem?"

"Just remembering it. *Sweetest love, I do not go, for weariness of thee*," Darby said, gathering her close. "You see, the poet is afraid because he has to leave his beloved: *When thou sigh'st, thou sigh'st not wind, but sigh'st my soul away*. Because if something should happen to her, his soul is in her keeping."

Henrietta blinked. "*Nothing* is going to happen to me! Haven't you been listening to Ortolon all these months?"

Darby ignored her. "He says, *Thou art the best of me.* And that's true. *Thou* art the best of me."

"I thought I wrote the love letters in this family," Henrietta whispered, turning her face up to his.

His mouth touched hers. "He tells his lover to pretend that the time they spent apart is just a long sleep. Oh God, Henrietta, if anything happens to you, my life would be nothing more than a sleep."

"Sleep? You look awful, Darby!" She peered at him. "Haven't you slept?"

He ran a hand through hair that was already on end. "No."

"Why not?" She winced and clutched his hand again. "My goodness. These pains *are* getting stronger. Why didn't you sleep?"

He said it into her hair. "If I sleep, I might miss an hour or two with you. And—" he couldn't finish.

"Nonsense!" But she turned it into a kiss. "I'm not even feeling all this terrible pain that women complain about. I think it's because I'm so used to discomfort. I truly think, Simon, that I won't even feel very much pain at all—"

Her hand tightened, and she blinked.

"OW!"

Uncivilized Behavior

Dr. Ortolon didn't know what was the most difficult: the labor itself, or the husband. Of course, it was often that way. As the premier *accoucheur* in London, he'd found that men could be quite as troublesome as their wives. But this husband outdid the entire gender, even the royal dukes, who combined sentimentality with bullheadedness.

Mr. Darby had seemed a logical man throughout the pregnancy. He appeared rational during those consultations at which he appeared, expressing a measured level of concern for his wife.

But in the last week or so, the man had come unhinged. In fact, he had apparently changed his mind about the pregnancy.

"It's a bit late for that," Dr. Ortolon said with a rusty chuckle. Of course, he laughed alone. Mr. Darby was pacing the entrance hall like a wild animal. And when Ortolon headed up the stairs, the man raged at his side uttering threats and generally impolite remarks.

And then he followed Ortolon straight into the birthing chamber!

Lady Henrietta was in some discomfort by that stage, although she was controlling herself well. Mr. Darby barged to the head of the bed and began speaking to his wife. When Ortolon suggested that Mr. Darby leave so that he could conduct an examination, the man swung around with one of the most uncivilized expressions Ortolon had ever seen on a gentleman's face.

"Don't even suggest it," he snarled.

Ortolon fancied he could see bared teeth. He gave in. It did seem to distract his patient to have her husband in the room, and that was all to the good.

The labor progressed nicely while Lady Henrietta scolded her husband for his rudeness and general indecency for remaining in the chamber.

Later, as labor grew more acute, his patient amused herself by shrieking at her husband. Normally the mothers-to-be had a tendency to berate the attending doctor, and Ortolon always found that this disordered his nerves. Yes, he thought to himself, husbands could be quite useful in the lying-in chamber, if one could just get around the impropriety of the whole affair.

In the end, it was a normal birth. Disappointing, almost. As an artist of the profession, Ortolon rather enjoyed the violent race against death offered by a difficult birth.

"Quite commonplace," he told his patient.

She looked up at him. It was a familiar picture. Her hair was dark with sweat and plastered to her forehead. She was white with exhaustion, and there were dark circles under her eyes.

But her eyes shone as she looked at the little bundle in her arms, a bruised ugly little lump of humanity who was already suckling with some enthusiasm.

"What will you call the boy?" Ortolon said, washing his hands once again and preparing to leave.

"Call him?"

Lady Henrietta appeared to have lost track of his question as she traced the little whorls of her baby's ear.

The baby's father answered. "John," he said. "His name is John, for the poet, John Donne."

Naming a child after a poet! What a heathenish idea. Dr. Ortolon was horrified to see that the man's eyes were shining with tears. He snapped shut his black bag and left as quickly as possible.

~ 46 ~

For Love of Johnny

Henrietta could hear the girls coming all the way down the hallway. Their voices were echoing off the walls, as excited little girls' voices had a tendency to do. Anabel shrieked with laughter, and then she heard Millie saying, "Now calm down, girls, do. You don't want to frighten your little brother half to death. He's only a babe, after all."

The babe had just drunk so much milk that his little stomach was stretched tight as a drum. He lolled in the crook of her arm, looking as drunk and pleasured as a sailor on leave.

His father strode in from the adjoining dressing room just as Anabel and Josie burst into her chamber. Anabel was an unsteady runner, but what she lacked in stability, she made up in speed. She made it to the rocking chair first.

"Mama!" she shrieked.

"Don't wake the baby!" Josie scolded, but it was too late.

John Darby opened his eyes and looked around in a dazed sort of way. He had just begun recognizing people's faces. The girls hung over him, bumping heads as Josie crooned, "Johnny! Johnny! Smile for me! Smile for me!"

So he did, of course. Who could not? There were his two

sisters, their faces shining with joy and pride. His belly was full. And his mother was near. He even heard a deep voice saying something or other—and he recognized that voice as well.

He opened his mouth into a joyous, toothless grin—and burped. He kept smiling as a small torrent of milk poured from his mouth.

He was a little surprised when the two faces above him whisked away and the air filled with squealing. But his mama patted him dry.

"It's just a little bit of spit-up," she said, and then the person with the deep voice came and picked him up.

John tried to focus his blurry vision, but there was no way a babe could take in the elegance of the man holding him.

"Oh Darby, don't!" Henrietta said in some anguish. "Not when you're wearing court dress, darling! You know that—"

"Nonsense!" Darby said, dropping a kiss on his son's plump little nose. "John just burped, didn't you? He's all done with that foolishness now."

"I doubt it," his mother observed. "And I've been meaning to inform you that this is entirely your fault. No one in *my* family was given to vomiting on a regular basis."

"I did!" Anabel shouted, hopping up and down next to the bed.

"You still do!" her sister retorted.

Insulted, Anabel broke into a howl.

Henrietta smiled at her. "Your stomach has been quite settled for the past six months, hasn't it, Anabel? That problem is in your past."

"Anabel was well over a year old by the time her stomach settled," Josie said, demonstrating the sharp intelligence that was already challenging her governess. "That means that Johnny has months and months of this behavior ahead of him. Yuck!"

Simon Darby grinned at his little sister, and turned to his wife. "I should leave," he said. "The Regent has—"

But at that moment, John felt an uncomfortable pressure in his throat. He blinked and opened his mouth. A strange dry cough emerged.

"Simon!" Henrietta said warningly.

"Oh *shit*," John's father barked.

Out came milk, slightly curdled by now, emerging with the force of a cannonball and stopping only when it encountered a waistcoat embroidered with gold leaves.

His mother was laughing; the girls were screaming; his father was swearing. Milk dripped from a coat lined with silk and trimmed with cherry floss.

John frowned. His stomach felt empty. Hungry. His little brows drew together into a frown and he let out a bellow.

"Don't you think it's rather unfair?" Henrietta said.

Darby handed her the child and raised an eyebrow, delicately shaking drops of milk from his lace cuffs. "What's unfair? The fact that my man just spent forty-five minutes dressing me for court and now must begin from scratch?"

"No. The fact that John clearly inherited both Josie's voice and Anabel's weak stomach."

Her husband bent down and tucked a curl behind her ear. "He has your sweet eyes," he said, his lips just touching hers.

Henrietta's heart thumped. "I love you," she whispered.

Darby ran a finger down her cheek. "Not as much as I love you."

A Note on What to Expect in the Toddler Years, Circa 1815

I used to believe that the age of parenting best-sellers began with Dr. Spock. I certainly grew up with the idea that Spock was the greatest expert on children who ever lived. One of the many-times retold tales of my family is the night my father attended an anti–Vietnam War rally and found himself in the same jail cell as the great doctor himself. Family legend has it that my excellent sleeping habits stem from this brief imprisonment, during which my father extracted advice on how to make his baby daughter sleep.

But, in fact, Dr. Spock's child-rearing books are merely part of a long tradition. As far back as the Renaissance, books advising all sorts of child-rearing practices have gone into multiple editions. Barthélemy Batt's *The Christian Man's Closet* (full of helpful advice for fathers) and Thomas Tryon's *A New Method of Educating Children, or Rules and Directions for the Well Ordering and Governing Them During Their Younger Years*, were two early best-sellers in the tradition. Perhaps the best advice of all came from the dissolute second Earl of Rochester, who lived from 1647–1680. "Before I was married," he reportedly said, "I had six theories about how to bring up children. Now I have six children and no theories!"

And One Final Note,

For those of you who are planning to advise me, with reference to *Dr. Spock's Baby and Child Care*, that children do not spit up after the first three months: Anabel's afflictions are taken from life. My daughter Anna is ample proof that weak stomachs can last well over a year.

OH! THE SCANDAL!

A runaway heiress, a letter that was never meant to be sent . . .
A celebrity in disguise, a womanizing duke . . .
There are *such* goings on in the Avon Romance Superleaders. . . .
It's as shocking as the headlines you read in the gossip columns!

But there is much more than mere scandal; there is love—sometimes unexpected, sometimes unpredictable . . . and always *passionate! These new love stories are created by the best and brightest voices— Cathy Maxwell, Patti Berg, Eloisa James—and there is one of the most beloved romances ever, as created by Laura Kinsale.*

So don't miss the scandal, the sizzle . . . and the chance to read about some truly handsome men!

WAYWARD HEIRESS BOLTS TO SCOTLAND FACES RUIN IN EYES OF SOCIETY!

**"I'm furious!" states her father. "I've arranged a
perfectly good match for her, and the ungrateful chit
repays me by doing this!"**

In *New York Times* bestselling author Cathy Maxwell's *Adventures of a Scottish Heiress*, Miss Harrell takes one look at her proposed husband and runs as fast as she can—to Scotland and the protection of her mother's family. But before she reaches the border she's tracked down by Ian Campion—a powerful soldier-turned-mercenary hired by her father to haul her home. But before he can get her back to London, the two begin a romantic adventure they never expected . . .

It was Abrams who broke the somberness of the moment. "Let us not be too grim, eh?" he said. He rose, offering his wife a hand up as he did so. "The future can wait until the morrow. Tonight, I need my sleep."

Madame nodded. "You are right, my son, and very wise. Come, Viveka. You will dream tonight and, in the morning, tell me every detail. Then perhaps we shall know more."

"I don't know if I'll be able to sleep," Lyssa answered.

"Keep the card close," Duci advised. "Your Knight will protect you."

She said the words in earnest and yet they sounded strange, because, for a moment, it had been the Knight that had frightened Lyssa. Her uncertainties dissipating, Lyssa laughed at her own gullibility. Neither Reverend Billows nor her father would be pleased.

Madame rose. The Gypsy gathered the cards while her

husband put away the folding chair and the reading table. No one seemed to notice that Lyssa still had the Knight of Swords. She stole a look at it and then turned to secretly tuck it into her bodice—

And that is when *he* appeared.

He stepped out of the darkness into the waning firelight, as if appearing out of nowhere.

For a second, Lyssa thought her eyes deceived her. No man could be so tall, so broad of shoulders. Smoke from the fire swirled around his hard-muscled legs. His dark hair was overlong and he wore a coat the color of cobalt with a scarf wrapped around his neck in a careless fashion that would have done any dandy proud. His leather breeches had seen better days and molded themselves to his thighs like gloves. A pistol was stuck in his belt and his eyes beneath the brim of his hat were those of a man who had seen too much.

Here was her Knight come to life.

He spoke. "Miss Harrell?" His voice rumbled from a source deep within. It was the voice of command.

Lyssa lifted her chin, all too aware that her knees were shaking. "What do you want?"

The stranger smiled, the expression one of grim satisfaction. "I'm from your father. He wants you home."

Ian was well pleased with himself. His entrance had been perfect—especially his waiting until *after* the card-reading mumbo jumbo. At the sight of him, the self-styled "Gypsies" turned tail and scattered off into the woods. They knew the game was over. But best of all, the headstrong Miss Harrell stared up at him as if he were the devil incarnate.

Good.

This task was turning out to be easier than he'd anticipated.

With a coin slipped here and there in the dark corners of London, he'd learned of a wealthy young woman who had hired some "Gypsies" to transport her to Scotland. Supposedly, the heiress was to stay hidden in the wagon, but after a time, she had felt safe enough to show herself along the road and thus became very easy to track. More than one person, upon seeing the miniature, told Ian that the young lady's red hair was a hard thing to forget—especially among dark-haired Gypsies.

Now he understood why they had felt that way. Here in the glowing embers of the fire, the rich, vibrant dark red of Miss Harrell's hair with its hint of gold gleamed with a life of its own. She wore it pulled back and loose in a riotous tumble of curls that fell well past her shoulders. It was a wonder she could go anyplace in Britain without being recognized.

And her clothing would catch anyone's eye. It was as if she were an opera dancer dressed for the role of "Gypsy" . . . except the cut and cloth of her costume was of the finest stuff. The green superfine wool of her full gypsy skirt swayed with her every movement. Her fashionably low white muslin blouse was cinched at the waist with a black laced belt and served to emphasize the full swell of her breasts. She must have had some sense of modesty, because she demurely topped off the outfit with a shawl of plaid that she wore proudly over one shoulder.

It was a wonder she didn't have hoops in her ears.

Her awestruck silence was short-lived. She tossed back her curls, ignored his hand, and announced, "I'm not going with you."

"Yes, you are," Ian countered reasonably. "Your father is paying me a great deal of money to see you home safe, and see you home safe I will. Now come along. Your maid is waiting at an inn down the road with decent clothes for you to wear."

Her straight brows, so much like her father's, snapped together in angry suspicion. "You're Irish."

Ian's insides tightened. Bloody little snob. But he kept his patience. "Aye, I am," he said, letting the brogue he usually took pains to avoid grow heavier. "One of them and proud of it."

She straightened to her full height. She was taller than he had anticipated and regal in her bearing. Pride radiated from every pore. A fitting daughter to Pirate Harrell. "I don't believe you are from my father. *He* would *never* hire an Irishman."

"Well, he hired *me*," Ian replied flatly, dropping the exaggerated brogue. He rested a hand on the strap of the knapsack flung over one shoulder. "The others couldn't find you. I have. Now, are you going to cooperate with me, Miss Harrell, or shall we do this the hard way? In case you are wondering, your father wants you home by any means *I* deem necessary."

Her eyes flashed golden in the firelight like two jewels. "You wouldn't lay a finger on me."

"I said 'by any means I deem necessary.' If I must hog-tie and carry you out of here, I shall."

Obviously, no one had ever spoken this plainly to Miss Harrell before in her life. Her expression was the same one he imagined she'd use if he'd stomped on her toes. The color rose to her cheeks with her temper. "You will not. Abrams and my other Gypsy friends will come to my rescue. Won't you, Abrams?" she asked, lifting her voice so that it would carry in the night.

But there was no reply save for the crackling of green wood in the fire and the rustle of the wind in the trees.

"Abrams won't," Ian corrected kindly, "because, first, he knows he's not a match for me. I have a bit of a reputation for being handy with my fists, Miss Harrell, and that allows me to do as I please. And secondly, because he's no more a Gypsy than I am. Are you, Charley?" he called to "Abrams."

"Who is Charley?" Miss Harrell demanded.

"Charley Poet, a swindler if ever there was one. You probably think Duci is his wife?"

"She is."

Ian shook his head. "She's his sister. And your fortuneteller is his aunt, 'Mother' Betty, once the owner of a London bawdy house until gambling did her in."

"That's a lie!" a female voice called out to him. "The house was stolen from me!"

"Is that the truth, Betty?" Ian challenged. "Come out of hiding and we'll discuss the matter."

There was no answer.

The color had drained from Miss Harrell's face, but still she held on to her convictions. "I don't believe you. I've been traveling with these people and they are exactly what they say they are—Gypsies. They even speak Romany."

"Charley," Ian said. "Get out here."

A beat of silence and then sheepishly, Charley appeared at the edge of the woods. He was slight of frame, and with a scarf around his head Ian supposed he could pass for a Gypsy. "Tell Miss Harrell the truth," Ian said with exaggerated patience.

THE D—— OF J—— TO DUEL AT DAWN
NOTORIOUS NOBLEMAN TO
CHOOSE HIS WEAPON
AND DEFEND HIS HONOR

**Friends are concerned that this "brilliant" and
"dangerous" man may tempt fate once too often.**

Who could ever forget the first time they opened the pages
of *New York Times* bestselling author Laura Kinsale's *Flowers
from the Storm*? It's one of the greatest love stories of all
time.

If you haven't yet experienced its powerful magic—and
the exquisite love story of London's most scandalous rake-
hell and the tender woman who saves him—you are in for an
experience you'll never forget.

"How long ago did you lose your sight, Mr. Timms?" he
asked.

Maddy stiffened a little in her chair, surprised by such a
pointed personal question. But her papa only said mildly,
"Many years. Almost . . . fifteen, would it be, Maddy?"

"Eighteen, Papa," she said quietly.

Jervaulx sat relaxed, resting his elbow on the chair arm,
his jaw propped on his fist. "You haven't seen your daughter
since she was a child, then," he murmured. "May I describe
her to you?"

She was unprepared for such a suggestion, or for the light
of interest that dawned in her father's face. "Wilt thou? Wilt
thou indeed?"

Jervaulx gazed at Maddy. As she felt her face growing hot,
his smile turned into that unprincipled grin, and he said, "It

would be my pleasure." He tilted his head, studying her. "We've made her blush already, I fear—a very delicate blush, the color of . . . clouds, I think. The way the mist turns pink at dawn—do you remember what I mean?"

"Yes," her father said seriously.

"Her face is . . . dignified, but not quite stern. Softer than that, but she has a certain way of turning up her chin that might give a man pause. She's taller than you are, but not unbecomingly tall. It's that chin, I think, and a very upright, quiet way she holds herself. It gives her presence. But she only comes to my nose, so . . . she must be a good five inches under six foot one," he said judiciously. "She appears to me to be healthy, not too stout nor thin. In excellent frame."

"Rather like a good milk cow!" Maddy exclaimed.

"And there goes the chin up," Jervaulx said. "She's perhaps a little more the color of a light claret, now that I've provoked her. All the way from her throat to her cheeks—even a little lower than her throat, but she's perfectly pale and soft below that, as far as I can see."

Maddy clapped her hand over the V neck of her gown, suddenly feeling that it must be entirely too low-cut. "Papa—" She looked to her father, but he had his face turned downward and a peculiar smile on his lips.

"Her hair," Jervaulx said, "is tarnished gold where the candlelight touches it, and where it doesn't . . . richer—more like the light through a dark ale as you pour it. She has it braided and coiled around her head. I believe she thinks that it's a plain style, but she doesn't realize the effect. It shows the curve of her neck and her throat, and makes a man think of taking it down and letting it spread out over his hands."

"Thou art unseemly," her father chided in a mild tone.

"My apologies, Mr. Timms. I can hardly help myself. She has a pensive, a very pretty mouth, that doesn't smile overly often." He took a sip of wine. "But then again—let's be fair. I've definitely seen her smile at you, but she hasn't favored me at all. This serious mouth might have been insipid, but instead it goes with the wonderful long lashes that haven't got that silly debutante curl. They're straight, but they're so long and angled down that they shadow her eyes and turn the hazel to gold, and she seems as if she's looking out through them at me. No . . ." He shook his head sadly. "Miss Timms, I regret to tell you that it isn't a spinster effect at all. I've never had a spinster look out beneath her lashes at me the way you do."

WHERE IN THE WORLD IS JULIET BRIDGER? CULT MOVIE STAR-TURNED-NOVELIST LEAVES PARTY SAYING SHE IS "SICK AND TIRED OF CAVIAR!"

"One minute she was enjoying the party,"
said her personal assistant, Nicole, "the next
she was driving off wearing her designer gown."

In Patti Berg's *And Then He Kissed Me* blonde bombshell Juliet Bridger has had it—too many cocktail parties, too many phone calls from her jailbird ex, too many nasty items in the gossip columns. So she disguises her identity and runs . . . straight into the arms of Cole Sheridan, a small town vet with troubles of his own . . .

He moved to the passenger door, rested on his haunches, and peered at the woman through the window. "What's the problem? Out of gas? Engine trouble?"

"I have absolutely no idea." She scooted as far away from the window as humanly possible, as if she thought he might punch his fist through the glass, latch on to her, and drag her out through the jagged shards—then eat her alive. "If you don't mind, I'd appreciate it if you'd go away."

Ungrateful female.

"You gonna fix the car yourself?"

"That's highly unlikely."

"You expecting a miracle? A heavenly light to shine down on this junk heap and make it start?"

"I expect no such thing." She sighed heavily. "Look, you could be the nicest guy on the face of the earth; then again, you could be Ted Bundy's clone."

"I'm neither," Cole bit out, her frostiness and his annoyance getting the better of him.

"Okay, so you're not nice; so you're not a mass murderer, but my dad taught me not to talk to strangers and, believe you me, I've watched enough episodes of *Unsolved Mysteries* and *America's Most Wanted* to understand not to accept help from people I know nothing about. Therefore"—she took a deep breath and let it rush out—"I wish you'd go away."

That would be the smart thing to do. Get the hell home before Nanny #13 walked off the job, but he couldn't leave the woman in the middle of nowhere, alone and stranded. Not in this heat.

"Look, lady, this hasn't been the best of days. My frame of mind sucks, and I'm in a hurry. Trust me, killing you doesn't fit into my schedule."

"All it takes is one quick jab with a knife or an itchy trigger finger and I could be history."

"I haven't got a knife, haven't got a gun, and I'm almost out of patience. If you're out of gas, just say so. You can sit right there, safe and sound behind locked doors, while I siphon some gas out of my truck and put it in your tank."

"The car's not out of gas. It simply backfired and died."

"Considering the lack of attention you've given the thing, I'm not surprised."

Even through her rhinestone glasses, he could see her eyes narrow. "I just bought the *thing* three days ago and before you tell me I got screwed, I already figured that out. Now since you're in a hurry and I'm not"—she attempted to shoo him away with a brush of her hand—"I'll wait for the cops to come by and help me."

Damn fool woman. "This isn't the main road and it isn't traveled all that often. If I leave, you could sit here for a day or two before someone else passes by."

She glared at his unkempt hair, at the stubble on his face, at his white T-shirt covered with God knows what. "I'll take my chances."

"You always this stubborn?"

"I'm cautious."

"Foolish is more—"

"Do you have a cell phone?" she interrupted, holding her thumb to her ear, her little finger to her mouth, as if he were some country bumpkin who needed sign language to understand the word "phone."

"Yeah. Why?"

"Perhaps you could call a tow truck."

"This isn't the big city; it's the middle of nowhere. There's one tow truck in town and it could be hours before Joe can get away from his gas station to help you."

"I'll wait."

"It's gonna be one hundred two degrees by noon. You sit in your car for a couple of hours you just might die."

"I get out of my car, I might die anyway."

He didn't have time for this. "Fine. Suit yourself."

Cole shoved away from the MG. Getting as far away from the crazy woman as he possibly could was the smartest thing to do. As bad as this day had been, he was sure it would get far worse if he stuck around her any longer.

He was just opening the door to his truck when she honked her horn. The squeaky beep sounded like a chicken blowing its nose, and the ghastly noise rang out four times before he turned. The confounded woman wiggled her index finger at him from behind her bug-spattered windshield, beckoning him back.

Shit.

Cole glanced at his watch. He glared at the woman, then, shaking his head, he strolled back toward the car and stared down at the face peering through the window. His jaw had tightened but he managed to bark, "What?"

She smiled. It had to be the prettiest smile he'd seen in his whole miserable life—but it was also the phoniest. "You will call a tow truck, won't you?"

Leave it to a woman to use her feminine wiles to get what she wanted. Leave it to a woman to be a pain in the butt.

LOVE LETTER GOES ASTRAY
MEMBERS OF THE *TON* ARE AGHAST
AT SUCH IMPROPER DISPLAY OF AFFECTION

**"I never thought Henrietta could inspire such passion,"
said her bosom pal, Lady Esme Rawlings. "Especially from
a man like Simon Darby. He's so cool on the outside, but
clearly there are unseen fires burning there."**

⁓

In Eloisa James' *Fool for Love*, Lady Esme Rawlings thinks she
can manage her friends' romances, so she concocts a plan to
have a love letter—proported to be written by the inscrutable
Simon Darby—"accidentally" read aloud at a dinner party.
Now, the only way the reputation of her friend Lady Henrietta can be saved is to marry Mr. Darby . . . quickly.

🍃

Slope played his part to perfection. Esme waited until after
the soup had come and gone, and the fish had been eaten. She
kept a sharp eye to make certain that Helene and Rees weren't
going to explode in a cloud of black smoke, because then she
would have to improvise a bit, but besides the fact that Helene
was going to get a stiff neck from looking so sharply away
from her husband, they were both behaving well.

The roast arrived and Esme sent Slope for more wine. She
wanted to make certain that her part of the table was holding
enough liquor to respond instinctively. Mr. Barret-Ducrorq
was ruddy in the face and saying bombastic things about the
Regent, so she thought he was well primed. Henrietta was
pale but hadn't fled the room, and Darby showed every sign
of being utterly desirous of Henrietta. Esme smiled a little to
herself.

Just as she requested, Slope entered holding a silver salver.

Speaking just loud enough to catch the attention of the entire table, he said, "Please excuse me, my lady, but I discovered this letter. It is marked urgent, and feeling some concern that I might have inadvertently delayed the delivery of an important missive, I thought I would convey it immediately."

A little overdone, to Esme's mind. Obviously, Slope was an amateur thespian. She took the note and slit it open.

"Oh, but Slope!" she cried. "This letter is not addressed to me!"

"There was no name on the envelope," Slope said, "so I naturally assumed it was addressed to you, my lady. Shall I redirect the missive?" He hovered at her side.

She had better take over the reins of the performance. Her butler was threatening to upstage her.

"That will be quite all right, Slope," she said. Then she looked up with a glimmering smile. "It doesn't seem to be addressed to anyone. Which means we can read it." She gave a girlish giggle. "I *adore* reading private epistles!"

Only Rees looked utterly bored and kept eating his roast beef.

" '*I do not go for weariness of thee,*' " Esme said in a dulcet tone. " '*Nor in the hope the world can show a fitter love for me.*' It's a love poem, isn't that sweet?"

"John Donne," Darby said, "and missing the first two words. The poem begins, '*Sweetest love, I do not go for weariness of thee.*' "

Esme had trouble restraining her glee. She could not have imagined a comment more indicative of Darby's own authorship. He actually knew the poem in question! She didn't dare look at Henrietta. It was hard enough pretending that she was the slowest reader in all Limpley Stoke.

" '*Never will I find anyone I adore as much as you. Although fate has cruelly separated us, I shall treasure the memory of you in my heart.*' "

"I do not believe that this epistle should be read out loud,"

Mrs. Cable said, "if it truly is an epistle. Perhaps it's just a poem?"

"Do go ahead," Rees said. He appeared to have developed an active dislike of Mrs. Cable. "I'd like to hear the whole thing. Unless perhaps the missive was addressed to *you*, Mrs. Cable?"

She bridled. "I believe not."

"If not, why on earth would you care whether a piece of lackluster poetry was read aloud?"

She pressed her lips together.

Esme continued dreamily, " '*I would throw away the stars and the moon only to spend one more night—*' " She gasped, broke off, and folded up the note, praying that she wasn't overacting.

"Well?" Mrs. Cable said.

"Aren't you going to finish?" Mr. Barret-Ducrorq said in his beery voice. "I was just thinking perhaps I should read some of this John Donne myself. Although not if his work is unfit for the ladies, of course," he added quickly.

"I believe not," Esme said, letting the letter fall gently to her left, in front of Mr. Barret-Ducrorq.

"I'll do it for you!" he said jovially. "Let's see. *I would throw away the stars and the moon only to spend one more night in your arms.*'" He paused. "Sizzling poetry, this Donne. I quite like it."

"That is no longer John Donne speaking," Darby remarked. "The author is now extemporizing."

"Hmmm." Mr. Barret-Ducrorq said.

"Did that letter refer to a night *in your arms*?" Mrs. Cable asked, quite as if she didn't know exactly what she heard.

"I fear so," Esme said with a sigh.

"Then we shall hear no more of this letter," Mrs. Cable said stoutly, cutting off Mr. Barret-Ducrorq as he was about to read another line.

"Ah, hum, exactly, exactly," he agreed.

Esme looked at Carola, who turned to Mr. Barret-Ducrorq and sweetly plucked the sheet from his stubby fingers. "I think this sounds precisely like the kind of note that my dear, dear husband would send me," she said, her tone as smooth as honey and her eyes resolutely fixed on the page, rather than on her husband. "In fact, I'm quite certain that he wrote me this note and it simply went astray."

Esme could see that Mrs. Cable was about to burst out of her stays. Henrietta was deadly pale but hadn't run from the room. Tuppy Perwinkle was torn between laughter and dismay. Darby looked mildly interested and Rees not interested at all.

Helene raised her head. She had spent most of the meal staring at her plate. "Do read your husband's letter, Carola," she said. "I think it's always so interesting to learn that there are husbands who acknowledge their wife's existence."

Esme winced, but Rees just shoveled another forkful of beef into his mouth.

Carola obediently read, " *'I shall never meet another woman with starlit hair like your own, my dearest Henri—'* " She broke off.

All eyes turned to Henrietta.

"I'm sorry! It just slipped out!" Carola squealed. "I truly thought the letter must be from my husband."

Henrietta maintained an admirable calm, although a hectic rose-colored flush had replaced the chilly white of her skin.

To her enormous satisfaction, Esme saw that Darby was looking absolutely livid.

Mrs. Cable said, "Who signed that letter?"

Carola didn't say anything.

Mrs. Cable repeated, "*Who* signed that letter?"

There was an icy moment of silence.

Esme said gently, "I'm afraid it's too late for prevarication, Carola. We must look to dearest Henrietta's future now."

Mrs. Cable nodded violently.

"It is signed Simon," Carola said obediently. She looked straight at him. "Simon Darby, of course. It's a quite poetic letter, Mr. Darby. I particularly like the ending, if you'll forgive me for saying so. After all, we have already read the letter."

"Read it," Lady Holkham said in an implacable voice.

" *'Without you, I will never marry. Since you cannot marry me, darling Henrietta, I shall never marry. Children mean nothing to me; I have a superfluity as it is. All I want is you. For this life and beyond.'* " Carola sighed. "How romantic!"

Then Henrietta did something that Esme had not anticipated, and which was absolutely the best of all possible actions.

She slid slowly to the right and collapsed directly into Darby's arms.

LISA KLEYPAS

New York Times Bestselling Author of
Lady Sophia's Lover

When is love . . .

Worth Any Price

0-380-81107-3/$7.50 US/$9.99 Can

Marry a nobleman who would control her—never!
So Charlotte runs to the protection of Stony Cross Park.
But it is there she is captured by Nick Gentry, a treacherous
foe reputed to be the most skillful lover in England.

And Don't Miss

WHEN STRANGERS MARRY
0-06-050736-5/$7.50 US/$9.99 Can

LADY SOPHIA'S LOVER
0-380-81106-5/$7.50 US/$9.99 Can

SUDDENLY YOU
0-380-80232-5/$6.99 US/$9.99 Can

WHERE DREAMS BEGIN
0-380-80231-7/$6.99 US/$9.99 Can

SOMEONE TO WATCH OVER ME
0-380-80230-9/$7.50 US/$9.99 Can